QUEEN OF THIEVES & CHAOS

ALSO BY K.A. TUCKER

Ten Tiny Breaths

One Tiny Lie

Four Seconds to Lose

Five Ways to Fall

In Her Wake

Burying Water

Becoming Rain

Chasing River

Surviving Ice

He Will Be My Ruin

Until It Fades

Keep Her Safe

The Simple Wild

Be the Girl

Say You Still Love Me

Wild at Heart

The Player Next Door

Forever Wild

A Fate of Wrath & Flame

Running Wild

A Curse of Blood & Stone

The Hustler Next Door

A QUEEN OF THIEVES & CHAOS

K.A.TUCKER

This book is a work of fiction. Any references to historical events, real people, or real places are used fictitiously. Other names, characters, places, and events are products of the author's imagination, and any resemblance to actual events or places or persons, living or dead, is entirely coincidental.

ISBN 978-1-990105-30-2 (paperback)

ISBN 978-1-990105-29-6 (ebook)

Edited by Jennifer Sommersby

Cover design by Hang Le

Published by K.A. Tucker Books Ltd.

Manufactured in the United States of America

To my family, my anchor.

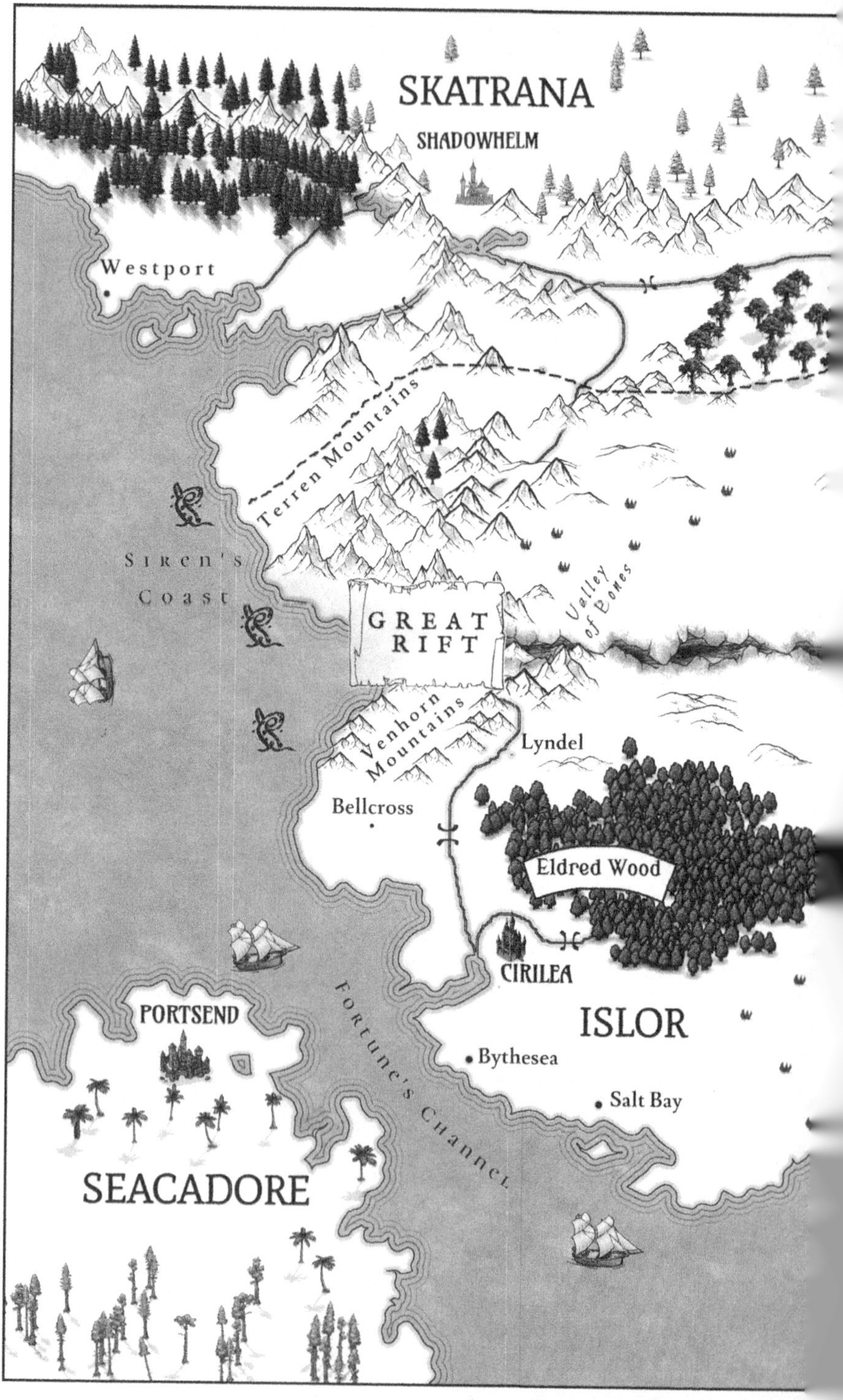
SKATRANA
SHADOWHELM
Westport
Terren Mountains
Siren's Coast
GREAT RIFT
Valley of Bones
Venhorn Mountains
Lyndel
Bellcross
Eldred Wood
CIRILEA
PORTSEND
ISLOR
Bythesea
Salt Bay
Fortune's Channel
SEACADORE

Bentsend
N
Gulf of Nyos
Dead Wood
YBARIS
MORDAIN
NYOS
To
Espador & Udrel
ARGON
The Grave Deep
Mount
L'Or
Endless
Sea
Hawkrest
Plains
of
Aminadav
Fernhoth
KIER
Gulf of Ostros
Kettling
OSTROS
Ratheus

1
SOFIE

Sofie could finally see.

After three centuries of agonizing and pleading, of empty promises and seemingly unconnected schemes that had driven her to the brink of madness …

The moment she dragged her kneeling, naked form from the cobblestones of the sanctum, stood to greet the Fate of Fire, and saw the anticipation in his harsh features, Sofie knew something monumental had shifted in their favor.

"She has done it? She has released the nymphs?" Hysteria clung to each syllable.

Malachi strolled around the stone casket holding the two corpses, his corporeal form as magnificent as it was terrifying. "The process has begun." His deep voice rumbled; the corners of his mouth twitched with delight as he reached down to graze a finger across Romeria's perfectly preserved cheek. "Whether she realizes it or not."

Sofie pressed her hands against her stomach to contain her excitement. "How much longer?" How much longer before she would feel Elijah's arms wrapped around her shoulders again?

"Soon, my love. Very soon." Malachi lifted his gaze to her. "Until then, I have a task for you."

2
ROMERIA

A peal of shrill laughter within the castle competes with our footsteps, earning Jarek's scowl.

I peer up at the formidable legionary who towers over me, his sculpted body wrapped in leather, his sable-brown hair freshly shaved along the sides and braided at his crown in three thick cords gathered at his nape. "Come on, you can't dislike *children*."

"Can't I?" His eyebrow arches, amusement painted across his angular but handsome face. "Let me show you what happens when the blood lust hits them for the first time, and we will see how cute you think those feral little monsters are then."

I grimace, recalling Zander's menacing description of the Islorian immortals when they're learning to feed. "*Mortal* children," I amend.

"They're *slightly* less feral. Equally irritating." His gaze surveys our limited surroundings, as if expecting a threat to materialize from the walls at any second. "And they don't belong here," he adds quietly.

Another squeal of childish laughter ricochets, the echo eerie within this hollow kingdom that thrums with ancient magic.

"Do any of us?" I opened the mountain wall three days ago, and since then, we have scoured every corner of Ulysede, finding signs of a thriving city—food stores, clothing, floral blooms decorating windowsills—but no life beyond livestock, songbirds, and the odd stray cat. Elisaf found an armory full of gleaming metal—enough to outfit a small army—each breastplate emblazoned with Ulysede's two-crescent-moon emblem, as well as a treasury vault filled with gold coins stamped with the same, but no one to wear the armor or collect payment.

It's as if Ulysede was built and then frozen in time, waiting for us. To what purpose, though, we still don't know.

It's an unoccupied city bordered by sheer, unscalable mountain walls on all sides, but only a fool would believe we're within the mountain, and an even bigger fool would think we're still in Islor. When that ancient wall of nymph scripture known as Stonekeep parted and we stepped through those main gates, we were stepping beyond our realm. The fact that two moons hang in the sky every night confirms it.

I study the painted ceiling that lines this hallway—an illustration of a teeming market with people selling wares, surrounded by horses and wagons and soldiers with Ulysede's crest on their breast plates. The white sandstone castle with royal blue spires and soaring parapets is full of these lively murals, with no hints about who these people are, or from what time.

Are they depictions of the past?

Or perhaps a hopeful future?

I suppose *I* belong here, seeing as it was *my* blood—an inexplicable combination of Princess Romeria, heir to the throne of Ybaris and daughter to Aoife, the god of Water, and Romy Watts from New York City, unwitting key caster masquerading as a human thief—that unlocked the secret of Ulysede. A crown of thorns on a prickly throne was waiting for *my* head.

The question remains, now what?

Jarek and I step into the grand hall as a little girl—one of Norcaster's humans rescued from their keepers' cages—darts past, chased by Eden in what appears to be a game of tag.

"I caught you!" Eden declares, encircling the child in a hug, earning another shrill scream of glee.

The corner of Jarek's mouth twitches, and I doubt it's on account of the child. My lady maid is the only one who seems capable of dulling his razor-sharp edges.

Upon seeing us, Eden releases the girl and bows. "Your Highness!" Her innocent blue gaze rakes over the black breeches and tunic I dug out from the expansive and stocked closet, and her forehead furrows. "Was the gown I laid out not to your liking?"

"She can't train in skirts," Jarek answers before I have a chance to respond.

I roll my eyes. He's been relentless in his demand that we spend time each day in the castle's sparring court. Of all the things I still need to learn, throwing a dagger doesn't seem vital, but I *am* improving. The blade no longer bounces off its target. "It's a beautiful dress." The closets of the queen's chambers are full of them, and they all fit as if custom-made with me in mind. "But"—I gesture at my outfit—"this is way easier for *moving around*, in general."

"Yes, I suppose so." Eden bites her lip, her focus flitting to Jarek. Where their interest in one another has landed, I can't say. The only time he leaves my side now is when I'm behind my bedroom doors with Zander, and even then, Elisaf has seen him roaming the halls late into the night.

The little girl has tucked herself into Eden's skirts, her attention shifting from me to Jarek. I remember her, peeking out from the gaps in the wagon outside of Kamstead—the tiny village with air that reeked of burning flesh. Where before she wore tattered clothes and smears of soot, now she's freshly washed and donning a sunny yellow pinafore.

I wonder which of us scares her more—the warrior with countless blades strapped to his leather-clad form, or the Ybarisan princess turned Ulysede queen with poison in her blood and untold magic coursing through her limbs?

I offer her a gentle smile. "What's your name?"

"Betsy, Your Highness." She attempts a curtsy and loses her balance, stumbling a step. It could be her age—she can't be more than five—or that she's had little practice in formalities, coming from the north where the idea of bowing to royalty is shunned. Either way, Corrin would be appalled.

"Do you like it here so far?"

Her head bobs in fervent agreement, but then she falters before throwing a pointed finger upward. "Is that really a nymph?"

I follow her aim to the stone statue in the center of the great hall, the creature at least ten feet tall, clothed in spiked armor, as if ready for battle. Its jagged wings appear designed as much to spear opponents as for flight, the claws on its hands primed to gouge enemy flesh. When I first laid eyes on it, I mistook it for a daaknar. "We think so." There are countless versions of these winged creatures throughout Ulysede—from fearsome gargoyles to dainty, humanlike figures and a myriad of forms in between. I assumed the latter were the true ones, the nymphs who speak to me through their childlike laughter that only I can hear, but Gesine warned me to not assume anything. The seers have seen this terrifying version hovering over us just as readily, and so far, their visions have not steered us wrong.

Betsy tips her head back to study the menacing creature. "How could something so dreadful make a city so beautiful?"

Eden hushes her, stealing a guarded glance upward as if the stone can hear the harsh judgment.

Maybe it can.

While stepping through those gates has brought a sense of safety and hope, I can't shake the spine-tingling sense that we're not alone and that this place is not all that it seems.

I take a deep breath to calm the dash in my heartbeat that comes every time I acknowledge that looming worry and smile to hide my apprehension. "I don't know, but I'm glad they did." It's the haven we so desperately need, as Zander decides the right next move to save Islor, and I embrace these newfound key caster abilities.

Footfalls sound, drawing our attention up the grand staircase where Elisaf trots lithely. No one would guess that my night guard was torn apart by a beast only a week ago, moments from closing his eyes and never reopening them. He stalls on the landing when he sees us, a slight head dip in greeting, and I know Zander must have sent for me.

"Is there anything else you require at the moment, Your Highness?" Eden asks.

"I'm good, thanks." It doesn't matter how many times I push her to drop formalities, she slips into them as readily as a person breathes.

"In that case, I heard Mirren found ingredients for bread pudding."

Betsy's face lights up with the prospect of a sweet treat.

"Your Highness." Eden curtsies, her eyes flittering to Jarek's briefly to add, "Commander," before she ushers the little girl toward the hall that leads to the castle kitchen.

Jarek's gaze trails her for a few beats before snapping back to focus.

"So … 'Commander,' huh?" I tease with a sultry lilt as we continue through the massive, empty space, heading for the stairs. Does Jarek have the same desire for Eden now that he no longer needs her blood? At least, not within these walls, where the two-thousand-year-old curse that created "Malachi's demons" has vanished. None of the Islorian immortals have felt so much as a twinge of that undeniable craving since crossing through the portcullis. It's a reality that has noticeably lifted Zander's mood.

"That is the title you granted me, is it not?" Jarek responds dryly, not the least bit fazed.

"It is." And only after Zander's urging that a queen needs to surround herself with trusted advisors. I couldn't think of a better warrior at my right hand than the lethal one who has proven his loyalties to Islor outweigh the prejudices he holds toward Ybaris and Mordain. "But why am I picturing some weird commander-and-servant role-playing thing between you two now?"

"Because you're a pervert," he throws back.

I mock gasp. "Is that how you talk to your queen?"

"Because you're a pervert, *Your Highness*."

I snort at his lack of deference, but I appreciate it all the same. Jarek and I have had our share of differences—the surly warrior has openly loathed, distrusted, and wished me dead on many occasions, and I've returned the favor in kind—but ever since the battle against the saplings and that monstrous grif, there is a current of respect and unspoken trust between us. It's just buried beneath a thick layer of arrogance and attitude.

It's not the only unspoken thing between us. I hinted at my truth one quiet night in a field, before the saplings crept in like shadows, merth cord dangling. Once Jarek knew it had to do with the fates, he shut me down, not wanting to hear the rest. Since arriving in Ulysede, he has stood by my side as Gesine gave me caster lessons, but he has never asked for an explanation, and I have never offered one. I've certainly never admitted what I am.

"Did he tell you to drag me out of bed if I wasn't already up?" I call out as we ascend the steps.

Elisaf's deep brown eyes crinkle with his smile. "His Highness waits in the war room for you. He insisted the queen be present to discuss pressing issues."

The queen. Will it ever not feel like he's talking about someone else?

"Like what? Your lordship?" It's been a running joke between us ever since Elisaf intercepted one of Atticus's letters that declared gold, land, and title to the person who captured the traitorous Ybarisan princess and delivered her to Cirilea. "Have you found any land in my *vast realm* that appeals to you?"

"In fact, I have, Your Highness. There is a quarter across the river that seems primed for agriculture. It has a few acres of cultivated land, and a pen with pigs and hens. Fearghal has taken to feeding them."

"Sounds like you want to be a farmer." The nymphs really did think of everything.

"Maybe he will be better at handling swine than he is a sword." Jarek's boots scrape against the marble as we climb. The warrior can move as quietly as a cat when he wants to.

"And yet it was *you* who was bested by a sapling," Elisaf answers nonchalantly.

"*Five* saplings, wielding raw merth," Jarek snaps, his hand absently rubbing his chest where I found the dagger embedded. It took all of Gesine's healing power to keep him alive.

And if I allow this verbal sparring contest to go on, it's liable to come to blows. "What *pressing matters* does Zander need to talk about?" He abandoned me in our bed hours ago, leaving with nothing more than a kiss against my forehead and a gentle goading not to sleep too long—that we have much work and not enough time.

Elisaf's expression shifts, all traces of humor gone. "Decisions that cannot wait, I'm afraid. About what comes next."

"So ... the usual," I mutter as we march up the stairs.

We discovered Ulysede's war room on our second day, high in a tower overlooking the river and the city beyond. It's a refreshing contrast to Zander's war room in Cirilea—a round, windowless space on the ground floor of the castle. Here, daylight streams into the airy, sparsely furnished room through an expanse of windows. In one corner is a simple wooden desk with stationery and a wax kit bearing the two-crescent-moon emblem.

The focal point, though, is the slab of stone in the center, a current map stretched across its surface, the lands of Islor and Ybaris bisected by the great rift. Another inexplicable thing that raises questions in a city that has been sealed for tens of thousands of years.

"... reached Kamstead by now, which means they'll know we kept going north. That is, if they're not still scouring the villages around Norcaster."

My heart skips at the sight of Zander leaning over the table, his gauntlets cast aside to display cut forearms as his arms bracket the map. It's a common sight—his handsome face is rigid with the weight of Islor's problems, his golden-brown hair pushed back off his face, likely from a frustrated shove of his hand.

Even dressed in the leathers of a warrior, he looks regal.

And he's mine.

Had someone told the jewel thief from New York City that a red-haired sorceress would send her to an alternate world to inhabit a treacherous princess's body and chase a stone at the behest of the God of Fire, the girl would have laughed in their face and called them delusional.

And yet, here she is now, in love with a king who abandoned his throne and kingdom to save her life.

Zander has always felt larger than life to me, from the first moment we met on that riverbank outside Cirilea's gates, he in his suit of armor, his dagger primed to spear through my heart. In the days and weeks and months since, he has played every role in my life here, from executioner to captor to reluctant accomplice, unlikely ally, and suspicious lover.

But now he holds my heart, and he's my reason to keep accepting every new challenge this deadly world throws at me.

Zander breaks from studying the terrain to watch me stroll in. "I do not understand how you sleep so much." There's a hint of scolding in his tone.

I saunter over. "*Someone* kept me up late into the night."

"Someone kept *me* up, and yet I've already walked half of Ulysede." A glimmer of humor peeks through his steely mask as he slides his hand into mine for a moment of contact before releasing it. I've grown used to the two sides of Zander—the passionate man who will take his time admiring every inch of my flesh with his mouth, and the unyielding ruler with curt words and a brooding nature. Behind the privacy of our doors is the only time I'm treated to his affectionate side, but I don't mind. It's intoxicating, facing this stony version during the day and then watching him break for me each night.

In front of others, though, he is an exiled ruler solely focused on how to regain his throne and save Islor.

Both tasks seem impossible.

And now that the Legion feels satisfied there isn't a deadly threat lurking within these walls—not an imminent one, anyway—Zander has been spending all his time in here, pacing over his next move.

"You were talking about Telor and his army?" I eye the map and the path from our location in the Venhorn Mountains, south toward Norcaster.

"There is still no sign of his approach, or of the Ybarisans, but our scouts are only able to cover so much ground before they're forced to turn around to avoid nightfall."

Or more specifically, to avoid the saplings who emerge at sundown to hunt and are armed with paralyzing raw merth, a silver cord that Princess Ybaris gifted them in a deal we don't understand. It's already cost us two legionaries captured in Norcaster and additional lives lost during the attack on our journey here.

"Nothing from that sapling you've been … questioning?"

Abarrane stands on the opposite side of the table, her ripe-wheat-colored hair freshly plaited, a dozen blades strapped to her lithe warrior's frame. She wears her usual grim expression. "Nothing yet, but he will yield." Zander's Legion commander has been outside Ulysede's gates every night since we arrived, torturing the prisoner in a bid to find Iago and Drakon's location.

Yield or die. She isn't known for tame methods of persuasion. That he's still alive—and remaining quiet—is shocking.

"If he has not given up their location by now, I am not hopeful," Zander says, as if reading my mind.

"Then I will take a handful of legionaries and search."

"We cannot hunt aimlessly through these mountains looking

for two legionaries who may already be dead," Jarek says, joining the conversation.

Abarrane's eyes flash at her former second-in-command. "Then we draw them out."

"And if you draw out a hundred of them? Without those merth cords, I would say that is an even match, but *with* them?" He shakes his head. "You will find Drakon and Iago, when you are lying next to them, being fed upon."

"Then what do you suggest? Abandoning your brethren to those … those …" Her face twists with rage, the thin scar that runs from her forehead to her ear crinkling.

"We're not suggesting that." Zander shoots a warning glance at Jarek. For as coldhearted as Abarrane can be, she is fiercely protective of her warriors, especially those she trained as children. "But we have more pressing matters than rescuing two legionaries. Hudem is coming, and between this poison that circulates and Atticus's edict to execute humans without trial, Islor will soon tear itself apart."

"I hazard it already has," Elisaf says somberly.

"All the more reason for me to leave *now*."

"And do *what*?" My panic swells. It's not a surprise that Zander plans on abandoning the safety of Ulysede's gates to return to Islor, where a king's army hunts for him and the blood curse he despises so vehemently reclaims him. He's been talking about it since the moment we arrived. But it seems reckless, and I don't know how to make him see it.

"I *must* sway Telor to our cause. The western lords follow his lead. Even Rengard will abandon his neutrality if Telor stands with me." His voice bleeds with conviction.

"How many men does Telor have with him? A thousand, Rengard said?"

"Give or take."

"You have *fifteen* warriors, Elisaf, and *me* at your side." And I barely have a grasp on my affinities. I'm learning, and quickly, but right now, I would be more a liability that an asset.

"Eleven warriors and *not you,*" Jarek corrects, his jaw setting with willfulness. When I appointed him my commander, one of his requirements was that he claim Zorya, Horik, and Loth for his little Legion unit to protect against any threats within Ulysede.

Zander and Abarrane agreed.

As for me staying in Ulysede? *I* never agreed to that, but now is not the time to argue with the stubborn oaf. "You can't go out there against a thousand soldiers, Zander. That's suicide."

He smirks. "You might recall, I am not defenseless."

"No, you're not. Especially if you plan on killing them all at first sight." He only needed a single, small flame to raze an apple orchard with his powerful elven connection to Malachi's fire.

"That is not my plan," he admits. "But the longer we sit here waiting, the more time we give Atticus to learn where we are and send more soldiers to hem us in."

"I'm sure Atticus already has an idea of where we are." Vaguely, at least. But he would never expect a new kingdom within his own realm. I wish I could be a fly on the wall when he receives that news. "Okay, so then you want to talk with Telor first? Do you remember what happened the last time you talked with a lord? In the Greasy Yak in Norcaster? Let me remind you. You could have died, and he only had, what, twelve soldiers with him?"

Zander grits his teeth. "I won't make that mistake twice."

"No, but you could make another one. Telor has *a thousand* soldiers. *Plus,* there are the saplings to worry about."

"And anything else that crawls out from the shadows," Elisaf adds, smoothing a hand over his leathers. Beneath, his thigh is as strong as ever, but it wears countless silver teeth marks where the grif shredded it.

Zander pinches the bridge of his nose. We've had this conversation more than once, and it never ends in agreement. "Then what do you suggest, Romeria? That I continue to hide here within these pristine white walls?" He waves around us. "What kind of king is that?"

One who won't die. I bite back those words because they're selfish and they won't bend his will. "Can we wait a few more days to give the Ybarisans a chance to reach us? We know they travel through Kamstead regularly. They'll get the message we left. They'll come."

Abarrane sneers. "And you're so convinced they'll swear loyalty to you?"

"As far as they know, I'm still Princess Romeria of Ybaris, and they have sworn to her mother, and so her by default, right?" I force as much conviction as I can muster. I have no idea if they've figured out I'm a traitor to Queen Neilina's plans.

"And when they realize you are not the same princess?" Zander asks.

"We'll cross that bridge when we come to it. Just a few more days. You said so yourself—you need Telor to listen, and two hundred Ybarisans with their affinities would make him think twice before attacking."

"If the Ybarisans don't kill us first," Jarek says.

I spear him with a glare. *Not helpful.*

Zander folds his arms over his chest, his thoughts churning behind a menacing expression. "We are in a precarious position. We do not know what Queen Neilina has heard or gleaned, other than to assume she knows we are now aware of the poison's source. We do not know what command those Ybarisans may have received from her as they march toward us, for we know there is communication between them."

"And if the Ybarisans attack?" Abarrane asks.

"I would hope Ulysede's gates provide us ample protection. But if the Ybarisans attack—if *anyone* attacks—we will have no choice but to respond with fervor."

"It would be a show of good faith to Telor if we slaughtered these Ybarisans ahead of his army's arrival." Jarek's grin is wicked.

"You make it sound so easy." Zander's gaze is on the map again, on the realm he lost to his traitorous brother. "I do not want to find ourselves in a battle with the Ybarisans or Telor. We need allies, not enemies. We need every one of those men marching upon Cirilea with us."

"So we have a thousand soldiers with Telor, two hundred Ybarisans coming, possibly to attack us, and we're in a fortifiable city. Sounds like a *fantastic* time for you to head out there." I can't help my sarcastic tone.

His molars grind. "We will give the Ybarisans one more day."

I sigh with relief. One day at a time is all I can ask for.

"In the meantime, perhaps I can help you loosen that sapling's lips tonight." He nods toward Abarrane.

She smiles. "I welcome your aid."

I shudder at the thought of what Zander's methods of persuasion might be. I've seen him use fire before, in the bowels of Cirilea's castle, trying to pull information from Prince Tyree. At least they've kept the interrogations outside of our walls, so no one within Ulysede has to hear the sapling's screams.

"Enough about this. What has the witch discovered?" Abarrane demands, changing the subject abruptly.

I shrug. "A lot of books on things she's never seen in Mordain's archives. I'm going to see her after we're done here."

Unsatisfied with my answer, she pivots to Jarek, arching an eyebrow.

"She seems to be searching for something specific. She will not leave the library." Jarek's first order as Ulysede's commander was assigning Zorya to watch over Gesine's every move. The official line is that it's for her safety in this mysterious city, but I know Jarek. He doesn't trust her.

"Searching for what, exactly?" Zander's hard gaze is piercing.

He snorts. "You think she has explained herself?"

"She will *need* to explain herself if we are to believe where her true allegiances lie." Jarek isn't the only one who doesn't trust Gesine. Zander hasn't hidden his worry that Gesine will forever be loyal first to Mordain, the island of casters who hold no love for Islor and would execute me in a heartbeat if they knew I existed. It seems Zander's suspicion has only grown since Ulysede's gates opened.

"Can we *please* remember how invaluable Gesine has been?" I remind them all, anger flaring in my voice. "We escaped Cirilea because of her. We found *this place* because of her, and the blood curse is gone here. Some of us are alive because of her, and for *no* other reason." That, I aim at Jarek. "She's helped us and healed us all along the way while being threatened by all of you." And she has become a friend to me in a sea of enemies.

"But does she help for our benefit or hers?" Zander presses. "Do not assume a priestess driven by prophecy does these things out of the goodness of her heart."

"Maybe not." I'm no fool. "But you guys keep acting like she's some villain, conspiring against us."

Zander inhales deeply.

"I swear to all that is holy, if you use that condescending tone to tell me how I don't know Mordain," I push out through gritted teeth. This is another argument we've had too many times, with no relenting on either side.

My unspoken threat stalls his tongue on whatever he was about to say. "Whatever she is searching for is not more important than training you on how to wield your affinities. Do you see anyone else in *all* of Islor who can do that?" He throws his hands toward the map. "The future is where her focus *should* be, not sifting through ancient books about the past."

"You're right. So if we're done here …" I spin and march out, hoping my annoyance leaves a heady trail.

Jarek is a split second from stepping on my heels. "We are right to distrust her."

"Oh yeah? By the way, how's that scar on your chest? You know, from the dagger that basically killed you?" I throw back.

His lips purse. "Our paths will only align as long as they lead in the same direction as hers. She is Mordain."

"That's where she's from, not who she is."

"Keep telling yourself that if it makes you feel better." His smile is grim. "You'll soon learn there is no difference when it comes to their kind."

I remember thinking that the library in Cirilea was vast when I first stepped inside, with its four stories and iron spiral staircases. But Ulysede's library is in a realm of its own, sinking three stories within the castle, each one stretching beyond my line of sight. The rows of polished wooden shelves are endless and filled with books, most in the same language that marks the throne and the sanctum altar. The air smells of paper and ink and wood, but not musty, as one might expect of an ancient library. Densely filtered light peeks in from beyond stained glass windows high above, offering little in the way of illumination. Flaming lanterns compensate, igniting on their own—or by some unseen hand—as they sense a visitor's approach.

We discovered the castle's library shortly after arriving, and Gesine hasn't stepped foot outside of it unless forced to since, parking herself at a desk with an oil lamp and an ever-changing stack of books.

Zorya greets us within moments of entering. "What did I do to deserve such a punishment, Commander?"

Jarek smirks. "I could swear you said you loved books and casters."

"Then you need your ears cleaned." She scowls at Gesine, hunched over a desk, seemingly oblivious to our arrival. "The witch orders me around all day long. 'Find a book with this word, Zorya,' 'Look for a section with that symbol, Zorya,'" she parrots in a mocking tone. "And when I find them, do I get a thank-you?"

That the lethal warrior is even fetching books is surprising. It only confirms Jarek's claims that Gesine isn't aimlessly absorbing information. She's hunting for something specific, and she hasn't taken a break from it in days, except to give me a few quick lessons with my affinities.

"Where's Pan?" I look around for that impish face. "He's supposed to be helping you."

"He left. I have no idea where or why." Zorya rolls her one good eye—the other is hiding behind a leather patch, mutilated by a merth blade during the escape from Cirilea. "Probably off playing king again."

Not likely. The last time Jarek caught Pan sitting in my throne with the crown on his head, yelling commands to imaginary subjects, he promised to make a new seat cushion out of his skin. I'm pretty sure the mortal peed his pants.

Pan likely abandoned his task in the library because Zorya threatened to cut out his tongue for talking too much, and he knows she's not kidding.

"What is Gesine looking for?"

"How would I know? That would require her to speak to me. She hardly leaves this dark place. She has barely eaten. She has not bathed." She sniffs with displeasure. "Last night, I found her passed out on a book, drooling. I had to peel her face off the page." Zorya shakes her head. "I much prefer the version we traveled with. *This* version? She is different, and I do not care for it."

An edge of unease slips into my thoughts with her words. "Different *how*?"

Zorya shrugs. "Distracted and snippy. She speaks to herself. Mumbles, mostly. It's incoherent."

My panic swells as a new fear erupts. What if …

I abandon Jarek to Zorya and her foul mood and rush over to where the elemental caster sits, my apprehension growing with each step. "Find anything interesting?"

No response.

"Gesine?" My voice is sharper than I intend, buoyed by anxiety.

Her head snaps up. "Oh, Romeria, I apologize. I was so focused." Her eyes are lined with heavy bags, her black hair unbrushed, her dress rumpled. I'm not used to this disheveled version. It's a far cry from the serene caster I met in Cirilea's apothecary.

But her emerald-green gaze regards me with familiar shrewdness, and I allow myself a small utter of thanks before nodding to the book she was so enthralled by. "Anything interesting?"

"Yes, I think so. Well, interesting to me, anyway. I am not as adept at translating this language as some of Mordain's more astute scribes. The style of speaking is archaic, and it's taking me forever, but I *think* these books were written by scribes who existed before the age of casters." She reaches for one on top of a stack. "They describe these beings called mystics, which sound much like casters in that they were born with elemental affinities of varying power. They were not born to mortals, though. They were capable of breeding, and their affinities were passed down through each generation. Amazing, isn't it?" Her eyes light up with genuine delight.

"What happened to them?"

"I have not yet come across anything that explains their disappearance from this world. I'm sure it's somewhere in there." She waves a wayward hand toward the shelves. "Mordain has no knowledge of that time, save for those volumes found in Skatrana and the seers' visions. The fact that the nymphs protected this knowledge within Ulysede feels important."

"Is this why Zorya had to peel you off pages last night? Because you're so desperate to know about these mystics?"

"I'm desperate to know about *all of it*. There is so much to learn here." Gesine sinks back in her chair, a grave expression pinching her features. "So much to learn that could be valuable to our cause and, I fear, so little time left for me."

I don't have to ask where her mind has wandered because it's the same worry that had me rushing over here. A clock ticks over Gesine's head, the one that ticks over every elemental, counting down to deliver a fate they cannot escape, that of the change from powerful caster to frail seer. I would have succumbed to it too—

unwittingly—had I remained Romy Watts in New York City, and not inhabited this elven immortal form.

The inevitable outcome is still fresh in both our minds. We lost Ianca a little over a week ago, a withered version of herself, bundled in animal pelts and grasping at visions, her grip on reality faded.

When it will happen for Gesine, we can't be sure, but it's said the change comes between their third and fourth decade, and the stronger the elemental, the sooner.

Gesine is thirty-six and a powerful wielder of three affinities.

It could happen in four years, or four months, or four weeks.

It could happen tomorrow.

I hesitate. "Have you ... *felt* anything?" Wendeline once told me some elementals sense the beginning tugs on their sanity, while others may go to sleep lucid, only to wake up lost.

"Besides overwhelmed and unequipped?" She smiles weakly. "Perhaps this heavy worry plaguing me is sleep deprivation."

"Zorya says you were drooling."

Gesine groans, smoothing her palms over her face. "I've heard about that several times already. I suppose I was exhausted. I don't recall her carrying me to my room."

Only for Gesine to rush back here.

For what, though? I sense what Jarek and Zorya sense—that Gesine is looking for something specific. But if she hasn't openly shared it, she must have her reasons.

"I've been building those wards like you taught me. I think I've got it." Mainly on doors, using my affinity to Vin'nyla, the Fate of Air, to weave an impenetrable wall, stronger protection than any lock can provide. It took some practice. Four wooden doors lay in splinters from where Jarek kicked through before I finally mastered it. The last one, he crumpled in pain, confirming my ward was as hard as stone against his shoulder.

"You are picking things up quickly. And you don't need your ring anymore." She taps my bare finger where Princess Romeria's engagement ring used to sit, a powerful ornament made from token gold from Aoife and a dull white stone, origins unknown, but rumored to be that of the nymphs.

"It served its purpose. I no longer have to mask anything." My caster magic is a welcome buzz deep inside me, rather than the paralyzing noise it once was. And I've resigned myself to seeing Princess Romeria's face when I look into the mirror, rather than the one I grew up knowing. "What should we work on next?"

"Building a flame wall, perhaps?"

My eyes narrow. "You already taught me that, remember?" Though I did it myself the first time, based on need.

She blinks. "You're right, I did." Her gaze drifts toward the endless collection of books. "I'm so tired."

"Then you should take a break. There's nothing *that* important in here, right?" I try to keep the suspicion from my voice. She gets it from everyone else, she doesn't need it from me too.

"I'm afraid there might be," she says vaguely. "But it is too much for me to search on my own."

"Zorya and Pan have been helping, haven't they?"

"Yes, but it's still not enough." She shakes her head. "No, I need experts. Dozens of them." She hesitates, as if building up courage to say her next words. "There are those who could use their affinities to better direct their search."

"And where do you find those people, besides Mordain?"

She bites her bottom lip, and I know without her answer, that is exactly what she's aiming for. Zander warned me Gesine would make this request, and when she does, it is to be a resounding no. After how badly Wendeline betrayed him, I can't fault him for not welcoming more casters with open arms.

I can almost see the gears working in Gesine's mind, searching for a way to convince me.

"That would mean telling them about Ulysede and how we opened the gate, which would mean explaining what I am." A key caster. My very existence is an offense to them, punishable by death, as has been the case for two thousand years.

"I share your worries," she begins slowly. "But I do not mean the entire guild—"

"Can you really control that, though?"

"The scribes have managed to thus far, with knowledge of Ianca's summoning. For years."

"That you know of. You haven't been in contact with them in *how long*? Since before you escaped Argon? That was months ago. Everything has changed. So much is out in the open now."

She bites her lip. "I *trust* the Master Scribe to involve only those who are necessary."

"Well, *I* don't." And Zander won't entertain this conversation. "The last thing we need is for Queen Neilina to find out I'm not her daughter and to tell those two hundred Ybarisans who are on their way here." Hopefully. "She'll order them to kill me. They can't know I'm not Princess Romeria. We need them for when Telor's army shows up. And what happens if your Master Scribe decides prophecy isn't worth allowing a key caster to roam loose, let alone play the role of queen of Ulysede?" *Play* being the operative word. My voice escalates with my words as wariness swells.

"Prophecy has already foretold of the nymphs walking the earth again in the age of casters, and that means a key caster must survive culling. They are aware, even if they are not yet aware."

"That doesn't mean they'll sit back and allow it. You said so yourself, not everyone in Mordain values prophecy." I shake my head. "I'm sorry, Gesine, but it's too risky. Protecting this secret is what has kept me alive for this long." Even Zander would have killed me had he found out in those early days.

Her brow pinches with discomfort. "I suppose I should tell you, then, that it is too late. The wheels are already in motion."

My stomach clenches. "What do you mean, it's too late? What wheels?"

"The scribes will have heard the truth about you by now."

"How? Who told them?" My panicked voice echoes through the cavernous library.

She peers up at me with unremorseful eyes. "*I* did."

3
AGATHA

"Master Scribe, look what I can do!" Paityn holds up her index finger to reveal a tiny flame dancing at its tip, her giddiness radiating.

"Good for you. Show me again when it's three times the size. And practice in a clearing *out*side so you don't burn down the entire guild." I force a smile as I pass my pupil in the hall, but I don't slow, the scroll gripped tightly within my grasp. I should hide this letter I received—Fates, I should *burn* it—before someone discovers it in my possession, but Allegra will need it. Besides, if I know Allegra at all, she'll demand to see Gesine's words before she believes them.

I can hardly believe them.

A key caster from another realm in Islor, by Malachi's scheming? In my almost eight decades of life, I have never heard of such a thing. The archives did not hint of it, and I would know. I've spent my life immersed within the recollections of seers and scribes alike, their considerable knowledge at my fingertips.

Yet here we are, and I must now decide how to proceed.

I wish I had no need to involve Allegra. The guild's Second is too young and ambitious, her seamless skill with wearing various masks unsettling. She could rival Queen Neilina with all her cunning, and sometimes I fear I will find myself caught in a web of her making. It's no secret that Allegra pines to one day climb to the role of Guild Prime. The lengths to which she'll go to get there, though … those worries keep me staring at my ceiling into the late hours.

But of all the guild leaders within Mordain, Allegra is the only one who values the role of the scribes. The others mostly disregard us, both for our mediocre connections to our affinity and for the importance we place on our seers. We are the castaways, the ones with too little power to be of any real use beyond collecting knowledge and training the youngest casters on beginner skills.

Besides, I have no other option than to involve Allegra anymore. I lack the affinity needed to send a return letter to Gesine, and no one among the scribes is strong enough to ensure it reaches its recipient. We *must* keep these lines of communication open if we hope to gain more vital information about this key caster and what she means for the fate of all.

I cross the parapet toward the guild tower. Beyond is an expanse of rock and blue waters and, in the very far distance, across the channel, the jewels of Argon's castle sparkle in the sunlight. To the north of Nyos, the Isle of Mordain is a breathtaking view of mountains and lush green forests. As a child, I relished the days my teachers would allow us time within the meadows, collecting plants and fungi for the horticulturists and chemists.

Over the decades, I've held on to that small joy, taking my young pupils out in nature to test their budding skills before they move on to greater lessons. But the rough terrain has become treacherous for these old bones of mine as of late. I've been forced to abandon the outings to those fresher and more suited, relegating myself to the dank, dark tunnels where the scribes toil away thanklessly.

The city of Nyos itself is vast, a sight to behold, with the towering guild at the center perched high above, its pinnacles a bold statement for both casters and children waiting to find their spark. The guild is the first thing anyone sees as they sail across the waters from Ybaris, a magnificent monument designed by the skilled stone casters, artists by trade. But it is the city below that most returning to Mordain long for—the thriving streets of shops and cafés and cottage-like dwellings, of like-minded people living in a world that has committed them to servitude of the queen and her subjects.

Subjects who readily outcast them the moment they are born and tested and found to be something other than simple mortals.

The general council is already in session when I reach the heavy wooden doors. The two guards at the door eye me with unyielding gazes, their hands gripping the pommels of their swords. I've always found it needless to station sentries outside a chamber of skilled casters, the room already warded against a multitude of evils. Almost as silly as dressing these elite warriors in head-to-toe armor and equipping them with blades when their affinities are their most deadly weapons. But I suppose if the point is to make them appear menacing and the act of interrupting a council in session daunting, it is effective.

"Hello, Darius, Fatima." I nod, as if my only crime against the guild today is arriving late to a meeting.

Darius's crystal blue eyes flare with surprise. Of course they would assume that the old crow who trained them three decades ago would not recognize them behind those intimidating masks.

I lift my chin. "I hope you are both still practicing your flame progression." A trivial beginner skill, considering what they've learned since they were recruited to the Shadow squad.

Delight flashes in Fatima's eyes, and I imagine that wide-toothed grin from her childhood hiding behind the metal. "Of course, Master Scribe."

"Very well, then." I nod curtly toward the door, bolstering my nerve.

She yanks the handle. It opens with a noisy creak that earns a few glances as I duck into my seat.

"… Her Highness is beside herself with worry. She has not heard from either of her children in a full moon's cycle, but the latest messages arriving from Cirilea are ominous. They speak of Prince Tyree's capture and a bounty placed on Princess Romeria's head," Lorel says from her seat at the council table, ignoring my tardy entrance. The Prime is dressed in her formal crimson and silver attire, her hair pulled into a chignon—an indication that she has just returned from visiting Argon and is relaying words directly from the queen's mouth. "Furthermore, she has vowed revenge against Islor for the assassination of King Barris."

"And did she show you the body of this supposed Islorian assassin responsible for the king's death?" Solange asks, her husky voice almost a purr, the unspoken accusation hanging out like linen on a clothesline for all to see.

Lorel's lips purse, the lines of age crinkling the skin around them. She came up in Mordain two decades after me, but her time as Prime has aged her prematurely. "She did not reveal it, and it is not my place to make such a request."

"Surely, it would be seen as a reasonable one," Allegra pipes up from her seat opposite Solange. She also wears her formal crimson and silver dress, for no reason other than to stand out in the assembly. The two casters claim equal rank as Seconds, beneath the Prime. As the three governing guild members, they decide what is deemed important. The rest of us—the masters of each faction—are spectators, to provide answers and cajole into picking sides in the rare case when a vote is demanded. In the end, it is always Lorel's choice that prevails.

Solange's willowy frame is stiff within her seat, her lengthy chestnut hair bound with braids and coiled into a bun, making her features more severe. At thirty-eight years of age, she is the youngest Second in the guild's history. "I suppose accountability is a luxury we can no longer afford."

"And how would that be perceived by Her Highness, besides a sign of Mordain's mistrust?" Lorel's eyebrows arch in challenge.

The Second doesn't balk. "Fates forbid we appear anything but cowed by the Ybarisan queen." Solange is the only one who dares so brazenly challenge the Prime's decision making.

Few around this table are foolish enough to believe Lorel's decisions are driven by anything but her need to curry favor with Queen Neilina—and retain her anointed position. Even fewer are foolish enough to believe that our southern neighbors had anything to do with the king's demise. It was widely known that Neilina was opposed to any sort of arrangement with Islor and resented her husband for entertaining it.

"What of her response?" Allegra steers the conversation away from coming to blows. A wise move. While the youthful Second might be a natural conspirator, she walks the line of diplomacy so effortlessly, few see any hints of betrayal.

To that, Lorel's sagging features turn grim. "Her efforts to drum up support have been fruitful. Both mortal and elven armies march in masses not seen since King Ailill and Caster Farren tore the veil into the Nulling. She intends to rescue her children from Malachi's demons."

"And what is expected of Mordain?" Allegra asks, but we all know the answer. It's what we've been fearing for months.

"The elementals are organizing to leave for the front line." The Prime squares her shoulders as if preparing for battle herself. "I have committed the Shadows, our strongest healers, and our architects to join them."

Murmurs erupt around the table. Beside me, Master Healer Brigitta exhales, the only sign that sending her best and brightest to war concerns her.

"Mordain has not fought in a battle for a hundred years," Solange begins with forced calm.

"Is that not the very thing you train your Shadows for?" Lorel throws back.

Solange's teeth grit. The Shadows have been hers—to recruit, to teach—for nearly a decade, since the last Shadow Master passed. She's never had to send them to their deaths. "This is not Mordain's war."

"But we are allies, and that is what allies do—support each other."

I stifle my snort. Queen Neilina keeps an iron vise around Mordain's neck, holding our caster babies hostage if we don't comply with her every whim. We are not any more allies than Islor's mortals are allies with the keepers who enslave them for their lifeblood.

"I propose we hold a vote," Allegra says.

"The result will make no difference. Queen Neilina has requested our support, and as Guild Prime, I have granted it," Lorel declares, not a hint of a waver in her voice. "Those casters stationed around Ybaris will be ordered to gather. Light bringers, healers, architects … all are expected to march for the rift and play their part in aiding the queen's army."

The respective masters of those factions share worried looks. None have trained for war.

But Queen Neilina doesn't care.

Master Messenger Barra clears his throat. "Do we even know what is truly happening south of the rift? The information that has reached us is confusing at best."

And if anyone is hearing rumors, it is the faction who gathers them using their affinity to Vin'nyla, blessing the crows and ravens for their flights across the gaping chasm.

I wish I could trust Barra to deliver my letters to Gesine, but everyone knows the master has aspirations for Lorel's seat one day. Until the time comes, he remains in her pocket, hoping she'll whisper flattering words into the queen's ear about him. That he is even questioning the Prime's decisions now, however subtly, is a cause for concern. It means he's heard a great deal.

"And what new information has reached your casters?" Solange's lips are pressed flat.

"For starters, that King Zander has been exiled, and his brother, Atticus, has claimed the throne for himself."

"Their politics are not our concern," Lorel dismisses. "The queen will not negotiate with either."

"Yes, my Prime, but there are more concerning issues, about the poison that floats through the lands, infecting the mortals and killing the immortals when they feed."

"The poison is not new. We've already heard about this. If you recall, it is how Queen Esma and King Eachann died."

"Yes, but it is now believed that the source of that poison is Princess Romeria's own blood."

The room grows dead silent.

Lorel blinks several times. "Obviously a fable the Islorians are spinning to place blame on Ybaris for whatever problems Malachi's demons face."

Barra takes a deep, calming breath. A master losing their temper and snapping at the Prime has grave consequences. At minimum, it's a demotion. At worse, a sword through their throat. Master Horticulturist Maeve seated across from us can attest to that. This is only her second council session, having replaced the previous master after an untimely death for erupting at the Prime. "Perhaps, but I have received the same message from several sources—"

"It is impossible."

"I wouldn't say impossible," Allegra speaks up. "There is a way."

"Something of that magnitude would require a summons to the fates, a treasonous act that our elemental sisters are incapable of while collared and Queen Neilina herself forbade centuries ago." Lorel's voice rises with each word.

In the growing tension that fills the room, I feel the sudden, inexplicable urge to speak up and confirm that it is *exactly* what happened.

Allegra's cutting glare of warning stalls my words.

Lorel leans in closer. "Are you suggesting that, Allegra? That

Queen Neilina removed a collar and bade one of our sisters to summon a fate?"

Yes! I do not have to suggest it. I know for a fact she did. Ianca admitted to it.

But speaking the words out loud would mean admitting to all the scribes have kept over the years, and that would earn many of us a death sentence.

Allegra's features are unreadable. "I would never suggest something so traitorous."

"I should hope not." Lorel taps the table with her fist, as if that topic is laid to rest. "Speaking of elementals, Her Highness expects two new ones to replace Caster Gesine and Caster Ianca now rather than later."

"But our oldest are too young. They have not completed their training yet," Allegra says. As supervisor of elemental studies, she would know.

"I've relayed your concerns to the queen, and she is adamant we send them right away."

I duck before my sneer is caught. *Of course* the queen is adamant. Beatrix and Cressida are seventeen and fifteen, respectively. Young and fearful, and easier to persuade should the queen decide she need to tempt the fates again. That was Ianca's folly and the queen's triumph the last time.

Though prophecy always finds a way, I need remind myself, and if Malachi's end goal is to have the nymphs' full power grace these lands again, then I suspect he has been scheming for far longer than any of us suspect.

"The training our elementals have received will have to suffice. The rest, they can learn from their elder sisters in Argon. After all, there are nineteen of them," Lorel declares. Another matter worthy of debate but already decided.

No one makes mention of the two elementals who ran, or why. No one voices questions about how they escaped in the first place. To do so would mean admitting that one—or more—of those nineteen elementals left in Argon's jeweled castle likely aided in their escape.

"We are adjourned for today."

Chair legs scrape against stone as council members abandon their seats in a rush, many wringing their hands over the news that Mordain has been conscripted into Queen Neilina's war.

Allegra's head is held high as she strolls toward the door. "You were late today, Master Scribe." Reprimand hangs in her voice. "Walk with me so I may hear your inadequate excuses."

I scuttle out the door next to her, struggling to keep her fast pace while remembering that I once whipped her bare behind for eating her classmate's lunch. Along the parapet we march, down the stairs, and into the courtyard. The bronzed statue of Caster Yason draws a shadow over a group of stone casters as they take their lesson on the building's spelled doors.

"I beg you, slow down, please. These old legs are not what they once were."

Allegra huffs with annoyance but adjusts her speed. Her eyes —the color of an evergreen forest after a heavy summer rain— flitter about us to check for listeners. "Any news from our sisters?"

"Indeed, there is. We have lost Ianca to the change. It happened on their journey down."

Allegra winces. "Likely for the best, though. This way she cannot speak to her crimes. Not that Lorel would acknowledge them."

If Ianca's even still alive to speak at all. When Gesine wrote this message, Ianca was barely holding on. What a loss. The caster played a vital role in what has happened and what is to come. Her name will live on through the ages, as surely as Caster Farren's has. I would have loved the opportunity to capture her seer visions for our scrolls.

"And what of this resurrected princess?"

"She is not who she seems."

Allegra's brow wrinkles.

Again, I curse the need to involve the Second. But Allegra has played an important role in our ability to communicate—both with Gesine in Argon and with our sources in Cirilea—for years. Not without cost. In the rare occasion that the masters are called upon to vote, she always has mine, whether I agree with her stance or not.

Leading her into an alcove, away from prying gazes, I thrust the scroll into her hand.

She unfurls it, flips it over, studies it. "There is a tracer spell woven into this."

"I'm not shocked. Gesine was always quick to learn things she wasn't meant to." But it's a blessing because it also ensures our response to her will arrive where needed.

"Where is she now?"

"Traveling north toward Venhorn."

"*Venhorn*. She still hopes to discover something at this Stonekeep."

"She believes it is tied to this prophecy." A more astute pupil than Gesine, I have never known.

With another perfunctory glimpse around, Allegra unfolds the letter.

I watch her eyes dart back and forth until they flare.

"A key caster," she hisses, pausing to flash me a panicked look. "How is that possible? Affinities can't be gifted, even by the fates themselves!"

"I do not know, but the king of Islor is aware." Or former king. Gesine's letter confirms that rumor of his exile is true as well.

"And yet he does nothing … because he is still infatuated with her. Of course, it is as Aoife meant it to be," Allegra murmurs, still reading.

I don't need to point out the line after, where Gesine declares this version of the princess is genuinely in love with her once betrothed.

Allegra gasps. "Gesine is sure of it?"

"'She rose again as a Daughter of Many and a Queen for All,'"

I recite the scripture word for word. "I do not know what other puzzle pieces Gesine has cobbled together since sending this message. It arrived by common carrier pigeon." An exhausted bird with no affinities to aid in its travel, short of the one Gesine wove into the scroll to guide its path here. They were outside a city named Bellcross, heading north, when she got her hands on paper and coerced someone to send it. It's likely been weeks since, and much may have changed.

"What is …" She frowns at the scribble hastily added at the bottom of the page, as if added in a rush. "Ulysede. What is that? I've never heard of it."

"Neither have we." I point to the drawing of two intersected crescent moons. "But the seers have seen that symbol time and time again. No one has ever gleaned a meaning behind it. This is the first time we can tie anything to it." A single word. A name. What does it mean?

Allegra shakes her head, rolling the paper. "I do not like the idea of a key caster within easy reach of an Islorian king who is desperate to regain his throne. At what cost, Agatha? How long before this proves disastrous, and we are complicit?"

It's not the first time Allegra has panicked since I've brought her into the fold. It takes effort and skill to weave webs. One slip, and she will surely find herself caught, along with the rest of us.

I pat her shoulder and feel very much the elder scholar comforting a student. "She is still very unskilled. Gesine is guiding her, but it could take months, even years, before she is a true threat. Regardless, whatever happens, it is in the name of prophecy. We cannot meddle."

"It was Caster Wendeline's meddling that got us here," she reminds me.

"Or it is as it was always meant to be."

She sighs, my words seeming to calm her. "You will prepare a response?"

"Right away. I will have it in your hands to send by tonight." My history with Gesine reaches far back, to the days when I'd find her covered in dust and hiding in the scrolls, avoiding caster lessons. She knows my handwriting. Any author other than me and Gesine would withhold valuable information. But it is Allegra's skill that will ensure my response reaches its destination.

Approaching voices have Allegra shoving the linen roll into my pocket. "And when will Alara be ready to join the rest of the elementals for her training?" she asks loudly.

"She has found her spark to Aminadav, but the one to Aoife escapes her."

"You may as well send her to me, anyway. It seems I will have space soon."

"As you wish, Second." With a bow, I rush back to my underground haven.

"Will you finally find your answers, my dear girl?" I trace the swirls of scripture carved into the stone wall. Many thousands of years ago, the guild towers of Nyos were built atop a mountain of rock, honeycombed with caves that have since formed the scribes' territory. The nymphs were already nothing more than a fable by that point, a bedtime story to tell children, and this wall existed among us and our daily lives, without an explanation that many longed for. A bright and curious Gesine was one of them.

Footfalls scraping against stone warn me of an approach a moment before I hear the childish voice. "Master Scribe, you called for me?"

I break away from the mysterious scrawl. My pupil stands within the archway, her lengthy blond hair braided into pigtails. "I did, Alara. Pack your things. You will be moving to the elemental wing."

Alara's blue eyes widen. "But I thought I had to find my affinities before I could go there?"

"Normally, yes, but perhaps the Second can chase Aoife out of you where I have not succeeded." I would have, given more time. The girl is only eleven.

"But ... but ... I want to stay here, with you."

"What you and I want accounts for little."

Her bottom lip wobbles, and I turn my back before she sees the tears that threaten. Alara came to Mordain as an infant and stayed in the village outside the guild towers as all children do until they begin showing signs that their affinities are rising. She has been in my charge for the past two years and should remain with me for at least another. I know better than to grow attachments to these children, whose time with me is so fleeting, but she reminds me so much of Gesine with her voracious appetite for knowledge. "Perhaps, if you focus on your studies and have some free time, you can come back to visit." I feign to be busy with my focus on the nymph scripture. "Go on now. Get your things. Caster Joseph will escort you."

"Yes, Master Scribe." Her feet drag with reluctance, and a sob sounds before she is too far.

I allow myself a soft exhale. It is for the best.

"Master Scribe?"

I jump. "What did I say about sneaking up on me, Cahill!"

"I'm sorry. I wasn't tryin' to." His deep adolescent voice is full of regret.

I calm my breathing. "What is it?"

He peers down the tunnel. "What's wrong with Alara?"

"Nothing is wrong with Alara. She is moving to train with the elementals."

"Already?" Dismay shines in his pale green eyes, such a contrast to his tawny skin. The two of them have been inseparable since she arrived, he like a big brother to her. "Can't I go with her?"

"No, Cahill. We've discussed this before. Alara has powerful affinities to two fates. She will train as an elemental caster and then move to Ybaris to serve the royal family. Your place is here, with the scribes, protecting our past and our future."

"Because I am weak." He studies his shoes.

"No, Cahill, because your *affinity* is weak, just as all scribe affinities are weak. But we are strong of mind, and that is where you will be of most service." I smile at the boy of seventeen as I lie to him.

For, if anyone knew the truth, they would have him executed by dawn.

4
ATTICUS

"Where are you, dear brother?" The contours of Islor's terrain on the map blur as my thoughts drift.

I know where Zander is—or at least I can guess. The messages arriving have painted a clear path of his flight from Cirilea to Bellcross and beyond, heading north. He and whatever Legion warriors have survived are seeking refuge in the Venhorn Mountains. How many of them remain, though? There were plenty of their bodies left behind.

The bigger question is, what next? How long will the mighty *king* of Islor hide in those caves, living among the Nulling's beasts and saplings while that Ybarisan traitor's blood infests the kingdom he once claimed?

Not long, if I know my brother at all.

In my hand, the tiny cylindrical vial burns against my palm despite its chill. Boaz delivered it earlier this morning—found hidden in the pocket of a tanner's servant, in Cirilea for trade. The mortal didn't even see the execution square. He swings from a rope on the street. No ceremony. A swift and brutal message to those waiting and wondering, or still undecided about whether to contaminate themselves.

How did *no one* guess that it was Romeria's blood? Especially after what happened to the daaknar? In hindsight, it is obvious. Wendeline knew, but she spoon-fed us lies that we readily swallowed. That was our mistake, one of many. I will not make that same mistake again.

I hold the vial up to study the dark brown liquid. To be fair, it doesn't look like blood, at least not the fresh crimson I've taken from mortals' veins, and not the blood pouring from Romeria's nose when Tyree smashed her face against the dungeon cell bars. But fates know what happens when it's siphoned and stored in glass.

And the fates surely know, for a weapon such as the princess could only have come from them. An intoxicating, addicting, beautiful creature capable of ensnaring kings and their brothers alike.

Princess Romeria is at the root of all Islor's pain, whether she remembers herself or not.

My skin prickles with this persistent sense of betrayal. I can't shake the genuine horror splayed across Romeria's face as those Islorian lords screamed and the Ybarisans burned the day of the royal repast. As if she truly had no idea what was to come. As if she had been speaking truth all along about her memory loss.

I will admit, there were times I wanted to believe her. The Romeria who rose from a merth arrow seemed different from the one who helped mastermind the attack.

But, even with her memory loss, she is still at the heart of it all, and I was right to lay all the blame at her feet and call for her capture.

"I had no other choice," I say to the empty room, as if Zander's lingering presence might pass my words along. "We would have lost Islor together. I hope you can see that."

The door to my war room creaks open behind me. "Your Highness ..." The guard's metal armor clanks.

I still half expect my father to respond. But he has been dead and buried for nearly a full cycle of Hudem's moon, and I am now left to clean up his disastrous deal with Ybaris. "What is it?"

"I did not expect a king so adept at commanding armies on battlefields to spend so much time hiding alone," a female answers.

My spine prickles under the trill timbre of Saoirse's voice. "I'm not *hiding*. I'm thinking." Though I do miss the ease of leading thousands of soldiers to battle over maneuvering around this fucking royal court.

"I hope you do not find my presence a bother." She feigns concern.

Everyone's presence is a bother lately. Saoirse, Adley, Boaz ... they all have an opinion on how I should rule my kingdom and no qualms about blathering in my ear to share. I suppose this is what Zander faced, too, when he prematurely inherited the throne. But our father had been grooming him his entire life for the role.

I'm learning as I go, and most days, the ground beneath my feet feels like quicksand.

Taking a deep breath, I tuck away my annoyance and turn to face the future queen of Islor as she glides across the floor toward me, her willowy frame graceful, her smile demure. An effective cloak to hide the wraith beneath.

I will admit, Saoirse is far from unpleasant to look at. The first time I laid eyes on Lord Adley's daughter so many years ago, I thought her sharp features appealing, and I flirted without realizing who she was. As soon as I learned, my interest fizzled. It's not just her ties to Kettling—a formidable city in the east that pines for control and would usurp my family in a heartbeat if afforded the chance. She was meant for Zander, to forge an alliance, before my father got the idiotic notion to negotiate with Ybaris instead, a realm that has openly wished for our deaths for two thousand years.

Kettling is far closer to enemy than ally, but at least I know their motivations. Saoirse cares for nothing but to sink her claws into power. Her father, Lord Adley, surely dreams each night of ruling the realm, but he will be satisfied with having the king's ear while he waits for either his daughter's heirs to claim the throne or my death, whichever comes first.

Knowing Adley, plans for the latter are already in the works.

For the good of my realm and its people, I remind myself for the hundredth time since agreeing to this marriage proposal. Thankfully, I've succeeded at limiting my time around Saoirse thus far to avoid regretting it. "Is there something I can help you with?"

"Yes, I'd like your permission to cut the tongue from that seamstress who is making my wedding dress."

My eyebrows arch. "Surely, you jest."

"She is a marvel, yes, but her incessant nattering is too much." Saoirse stops a few feet away, drawing her index finger over the edge of the map. "She does not need her tongue to sew."

"This is Cirilea, where we pride ourselves on not arbitrarily maiming our household." If what I've heard of Kettling is true, the same cannot be said over there.

"I was only kidding." She sniffs, her disappointment palpable.

"Of course. I never doubted it." The more time I spend with Saoirse, the more I see why Zander would choose our parents' murderer over her. Zander's heart has always bled for Islor's mortals, and it's clear Saoirse only tolerates them as much as she needs them to survive and dress well. My heart doesn't bleed in the same way as my brother's, but I'm not vicious. "Anything else?"

"The assembly is gathering."

"I'm aware." The dull hum of voices carries as Islor's lords and ladies collect in the throne room. "Was there anything else you wished to discuss?" Or can we end this unpleasant exchange immediately?

"Given all that Islor has faced since last Hudem and the horrors we are facing *still* due to Ybaris's treachery, I think it wise to demonstrate a united front between Cirilea and Kettling."

"Isn't that the purpose of our marriage?" I drawl, feigning

humor where I feel none. Kettling may be a city, but it steers the entire eastern side of Islor, where Adley has been allowed to forge his own alliances for too long. Another mistake of my father's making.

"Time is of the essence, though." Her black eyes dissect my face, attempting to read me. "Your brother did not wait for tradition to seat *her* on the throne."

So that's what this is about. Saoirse wishes to use Zander's mistake as a precedent. She doesn't want to play queen in weeks or days. She wants to be queen *now*. The day after we announced our betrothal, she attempted to move her things into the queen's quarters, which I refused, not wanting her so close to where I sleep. Now this. I should have seen it coming.

"Returning to Islor's traditions would be beneficial for all," I say slowly.

"You don't think the spirits of Islor's lords and ladies would benefit from seeing us together, Atticus?" She edges in until she's inches away, tipping her head back to flash me a flirtatious smile. It's the first time she's ever addressed me by my name, and she does it with a sultry tone meant to sway me.

My cock doesn't so much as twitch.

I chuckle, a mask for the urge to grind my teeth. "Islor's lords' and ladies' spirits show no signs of suffering." At least not those lined up to see how they can benefit from this spontaneous change of ruler. I step away, putting distance between us as I return my focus to the map. "You will have plenty of time to listen to grievances after Hudem. Until then, I would think you should be more concerned with keeping up to date with the goings-on in your city. There is a poison ripping through Islor, after all." And if there was a city of mortals who wished their keepers dead, surely it would be Kettling.

"It is *you* who insisted Father and I stay within Cirilea!"

Because enemies should be kept close. "Yes, but I would have expected you to be consumed by frantically writing letters to the city wards during this *horrific* time to ensure the city is well managed."

"Father receives messages daily—" She falters, as if she's revealed too much, but it's nothing I don't know. My trusted captains have been tailing every eastern lord since I took power and reporting back to me. "Kettling's steward is handling it."

I arch a brow. "By locking servants in cellars, from what I've heard."

"To keep them from making poor choices that would force their keepers to punish them. I would think a cellar with food and water and a pallet is far more humane than a noose. Wouldn't you agree?" she counters, her chin lifted in challenge. "Besides, Kettling may be my home, but *all of* Islor are my people. My place is by your side now."

What a well-rehearsed answer. I force an easy smile. "Of course."

"Shall we?" She takes several steps toward the door that leads into the throne room, reaching for my arm. If I won't allow her a place on the throne beside me, escorting the king in is her consolation prize.

We haven't so much as held hands since this arrangement was made, and I have no desire to find out how prickly her body feels before I'm required to by marriage rite. "I will see you in there."

A flash of anger skitters across her face before she quells it. "As you wish, Your Highness." With a subtle nod of deference, she departs.

"It's what's best for Islor," I whisper for the hundredth time.

But I will not be manipulated by *anyone* ever again.

5
GRACEN

"Mika!" I hiss.

His index finger stalls a hair-width's length away from his baby sister's cheek.

I hold my breath as her lashes flicker, waiting for the first wail. But she settles again within her woven basket, none the wiser to her mischievous brother.

A slow sigh sails from my lips. "Fates help you if you wake her." She's mere days old, and it took an hour to coax her to sleep after her morning feed. I'm hoping I can steal an hour of rest myself after I set these tarts.

Mika flops back against the stone wall, his curly brown hair forming a halo around his little face. "I'm bored."

"What a nice problem to have." I dust my hands with a fresh coat of flour and return my focus to kneading pastry dough. The kitchen is quiet at this hour, the morning rush over and the afternoon one yet to start. Aside from Sena, who tends to the hearty and fragrant stew simmering over the fire, all is quiet.

Sabrina pokes her head in then. "Anything fresh from the oven yet?"

I nod toward the loaves of bread I pulled from the oven fifteen minutes ago, my way of granting her permission.

She glides over, her elegant lemon-yellow dress swirling around her legs as she moves. "I have been thinking about this *all morning*." Hacking off a chunk, she slathers it with butter and then takes a bite. She moans.

The beautiful blond tributary often leaves her spacious room on the ground floor to swap gossip and get a slice of the freshest bread in the castle kitchen. She's the only one of the tributaries who does. I think she's lonely and missing her family.

"So? Did the king call on you last night?" I ask.

Her shoulders sink with a crestfallen look. "No. It has been nearly a week."

"I'm sure it's because of the poison. It is causing such havoc." He was calling on her almost nightly not long ago. She would float in here the next day as if she had met and been blessed by all four fates themselves.

"Yes, perhaps." She sighs. "I have important tasks I should get back. See you later, Gracen. Mika." She winks at him and then she's gone.

What *important* task that could be, I can't imagine. None of these royal tributaries have any duties beyond offering their vein. They don't even make their own beds. Though, Sabrina has minded my children for me on more than one occasion, so I shouldn't judge too harshly. It's just a very different life than the one I had as a tributary.

"Where's Lilou?" Mika asks.

"Helping with the laundry." Likely playing with suds, but one less child to mind while I work is a blessing to me.

"Can I see what Silmar is doing?"

"If I believed that you'd make it to the stables, then certainly, you could. But you and I both know that you will not make it to see Silmar. You will get distracted and venture someplace you do not belong." In any one of the countless dark nooks and secret passages in the castle that my impish five-year-old son has a knack for discovering, causing the staff hours of grief while we hunt for him.

"But I won't this time. I *promise.*"

"Fetch me some pears while you are making promises you can't keep." I soften the scolding with a smile.

Mika drags himself up off the stone floor and ambles over to the bushel, his arms swinging aimlessly around him in an embellished sign of his frustration. But he's quickly distracted by the large, ripe fruit. "May I have one, Ma?"

"You may." I feel the wistful smile touch my lips. A request that I could never have granted in our former life, living under the cruel thumb of Lord Danthrin, our stomachs perpetually empty. When we arrived in Cirilea for the fair, Mika and Lilou were skin and bone, their clothing threadbare and hanging off them. I wasn't much better, all my body's energy going to the unborn child in my swollen belly, my cheeks sunken, my complexion pale. But several weeks here, and my children's ribs no longer show in the bath, their cheeks hold a healthy glow, and I'm treated to more smiles in one day than I'd see in a month in Freywich.

There is no one waiting to burn Mika's hand should he dare pick a rotten piece of fruit off the ground to quiet his grumbling belly.

And it's all because a Ybarisan princess had compassion for us.

A princess who was meant to be queen, who has since been painted an enemy to the crown and to Islor.

My smile evaporates. It cannot be. What they say of her … of her conspiracies and murderous plots … The woman whose blue eyes peered into mine from across the table of pastries, who saw our terrible predicament and *asked*—asked! That's unheard of for nobility—if I'd like to leave it, who saved us from a wretched life at the hands of Lord and Lady Danthrin, does not have murder in her heart. On that, I would stake my life.

But uttering such things within Cirilea are tantamount to treason, so I show my smile, and give silent thanks to the traitor who saved my family.

The door to the kitchen swings open with a force that only one household staff member dares use: a petite and fierce lady's maid who once scared me with her abrasive nature and blunt personality. That was until I noticed how she flinched at the marks and bruises on my body, scowled at the scar on Mika's skin, and slipped delectable grapes from her pocket into Lilou's palm.

"Do you ever *not* have food in your hand, child?" Corrin scoffs.

"You told me to eat more!" Mika fires back with indignation before flashing a wide, gap-toothed grin and then biting into his pear. He doesn't fear her either.

"Cheeky." She shakes her head, but there's no venom in her tone as she passes him. Her demeanor softens as she spots the sleeping baby, and a smile curves her lips. It was Corrin who screamed at me from within the walls of our family quarters to keep pushing, who held my daughter before I did, who has ensured my family and I have everything we could need since we stepped foot within these castle gates, without me ever asking. I used to think it was at the princess's bidding, but she is gone and we are still cared for, sheltered.

Corrin's gaze shifts to me, and the smile fades.

I hold flour-covered hands in the air. "I know … I said I'd rest another day, but I prefer to remain useful." Useful servants are the ones keepers don't let go of. And with a royal wedding around the corner, there are plenty of cakes to make.

"That is not it." She sighs. "You have been summoned."

"*Summoned*. It sounds so formal. By whom?"

Her throat bobs with a hard swallow. "By the king."

My jaw drops. "But … *me*?" I'm a baker. What need does the *king* have of me?

"We are not privy to an explanation, only a demand that you must come now. A guard waits outside."

"*Now*?" I look down at my soiled apron. "Should I not change?" Or at least clean up? The only other dress I have was an old one from Dagny that is too large on my post-delivery body.

"There isn't time for that. He is already in the throne room and waiting."

My bladder threatens to loosen with that added news. Given my recent delivery, there's a strong possibility of that happening. "Fine. I need someone to mind the children—"

"*All* of you have been summoned. Even the baby. I assume Lilou is with the laundress?" Corrin has shifted into her emotionless version.

I nod dumbly. My pulse races in my ears as I shuck my apron and hang it on the wall, the simple act suddenly a struggle. What reason could Islor's king have for demanding not only *my* immediate presence, but that of my children? In the throne room? Surely, not a good one. Especially not if he takes offense to how we joined his household, by Princess Romeria's will.

Oh, good fates. It clicks. "Is there an assembly today?"

Corrin pulls her shoulders back to feign a strong front, but her forehead is furrowed. "Yes, there is. Many of the lords and ladies are gathered."

Will *they* be there?

Will *he* be there?

What if …

My breathing labors under my panic, a wave of dizziness hitting me. It makes sense now. I *knew* this new life was too good to be true.

Corrin reaches out and squeezes my shoulder. She understands my fears. She saw the evidence of my time in Freywich. "You all wear the king's mark now, and while he is not his brother, have faith that he will make the right decision."

I swallow my terror and nod. "Come, Mika."

"Where are we going?" he chirps between mouthfuls, oblivious to the cloud of danger that whirls around us.

"To meet the new king."

I absorb as much calm as I can from the tiny sleeping bundle within my arms as my gaze wanders the hallway lined by gold pillars and sentries. I've seen much of the castle due to Mika's naughty antics, but I've never been in this part before.

Then again, I've never had need to visit the throne room until today.

Mika is ahead, mimicking the guard's march, but his short legs are unable to match the pace and it leaves him scrambling every few steps to catch up. If not for the dire situation, I would laugh at my comical son.

"I do not know how he keeps such high spirits for a boy who has seen much," Corrin says alongside me, Lilou's hand gripped within hers.

"Children are resilient." Far more so than I. The screams Mika let out while they made me stand and watch Lord Danthrin punish him still haunt me. It caused such damage and unending pain, I wasn't sure Mika would have use of his hand afterward. The village priestess with no true caster affinities whatsoever recommended they cut it off to offer him relief. But Lady Danthrin insisted we leave it to remind Mika—and others—of his folly.

As if a stump wouldn't remind everyone all the same.

In the end, I'm thankful for her cruel interference. If they'd cut off his hand, Priestess Wendeline would have had nothing to fix when we visited her that day. She took his pain away and gave him full use of it again.

Another traitor to the realm, according to rumor. What has become of the caster, I do not know. Some say she was burned in a fiery ball the night of the royal repast. Others insist she was executed along with the rest of Cirilea's casters. And yet a few swear she remains locked in the dungeon beneath the castle.

"Thank the fates for that." Corrin's focus is on the looming doors of the throne room ahead, her face grim.

I lower my voice from prying ears. "Please tell me, once we walk through those doors, what should I expect?" Of anyone in the household, Corrin will speak truth without rolling it in sugar first.

She worries her lips. "A show of power and of new rule."

That's what I'm afraid of. "At my family's expense?" We are a baker and three small children. We are no one. But perhaps that is the whole point. Our mortal lives mean nothing, and yet trading them will earn a lord's loyalty. *If* Danthrin has a loyal bone in his body.

"It's always at *someone*'s expense, isn't it?"

That does not alleviate my surging panic. "And this king? Is he like the last one?" Not that I ever met King Zander, but it's general knowledge throughout the castle that he was sympathetic to his mortal subjects and their plights.

Corrin's attention flitters to the guard, who is ahead and likely out of easy listening. Still, she slows her pace and drops her voice to a whisper. "He is young and brash, and much prefers his sword to diplomacy. Soldiers revere him and will follow him anywhere, including to seize his brother's crown."

"Is he kind?" Sabrina complains about the infrequent visits, wishing things would return to normal, which tells me he can't be cruel. I never wished for *more* evenings with Lord Danthrin, or any of the Islorians he passed me along to. I dreaded those nights and still wake in a cold sweat every time I relive them in my sleep.

Corrin's lips purse. The night of the mutiny, she stormed into our room and told us to bolt the door. The next day, she returned and calmly announced that there was a new ruler. Beyond that, she has never outwardly taken sides and has warned me to follow suit, for my own good. "King Atticus has an easy charm, but do not mistake that for kindness. Mortals are being hanged every day now, by his command. Some in the streets, without trial. He does not share the same soft spot for our kind that his brother does." She sighs. "I cannot say for certain how this will end, Gracen."

"You and I both know how this will end." With my family

stuffed into a wagon and dragged back to Freywich. "Please, Corrin, we cannot go back there. I would rather we all—"

"Hush now!" she hisses, before I can utter such horrendous words out loud. "You will survive this, as you've survived everything else. But you must keep your head up and your brave face on. For *their* sake"—she nods toward Mika—"and for yours."

"Even if I'm terrified?" Even if I'd rather jump into the river with my family than return to our old life?

"Especially then." Her eyes flash to mine. "But whatever you do, do not lie to him."

The two guards manning the enormous doors draw them open with ease, revealing the immense room and crowd beyond.

Nausea churns in my stomach. "Mika, stay by my side at all times, and do not say a single word," I whisper.

Countless heads swivel, and my stomach tenses under the rapt attention of Islor's lords and ladies, at least the ones who did not run home to safeguard their lands at the first signs of this poison. Most discount us immediately, but there are those who watch my little family tread along the marble aisle toward the steps, their keen interest on my children. I can guess what they see—the same thing Lord Danthrin hoped for when he *acquired* me: a high return on investment.

Even Mika senses the weight of the situation and falls back to cling to my leg as we walk forward, toward the stairs and the form seated above.

I take Corrin's advice and channel the same courage I dug up when Princess Romeria offered me a position within the castle, knowing that if I said yes and then she changed her mind, if I somehow ended up back in Freywich, we would pay dearly for my disloyalty.

"Your Highness. The baker and her family, as requested," Corrin calls out when we reach the bottom of the steps, followed by a curtsy.

I follow suit a split second later—a poor attempt, given the baby in my arms—and then right myself, keeping my focus on the swirls in the marble floor.

"Does the baker have a name?" a fluid but deep male voice asks.

After a moment's pause and an elbow to the ribs from Corrin, I realize I'm supposed to answer.

"Gracen," I croak and then clear the gruffness from my voice. "Your Highness."

"You seem more interested in the pattern on the throne room floor than in your king, Gracen." Humor laces his tone.

"I ..." I falter at how to respond. How else am I supposed to behave?

"Look at him," Corrin hisses.

My head snaps up as commanded until I meet the gaze boring down on me from above.

So *this* is the new king of Islor.

His muscular frame is partially slouched on the throne, his thighs splayed, a finger tracing his angular jaw, looking utterly bored by this event. But I imagine that's by design. My father once said lords and ladies are more apt to dance like court jesters before an uninterested king when they want to win his favor.

He is even more handsome than Sabrina claimed. His golden-blond hair is cropped short, but the ends wisp up around his crown, as if begging for the chance to grow long enough to form plump curls. I heard he led the king's army before and is said to be a proficient swordsman. His frame certainly suggests that. Corrin claimed he is young and brash. He's young-looking, yes, but he could be a mortal thirty or an elven three hundred.

And his piercing blue eyes dissect me.

"How long have you been under my employ, Gracen?"

I don't dare look away. "Since the Cirilean fair, Your Highness." The best weeks of my children's lives. I suppose all must come to an end.

"Since Princess Romeria stumbled upon you in the market and demanded you join the royal household?"

"She never demanded," I manage around a hard swallow. Corrin told me not to lie.

His eyebrow arches. "No?"

I shake my head. "She asked if I'd like to come here, and I said I would. Your Highness."

"Surrounded by soldiers carrying swords, with her children by her side, what else was my subject supposed to say?"

The blood drains from my face at the sound of that voice, but I can't bring myself to turn toward it. There's no need; I can easily picture Lord Danthrin, with his perfectly coiffed silver-white ponytail and his tailored suit and his wicked smile. He still thrives in my nightmares.

Lilou lets out a wail. It's echoed by Mika's sob. I promised them they'd never have to see that cruel lord again.

"None of that, children. Come now." Corrin herds them away, off to the opposite side of where Danthrin hovers. I sense him moving in, preparing to claim his property.

"The children seem *thrilled* to see you," the king drawls, as if this is amusing.

Lord Danthrin laughs—that forced, false sound that he uses around nobility to pretend he's pedigreed when he's a demon. "They probably missed their naps. They will sleep in the wagon on the way back to Freywich."

This can't be happening.

"No, Mama, please don't make us go back there!" Mika cries, finally realizing the gravity of the situation. The terror in his voice …

Fates, please help us. I squeeze my eyes shut but not before several tears escape, rolling down my cheek, falling.

The sudden stir within my arms tells me they've landed on my sleeping daughter, disturbing her slumber. She coughs as her tiny body stiffens and then her eyelids blink open.

"Shhh." My tense body sways, the instinct to lull her back to peace kicking in despite the doom that surrounds us.

A loud creak cuts through an otherwise quiet throne room—

the spectators' attention now rapt. The king has risen from his throne in a swift, graceful move, but his steps down are painfully slow by comparison as he descends to stand inches from me.

From this proximity, he is far more imposing. I struggle to keep my composure, my body trembling.

"Gracen ..."

The unexpected softness in his voice compels me to look up. Blue eyes the color of the spring hyacinths in Lady Danthrin's garden bore into mine. I imagine he's doing what all elven are adept at—seeing what we don't wish them to see. As a child growing up, I thought it was another empty threat delivered to small children by their parents when they misbehaved. But soon after Lord Danthrin collected me on Presenting Day, I learned how easily the immortals sensed our fear.

And how much some of them thrived on it.

Can the king read the terror that grips every inch of my flesh and bone now at the thought of going back to our old life?

"Please ..." It's barely a whisper and likely pointless. The king has been executing mortals every day since he took power. He hears people's appeals all day long and dismisses them with nary a blink. But all I have left is a mother's plea for mercy and a wish that, in this one instance, he may grant it.

Something raw sparks in his gaze, but it's gone in the next instant, so quickly that I think I must have imagined it.

Lilou's wails worsen despite Corrin's best efforts to console her, and numbness takes hold of me as we await the king's ruling.

"You've come here today to reclaim mortals you allege Princess Romeria took from you by force. Is that correct?" King Atticus asks, his voice steely, no hint of humor in it.

"That is correct, Your Highness. Gracen and the children. Three now, I see. An injustice that, righted, would go to great lengths toward rebuilding Freywich." Lord Danthrin sounds smug. He's convinced he has already won.

But ... *rebuilding Freywich?* What happened to it?

"Yes, that was an interesting turn of events. It's almost as if my brother found something in your lands that angered him. Why, oh why, would he go to the efforts of slaughtering the town's keepers?"

My eyes widen with shock. Those keepers were horrible but … they're all gone?

"For their allegiance to you, Your Highness," Lord Danthrin answers smoothly.

"Before they likely heard that I had claimed the throne?" The king frowns, as if that's doubtful. "But he also demanded your entire household for himself and burned your orchard." The king has shifted to that bored drawl again. "An orchard that you declared to my late father was not thriving. Year after year of a terrible blight, I believe you said."

"The Ybarisan whispers evils and tall tales in his ear, Your Highness, steering his temper and his hand." But Lord Danthrin's confident voice wavers.

Blight. What blight? I've never seen such a healthy and fruitful orchard as the one that stretches behind Lord Danthrin's manor, and I grew up in the Plains of Aminadav, where vigorous crops are abundant. My children and I spent many long days in that orchard, collecting its produce for meads and jams and delicacies.

"Tall tales, indeed." The king watches me closely, the corner of his mouth twitching. "Thank you. Your confusion is enlightening," he murmurs, so quietly I doubt anyone else could hear it. Taking a step back, his deep voice carries. "My brother has wronged Islor in many ways, but I cannot fault him for his righteousness, especially when it comes to the welfare of Islor's mortals. If he took such care to punish you, Lord Danthrin, I suspect it was justified."

"Your Highness—"

"I wonder, if I were to pay a visit to Freywich, would I find proof of the picture you painted for my father so he would spare you the hardship of paying the crown's tithe?"

"I … yes, Your Highness," Lord Danthrin sputters. "There is no longer any orchard to speak of. Nothing but charred remains."

"Convenient for you, wouldn't you say? Seeing as the penalty for lying to a king is death. What should the penalty be for lying to *two* kings?" The smile on his lips is so contradictory to the thinly veiled threat escaping them.

I dare steal a glance. Lord Danthrin's normally olive skin tone is sallow.

"Your Highness, if I may ..." An older, regal-looking man steps forward from the first row of seats. "Regardless of what may or may not have transpired in Freywich, Princess Romeria of Ybaris unlawfully claimed this lord's valuable property and, given she is a traitor to the crown and an enemy of the people, all that she has done should be undone. That property should be returned to its rightful owner." He caps that off with a dramatic flourish of his arms, as if his declaration is straight from the fates' mouths.

Who is this lord who speaks out of turn and contradicts the king in his own throne room? For my sake, I hope he doesn't hold the influence he thinks he does.

The king's jaw tenses before relaxing. "Did you collect payment for this exchange, Lord Danthrin?"

"Yes, Your Highness, but it was forced on me. I would gladly return—"

"That payment was made with the crown's funds, and therefore legitimate, regardless of who within the royal house claimed these mortals. Your request is denied. The baker and her children will remain in my household and I, their keeper."

My knees buckle under the weight of relief from his declaration.

The king is suddenly there, his hands gripping my waist, his arms beneath mine, holding both me and my baby upright.

Gasps fill the room.

"I wasn't going to drop her," I mumble as another wave of shock washes over me.

"I didn't think you would." But he remains where he is, his

hands lingering on me, his imposing form too close for my comfort.

I keep my eyes on the embroidered collar of his tunic as my cheeks flush, unsure what else to do or say except, "Thank you, Your Highness."

"How old is she?" he asks softly.

The unexpected question throws me off. "Only a few days," I stammer, adding a breathy, "Your Highness."

"Her name?"

I calm my nerves as best I can. "Suri."

He hums, and I feel it deep inside. "That's a beautiful name." After another beat, his hands slip away. He steps back. "You and your children may return to your quarters."

I find the courage to meet his gaze again. "Thank you for showing us your mercy."

He offers an almost imperceptible nod, but his expression is somber. "I hope when the time comes, you will show me yours." With that, he spins on his heels and strolls away, heading swiftly for a door in the back as if he can't get out of here fast enough.

"What did I tell you, a show of power." Corrin sidles up to me, Lilou in her arms.

"He asked for her name," I whisper.

"And which did you give him?" A hint of panic touches her tone.

I peer down at the tiny, innocent face in my arms, relaxed in slumber once again. "The one we agreed to."

Not the one I anointed her with in the wee hours, moments after her birth.

A traitor's name.

6
ZANDER

"You are *surprised* by the witch's betrayal?" Abarrane's tone carries its typical scorn. I can always count on my Legion commander to mock me the first private moment she finds. In this case, Elisaf's presence doesn't stay her sharp tongue.

"Nothing surprises me anymore when it comes to these casters and the lengths they will reach to ensure prophecy fulfills itself. That does not mean I cannot be furious."

Our voices echo through the tunnel in the mountain wall that separates Ulysede from the outside world. The first time we walked through here, these fifty paces felt like five hundred. But already the distance between the two portcullises is narrowing, the sense of the waiting danger beyond growing every hour since Romeria informed me of Gesine's secret message to Mordain.

An hourglass has been flipped, and it is spilling sand. How quickly? How long before Mordain's guild knows all there is to know about Romeria? Gesine could not say. But she freely admitted to securing paper, ink, and seal from Bellcross's sanctum when they retrieved Ianca and tasking one of Freywich's mortals with delivering a note to the priestess upon their arrival in Bellcross with Lord Rengard. From there, the priestess who kept Ianca hidden would know what to do.

"If it's any consolation, that is an impossible journey. Maybe the bird died over the rift," Elisaf offers.

"As impossible as Stonekeep lending itself to prophecy and giving us *this*?" I wave a hand around us. When Gesine had suggested there was more to this mountain than a sheer rock wall of ancient nymph writing, I laughed in her face. I will never make that mistake again. "She spelled the message for travel and is confident it will land in the right hands. She has proven more than capable of achieving her goals, so we must assume her scribes will soon know where to look for us."

"Are you worried what they will do when they find out we have a key caster?" Abarrane asks, more somberly.

"I am worried about many things, Mordain and otherwise." I sigh. "Gesine is adamant this Master Scribe is prudent. But if it should reach the broader guild, we must assume it will travel to Neilina's ears shortly after." And then she will know her daughter the princess is dead. What will that mean to her? "In any case, it is only a matter of time before the world knows there is a key caster again. This secret was never going to remain ours forever." But I'd hoped long enough to allow me a chance to regain my crown and right all that's wrong in my realm.

Abarrane scowls. "We have Neilina to worry about, and Atticus to worry about, and now this poison. We do not need an army of witches after us too."

All the more reason for me to leave the safety of Ulysede behind. But for the first time in my life, I'm paralyzed by indecision. Every choice I could make, every direction I could take, feels like the wrong one.

"I am ready when you are, Your Highness." Abarrane draws her sword as we approach the second gate where three legionaries stand guard, and it prompts Elisaf and I to draw ours. "Any movement tonight, Loth?"

"Nothing yet, Commander." Loth stands sentry next to the lever, an arrow nocked in his bow, ready to fire. "We sensed something earlier, but it vanished."

"The same as the previous night." Horik's hulking frame is strapped with a dozen weapons. I let his size fool me once in Cirilea's sparring court and assumed he would not be able to compete. I ended up pinned to the dirt beneath his blade and listened to Abarrane's mocking laughter for months after. He is one of the fastest of the legionaries. Couple that with his strength, and he is a force to be reckoned with.

Something tells me we will need that before long.

Abarrane's sharp gaze roves the dusk beyond the wagon, narrowing.

There is nothing from what I can see but the arid, craggy ground, speckled by boulders. A thousand shadows but no hint of threats hiding within them. "One of Telor's scouts, perhaps?" The sun has barely dropped past the horizon. It's still too early for the saplings, unless they've found adequate cover in a nearby hole, which is unlikely.

"Or one of Ybaris's," Elisaf offers.

"Be prepared for all of them. Loth? If you will."

He pulls the lever, setting invisible mechanisms within the wall in motion. The heavy iron portcullis draws upward smoothly.

I test the flames in the torches that line the tunnel, letting them flare under my affinity's touch. Each night, Ulysede ignites with light of its own accord, as if sensing our need. If the city didn't leave me so unsettled, I would appreciate its sentient abilities.

"Brace yourself, Your Highness," Abarrane warns. "The blood curse returns with a vengeance the first time."

"I'm prepared." I haven't stepped outside of Ulysede's gate since we arrived, but now I sense a strange tingle along my throat and a sting in my gums where my needlelike incisors drop.

Four steps out, I realize Abarrane wasn't exaggerating. An

overwhelming wave of need hits me, buckling my knees. I stagger, reaching for the wall to balance myself as my vision blurs. My incisors drop of their own accord, so fast they cut into my bottom lip. All I can do is breathe through it until it subsides into nothing more than an irritant.

When I pull myself upright, the legionaries are strolling for the wagon as if unfazed.

Like me, Elisaf struggles, still down on one knee. "Fates, this feeling …" He grimaces.

It is as terrible as when I was six years old and hit with the lust for blood the first time. "How many trips out here before your tolerance grew?" I call out. Abarrane has been through these gates every day since we arrived.

She flashes a smug smile over her shoulder. "Whatever do you mean?"

Elisaf casts a vulgar gesture—a rarity for him—and it earns her wicked laughter.

The air is noticeably cooler, another sign that wherever we go once we step through those gates, it isn't Islor. I scan the clear, star-filled sky, half expecting the same two moons that cast light in Ulysede each night. But there is only the one.

What will become of Islor after the next Hudem? If my foolish brother goes through with this arranged marriage, he will regret it, there is no doubt about that. Kettling will not honor any alliance when it comes to the crown. They will betray him. My father knew it, I knew it. But the decisions we've made have always been a thorn in Atticus's side. I shouldn't be shocked he'd do the opposite.

We navigate around the boulders, closing in on Horik and Abarrane. From this distance, my affinity can't reach the torch flame at the gate. "Why must the wagon be so far out?"

"When the sapling screams, that imbecile screams, and I recall a tongue lashing from *His Highness* the last time there was too much screaming for the princess's liking."

"The mortal is *still* alive?" Genuine surprise laces my tone. We took that mule of a man prisoner in Norcaster after he divulged information about Lord Isembert's deal with the saplings. We thought he might have more information to share.

"If he hasn't revealed anything by now, then surely he has nothing to offer," Elisaf says.

"On the contrary, he offers me entertainment while I work on the sapling. You should hear the stories he sputters to see what might save his vile life."

I shake my head. "The things that amuse you cause me worry, Abarrane."

Elisaf slows, his narrowed focus on the ground. He crouches.

"What is it?"

"Grass. A few blades." He plucks one from the ground and holds it up in proof.

Abarrane snorts. "Do you suddenly fear vegetation?"

He ignores her, peering up at me. "Do you recall seeing anything the day we arrived?"

"No. Nothing." Barren, dry soil, devoid of so much as a weed. It's been this way for as long as anyone can remember.

"And yet now there is grass. Here …" He stands and walks a few steps, then points. "And there too. As the land prepares for winter."

"It is coming up all over the place. I've seen it in the daylight," Horik confirms.

Elisaf's brow furrows. "What do you think it means?"

"I do not know. We'll get a better look tomorrow." Perhaps with Gesine, if we can pry her from the library.

Horik stops abruptly twenty paces from the wagon. "Do you smell that?"

"Piss and vomit?" Abarrane trails behind him. "For days now."

"No." He inhales deeply. "Rotten flesh."

His description rings an alarm bell in my head as Abarrane reaches him and inhales. "Fates, that is offensive."

My nostrils catch the stench a moment later and grim memories flood my mind, of a night long ago when Elisaf and I fought for our lives. "That is a hag."

Their agile bodies shift into a defensive stance, searching the surrounding darkness.

"It's likely in the wagon already, devouring its prey. Assume we've lost our source of information." We should have expected as much. These beasts from the Nulling still linger in the depths of these mountains, close to the rift. Normally they stay hidden, but with two powerful casters to draw them out—even tucked into Ulysede—it seems they can't resist the pull. That or this thing couldn't refuse an easy meal, and we basically left it bait.

Horik curses. "How did we not see it?"

"Because they are small and fast and intelligent enough to lie in the shadows until their best opportunity to strike." Unlike the grif that strolled up to us during the battle against the saplings. "Their scent is usually their only warning."

"I have waited my entire life to fight one of these." Abarrane draws another sword, excitement in her voice.

"And here I was, planning on living my entire life *without* fighting another," Elisaf mutters. "The last nearly bested us."

"It was not facing me." She prowls forward.

"Your arrogance is about to kill you. It is not hiding, it is *waiting* for you," I warn. "Move back now."

They heed my warning, their eyes never leaving the wagon.

"This is not the time to tempt a Nulling beast, especially one with claws that can slice you in half. Let us be finished with this one swiftly." Elisaf and I each draw a second blade, and I holler, "Loth! Flame!"

Seconds later, a fiery arrow is sailing in an arc across the sky, embedding into the wagon's evergreen canvas. It's all my affinity needs. The entire canopy erupts in a ball of fire, the blast of heat touching my skin.

With a shrill cry that resembles a daaknar's and echoes across the mountain range, the hag tears through the burning wall with swipes of its blade-like claws and launches itself toward us, its ragged cloak ablaze. At first glance, someone might mistake it for any one of us—walking on hind legs, arms at its side. But the moment it lifts its cloaked head, reveals its ghastly gray skin and black eyes, and opens its mouth to show off the four rows of jagged teeth ready to rip apart flesh, there's no mistaking this for anything other than the stuff of nightmares.

"It is small!" Abarrane declares with glee.

"We do *not* want to fight this thing!" I holler, cursing. "Move out of the way."

But it's too late. The hag wastes no time, launching itself at Horik, its body contorting unnaturally to avoid his first swinging blade, then his second, the cloth swirling with its movements, disguising its gangling limbs as they swipe through the air.

Horik grunts as its claws rake across his torso, dropping him to his knees.

With a battle cry to challenge any Nulling beast's, Abarrane leaps at its back, carving her blade through its spindly shoulder before spinning out of its reach.

The hag pivots, searching for its attacker, its teeth snapping at the air in anticipation. It can't seem to decide which of us to lunge at first.

Without warning, it decides I'm its next target. I move out of range at the last moment, but its claw catches my arm above my gauntlet, biting into my flesh.

I answer with a swift blade strike that slices into its side before it falls back.

Abarrane scowls. "Why doesn't it make a sound when wounded?"

"I do not think it feels pain like we do." My fists grip the pommels of my blades. "Draw it away from us."

Abarrane whistles to catch its attention. She sways from foot to foot, dangling her swords in a taunting manner as she steps backward, enticing it to follow.

It works, the fetid thing creeping forward.

I reach for my affinity, preparing to raze the hag and be done with this deadly charade.

"So it will not feel this?" With a deft tumble and powerful swing of her blades, Abarrane launches another offensive attack.

"Fates!" I yell, frustrated with her bullish nature.

But her blade's strike lands true, severing the hag's right leg. It topples to the ground. Tar-black blood sprays through the air as it drags itself away.

Finally ... "Stay back, Abarrane!" I launch my affinity at it, engulfing it in flame. A thick plume of smoke rises as its ear-piercing scream ricochets through the otherwise silent night, and the air grows pungent with the smell of decayed flesh alight. Only when its screams die down do I release my hold on the flame.

A charred black heap remains. "*That* is how you deal with these things," I snap.

"It is still alive." Elisaf points to the fingers on one hand. Even now, its nails claw at the dirt.

Abarrane marches over, streaks of its black blood across her forehead. "You ate my hostages." She stabs her blade into its throat and twists.

Its hand stills.

"And *that* is how you kill them."

"That scream will have been heard far and wide." Elisaf searches the darkness around us. "Possibly by Telor's men."

"Then perhaps that will make them think twice about coming any closer to the rift."

A groan pulls our attention. Horik has propped himself up with his sword, his free arm wrapped against his stomach. A gaping wound threatens to spill his insides.

Abarrane is at his side in an instant. "On your feet, warrior," she commands, but worry laces her voice.

"Have I told you how much I hate these mountains." Elisaf fits his shoulders under Horik's arm to help him walk.

I smirk. "Once or twice." I scan the trees, sensing eyes but unable to find their source. I could set fire to the perimeter and hope to catch whatever it is within the flames, but I decide against it. Horik needs immediate attention from Gesine and, besides, nothing good waits for us out here.

7
ROMERIA

Zander grimaces at the purple mark on my biceps, earned during one of Jarek's robust training sessions. "Why can't you heal yourself?"

"I tried, but it doesn't work like that." I hold up my arm in front of me to study my bruises, the silky white canopy over our bed providing an airy backdrop. The matching sheets have been pushed aside, leaving our bare skin to the warm night air flowing through the open windows. "Wouldn't that be nice, though?"

"Then Gesine should have healed it for you."

"It's nothing, and she's been a little busy putting Horik's guts back together." The gouge across his abdomen from the hag was so deep, I could see his intestines. He was pale when they dragged him in, and it took Gesine an hour to fix it and half a day to recover afterward.

I was no help either, too busy heaving from the gory sight. It seems I'm nowhere near proficient enough with my affinities to heal someone unless I have a two-headed beast hovering behind me.

I did, however, manage to close the gash on Zander's forearm. I admire my work now, tracing a fingertip along the thin silver line. "Do *all* these creatures leave scars?" A regular blade strike vanishes as if it never existed on elven skin, but merth wounds and marks from these *other*world beasts seem everlasting. I wear one on my hand, where Zander cut me the night I arrived in Islor. Oddly enough, the merth arrowhead that pierced Princess Romeria's heart left no evidence, but I imagine that has more to do with Malachi's touch when he brought this body back to life with me in it.

"Most things from the Nulling do, yes. And certainly, anything that crawls out of Azo'dem is especially difficult to heal." Zander leans in to kiss the scars on my shoulder, where the daaknar skewered me, leaving five jagged gouges that we spent weeks hiding with caplets and high-collared dresses to keep up illusions.

The affection ends with him scraping his teeth along my dewy skin, sending a shiver along my spine.

"Are you afraid of going out there again?"

He shifts his attention from my scars to the swell of my breasts, his lips grazing my nipples as he speaks. "Hags are rare. We're not likely to see one again for a few weeks, at least." More quietly, he adds, "I hope."

I tremble beneath the feel of his breath, fresh desire stirring in my core despite the morbid conversation. Then again, all our conversations are the same—talk of threats and treachery and imminent death. "I mean, because of the blood curse." I've sensed the change in him since we came to Ulysede. Sure, he's burdened by plenty of worries, and yet he seems ... lighter too. Now, when his mouth finds my neck, he isn't as reserved as he once was—as if he was afraid he'd forget himself. I've caught him dragging his tongue across his teeth from time to time and the marveled smile that follows, as if he can't believe those needlelike fangs are no longer waiting to descend.

Zander described the first few moments of stepping beyond Ulysede's gates the other night, of the crippling need that hit him, buckling his knees. But it was the dismay in his eyes that showed his true agony, of feeling that gnawing hunger again, a cancer returned.

"It will get easier, each time. According to Abarrane." He swallows. "But I will need to feed again before long once I'm out there. Of that, I am certain."

Because he is determined to save Islor by himself if necessary. He'll probably get himself killed in the process. I push my growing panic aside and smooth a palm over his angular jaw, pushing it back far enough that I can admire his handsome face. "That's fine. Fearghal should be back with his wife soon and has offered himself up as needed."

Zander's deep chuckle vibrates in my chest. "Is that to be my lot in life now that I am with you? Feeding off hairy old men that smell of ale and sausage?"

"Hey, don't knock him till you try him." The rugged mortal with missing teeth from the wild town of Woodswich has proven far more loyal than I ever expected when he sat down across from me in the Greasy Yak. I trail a fingertip down Zander's chest, somberness taking over. "I wish you didn't ever have to do it again. I wish we could stay here forever."

"Wouldn't that be nice." He runs his tongue over the top of his teeth. "It's like they no longer exist. I couldn't call on them if I wanted to."

"Imagine if it was like this *everywhere* in Islor?"

He rolls onto his back, giving me a sublime view of his naked form and all the hard, chiseled curves that come with it. "The entire keeper system would be meaningless. What would the lords and ladies do?" His gaze crawls over the vaulted ceiling, his thoughts wandering.

I resist the urge to climb on top of him. "They'd still lord over people, like they do in Ybaris. That wouldn't disappear overnight."

"They still hold the money and property and title," he agrees. "At least for the short term."

"The rich don't like giving up being rich. They'd fight to keep the laws the same, or close enough that they can keep their power. They wouldn't give the mortals any more rights, even though they don't need their blood to survive, because they'll never see the mortals as equal." Status quo in my world. My *old* world. I'll never see it again. That reality doesn't bother me anymore, but I am sad I won't see my father again. Now that I know the truth about him, about why he is the way he is, I wish I could go back and help him.

"You describe much of the east, I'm afraid. Led by Kettling, who is about to marry into the throne." His molars grind. "The mortals would revolt in droves."

"They're ingesting poison to kill their keepers. They're *already* revolting in droves, and they're willing to die for their freedom."

"It would be worse. There would be outright war."

"Maybe not … at least not at first, and not in places like Bellcross, with lords like Rengard." The Islorian impressed me, even if he doesn't trust me. I wish I'd had more time to get to know him.

"Few and far between. Telor is honorable as well, but I do not have the same friendship to lean on where he is concerned." Zander sighs. "I wish these seers' prophecy would give us the answers we need most." He smooths his palm over mine, matching our fingers against each other. "I wish they could help us choose the right course of action."

"By the right course of action, you mean, should you and I do it on the altar under the full Hudem moon?"

He grunts at my crassness, but his expression remains somber. "Gesine said the seers have seen the door opened in the age of the casters. Given all that has transpired with this place, we have to assume she is right and it is inevitable, one way or another."

"Maybe she is. She always seems to be. So we would be rid of this blood curse." One positive.

"At what cost? Malachi as king and the Nulling's beasts flooding these lands? How would we fight against them *and* a hundred nags and grifs outside Ulysede's gates?"

"There has to be a way. He was defeated once, right?" Both Malachi and Aoife, masquerading as king and queen. "How?"

"I can tell you how it *did not* happen, which is with all our lands and people so terribly fractured as they are today. Ybaris, Islor, and Mordain would have to work together." He scoffs as if the very idea is laughable.

"They did it once." When King Ailill tried to release the nymphs the last time at Malachi's behest and tore the veil into the Nulling. Wendeline said it took them fifty years to rid this world of the worst beasts and seal the tear.

"We did not have Neilina at Ybaris's helm, scheming so vindictively. Islor was not being ripped apart from within. I can't decide which is worse—the treacherous lords or the poison. I hazard it does not matter. I fear there are no alliances left to be made."

"That's not true." I curl into him, wanting to feel the warmth of his body against mine.

"What *is* true anymore? That we are alone. You and I, and fifteen legionaries and this palace with untold power we cannot wield without causing dreadful harm." He sighs heavily. "Atticus does not have the head for politics. He does not realize how precarious his situation is, how claiming the throne from me in such a public display has fractured the strength of it. For the first time since Rhionn, our enemies have seen it taken."

"Maybe you need to tell him that." We've heard nothing from Atticus beyond the letter we intercepted and what Rengard described. No communication between the two brother-kings.

Zander's chuckle is low and humorless. "He is a stubborn and pompous fool, too busy enjoying that crown he's coveted for so long to listen to anyone with wisdom."

I've seen only glimpses of the brothers' relationship, but anyone could read the power struggle that existed despite Atticus's carefree persona. Still, their connection seems deep. "Why didn't you have him executed when you found out he slept with Princess Romeria?" It's become easier to speak about the Ybarisan who once occupied this body as if she was some other being.

"Because he is still my brother." He pauses. "Why? Do you wish I had?"

"I don't know." What would the weight of executing his own brother feel like on his shoulders? "But at least then he couldn't have stolen your crown from you."

"No, but someone else would have likely tried by now. Besides, I know firsthand how persuasive and enticing the princess was. I can't fault Atticus for that betrayal." He rolls onto his side again to capture my lips with his. "Though she wasn't as enticing as this version."

"Are you talking about other women while in bed with me again? What did I say about that before?"

His lips curl. "That you would make me pay for it."

"Right … right … But how?" I pull away from his lips and roll onto my back, arching my body in a deep, dramatic stretch, the night air grazing the peaks of my breasts.

He accepts the blatant invitation, moving in on me in an instant, his mouth sealing over my nipple, his palm sliding up my inner thigh. A soft moan slips from me as his touch slides across my center, and my legs part to grant him better access. "I suppose this is a start."

His chuckle against my flesh sends an electric current along my nerves, stirring a fresh, deep wave of need in my core. Our little games never last long. As soon as I feel the heat of his body against mine, I'm done for.

"Do you know how hard it is to keep myself from touching you when we are outside these chamber walls?" He echoes my thoughts as his fingers tease me. "All I can think about is getting back here with you."

"While you're planning war? How romantic."

He ignores my crack. "And then when I finally have you here …" He lifts himself onto one elbow to give him a better view of my naked body. His heated eyes rake over me, stalling on my thighs to watch his hand work me over. "I can never get enough."

"Good. I don't ever want you to." I roll my hips against his touch.

With a groan, he's moving and shifting down to hook my legs

over his shoulders. His breath skates across my damp core, turning my breathing ragged.

With a devilish smile, his mouth closes over me—

Knuckles bang on our door, followed by a loud "Romeria!"

"Is it too much to ask that he shows a little deference to his queen?" Zander complains.

"It's Jarek. If the door wasn't warded, he'd be standing at the end of our bed."

"And then I would have to kill him.".

I curl my hand around the back of his head, pulling him back to me, even as I holler, "What!"

"You're needed at the gate," comes the booming response.

"*Now*?" Zander and I exchange wary looks. It's the middle of the night. "Who needs me?" I holler, at the same time Zander calls out, "For what?"

"The Ybarisans have come."

The clomp of horse hooves along the cobblestones is especially eerie at this late hour. "Tell us everything you know about this captain," Zander demands as we ride for the gate, the path lit by flaming lanterns. He wears the mask of Islor's stony king again, and his tone is especially harsh. The news of Gesine's secret message to Mordain hasn't helped their relationship.

I'm not happy with her either, but I can't waste energy on anger right now. Besides, I know she didn't do it maliciously.

"Kienen, you said," Gesine repeats, blinking the sleep from her eyes as she rides behind Zorya, clinging to the warrior's waist. We found the caster face down in a book in the library, a blanket drawn across her slender body, I assume, thanks to that same warrior who guards her day and night.

I watch her closely; her growing worries about the coming change have taken root in mine. But in this case, I think her confusion has more to do with being woken from a dead sleep and thrown onto a horse within minutes.

"Yes, I know of whom you speak. A soldier who was often at Prince Tyree's side. He was respectful to the elementals. Far more than others, including the prince himself. He seemed a trusted advisor, always ready with his blade."

"So we cannot put any hope in him." Zander's expression is hard.

"I did not say that, but I would be wary. He is beholden to Ybaris, but if he is at these gates now, he must have loyalty for his princess."

"He might be looking for direction, now that Tyree is gone," Elisaf offers, riding opposite Zander.

"Or it is a mission to gather information to feed back to Neilina," Zander throws back without missing a beat. "Surely he would have heard what is happening within Islor."

"It would be wise to assume so, yes. At least the rumors."

"Of which there are many." Zander's gaze flitters to me, and I know what he's worried about.

"Rumors that likely won't point to me," I remind him. Those in Norcaster would assume Zander controlled the ring of fire and that anything else inexplicable could be tied to the caster who travels with us. Talk of the princess's glowing silver eyes would likely be dismissed as a fable—a way to villainize me more. The only people who could speak to my caster abilities are in Ulysede with us. "How well would Kienen know Princess Romeria?"

Gesine frowns in thought. "Not well, if I had to hazard a guess. The princess spent much of her time with Neilina, and she and her brother were not particularly close."

"Only close enough to mastermind an attempted coup and slaughter of a royal family," Zander says dryly.

"If he doesn't know her well, then that works to our advantage. I say we play this carefully until we get a good read on him. As far as he's concerned, I'm still Princess Romeria from Ybaris." As much as I hate playing her.

"With the exiled king you plotted to kill and his Legion in tow?" Jarek raises a doubtful eyebrow. "How will you explain that?"

"I don't know yet. I need to feel him out first." I always do my best thinking while in the thick of trouble, and I've found myself in *a lot* of trouble over the years. It'll come to me. It always does. It *has to.*

"And all this?" Zorya nods at a statue of a nymph.

"Tell him it was Mordain's doing," Gesine answers for me. "He is a soldier. He would not know the intricacies. It's highly unlikely he would understand how our affinities work, and what we are and are not capable of."

Has Kienen heard about Gesine's escape? Will he see her as a traitor to his country?

Zorya grunts. "That makes at least two of us."

"None of the Ybarisans captured with Tyree knew of Neilina's plans, and I imagine Abarrane was quite thorough with her methods. The prince must not have divulged much," Elisaf adds.

"So, we go in assuming he's here to answer his princess's call and confused as hell." That, I may be able to work with.

"There were many in Ybaris who were tired of going hungry each winter from poor crops and welcomed an alliance between the nations. I cannot say which side this soldier is on."

"The side that has been peddling poison," Jarek reminds us. "And what of his affinity?"

Gesine pauses in thought. "I cannot recall, but I imagine it is not remarkable, *because* I cannot recall."

"He'll have to rely on a warrior's skills rather than a coward's. Good. Let me bring him in and find out what he knows." Jarek's toothy grin brings back thoughts of the dead keepers from Freywich.

It makes me shudder. "You can't go around torturing people we need, and we *need* these Ybarisans."

"She is right. Whether we like this or not, we need alliances, even the unsavory ones," Zander admits, his voice heavy with reluctance. "If anyone can fool the male, it is Romeria."

"Is that a compliment? I can't tell."

He smirks. "Play your role and lie about your new affinities if it comes up. Blame Mordain for chasing prophecy to Ulysede. At least that is the truth."

"And if he is not convinced?" Elisaf asks.

"Then we kill him where he stands." Zander's horse speeds up, moving ahead of us.

So, if I screw this up, I get to watch this Kienen die. "No pressure."

"You will do fine," Gesine says.

"Will you shield us, just in case?" I've been practicing and I'm getting better at it, but I don't think I'll be able to focus on that *and* the lies that come out of my mouth.

Her smile is wan but authentic. "Of course, Your Highness. Always."

I haven't stepped inside this tunnel since we arrived in Ulysede, a rivulet of blood dripping from my hand and an unknown world ahead. Now as we move along it again, the lanterns flicker and ominous shadows crawl over the arched ceiling.

Six legionaries stand before the closed gate, their arrows nocked and aimed outward into the darkness.

And on the other side waits a single form.

Zander sidles his horse next to mine. "Are you ready for this?"

I swallow my nerves. "Yes. Why?"

"Because I can practically see your pulse in your throat."

My heart *is* racing. And his uncanny—and sometimes annoying—ability to sense it has only grown stronger since we arrived here, rather than vanishing along with his need for mortal blood. "I'm remembering what happened the last time I played Princess Romeria with a guy on the other side of iron bars." Tyree did not care that I was his sister by blood when he smashed my face into them.

"That will not happen this time." He nods toward Gesine, whose green eyes cast a dull glow. The shield is already up, and it takes almost none of her power.

I can't wait to have that kind of control.

"Remember, *you* are in command here. I am just a fleeing, enamored king, bending to your will."

"As if you can handle not saying something. I give you two minutes."

His lips curve. "Care to wager?"

"What are the stakes?"

"I'm sure we can agree to something suitably depraved once we're back behind the safety of our chambers." He drops down off his horse, prompting me to do the same, and then juts his chin forward subtly. "Lead the way, my queen."

The legionaries part ways, their weapons still drawn, allowing me through.

The face that stares back at me through the gate is full of youth and caution. Kienen couldn't be more than late twenties by mortal standards, his clean jaw giving him a boyish, almost innocent, look. But his leathers and four blades strapped to his honed frame suggest he's far from it. "Your Highness." He falters, his focus skittering to the arrow aimed at his head three feet away, but then bows.

Right. I have a role to play.

I ignore the cold air breezing in beyond the gate and assess the situation. A small horde of Ybarisan soldiers waits at his flanks, some twenty feet back, the darkness a suitable veil. Their hands are free of weapons, but I know they wouldn't need them to cause me harm, not with their elven affinities.

Still, this isn't a great way to start a conversation.

"Lower your weapons."

"Are you certain?" Jarek's raspy voice comes from directly behind me.

If I wasn't already on edge, he would have startled me, sneaking up to serve as a looming wall behind my slight frame. But I've seen how fast Jarek can move. He'd shield me before anyone could draw an arrow, despite Gesine's protection.

At least he has the good sense not to contradict me in front of them. "Ybarisan soldiers have no reason to harm me. I am their princess."

A few beats pass and then, from the corner of my eye, I watch the arrows lower.

Kienen clears his throat, his stance still rigid. He's no less relaxed. Is it from confusion or fear or anger? "I apologize for the delay. When we received word that you were waiting for us in these mountains, we were not sure if it was a trap." His gaze skims over the legionaries. He's still not sure, it seems.

He's confused, I decide.

"You've been watching us from the trees," Abarrane states.

"Yes." He appraises her frame. Or her weapons. "Did you get what you wanted from whatever poor creatures you tormented in the wagon?"

"Besides my enjoyment?" Abarrane bares her teeth. Even without her fangs, she looks menacing.

If it unsettles Kienen, he does a good job of hiding it. "We saw you defeat the hag the other night. It was impressive."

"So good of you to lend a hand."

The faintest twitch of a smile touches his lips. "I would have, if we were sure we wouldn't end up under your blade next. Besides, it seemed you had a skilled fire wielder to help you."

Zander remains quiet. Likely chewing on his tongue to keep from taking control of the conversation.

Has Kienen figured out who this fire wielder is? How much does he know? "How many of you are left?" I ask instead.

As if only then remembering that his princess is here, he stiffens even more, any hint of humor on his face vanishing. "Two hundred and fifty-four, Your Highness."

I resist the urge to meet Zander's eyes. That's more than we expected. That's good … as long as they'll follow me. And bad if they won't. "Where are they now?"

"They wait south of here for a rider to confirm it is in fact you here, with the Islorians." His brow furrows, and the unspoken question hangs.

"I have a mutual interest with these particular Islorians."

"It seems so." He sizes up the vacuous tunnel. "We've passed through this barren tundra, and there was nothing but a stone wall of script before. Yet now there is a grand gate and greenery sprouting, even as a snowfall threatens." He pauses, as if waiting for an explanation.

Grass sprouting, along with tree saplings and the hint of other shrubbery, more each day. When we asked Gesine about it, she had no answer, but her frown was deep. "Mordain's casters have their value."

"Yes, Your Highness." His gaze flitters, I assume, toward Gesine. He nods before returning his focus to me. "I have something for you." He reaches into his vest.

Arrows are aimed at him instantly, freezing his hand.

He lets out a deep, slow breath as if it might be his last. "A letter, from the queen."

I knew Neilina was communicating. Tyree admitted as much from his cell, informing me that she was *disappointed* in us for our failure. I struggle to keep my sneer from my expression and wave off the arrows again.

Kienen slips the folded parchment out and slides it through the bars.

And what does Mother Dearest have to say to me? I can't wait to find out. The forest-green seal is still intact. "How long ago did you receive this?"

"Almost a full moon cycle, Your Highness. After the prince left." He hesitates. "He and the others have not yet returned. They have not sent word."

"They won't. They were captured and executed in the Cirilean square."

Kienen flinches at the news, and I feel a stir of regret at my callousness. For all I know, they were good friends, like Zander and Elisaf are close.

And *I* am supposed to be Tyree's sister. I soften my voice to add, "My brother was taken prisoner and locked in the tower when the others died. He's likely dead, but I can't be sure. We were driven from the city by the king's brother and his army before I could help him." Help him by driving a merth blade through his heart. A blatant lie woven into the truth.

Kienen's eyes widen. "So, that is not simply a rumor. Prince Atticus overthrew the king?"

"King Atticus now. Yes. You remember him?"

"Certainly, Your Highness. From the escort south. He was difficult to read. But we did not anticipate a bold move such as that."

Atticus *is* difficult to read. He has a relaxed, playful demeanor that appeals. But I've seen his treacherous side now firsthand, the way he used me as a scapegoat for his benefit.

Does Kienen know that Princess Romeria slept with him on that escort south? If he does, he feigns cluelessness well.

"There is an Islorian army heading this way—"

"How many days away?" Zander blurts, unable to bite his tongue any longer.

Kienen's attention flips to him. "Two, at most."

Zander sighs, and I can't tell if that's relief or worry. "They are from Lyndel, sent by my brother to apprehend us."

"*Your* brother." His eyes widen a second time as the pieces click. "*You* are King Zander."

"I am," Zander answers cooly.

"And you are now *here*, with *our* princess."

"*Your* princess, who brought poison into my lands. The same poison that is now flowing through villages and towns from Bellcross to Salt Bay to Hawkrest, thanks to *your* efforts."

"Zander," I warn sharply but grit my teeth against the urge to tell him outright to shut up.

"What? I figured he should know we are not clueless to Ybaris's scheming." He stares Kienen down as if in challenge.

Kienen matches the stare, but I'm sure the wheels in his head are spinning, unable to come up with a reasonable explanation for why he—or I, for that matter—haven't been cut down, if Islor already knows of Ybaris's plan. "Your Highness, are you here of your own volition?" he asks carefully, his eyes flittering to mine.

He's worried I'm a prisoner. That's the only explanation he can come up with. Of course, that makes sense.

I offer him a reassuring smile. "I'm not being held or threatened. I barely escaped from Cirilea with my life. If not for the king and his legionaries, I would be dead." My luck would have run out by now, even with Gesine by my side.

"I lost a great many legionaries protecting *your princess*," Abarrane hisses.

Kienen works an answer around in his mouth, as if testing it. "Then it would seem Ybaris owes a debt to Islor's exiled king."

I see my opening. "On our way here, the saplings attacked our camp."

"Yes. We found the group perished in a field south of here, along with a charred Nulling beast." He looks to Zander. "That was you?"

"Who else could it be?" Zander's testing him, looking for any hint of rumors that might be floating about me, about my powers. But it's smart. Let the Ybarisans think Zander's affinity is strong enough to kill a grif. It'll make them think twice before challenging him.

Kienen nods once. "Impressive."

"Where are the rest of the saplings hiding?" I ask.

His assessing gaze lingers on Zander another beat before shifting back. "In the mountains, I imagine."

"You don't know?" They must have a home base.

"They haven't been overly receptive to aiding our cause as of late, with the rumors that Her Highness did not survive the attack on Hudem. And since Prince Tyree left, even less so."

"Clearly those rumors were wrong."

"Fates be merciful for that." He dips his head in deference. "This far in the mountains, news travels over ten thousand tongues and when it arrives, it's laden with falsities. Not long ago we heard that Her Highness had not only survived but sat on the Cirilean throne. We thought it impossible that the king would ever—" He cuts off, catching himself with whatever he was going to say. "That he would ever accept you again. We assumed it a tale spun by drunks around a campfire. No one believed it. And the saplings are convinced that the bargain made with Ybaris is broken. They are no longer allies to us."

"They have all that raw merth cord." That we assume Princess Romeria brought with her because the Terren Mountains in Ybaris is the only place it grows, but I don't know for sure. I have to be careful what I say.

"A conciliatory prize, according to them. They do not believe the queen will ever deliver on her promises. They do not think Mordain will support her."

Which means this deal between Ybaris and the saplings was about more than some paralyzing weeds to help catch their meals.

"As for the ones who attacked your camp, they likely did not realize you were among the Islorians."

"Or maybe they did. It's impossible to trust anyone. Hence ..." I wave a hand toward the arrows, lowered but still nocked. "Can you reach the saplings in the mountains?"

"They are a quarter-day's ride from here." He pauses. "Do you have a message for Radomir you wish me to deliver?"

I resist the urge to ask who Radomir is. Princess Romeria wouldn't ask that. I assume he's the sapling's leader.

Before I have a chance to speak, Abarrane steps forward, her dagger in her grip as if there isn't a gate separating them. "You will show me *exactly* where those vermin are hiding."

Kienen is unfazed by her sudden venom. "You wish to enter a cave with hundreds of saplings waiting to feed off you?"

"No. I wish to rescue my warriors."

"You won't succeed. *We* don't even go up there. I would not recommend it."

"Do not feign worry for me, Ybarisan," she spits out.

Kienen's expression is stony as he shifts to me. "What is *your* order, Your Highness?"

Abarrane growls.

If this situation weren't so tense, I might smile. Kienen has a spine. "If Telor is two days away, we need you *here*, Abarrane, not running into caves that you won't come out of." Not with hundreds of saplings and God knows how much raw merth. I shudder at the thought of that many immortals, with their sunken cheeks and bulging foreheads. "Radomir has two legionaries captured in Norcaster, and I am demanding that he return them to us immediately. Come back tomorrow night with him *and* the warriors, along with the rest of the Ybarisan army."

Kienen's face tightens. "I do not know that Radomir will agree to such a demand, Your Highness. As I've said, they do not have much faith in Ybaris anymore. He may agree to release the warriors, but I cannot see him traveling here."

"Tell him I'm alive and I always keep my word." I hold my breath, hoping that's vague enough. Whatever bargain they struck, the prize was enough for that sapling to come to Cirilea to help Ybaris in their attack.

"Unless he'd prefer we seek him out in his home and help him see the light," Zander adds, that cool, calm edge to his voice scarier than all of Abarrane's barking. "Do let him know how you found his companions and that Nulling beast."

"I will share both your messages." Kienen bows. "Do you have a letter for the queen that I can send with the taillok?"

His request throws me off. "Uh … I'll have one ready by the time you return."

With a fleeting look toward the legionaries and their nocked arrows, as if one might land in his back, Kienen marches toward his waiting horse. As one, they turn and ride off.

"I do not trust him," Abarrane declares. "He is too young and smug. And Ybarisan."

"We do not have a choice. But if he shows up here tomorrow night with Drakon and Iago and two hundred and fifty-four Ybarisan soldiers, then we know we can put at least *some* trust in him," Zander answers. "Well played, Romeria."

"Thank you." I let out a deep exhale. Only now do I feel how stiff my body was, how much tension coursed through my limbs.

"Why bring the sapling here?" Jarek asks.

"Because Ybaris made a deal with them that involves Mordain. Don't you want to know what it was?"

"The more information, the better," Zander agrees. "Though if they've discovered what we did to their kind, no bargain may be sweet enough to win him over."

"I do not want to win him over. I want to kill him." Abarrane sheathes her sword.

We retreat to our horses, the queen's letter firm within my grip, teasing my curiosity. "What is a taillok?"

Zander smirks. He's always amused by my ignorance. "The queen's messenger. A bird of a sort. I have only ever seen it once when it arrived with a letter to Cirilea."

"We believe it arrived through the Nulling," Gesine confirms. "It is guided by Mordain's hand, it travels at impossible speeds, and it never misses its mark. As far as we know, it is the only one left in existence, and the elemental who steers it acts by Queen Neilina's order. However, if we can get hold of it, I may be capable of respelling it to our advantage."

"So you can send more secret messages to Mordain?" Zander quips before shifting his focus to me. "What does the letter from Neilina say?"

With a deep breath, I break the seal and unfold the crisp paper, my insides suddenly in knots, as if she might somehow know that an impostor reads her words. This is the elven at the heart of *everything* Zander and Islor now face. She is part of the reason I'm in this world.

The handwriting is floral, the ink a deep, dark crimson. "It's addressed to Tyree." That makes sense. If this came a month ago, I was still in Cirilea, and Zander hadn't yet lost his throne. "She's received word that I'm still alive and within the castle. Her sources aren't sure to what extent Zander trusts me."

"We knew she had spies within the city walls," he says. "What else?"

I read the next lines.

And my stomach drops. "They're going to cross the rift. They plan to start a war."

8
ATTICUS

By the time I reach the top step of the tower, my thighs burn. I've spent too much time pacing around my war room. I must get back on my horse and among my men.

Though, my weakness is more likely because I haven't fed in a week. A stretch unheard of for me. I've been so preoccupied, I'm only realizing it now.

"Enjoying your accommodations?" I drawl, ignoring the fetid stench that greets my nostrils. "I imagine you're not accustomed to such luxury."

Prince Tyree sits on the straw pallet, his back against the wall. "I haven't seen any signs of luxury since I stepped foot inside this squalid country of yours. I do not think Islorians know what that is."

I smile at his response. Even caged and facing imminent death, his dark hair matted, his face covered in scruff, he keeps his arrogant chin high. I respect that. "Open it," I order the guard holding the key.

Within moments, I'm pacing inside the cell. From here, the scent of his Ybarisan blood is more potent. Despite myself, I inhale that sweet smell. On Romeria, it used to rile my senses almost to the point of losing control. Once, during a heated night in her tents, I nearly did. She stopped me, insisting she couldn't give me that part of her.

Even though she was giving me *every* other part.

In hindsight, I should have been suspicious, but how would I ever suspect such a thing as tainted blood?

Tyree's blood will be as ruined as the three Ybarisans who died during the royal repast. Knowing that quells my taste for it. "Leave us."

The two guards are gone in seconds, their armor clattering on their climb down the steps.

"Not worried I might overpower you?" Tyree asks coolly as I wander toward the window that overlooks the arena.

I give his limp body a once-over. The multiple merth blade wounds covering his arms from Abarrane's sessions are in various stages of healing. "And how would you do that? You're injured and weak. With those cuffs, you will have no access to your affinity until I deem it so." Thankfully, Zander returned the tokens to the family vault after removing them from Romeria's wrists. The first thing I did when I decided to keep Tyree alive was secure them to his. He's too valuable to risk losing to festering infection, especially now that we don't have a healer.

"Is it true you were born without an affinity? What must it feel like to be impotent?"

I answer with a laugh. He's trying to get a rise out of me. "I didn't need an affinity to raise an army and claim a kingdom, did I?"

"I suppose not. You are the great and powerful *King* Atticus, after all," he mocks.

I tap my boot against his tray of food that sits on the floor, untouched. "Not hungry?" The stew they delivered the other day was laced with ground meat. The guards reported him curled into a ball for hours, writhing in agony.

"Not particularly." He sighs, and all humor slips from his voice. "What do you want?"

I peer out the window at the gallows and the bodies dangling.

The executions are happening daily now, each time a new mortal is discovered with tainted blood—when their keeper dies violently—or is found with a vial hidden in their clothing or their quarters.

Mortals who thought their lives would somehow change for the better through murder. Cobblers and farriers, seamstresses and cooks. Simple people, desperate to be free of their duties. In the end, standing at the gallows, they all plead for mercy from their king.

But their king doesn't grant it. He mustn't, because to do so would be to show the same weakness as the previous king. So instead, he hardens his heart and watches them hang, punished for Ybaris's betrayals.

I haven't had to punish them all, though.

That family presented in front of the assembly still lingers in my thoughts, days later. Anyone with half a sense could see those children had been terrorized by the minor lord from Freywich. I'm certain that's why Romeria rescued them with a bag of coins.

Gracen … that was the baker's name.

The moment I laid eyes on her, I could see why Danthrin appeared before my assembly, insisting she be returned. She is stunning—for a mortal, dressed in worn clothes, dusted in flour. Her features are delicate and refined, a contrast to a wild mane of curly blond hair she attempts to tame with ties, and a smattering of freckles across the bridge of her nose. But it was the intensity in her blue eyes that caught me off guard. For a mortal of perhaps twenty-five, they revealed more depth than many of the century-old elven who hold court positions. Or maybe it was the way she pleaded with me to save her, and then gazed up at me with admiration that momentarily seized my breath.

Had Gracen been brought to Presenting Day in Cirilea, the crown would surely have claimed her as a tributary. If I had seen her?

I would have declared her mine in an instant.

I don't doubt Danthrin fed off her regularly—how could he

resist?—but he's obviously bred her too. The mortal has already produced three healthy offspring with no husband in sight. The fear and loathing that radiated from her body when Danthrin spoke told me all were likely sired by different mortal men, and none of the experiences were pleasant.

She trembled as I stood before her, like a terrified lamb knowing it would be sent to slaughter. Has any male ever been gentle with her? The way her body stiffened when I gripped her waist would suggest not, but that could have been that *the king* was the one touching her.

The cold look in Danthrin's gaze promised he had far worse planned for her return to Freywich. Punishment for daring to accept Romeria's offer, if only for her children's sake. Surely, Gracen would ingest poison to be free of a keeper like that, and I would not blame her.

But then I'd have to hang her, all the same.

At that moment, I felt a glimpse of Zander's anger toward our kind. It took *everything* in my power not to draw my sword on the pompous ass, but executing even a lowly lord won't win me the allies I need among the many detractors I'm facing. Denying the lord was already risky enough, given his tangle with Romeria and Zander.

And then fucking Adley, with his *wise words* in front of the assembly, didn't help.

I sigh heavily. "So many mortals are losing their lives because you promised them something you can't deliver. Are you proud of what you've accomplished? All these corpses to look upon each day?"

"Who says we are not delivering on our promises?"

"Maybe you are," I admit. Promises to whom, though? Islor is in turmoil, gripped by fear and growing fragile because of it. "What *was* Ybaris's plan the night you killed my parents, anyway?"

Tyree shakes his head. "Of course, you would have the gall to ask."

I shift into an easy, conversational tone. "Come on, it can't hurt you to tell me now. I've always considered Neilina cunning. I'm *dying* to know how she could be stupid enough to think she'd succeed at securing Islor's throne."

Tyree smooths a palm over his jaw. It hasn't seen a razor in weeks. Finally, my taunts seem to work. "We had people positioned and ready. They were to stab the royal family and their tributaries with merth blades in the first moments after they were incapacitated from the poison."

"Simple, but clever." And an echo of what Neilina did to her husband, at least the stabbing part. "And Romeria?"

"She was to be injured enough that it looked like she was also a target but fended off her attacker. She would identify Kettling for the attack. Retaliation for putting a Ybarisan on the throne. Everyone knows they opposed the marriage."

"And you thought Islor's lords and ladies would simply allow Ybaris to claim the throne?" I laugh.

He smiles, but it doesn't reach his crystal blue eyes. So much like Romeria's. "We knew there would be significant turmoil between the east and west, but we would have taken control of Cirilea and locked the gates. It was supposed to fall to us that night. It would have, had you not brought so many of your soldiers within the walls."

I hum. "Romeria tried to dissuade me." In the days before, she sought me out in the depths of the gardens late at night and pleaded with me to keep the army outside for the celebration. She said Ybaris would feel threatened by so many of the king's men there on the day of her wedding. She almost had me convinced too. Her methods of persuasion were impossible for me to resist.

And yet in this, I resisted.

"I guess she wasn't convincing enough."

"No. She wasn't." I'll never be able to explain the gut feeling I had that morning, but I'll be forever glad I listened to it. "So Ybaris would control Cirilea, and then what?"

"In the weeks and months following, while Islor was in

turmoil, we would distribute the vials of poison throughout Islor."

"How many did you bring, by the way?"

He shrugs. "It doesn't take much to sow panic."

He's not wrong in that regard. Already, the reports coming from towns and villages across Islor brim with stories of keepers accusing their servants of plots of murder without any proof.

"As the Islorians fell, we would convince them of a sickness plaguing their mortals that only Mordain could fix."

"At what cost?"

"One my mother would negotiate."

"Let me guess …" There's only one thing she has ever wanted—Islor. Well, two … Islor, and all of us, dead.

"No one was ever to suspect my sister's blood as the culprit of this mysterious illness."

"Or that your mother summoned the fates to accomplish that? Was anyone supposed to know that?" Neilina's treachery is obvious to anyone with half a mind. The night of the tournament, when Tyree's haunting laugh echoed across the silent arena, the shock on my brother's face was genuine, but understanding followed closely. He'd had all the puzzle pieces for far longer than I did, and he was too blinded by Romeria to see the big picture.

What else did he hide from me?

"My mother is nothing if not resourceful," Tyree says.

"She didn't expect her whole plan to be foiled by Mordain, though, did she?" By one caster—someone my family trusted. Someone who clearly knew about the tainted tributaries but, instead of warning us, took steps to ensure my parents died earlier in the day.

I supposed I could thank Wendeline for her actions, because it sounds like, had she not, we'd all be dead. Perhaps I'll pay her cell beneath the castle a visit one day, when I'm sure I won't kill her on sight.

"Not by Mordain. That caster is an exile. *Was* an exile? Did she die in the execution? I watched, but I couldn't tell who was who."

I ignore his question. "What about the caster who fled Ybaris and sailed to Cirilea and helped my brother and Romeria escape? Ianca, I believe was her name? Or was it Gesine?" Zander gave Boaz two possible names and a physical description that matched the caster in the skiff the night they escaped Cirilea. According to Boaz, she created a wind and wave strong enough to destroy the Rookery had she turned it on us. Instead, she took them out to sea.

Tyree purses his lips, as if toying with an answer. "Whoever she is working with, it isn't Ybaris."

My gut tells me to believe him. "Regardless, we're aware of her, and we're aware of the poison. Soldiers and keepers are searching for these vials, and mortals know what will happen should they be found with one." I point out the window toward the gallows. "We'll find them all soon enough, and the fear will dissipate." I force confidence into my voice. "And Ybaris will fail miserably with their foolish plans, yet again."

Tyree nods slowly. "It sounds like you have it all figured out."

Not everything. "What is your mother planning next?"

"You'll have to ask her." He stretches his legs, as if setting in for a leisurely conversation. "I'm sure she'd accept an invitation for high tea from the usurper king if he asks nicely."

Smug prick. "I think she's going to cross the rift and attack." Recent messages from the rift confirm a growing army. The meager sources I have within Ybaris paint a picture of fury. The people believe the lies Neilina has sown and cultivated—that Islor assassinated their beloved king from within his own borders and is about to murder their princess and prince. According to some rumors, it has already happened. Now people gather for retribution. "When?"

Another lazy shrug, but I sense he's lying. He knows what she plans.

"She's not known for her patience. Neither is the commander with whom she shares her bed. By the way, was it Tiberius who stabbed your father, or did she do her dirty work herself?"

He grins. "My mother has always preferred to keep her hands clean."

He's not even denying it. Either he's given up on living or it amuses him that his father is dead. Neither are my problem. "I think she'll cross soon, while she thinks Islor is in turmoil and there will be no one to resist her." I watch Tyree's expression, but he gives nothing away. "Is she willing to negotiate?"

"Depends. What do you have to offer?"

A thought has been brewing in my mind. "A royal wedding."

Tyree barks out a laugh. "You're not my type. Besides, I've heard you're already betrothed."

"Don't remind me," I mutter before I can stop myself. "Where did you hear that?" He's been locked in this cell since the royal repast, shut out from the world, save for the executions below.

"Your guards gossip when they think I'm asleep." He drops his voice in a mock whisper to add, "For what it's worth, they think it's a bad match."

Don't we all. Marriage has never been on my list of things to do, even when I was a spare prince. And to Saoirse, of all suitors ... Thank the fates for separate bedchambers. I would never trust sleeping next to her. "Sometimes bad matches are the only ones available. My sister will come to realize that too."

"Princess Annika, with her long blond curls and penchant for young men's blood." He twirls a piece of straw in his fingers, his focus to it. "I suppose I could do worse."

"And she could do far better."

He shifts and stretches out on his pallet, his arms cradling his head. "By all means, go and try to save Islor, *King Atticus*."

I sense I'll get nothing more from him today. That's fine, I've gotten enough.

"Do enjoy your meals." I saunter out, feigning ease with having a Ybarisan at my back.

Boaz strolls into the war room. "You called for me, Your Highness?"

"Yes." I test the wax with a tap of my finger to ensure the royal seal has hardened. "I need this taken north to the rift. Official communication with Ybaris." As opposed to using a chain of pigeons and covert messengers with scrolls up their sleeves, which may or may not succeed in delivering vital information. "It's for the queen."

"Immediately, Your Highness." He collects the letter and studies it, as if choosing his words delicately.

"What is it?" I ask, unsure of his hesitation.

"The contents … I am wondering what it may contain."

Because I haven't discussed it with him first, he means. I've known Boaz since I was running around with a wooden stick for a sword, annoying my twin sister and envying my older brother. I have few constants left in my life. He is one of them, acting as a reliable advisor, as he did for Zander, and before him, my father.

But lately I feel like I've had too many voices in my ear, trying to steer my actions, and none of them have been particularly helpful. This decision, I've come to on my own. "I've informed Neilina that I have her son and will soon have her daughter. If she attempts to cross the rift with an army, as I strongly suspect she is planning, then it will be met with their body parts after a public execution, and I will make sure to tell them she could have stopped it."

"That sounds … an effective threat."

"It's not a threat. It's a promise. But I'm also offering her an olive branch. A marriage between Annika and Tyree."

His brow furrows. "Is Annika aware of this?"

I chuckle, though none of this is funny. My relationship with my sister has always been tepid at best. Since Zander ran, she's been outright hostile with me. "Not yet, but she will do as required, as we all must."

But Boaz isn't convinced. "Need I remind you that the last marriage pact with Ybaris did not turn out as planned."

"I still have the scar on my chest to remind me of that, thanks." I rub a hand over the spot where the merth arrow skewered me. To think it was the same caster who sent my parents to their death who rushed to heal me. "But the throne will go to Annika should I die before I sire a child, putting all of Islor within easy reach of Tyree."

"And you'll have Tyree scheming to ensure that happens from one side, while Adley schemes from the other. You cannot trust either of them, Your Highness."

This is why I didn't seek his counsel before the wax seal hardened. "I'm well aware of the risks, Boaz." As well as the bleak reality. "I must keep Neilina away from the rift while we deal with this poison, and if she believes she can still gain power in Islor without waging an all-out war, perhaps this plan will buy us time."

"I suppose that could work."

"See? Zander accused me of always reaching for the sword first, but I'm suggesting we *avoid* a war. Wouldn't he be shocked. I can be pragmatic, after all."

His lips twist with grim amusement. "So you do not plan on marrying Tyree to Annika?"

"Perhaps I will. Perhaps not." My sister is beautiful, and Tyree didn't sneer at the idea, but he could have been imagining ways to snap her neck the second he has a chance. "Islor needs casters and, if these hangings continue for too long, we will also need mortals, ones not tainted by poison. Neilina's scheming hasn't gone all as planned, and both her children are now trapped within our borders. One is my prisoner. Having her son near the throne would be more advantageous to Neilina than him in pieces." I wander to the map and pick up a random marker. "But it is a gamble."

"As are all decisions made by a ruler." Boaz's unfriendly gaze wanders around the circular war room. "Your father would spend days at this table, toiling over the right decision, and then when he made it, he would doubt himself mercilessly."

Mention of my father pricks my chest. "I recall." Because I spent many of those days at this same table, disagreeing with his every move. Now I'm on the other side, and I feel his frustrations.

"But he always insisted it was best to choose a course and stick with it through the hurdles."

"His choices have given Kettling too much influence and allowed Ybaris into our borders to kill him and destroy Islor. The hurdles feel insurmountable." As king, his complacency and desire for diplomacy inspired too many mistakes. Still, I miss him. "I will follow this course of action until another one proves more beneficial to Islor, and then I will pivot without an ounce of regret."

"It sounds like you have given it much thought." He holds up the letter. "I will send this with our best riders immediately."

"Without Adley's knowledge." The less information that snake has, the better.

Boaz grimaces at the name. He hates Lord Adley more than I do. But not as much as Zander does, I'm sure. How much my brother must regret not having that lord executed as his first order of business. "Of course. If that is all?"

"Yes." The dull headache from earlier has traveled between my eyes where it sits, a constant irritant.

Boaz is halfway to the door when I blurt, "Wait."

"Yes, Your Highness?"

"Have Sabrina sent to my chambers." I'm in need of some respite in my life, even if only for a few short hours.

"Good evening, Your Highness."

I lounge in a wing chair, watching my tributary saunter in. The fireplace blazes next to me, chasing away the dampness that clings to the air from the falling rain. "Sabrina, thank you for coming."

"When you call, I come." A coy smile curves her lips at the double meaning, earning my chuckle.

She always lightens my mood within moments of arrival, before I've even laid a hand on her. My tributary before Sabrina—Genevieve, whose blood was tainted the night of Ybaris's attack—was also pleasant to look at and perfectly willing, but not as responsive as this one.

I sense Sabrina's pulse racing, and it stirs my growing need on more than one front. The first time I was with her, I mistook her reaction for nervousness, until she pushed her gauzy white sleep dress off her shoulders and let it fall to the floor. I realized then that it was excitement I was reading. Later, she admitted that it was the first time she had ever enjoyed her role as tributary. And I, in turn, enjoy her as much as any king can enjoy a transactional relationship with a mortal servant, while ignoring her aspirations. I sense them in all tributaries when they slink into my bed. Those delusions that they will be different from all those before them, that they will be special enough to win over my royal immortal heart, that I'll break all the rules and choose only them.

But none of them have any clue what it means to be queen of Islor.

The guard who escorted her stops beside her, and Sabrina's body tenses.

I groan. "Must we do this *every* time?"

"To ensure her blood is pure, Your Highness, yes," he answers with forced patience. We go through this same song and dance every time Sabrina comes to my rooms.

I wave him off. "But Sabrina would *never* harm me."

She shakes her head. "*Never*, Your Highness."

The guard's mouth twitches. "Captain Boaz says to remind His Highness that her blood can be tainted without her knowledge and that he'll execute me if I don't perform my duty."

"We wouldn't want you executed." Maybe I should stop being a prick about it. Boaz can be overenthusiastic at times. He *will* put a blade through this guard for disobeying an order, and he won't wait to hear my thoughts on the matter. "Be quick about it, though, if you will." I'm already half undressed, several buttons of my tunic unfastened, my weapons cast aside.

My appetites gnawing.

"Of course, Your Highness."

Sabrina shifts her lengthy blond hair off to one side, but her smile is gone. No one else is permitted to feed off her now that she is mine, and she *hates* this part, she's admitted as much. But she tips her head to the side, exposing her long, delicate neck.

"It'll only take a few seconds, and then I'll make it up to you, I promise." I rake my gaze over her curves.

The guard opens his mouth to call two needlelike fangs to emerge. He leans in and sinks them into her flesh, earning her wince.

My own teeth descend in anticipation of that taste.

And then the guard drops, his bloodcurdling scream ripping through the calm.

9
GRACEN

Sleep is welcoming me into its warm embrace when a commotion outside our door yanks me from it. Voices, so many voices. Deep ones, barking orders. Fists, pounding. Somewhere in the mix, I'm sure I hear Corrin.

A candle burns within its holder in our windowless bedchamber, granting just enough light for me to find my way around should Suri need me in the night. Beside me, Mika's and Lilou's breathing remains slow and deep. Not for long, if this keeps up.

With my heart pounding in my throat, I slide out from under the blanket and tiptoe to the door to see if I can glean what's going on. It doesn't sound like anything good. Fates, it can't be another uprising, can it?

I've just pressed my ear against the door when a fist bangs against the other side, causing me to jump back, a pained rattle in my head. "Open this door now!" an angry male voice booms. It can only be a guard.

"She has young children asleep in there!" I hear Corrin scolding. "Can you not come back in the morning?"

He ignores her pleas, his fist pounding against my door again. "Open the door now, king's orders!"

"Mama, what's happening?" Mika sits up, his eyes still half-closed from sleep. Beside him, Lilou stirs.

"I'm not sure, but don't worry." At least Corrin is there. She wouldn't let anything bad happen to us.

A whimper sounds from the crib.

"Open this door now!"

"Yes! Just a moment!" My hands tremble as I fumble with the latch that secures it, and then I rush away.

Two guards in full armor barge in, their size eating up our meager room.

"You take that side, I'll take this one," the one says to the other, each carrying a lantern. "Everyone out of their beds now! Stand over there," he barks, pointing to a far corner.

"Children, come." Corrin ushers them over. They scamper to her side, Lilou's thumb in her mouth to soothe herself as she stumbles.

I collect Suri from her cradle and calm her as the two guards toss sheets and blankets, overturn our pallet, and rifle through our belongings.

Searching for something.

"What has happened?" I whisper, rocking my baby.

Corrin smooths her palm over Suri's forehead. "They did not say, but if I had to guess, someone in the castle has been poisoned."

"Dear fates." There hasn't been a case within these walls since the royal repast. "Please tell me it was not the king."

"It's not likely. The captain would insist on a tester." But worry mars her face.

The guards shift their focus to stones in the wall, exploring for any loose ones that may prove good hiding spots.

"Search them all! Search for secret pockets!" a deep voice demands from the hallway and heavy footfalls march past. I recognize that voice—it's the captain of the king's guard, a stone-faced Islorian who never smiles. He's known to be harsh.

The two guards abandon the loose stones and charge for our corner, each yanking one of my children away.

Lilou sobs as one rifles through her night clothes and paws at her tiny limbs with rough hands. Mika's bottom lip wobbles but otherwise, he remains quiet as he is thoroughly searched.

My anger flares, but I bite my tongue. I have yet to meet a gentle soldier when they're following orders, or a sympathetic one when they're questioned.

"They're children," Corrin scolds, but she doesn't move. She knows her place too.

"Search the baby," the one who seems in charge commands, unfazed.

The other casts Lilou aside and reaches for Suri.

I flinch on instinct, turning away from him.

"Everyone is to be searched!" he bellows, grabbing my arm.

Not with those hands, they won't. "Stop!" I hang on to Suri tight. "You're going to hurt her!" Or worse, make me drop her.

"What's the problem here?" a new voice demands.

The guards stiffen immediately, coming to attention.

The king himself enters our bedchamber, a regal presence despite his disheveled attire—his white tunic untucked and half-buttoned, as if he was caught by an emergency while undressing.

I don't know whether to be relieved or terrified. Since when does a king visit the servants' quarters?

"She refuses to let us search the infant, Your Highness."

"I haven't refused. I just ... she is a newborn, and you are too rough."

"When was the last time either of you held an infant?" Corrin waggles a finger at the guards.

Their blank glances at each other answers her question.

"You can't jostle them about. They need their head supported!"

The king surveys our toppled room and my two children, both crying, though Mika is trying to muzzle it. "Fix the pallet and then move to the next chamber," he tells the guards. "Corrin, I'm sure there's something sweet in the kitchen that might soothe them?" He sounds so calm. It's in such conflict to the chaos his order has stirred. Shouts and clatter come from every direction.

"I'm sure I can scrounge up an apple fritter or two."

Mika's eyes light up at his favorite.

With a hand on each child's shoulder, Corrin guides them out, offering a pointed glare at the guards on her way past. It would be comical if I weren't so frightened.

"The servant and her infant have not yet been searched, Your Highness," the larger, meaner of the two declares.

"Thank you. That will be all."

They stroll out, but the king stays, pushing the door shut, closing out the madness beyond.

My nerves spike with just the two of us in a room together. I've found him in my thoughts these past days far more often than any mortal servant should ever allow thoughts of her king. I keep telling myself it was because he was kind to my family when others would not have been. Yet, it is his handsome face and the soft, seductive lilt of his voice when he spoke only to me that I've lingered on.

Entirely inappropriate thoughts, and ones I never expected I'd have for any male after what I've been through, immortal or otherwise, let alone *the king*.

Fortunately, the only thing he's likely to read in me right now is my genuine terror.

"I don't think I have ever been in the servant quarters before." His back remains to me, allowing me the opportunity to study his broad shoulders. "It is dark and damp."

"It's more than adequate, Your Highness."

"Is it?" He turns to regard me. The buttons on his tunic gape. Even in the dim candlelight, I can make out the padded muscle around his collarbones.

I drop my gaze before I'm accused of ogling. "When we lived in Freywich with Lord Danthrin, our sleeping quarters were in a small dirt cellar with all the other servants. At least ten at any given time. There were vermin everywhere. Far more than here." The cats in the castle are plentiful and plump.

"Why am I not surprised to hear that." His lips curl with disdain.

"This is more private. Quiet. *Usually,*" I add, and then regret the word the moment it's out of my mouth. It sounds like a criticism, and I would never want to be accused of such a thing.

"Yes." He bites his bottom lip. "Sometimes I forget how passionate the guards can be when carrying out orders."

Passionate. That's one word for it.

"I am sorry."

My mouth drops. Did a king apologize to me? "These are difficult times, Your Highness," I murmur in a stupor.

Suri fusses in my arms. She could do for another feeding, but I'll have to wait until the king is gone.

He sighs, his steps slow and deliberate as he wanders through our room. "My tributary was discovered to have tainted blood tonight."

I gasp. "Sabrina?"

"Yes. You know her?"

"Of course. I see her every day. Sometimes she minds Lilou and Mika for me."

"A guard died. A terrible death." Strolling over to where the woven bassinet lays upside down, he bends over and rights it, then fixes the blankets. Or attempts to. He hasn't the first clue how to make a bed. It's … endearing. "I don't think she knowingly took it—"

"No, she wouldn't have. She—" I cut myself off before I say what I was going to, that Sabrina is madly in love with him. And then I realize I interrupted the king midsentence. A fresh flare of anxiety hits me. "I mean, she never once complained about her duties where they involved you, Your Highness."

"I imagine she did not." His full lips curve with a secret, and I can only imagine the thoughts flowing through his mind. Sabrina practically floats around the castle the morning after she's called to him. According to her, he's *generous* with his tributaries.

I smiled and nodded when she confided that, not understanding what she meant. My experiences with males have never been for my benefit, and the only thing they were generous with was pain and humiliation.

The king's eyes graze our scattered clothes. "She has not left the castle walls since she last visited my rooms, which means someone within the castle dosed her. Likely someone in the kitchen."

My forehead furrows as I rifle through all the faces and names that pass through each day. "I haven't seen anything suspicious."

"And yet it happened, which is why the guards now search everyone's room. We felt it prudent to do so before anyone had a chance to hear about the death and hide evidence."

"And you came to join the search, Your Highness?"

"I came down here because I could not sit in my rooms, waiting. I was hoping to find the culprit myself." He stretches our blanket out over the bed. "I didn't know the guard's name." Remorse fills his voice.

"You're a king. You can't be expected to remember names."

"My brother would have." He glares at the low stone ceiling, but I sense his thoughts far away. Does he regret what he did to King Zander? Does he feel justified?

I hesitate. "What will you do to Sabrina?"

"I don't know yet." But his jaw clenches, as if the options are limited and all unpleasant.

I have yet to hear of a tainted mortal allowed to live since King Atticus took the throne.

My heart aches for the young woman.

"Come, this can be done quickly, and then you can go back to sleep. Or whatever needs you must tend to." He gestures toward the bed, but his focus is on Suri, rooting for a nipple to clamp onto. The top buttons on my nightdress are unfastened for easy access, leaving the collar plunging to near indecency. In all the turmoil, I hadn't fixed myself.

"Yes, Your Highness." I lay her down and unravel the blanket that swaddles her little body until she's in only her diaper. Unfastening the pins, I peel cloth away, leaving her naked to the cool night air. "Nothing hidden there. Though I wouldn't even know what to look for."

"A tiny glass vial of liquid." He watches her as she kicks her legs, her face growing red with her wails. "I can't remember the last time we had an infant living within the castle. Decades, at least."

"They bring great joy and even greater worry." Especially in this evolving world.

He sighs. "You can put her out of her misery now."

I bundle Suri up, giving her my fingertip to calm her, while my other hand covertly tugs the sides of my gown together, so I'm less exposed. Is there any point, though?

"*Everyone* must be searched," the king confirms, answering my unspoken question.

"Yes, of course." But I remain frozen where I stand as dread takes over. This feels so much more intimate than having the guards jostle me and then move on.

"Gracen."

My eyes flash to his. He remembered my name?

He towers over me, examining my face. "Would you rather I call the guards back in?"

I shake my head.

His head is cocked as he studies me. "How would you prefer this done, then?"

Not at all would be nice. "Could Corrin—"

"No." The answer is so abrupt, it startles me. He sighs, his tone softening. "Corrin was Princess Romeria's lady maid and loyal to my brother. The only reason she's still alive and in her position is that she was equally loyal to my parents, and she runs the castle's household better than anyone else. But I am not a complete fool. I only trust her so far."

"That is fair."

Blue eyes bore into mine, narrowing. "You still falter. Why?" There's a hint of suspicion growing. It's *never* a good thing to have a king suspicious of you when someone just tried to kill him.

My face flushes. "Mortals are far more modest than Islorians, Your Highness." And I'm struggling to decide which would be less mortifying: having this Islorian male's gaze on me, or his hands. My body hasn't healed from childbirth yet.

And he is a king.

He nods slowly as if digesting my apprehension and searching for a solution around it. And then a twinkle sparks in his eyes. "Would it help if I ..." He reaches for a button on his tunic, unfastening it, then another. Half were already undone when he arrived, and now they're all undone, and he's reaching for the hem to pull his shirt off.

"No!" My hands fly to his, clamping over them, stopping them from their work. The brief contact spikes my heart rate, but then I pull back as if burned, realizing I've touched him without his permission. "I'm so sorry, Your Highness."

He doesn't seem offended, though, his lips curved with amusement. "I was just trying to even the playing field."

"That is kind, but there is no need for it." And there's no avoiding this. At least it's dark. With a slow exhale, my stomach churning, I reach upward, to the collar of my nightgown.

"Stop."

My hand freezes.

He sighs heavily and steps closer, until he's looming over me, the heat from his body radiating against my skin. His eyes remain locked on my face as his hands fumble with the soft fabric folds of my nightgown, grazing my thighs in the process. "Are these the only pockets in this nightgown?"

"Yes, Your Highness, and you will always find them empty of anything harmful to you." I swallow against my nerves and look up, praying he sees only sincerity. "I would *never* harm someone who showed my family such mercy as you have."

His eyes settle on my mouth. He has such long lashes. "I would hope not, because there are far worse Islorians out there than I who wish to sit on this throne."

"Yes, you are about to marry one." The seamstress Dagny claims a daaknar would be friendlier than the Lady Saoirse.

The king's eyebrows climb halfway up his forehead with genuine shock.

"I mean … I …" I can't even come up with a suitable excuse for my idiocy. I am usually much smarter than this. Why did my lips loosen for him?

I tense as the king's hand settles on my throat, his cool fingers curling around it. He could snap my neck with no effort, squeeze until the airflow cuts off. Suddenly, this dank little room blazes, as my pulse hammers in my veins, and I wait for him to dole out my punishment for insulting his future queen.

But he doesn't squeeze or otherwise threaten me injury. His thumb smooths a circle against my skin while his gaze roams over my face, before slipping down to my exposed neckline. Heat flares in his eyes. If the guard died while testing Sabrina, then the king hasn't tended to *his* needs yet tonight.

He leans forward.

And I brace myself for the prick of those fangs, the pull against my flesh, as if my very vein is being tugged through my skin.

"If anyone asks, you undressed for me, and I searched you *thoroughly*," he whispers, his lips grazing my earlobe, sending an unexpected wave of pleasure through me to combat the fear. "We don't want Boaz circling back for his own inspection."

I swallow. "Yes, Your Highness."

He lingers another long moment before pulling away abruptly and stalking toward the door. Throwing it open, he marches out without a look back.

I can't say how long I stand there, but eventually Suri's cries can't be ignored.

By the time Corrin returns with my other children, I've fed and tucked her in and righted our room. The chaos within the servants' quarters has faded, the guards searching for the perpetrator elsewhere. It doesn't sound like they've found one here. I can't decide if that's a good thing or a bad thing.

"So?" Corrin asks. "Did the king give you much issue?"

"None at all." He is far different from what I expected. Playful at times, almost boyish. "You were right. He can be rather charming." And seductive, whether that was his intention or not. Surely not. What purpose would a king have for seducing a mortal baker with three children in tow?

My cheeks flush under Corrin's weighty stare.

10
ZANDER

"They're not coming." Abarrane paces along the inside of the gate like a caged beast. "We should *never* have let that Ybarisan ride off. If you had allowed me, I could have—"

"He said it was, what, a six-hour ride? That's half a day, there and back. *Plus* time to convince this Radomir guy, who can only travel at night, to release Drakon and Iago. Have some faith, Abarrane." Romeria says this, and yet she paces too.

"Faith in whom, exactly?" she sneers. "The Ybarisans or the saplings? Do you know what you ask? Both sides are murderers and thieves. One has been plotting to kill us and take our land, and the other plot to take our blood and then kill us."

"I get that. But torturing Kienen for information would have gotten us *nowhere*. It would have been stupid—"

Jarek inserts his enormous body between the two bickering females before I can react. The rest of the legionaries remain where they are, not foolish enough to get in the middle. "I cannot stand relying on them either, but this plan offers at least a chance for *some form* of arrangement," he says.

"Well, don't you sing a different tune now," Abarrane growls.

"A pragmatic one? It's the only realistic chance we have of getting Iago and Drakon back."

She sniffs. "I still think we should let Ybaris and Lyndel battle each other."

"We will need *all* of them fighting alongside us for what is ahead, if Queen Neilina's letter hints at the truth," I add coolly, hoping my words will end the quarreling. An impossible task, I'm sure, but I'm searching deep for hope. Telor has been a friend for many years. Not the same sort of friend as Theon Rengard of Bellcross, but one nonetheless.

Abarrane spins on her heels and marches to the far side to calm her temper.

I can't blame my commander for her doubt or her anguish. Neither the saplings nor the Ybarisans can be trusted. We don't even know if the two legionaries are still alive. But what we do know now is that Neilina plans to cross the rift at the height of the Hudem moon with a mighty army that will take advantage of Islor's growing dysfunction.

We spent most of our time since Kienen rode off strategizing what comes after this encounter, but there are still too many unknowns in front of us to make solid plans. All I *do* know is that I must put aside my plot to march on Cirilea and regain my throne. For the good of Islor, our focus must shift to the rift.

Suddenly, Jarek's head jerks outward. "Do you hear that?" His ears have always been among the keenest.

Everyone freezes as we listen intently.

"I hear it too," Elisaf says a second later, just as I catch the faint, familiar sound.

Romeria scowls, frustrated that her kind's senses aren't as strong. "What is it?"

"Hooves." Many of them.

"Look!" She points to a single torch in the far distance. It's joined by another, and then they multiply. "Is that them?"

"Telor would not ride his men through the night in these mountains." They would camp with a tight perimeter against any unwanted beasts.

I sense Romeria's heart racing, a palpable expectation radiating from it, combined with relief. I hope I never lose the ability to read her in that way.

She smiles. "Okay, this is good, then. They're coming like we asked."

"As you commanded," Jarek reminds her and nods his approval.

"Right. I didn't think they'd listen."

"Why don't you give them some added light for their approach to Ulysede's gates, Romeria?" Gesine coaxes, the caster remaining in the corner. "As we practiced."

Romeria nods and then steadies her gaze on the nearest woodpile the legionaries and mortals spent the day stacking. A dozen identical stacks fan out across the arid plain, strategically placed for our defense as needed.

For several beats, nothing happens.

And then suddenly, it erupts in a burst of flame.

The smile of pride that stretches across Romeria's beautiful face reminds me of the one she wore the morning I caught her teasing water into waves and chased the nearby ducks from their reed beds. I could spend all day admiring it, if given the opportunity. But now is not that time.

"Let me offer you help." I pluck a spark from the lantern with my affinity and launch it outward. The barren space erupts in a chain reaction.

"Couldn't help yourself, huh?" She cuts an annoyed glare my way, earning my chuckle.

"You must conserve your power, Romeria, in case we need it shortly. I suspect we will know quickly whether they come as friend or foe. Gesine?"

"I will be ready, Your Highness, though my shield will hold only so long against that many Ybarisans."

"Our blades will do the rest," Abarrane declares. As if the legionaries share one mind, they notch their arrows simultaneously.

There is nothing left to do now but wait and watch.

And hope we have not made a grave mistake.

The cavalry approaches in tight formation. The closer they come, the more it is clear this is not some rabble of warm bodies handed swords and sent across the rift to die. Their clothing is fine and fitted, their weapons gleam from a soldier's polish, and they carry themselves without any hint of fear.

Someone barks an order, and the rows come to a sudden halt near the charred wagon and hag's corpse.

"What now?" Romeria whispers, her eyes steady on the faces ahead.

"Now we wait for them to concede. And remember, you rule here. Remind them of that and give them *nothing* they can share with Neilina. There may be more of them, but we hold the power. And do not allow them inside Ulysede." Some secrets must be guarded.

Her nod is subtle.

Long moments of staring across from one another in silence pass until, finally, the line parts and several horses move forward —one carries an extra rider, draped in a ratty wool cloak and struggling to sit up. The mangy red beard is unmistakable, even from here.

I sigh with a mixture of relief and dismay.

There is no hint of Iago.

"Open the gate," Abarrane hisses.

"Commander," I warn as the metal bars begin to rise. When she doesn't answer, I step closer. "If you were Radomir and you did not think you'd walk away from this exchange, would you hand over both bargaining chips at once?" At least, I hope that's the reason for only one returned legionary.

She inhales through her nostrils. "No."

"Perhaps keep that in focus before you charge out there."

Kienen breaks through the line of soldiers on his horse. "Help him to the gate!"

The rider with Drakon hops off the horse and attempts to

guide him down, but the legionary is too big and too weak, and the Ybarisan struggles to keep him from crumbling.

With a curse, Jarek charges forward to help, passing the threshold without thought. A bad judgment call by Romeria's commander, driven by loyalty for his friend. He drops to one knee immediately, the need for blood crippling him as it did me the first time I stepped through.

It would have been fine—an embarrassment for the Legion commander, showing his weakness, but nothing more.

But then Romeria rushes out to aid him.

"*No!*" I roar.

The next few seconds happen in slow motion, and yet too fast for us to react.

Romeria, reaching for her commander's arm to help him up.

Jarek, catching the sweet scent of her Ybarisan blood and, unable to control himself in that moment, rearing up on his feet to grab her by the chin, his incisors elongated.

Romeria, eyes widening as she comes face-to-face with the warrior, realizing her mistake, seeing what's about to happen.

I grasp for flame with my affinity, hoping to stop this before it's too late.

But before the spark can reach him, Jarek is in the air, landing on his back in the dirt some distance away.

It only takes one look at Romeria—her eyes glowing silver, like that night in Norcaster, when she freed the mortals trapped in the pillories—to realize she was the one who sent him flying.

And now the ring of Ybarisan soldiers wear expressions of shock, confusion, and suspicion.

Even with my worry, a flare of pride swells in my chest. She is quickly learning to wield her affinities to protect herself. In this case, though, it was likely more about protecting Jarek. If he'd bitten her, he would be a corpse rather than winded.

"Fool," Abarrane scoffs. "He has been too busy playing babysitter inside to grow accustomed to the outside world." She charges out with Loth, stalling by Romeria several beats, long enough to whisper, "I can't wait to hear your explanation for that," and then she and Loth march forward. They waste no time collecting Drakon from the ground and hauling him back past the gates to settle him against the wall for support.

The other legionaries attempt to keep their focus on the threat ahead while offering nods of greeting for their comrade, a normally loud and boisterous warrior who slumps where he sits, his face drained of color.

Jarek has climbed to his feet and moves slowly to Romeria's side, as if nursing an injury. They exchange a wordless look—Romeria's laced with apology for her mistake, Jarek's with regret for his—and then the warrior winks at her. The only communication, but it's enough.

If I couldn't feel Romeria's pulse race every time I approached her, if I ever doubted her feelings for me … I might insist she find a new commander, one less devoted and powerful and male. Still, my jealousy spikes at their growing connection.

The chaos of the last few minutes seems to have unsettled the Ybarisans. Their horses shift their weight, likely sensing their rider's unease.

Kienen finally dismounts and approaches. His weapons are sheathed, but that provides me no comfort.

I move to step out.

Abarrane's sudden grip of my arm stops me. "You have only been outside once. You will not fare much better than Jarek did, especially around her," she warns. "Islor's king *cannot* appear frail before them."

"They are sitting ducks out there." Two hundred and fifty-four Ybarisans on horseback against two.

"She has proven herself more than once. Trust that she can handle this, one way or another."

I grit my teeth and plant my feet, but keep a strong hold of my affinity, ready to engulf the entire company in flame if needed.

"Your Highness." Kienen bows. His eyes flip between Romeria and Jarek—surely, he has questions for both—before settling on

Romeria. "We were able to negotiate the release of one captured legionary."

"I see that. And the other?" Romeria asks calmly, sounding more like a queen, born and raised, each day.

"Will be released when we know your promises are as credible as your threats." The wall of horses shifts again, and a rider passes through a sizable gap, tucked in a cloak. Even still, the glow of the fire illuminates the sunken cheeks of the sapling.

My lips twist with distaste at the sight of the abomination. Of all the dark creatures within my lands who wish to kill us, these are the only ones that stir my apprehension. And now that they're armed with merth ...

"It seems you may not have failed after all. At least, not yet," he croons.

Romeria gasps. "*You.*"

11

ROMERIA

I never got a good look at the sapling that night on the bridge, when he bound Annika with merth and tossed her over, assigning her a slow death. But the moment I hear those words and that voice, a wave of déjà vu slams into me.

"It's good to see you again," I force, trying to hide my surprise. Several dozen cloaked figures move forward on horseback to form a line behind him. More saplings.

The Ybarisans have shifted away, carving out empty space around them. They seem as uncomfortable around these creatures as the Islorians are.

Radomir's chuckle is dark, as if he doesn't believe me. "I was sure you had perished, but you have proven more formidable than I expected." He brings his horse closer, the light revealing his sunken cheeks and a tattooed design that crawls up his neck. It was easy to see these saplings as monsters rather than men when they were attacking us in the night. But listening to him speak now reminds me they were once like Zander and Jarek—Islorian immortals who then fed on their own kind and turned into these hideous cannibal-like creatures.

"That's close enough," Jarek growls, drawing two swords in an instant, reminding me how fast he can move, how fortunate we both are that my affinity to Vin'nyla moved even faster moments ago.

I can't believe I nearly killed my commander with my own stupidity. What was I thinking, charging out like that? The truth is, I wasn't thinking. I was *feeling,* and seeing Jarek crumble in front of potential enemies charged my actions. But now is not the time to chastise myself.

I force myself to meet Radomir's gaze. What the hell did Ybaris promise these vile, black-eyed demons? Wealth? Power? Land? What does a sapling wish for besides a constant vein to satisfy their thirst?

It has something to do with casters, that much we know. "Kienen told us you doubt Mordain's support."

"We may hide in these mountains, but we hear things."

"Such as?"

He flashes a smile, showing off jagged, pointed teeth.

It's everything I can do to keep from shuddering.

"That Mordain is the reason Cirilea did not fall to you that first night."

Radomir has reliable sources, then. "Not Mordain. A few casters working on their own."

"To what end?"

"Does it matter?"

His eyes wander past me, into the tunnel behind us, and they flare with shock. "All those years of hiding in holes within the ground, starving while feeding information to your cause, and your queen did not think my people may find value in a place like *this*?"

"You know about it now."

"By design or desperation?" His lips twist with disdain. "After decades of service, Queen Neilina promised us the sun, and yet here we are, *still* dwelling in darkness. Meanwhile, three score of my men lie in a smoldering heap in a field south of here, and you arrive, doling out threats and expecting continued alliance."

He sounds well educated. Who was he once? "Your men attacked us."

"And they will continue to do so, by my orders or those who follow, should you kill me."

"Why? Our deal isn't over." Whatever it was.

"Forgive me if I do not rush to Ybaris's aid again, but you are as treacherous as your mother, something *others* have not yet realized."

A dig at Zander, clearly. And a fair one, for an outside observer. That he's surrounded by Ybarisans and still throws out insults and threats like he's hiding behind a wall of protection is brave. He hasn't shown a hint of fear.

"It sounds like we have no more use for you, then." Jarek takes a menacing step forward.

As one, the saplings shift their cloaks aside to reveal the coiled strands of glowing silver merth strapped to their sides and the swords already drawn.

No wonder the Ybarisans are giving them a wide berth. Just being near drains their strength.

Radomir has no chance of riding away tonight, unless they expect the Ybarisans to stand by idly and watch. Or worse, join in.

Or all he cares about is killing *me* before Jarek ends him.

Kienen's hand sits on his pommel, but it's sheathed. He might be waiting for an order from me, but he could just as easily be waiting to see this play out. The Ybarisans around him shift uneasily in their saddles, glancing to one another.

In this perilous moment, my affinities rise to the surface, crackling beneath my skin, begging to be unleashed, and I know I could kill them—*all* of them.

But Radomir's words strike a chord.

Queen Neilina promised us the sun.

Of course.

"Would you like to see what's inside this mountain?" I blurt.

"Romeria!" Zander barks in warning.

I ignore him. This is the opposite of telling them nothing. This is telling them *everything*. But if I'm right … "Would you like to see Ulysede, Radomir?"

Radomir's eyes narrow with suspicion.

"You won't be harmed, you have my word."

"Your word means nothing."

"Keep provoking me." Jarek grins in a way that begs for it.

"Aren't you curious to see what you've been missing all these years?" I gesture toward the gate. "Only you, though."

The sapling studies the tunnel ahead, then his men at his back. "If we do not return to our stronghold by tomorrow's nightfall, they will peel the skin from your legionary, strip by strip. They will do such hideous, vile things to him. Things your worst nightmares could not even conjure."

"Fair enough." I nod toward Kienen. "You're coming too."

I'm sure I heard Zander's groan.

Kienen seems even less excited about the prospect, his wary gaze drifting over Jarek, who morphed into a thing of Ybarisan nightmares not five minutes ago. But I am his princess, and I see the moment he accepts he has no choice. "Aziel. The men are yours."

A Ybarisan with lengthy dark hair nods once, his expression hard.

Wearing a look of resignation, as if he's heading to his death, Kienen guides his horse forward.

"Relax." Jarek backs away from its path, a taunting smile on his lips. "No one here wants your toxic blood."

Radomir follows behind the Ybarisan. "What about *my* blood?"

My commander's grin turns into a grimace, earning Radomir's laugh.

"On foot, sapling, and leave the merth behind," Abarrane barks, sparing me a glare that promises I'll be getting an earful from her later. That she hasn't openly argued with me in front of them is an improvement, though.

Radomir obliges, tossing the glowing cords and reins to his

closest sapling and dropping from his saddle. He strolls toward me.

Jarek steps between us, his swords ready.

From this proximity, I see the sinewy skin pulled taut across his cheeks, like he's been starved.

"What's the matter, Romeria? You once told me my face wasn't as unappealing as you had imagined."

I swallow against my shock. Apparently, I *have* been this close to the sapling before. "I guess I was a good liar?"

He chuckles. "Don't I know that."

Once they're past, Jarek leans in and whispers, "What part of 'give them nothing' did not sink into that thick skull of yours?"

"Zander said we need allies, not enemies."

"Saplings make target practice, not allies. You have nothing to offer that will earn their loyalty, unless you plan to deliver them our veins."

I hope that's not true. "Would you please trust me for once?"

With a deep inhale and a shake of his head, Jarek guards my back as, together, we trail Kienen and Radomir past the entrance to the tunnel, and the portcullis descends behind us, leaving the rest of the Ybarisans and saplings on the outside.

Loth and Horik dive for Drakon, helping him onto a horse. He'll need Gesine's healing touch.

Zander shakes his head at me—I've earned myself an argument later; he obviously shares Jarek's doubts—before warning, "Any foolish ideas will be dealt with harshly." Every lantern within the tunnel suddenly flares with a burst of flame, the heat grazing my cheek.

Radomir strolls forward. "I've always found it ironic, how horrified you are to be treated in the same way you treat your mortals."

"We do not trap our mortals and feed on them until they wither into nothing," Abarrane snaps.

"Because you've subjugated them to two millennia of slavery. It's all they know, and they follow like sheep. At least they *did*. But now they have an effective weapon, thanks to your gracious neighbors." He peers back over his shoulder to wink at me.

"And how does that benefit you, sapling?" Abarrane draws another sword, for show. "Without us, you die too."

He sighs, his voice suddenly somber. "We all must die, eventually."

Silence falls over our company, save for the horses' clomping hooves, but the tunnel brims with tension. Radomir strolls at the front of the line, hidden within his cloak as if unbothered by the enemies at his back. He's a tall creature, his heavy cloak making his presence seem larger.

Kienen follows closely after, the suspicion radiating from him enough for the two of them. He assumes he's heading to his death. If he doesn't react the right way, I fear he is.

And the way Zander's attention is locked on both the sapling and the Ybarisan, looking for any excuse to set them on fire, would make anyone believe the pyres are already built and waiting.

The trek to reach Ulysede feels eternal, giving me enough time to doubt my choices ten times over.

"Fates," Kienen whispers, his head tipping back as he takes in the night sky beyond the mountain wall.

"Not what you expected?" I ask.

"I did not know what to expect." He peers up at the two moons shining bright, his words a mumble I barely catch. "Certainly not this."

Radomir wanders farther in, his steps slow and staggered as ours were the first time we entered.

My stomach sinks. Was I wrong?

"What is this place?" The air of arrogance that tinged his words outside is absent. Now, only awe remains.

"This is Ulysede." I hesitate, but only for a second. Zander ruled his kingdom on secrets and lies, and where did that get him but exiled? "It was built tens of thousands of years ago and sealed, waiting for prophecy to unfold."

Zander's warning gaze burns into the side of my face. "Romeria—"

"That time is coming."

"Why do I feel so … *off*? I can't explain what it is, but…" Radomir slowly turns.

I gasp at the face staring back at us, still obscured within the depths of a cowl. Gone are the bulging forehead, the sunken, sinewy cheeks, the lifeless black eyes. Now, an Islorian male with striking features stands before us. Handsome, many might say.

"Fates." Zander is equally stunned.

Everyone is.

When Radomir realizes we're all staring at him, gobsmacked, his panic stirs. "What have you done to me?" He shuffles back several steps, looking ready to bolt.

My smile stretches, unbidden. For a moment, I thought I'd gotten it *all* wrong. "I've kept Ybaris's side of the deal."

He frowns, not understanding.

"See for yourself." Zander hops from his horse and pulls out his sword.

Radomir draws his in reaction, backing up.

But Zander holds his up unthreateningly, allowing the polished metal to shine within the firelight.

Shock slams into the sapling's face as he catches his reflection in the blade. His sword clatters to the ground as he reaches up to grope his cheek with his fingers, as if to confirm the reflection is his.

Sympathy pricks me. I once found myself doing the same thing, the night I took off my ring in the apothecary and saw a stranger looking back at me in a mirror—my face in this new world.

"Is this real?" Pushing the cowl off his head reveals a mane of lush brown hair to replace the stark white from before. He studies his hands as if they're someone else's.

"You wanted to see the sun again, didn't you? That was the deal you made with Queen Neilina."

"To see its beauty … feel its warmth."

"Within these walls, that will happen."

His mouth gapes as his attention flickers between me and his reflection. And then an unexpected sob wrenches from his throat and he drops to his knees. "You have no idea what this means." Tears stream down his cheeks.

Despite the evils his kind has committed—what they are—watching this moment softens my heart for the wretched man. Even for a moment.

"I think I can imagine." Zander's jaw tenses, not unaffected by this raw display of emotion either. He has wished for an end to the blood curse for centuries, but he's never been deprived of the sun's warmth. He wasn't visibly transformed into a monster.

"I never expected …" Radomir's words break off with breathless laughter. "Neilina honored our agreement, after all."

Zander and I share a look, and he nods. He's figured out what I have: that Neilina promised the saplings she would have their curse reversed. But she can't do that without summoning the fates, and the fates do not reverse summons granted. The only beings who can effectively undo what the fates have done … are the nymphs.

"Queen Neilina did not honor anything. I doubt she ever had plans to. She doesn't even know this place exists." I'm sure she will soon, though.

Radomir's focus shifts to Gesine. "This was Mordain then, caster? You have done this for us?"

"No. I am not capable of such a feat. Nor is Mordain as a whole, beyond our ability to share our knowledge of prophecy. If you are looking to thank someone, look no further than to the queen of Ulysede."

"This city has a queen? Where is she?" He looks around. "Can I meet her?"

"You already have." Gesine gestures at me.

I harden my resolve, knowing that what I'm about to say is a death sentence if either Kienen or Radomir so much as twitch in the wrong direction. "Queen Neilina and I no longer see eye to eye on the right path forward for Ybaris and its people. Whatever bargain you made was with her, not with me. This"—I gesture at his face—"is my gift to you, but it has strings attached."

Realization forms on Radomir's face, and I hold my breath, waiting for his reaction.

He drops to his knees. "How can I repay you for this extraordinary gift, Your Highness?"

I steal a glance Zander's way. I can't read his face, but it doesn't matter. We don't have time to waltz around the truth. "I need an army."

12
ATTICUS

"Are you trying to defeat me or dance with me?" I tease, deftly stepping out of reach of Kazimir's sword.

"Certainly not the latter. You're a terrible dancer." He dives forward with another mighty swing. Our blades meet with a noisy clang that echoes far past the borders of the sparring court this early in the morning, but I spin, and in a short second have the tip of my sword pressed against his throat.

Kazimir has fought in the king's army by my side for decades. He's an exceptional swordsman, both in practice and on the battlefield. But even he can't challenge me the way Zander can.

"The captain should be mindful of injuring His Highness, now that we do not have a healer handy."

Tension grips my body instantly with the grating sound of that voice. My brief respite is over. "Lord Adley! You are interrupting my morning sword work. This *must* be important." I infuse casualness into my voice to hide the fact that I'd like to cleave his head clean off his pompous shoulders. With a chin jut toward Kazimir, I hand my blade off to a servant, exchanging it for a towel to wipe the sweat from my nape as I close in on my future father-in-law.

He's dressed as finely as usual—with gold thread woven through his fitted silk vest, as if he thinks himself king. "I received word about your ordeal last night and thought it imperative to see you immediately. Terrible thing to have to worry about within the castle walls." He emphasizes that with a furrowed brow. "Has the captain of the king's guard apprehended the culprit yet?"

"Not yet, but I'm sure he's closing in." They suitably terrorized the entire castle staff in their zealous search.

Adley hums. "They have so much on their plates already. I would be more than happy to enlist my soldiers to help."

"No need. I prefer them right where they are." Half of them outside Cirilea's wall, the other half scattered across the east, hunting for poison.

"Very well." He smiles, as if my continued refusal to allow Kettling's army inside my city doesn't make his teeth grind. "I do applaud you for your swift actions. It was wise of you to close the castle to outsiders, and limit the opportunity for your enemies to act again."

I have plenty of enemies still left within the castle. I'm looking at one now. Thankfully, I've relegated them all to the west wing to minimize contact. "I'm pleased to receive your approval. I *do* seek it so."

If he catches the sarcasm in my tone, he ignores it. "And the tributary? Has she provided any insight?"

"Besides that she never took the poison willingly? No. There was nothing out of the ordinary in her days leading up to last night." If there had been, Boaz would have gotten it out of her. I told him to go easy on her, but I don't know if those words exist in his vocabulary.

"The culprit knows what they're doing, then. When will you hold her execution?"

The thought of watching Sabrina hang stirs my anger. The mortal has only ever wanted to satisfy me. She's an innocent pawn in someone's game, and now she sits in a dungeon cell, awaiting judgment. "I haven't decided yet." But I will miss her, regardless.

"You mustn't wait long. Swift and severe punishment, visible to all, is critical."

"I haven't lacked in that regard." I make a point of sighing heavily. "Is there another reason for your visit, Adley?" He hates when I drop his title. I do it as often as possible.

"In fact, there is." He pauses, notices Kazimir standing nearby. "Surely, you have something more important to do than eavesdrop on His Highness's courtly conversations?"

"No, actually, I don't." Kazimir's expression remains stony.

I give him a nod to move away, struggling to hide my amusement. We both know I'll repeat everything Adley says the moment he's gone, but giving the lord the illusion of respect—albeit reluctantly—is to my advantage.

Satisfied, Adley shifts his focus back. "Given all that is transpiring in the kingdom, I feel it would be prudent of His Highness to reevaluate things."

"In what way?"

"The royal wedding, for one. You have arbitrarily set it for Hudem, but I would advise there is no need to wait—"

"We are not moving up the date of the wedding. Do not suggest it again." If it were up to Adley, we would have been married within an hour of announcing the union. He's stopped just short of accusing me of stalling. But I'm walking a fine line here, and I do need to keep up pretenses. "The castle staff is working hard to prepare for the date we've set. I do not want to overburden them. They've already been through so much."

His fleeting grimace morphs into a smile. "Very well. Might we also discuss Islor's traditions of Presenting Day?"

"Presenting Day isn't until *next* Hudem." The first of the year, when mortals of a certain age are offered for bidding as tributaries.

"Precisely. Which gives the mortals more time to organize, more time for this poison to find its way into their veins. If we were to move Presenting Day up to *this* Hudem and lower the age requirement, we could claim the children—"

"The *children.*" I glare at him as I repeat his words.

"Yes. Before they are corrupted by the Ybarisan poison that your predecessor allowed to run rampant."

I don't know what Zander *allowed*—how much he knew about this poison—but I know he didn't want what's happening in Islor. But Adley takes any and every opportunity to highlight all the ways my brother went awry. "And what age would you suggest is suitable?"

"Well …" He frowns, pretending to consider this question. "It is really a matter of what age a mortal parent may dose their child, is it not?"

"So you are suggesting we pry babes from their mother's arms." An image of my mortal baker with her three little children hits me, and my rage swells.

"It is these very mothers who are dosing their unwitting children and condemning them to death. Need I remind you of Hawkrest?"

My mouth sours with a bitter taste. "You need not." Zander fled, and I was forced to witness the life drain from their young bodies until the glowing marks Wendeline branded on their hands faded. What choice did I have, hours after overthrowing him from his seat, but to do the opposite of what he wanted? What Romeria wanted. "And what would the keepers do with these *children* until they reach a respectable age to serve as tributaries?"

"Why, care for them in a safe and protected environment, of course. Just as you are doing now, with your staff."

"Keeping them within the castle walls isn't the same as keeping them in cages."

"I did not suggest cages, Your Highness." Adley paints his face horrified. He could play a court jester in one of our productions, his acting skill impeccable. "Bartering children is not the most palatable solution, but it is better than seeing them executed. I've spoken to several of the other lords and ladies, and they are all in favor of this plan. We could announce it during the next assembly."

I sigh. I would hate to agree with Adley, but in this case, he may be right, at least about moving up Presenting Day. "I'll consider your request."

"It would go a long way to curry favor. There are still those within Islor who are apprehensive about the future direction of—"

"I said I'll consider it." I sharpen my tone, enough to tell him not to needle me. Adley's so good at it.

"Of course, Your Highness. That is all I ask. Until then, I think I will enjoy a lovely morning stroll through the garden." Adley bows with a flourish and wanders toward the path.

Kazimir's boots scrape across the sandy ground on his approach. "'If I may …'" He mocks Adley's standard line. "What was that about?"

"Besides giving my balls a good fondle while he claws at power?" I relay Adley's request.

"He wants to claim children now. Why am I not surprised." Kazimir grimaces. "What will you do?"

I shake my head. "Even now, keepers are locking up their servants of all ages to protect themselves." And how can I blame them? I'm doing the same. I just have the luxury of a castle and guards.

"Do you believe he had nothing to do with last night's poisoning?"

"Why would he?" I watch Adley disappear behind a hedge. "Kettling doesn't benefit if I die before Saoirse sits on the throne."

"No." Kazimir scowls after him. "But he's up to something. I feel it in my bones."

"That's what you're here for, isn't it? To find out?" I tease, but there's nothing false in my words. Kazimir is my most trusted advisor. I would have replaced Boaz with him my first day as king, but I need Kazimir free to move about Cirilea, gathering information on traitors and plots, not bogged down by daily duty. "Have you heard from Rhodes?" My other trusted captain who has been tasked to be my eyes and ears within Cirilea, tailing Adley's allies.

Kazimir nods. "He followed Lord Stoll into the Goat's Knoll last night."

"And who was the lord of Hawkrest meeting with?" I ask, but I'm sure I already know the answer.

"The owner of the tavern."

"Of course." Bexley deals in information as readily as a fishmonger peddles his daily catch.

"Would you like me to compel details of their conversation from her?"

I chuckle. "You won't compel her to give you *anything* she doesn't want to give, and it'll cost you far more, believe me." I've relied on Bexley for one thing or another since the first night I slinked into her establishment decades ago, pretending to be another Islorian passing through. Somehow, she knew who I was with one glance. She's one of my greatest allies and yet likely the most dangerous immortal within Islor, if not beyond our borders. Bexley looks out for Bexley, and she does it well.

"I'll pay her a visit myself as soon as I'm able." Behind us, blades clash as several guards move in for their morning practice. "But right now, I need to clear my head."

13
GRACEN

"We do not have time for this, do we, little one?" I coo. Suri wriggles within her sling but settles against my chest, content to sleep in her cocoon. I ease the heavy door open. "We have fruitcakes and gingerbreads and compotes to make for a royal wedding. And yet we are searching for your brother. *Again*." Mika disappeared an hour ago while I was nursing the baby. I've checked all his favorite hiding spots so far, to no avail.

I hold my breath as I slip through the door. Servants aren't permitted to wander freely about this part of the castle, but the guards are too busy searching for the source of that poison to help hunt for a mortal child. When I approached one to see if we could check the library—they've found Mika hiding in here before—he waved me through with a grunt of "Go find the brat yourself."

But tributaries are allowed by escort, and Sabrina told me the castle library is a marvel. I see now that she was not exaggerating. It seems designed to be part collection of books and part garden. Around the outside are where the bookshelves reside, four floors of them, each with its own staircase. I've never seen so many books in my life.

But the center of the library is just as impressive, filled with full-size trees and weeping vines, and a stream with carrot-orange fish gliding through.

There are likely countless places to hide within here. No wonder my naughty son would risk the guards' wrath to venture in. It doesn't appear like there's anyone here to cause us any trouble.

"Mika?" I call out, choosing the nearest book aisle to begin my search.

Up and down the empty sections I wander, admiring the spines, curious what knowledge one could find. There are so many noble-born staying in the castle ahead of the wedding, and none of them are here. It's disappointing. If I had all their freedoms, I would be here every day, learning.

Lord and Lady Danthrin have a library in their manor, but it is just a small room, and none of the books have such elaborate spines, designed by an artist's touch. I reach up to graze one with my fingertips, to test what it feels like.

"What are you doing in here?" a crisp voice demands.

I startle and spin around, finding myself facing an Islorian female with a curtain of straight black hair. "Milady." I bow, my heart stuttering with fear. "I apologize, I'm looking for my son. He has a habit of sneaking off."

"And do you think he is hiding within that book?"

"No, milady. But we do usually find him in tight spots."

Her attention drops on the sling, as if only then noticing I carry a baby with me. "You're the castle baker. I recognize you."

"Yes, milady." She was obviously at the assembly. My focus was on no one that day but the king and my children. Is she someone important?

Her dark, hostile eyes comb over me, stalling on my unruly hair, and I fight the urge to smooth a hand over the braids I struggled with this morning. "Atticus was generous with you and your little family."

Atticus. She uses the king's name as if she knows him well and wants me aware of that. "Yes, he was merciful." Not only the day of the assembly, but last night, alone in my chamber. He could have demanded *anything*, taken *anything*, and I would have had to comply.

She takes a step closer. "I would not have been." The coldness in her voice sends a shiver through my spine. "Why did that Ybarisan traitor bring you here? Was it so she would have a loyal spy within the household?"

"No—"

"So you could move about the castle unnoticed, fooling everyone with this innocent act while you supply her with information that she could use against us?"

"No!" I swallow. "I never saw Princess Romeria again after the day she rescued us from Lord Danthrin."

"No, *Your Highness*," she hisses, grabbing hold of my biceps and jerking me toward her.

Highness. That means … *this* is Lady Saoirse? Our future *queen*?

Fates have mercy on us.

"Settle down, Saoirse. You do not wear that title yet," a deep voice calls out behind us.

I recognize it immediately, and my heart skips several beats with excitement, despite my fear.

She sneers at me as if she sensed my reaction—she likely did—before plastering on a smile and turning to greet him. "Your Highness! What are you doing here?"

"Keeping you from tormenting my staff, apparently." The king strolls leisurely along the narrow corridor in breeches and a white tunic that hangs loose and is marked with dirt and lines of blood along the sleeves and chest. "What are *you* doing here?"

"I was perusing your collection to see if there was something of interest for me when I discovered your baker snooping."

"*Snooping* through *books*. Yes, that sounds positively treasonous." His expression is even, unreadable, as he winks at me. "Release her now."

She does as ordered, dusting her hand against her skirt as if it's coated in filth.

"And did you find something of interest?" The king nods toward the book tucked under her arm.

"Besides this servant of Princess Romeria's who is not where she should be?" She smiles tightly and slips out the book. Its gold binding glints despite the lack of light. "I thought I should educate myself on my future husband."

"Master Sicily's collection on the royal family." The king hums. "I can't say how much of my escapades are accurate. He never interviewed me."

"I will make sure the historian is more thorough going forward, beginning with our nuptials." She steps toward him.

He smoothly shifts out of reach of her grasp. "Enjoy the rest of your day, Lady Saoirse."

The dismissal is obvious, and by her clenching jaw, not appreciated. "Your Highness." With a scathing glance at me, she marches away.

The king watches her disappear around the corner before turning his attention back to me. "So? What do you think of my bride-to-be?"

"She is …" I fumble for a suitable lie.

"Oh, that's right, I think you shared your feelings already." He chuckles, and it softens the hard features of his face. "Don't worry, I share those thoughts."

"Then why?" I find myself blurting. I immediately regret it. "I mean … excuse me for my disrespect, Your Highness—"

"For the good of the kingdom." A somber expression takes over his face. "To unite Kettling with Cirilea, two powerful sides that seem to be moving farther apart with each day, but especially after the betrayal by the Ybarisans."

I hadn't expected an answer. I swallow. "That is a noble reason." Though sad that he feels he must hitch himself to that terrible elven, but I can't feel too sorry for him. He didn't have to take his brother's throne.

"We will see. Things are more complicated within these walls than they are on a battlefield."

Speaking of battlefields ... "You're bleeding." I nod toward his sleeve.

He tugs at his collar, pulling it down to reveal sculpted muscle over a shoulder where a sword slash still weeps. "It is nothing. It will close by tonight, even without a healer's aid."

"I've always envied your kind's healing abilities." My body is still recovering from childbirth.

He peers down at the small bundle against my chest. "She is much quieter than she was last night."

Last night ... Those few quiet, intense moments between us that I have replayed over and over in my mind since I reclaimed my spot in bed, unable to make sense of it.

Even now, thinking about all that transpired, my adrenaline races.

The tiny flick of his eyebrow tells me he's caught the reaction, but he doesn't pry for my thoughts. "Did Saoirse hurt you?"

My arm aches and will no doubt wear bruises, but I shake my head. "No, Your Highness."

He nods, his lips pursing as if he knows I'm lying but doesn't want to call me out for it. "What *are* you doing in the library?"

"Oh." I smile sheepishly. "I'm sorry if I've overstepped my bounds, Your Highness, but I'm looking for my son. He has a habit of finding places to hide. Unfortunately, this castle has many of them."

"Unfortunate for you, but not so for him." He chuckles. "And you think he's in here?"

"He's not anywhere else I've checked, and the guards have found him in here before. They weren't willing to help with the hunt this time, but they waved me through."

"I imagine they are occupied with more pressing matters than a mischievous little boy."

"Yes, of course." They're searching for whoever tried to kill the king.

"Let's try this way." He gestures down an aisle.

Let's? As in let *us*? "*You* are going to help me look for him?" I can't hide the shock in my voice.

"I was a mischievous boy in this castle myself, once. I have a few ideas." He pauses. "Unless you'd rather not have my help?"

"No, of course I would love it. It's just … I'm sure the king has far more important things to focus on?"

He sighs heavily. "Actually, I could use the distraction. Come."

I move in his direction, catching his scent—clean sweat and worn leather. Sabrina says he practices in the sparring court every morning. That must be where he earned his injuries. I would love to watch him there, if I could find an excuse to knead dough outside.

We walk alongside each other, our footfalls the only sound in the library. There's an easy quiet between us, and yet I can't seem to calm my nerves as my thoughts whirl. What if I hadn't stopped the king from undressing last night? Surely his offer was in jest, but if it wasn't …

I can still feel his warm hand against my throat. What if he had decided to take what he wanted from me? Would it be as terrible as every other time I've experienced it? Or would he be gentle, as Sabrina claimed him to be?

My pulse hammers in my veins.

The king clears his throat and murmurs, "This way," slipping a hand against the small of my back to steer me down an aisle three over.

I stiffen instinctively. Lord Danthrin and his *guests* used to coax me with gentle touches and soft reassurances, and it always led to unpleasant experiences.

"Have you ever been inside a library?"

"Not like this one."

"It is quite impressive." He removes his hand.

I instantly feel the loss. "My previous keeper had a collection of books. Mainly from Seacadore. Lord Danthrin has a fascination with those lands. But I was never allowed to touch them, let alone read them."

"You can read?" He doesn't hide his surprise, and I can't blame him. So many mortals can't.

I nod. "When I was born, our keeper gifted my parents a book. It was about a mortal girl named Hania, who went on a grand adventure to Kier and beyond—"

"There's a beyond?" Humor laces his voice.

"You tell me. You are the one with the map." I feel my cheeks flush. "But there was a beyond in this story, a land where—" I falter.

"A land where ...?" he pushes.

"Where mortals live free, and immortals live in hiding."

He harrumphs. "If such a place exists, I should think I will not be visiting."

"It was only a silly fable, of course. Anyway, our keeper taught me to read it. I wish I still had it." I hadn't been allowed back to the house to collect my belongings after Lord Danthrin purchased me. I was barely allowed to hug my parents goodbye.

I feel the king's gaze on me as we walk. "I'm happy to hear there are good keepers out there."

"Yes, Cordin was kind and fair." That's probably what made where I ended up so much harder to stomach.

As if reading my mind, the king asks, "How did Danthrin acquire you?"

"On Presenting Day in Baymeadow. It is a larger village near—"

"The Plains of Aminadav. Yes, I have men from the area." His brow furrows. "Freywich is many days' travel from there, is it not?"

"Yes. Lord Danthrin was there for trade at the time. Selling mead, if I recall."

"Before this terrible blight that devastated his crops?"

I steal a glance at the king to see his doubtful smirk. He knows my previous keeper lied to the crown to avoid paying tithe. Why didn't he execute him for it?

"So that is the only book you've ever read? This fable of the mortal girl on an adventure?" he asks before I have the chance to ask my question.

"The only one. I could probably recite it line for line."

The king slips behind an iron circular staircase, crouching down to inspect a small nook in the wall.

I admire his broad shoulders, his powerful thighs.

"No little mortal boys hiding in here." Sliding back out, he leads us in another direction. "You must feel indebted to Princess Romeria after what she did for you. Rescuing you from a keeper like that."

I hesitate, afraid the truth will lose me favor with him.

"It's all right." He smiles softly. "I just pray that never outweighs your obligations to me as your king."

"*Never*, Your Highness."

He nods, more to himself. "And how are you finding your time here?"

"Wonderful. I am thankful every day for … I'm thankful." *For that traitor.*

"Have you made many friends?"

"Uh … a few. Corrin, for one."

He snorts. "I didn't think that one was capable, with all her bossing around."

"She terrified me at first," I admit.

He leans in to mock whisper, "She *still* terrifies me half the time."

"She does *not*." My laughter erupts unbidden upon the comical image of this battle-hearty Islorian commander—and *king*!—afraid of a tiny mortal whose forehead reaches his chest.

A secret smile touches his lips, and my cheeks flush.

"Who else have you befriended since?"

I sense he's gathering information on me, but I don't mind. I have nothing to hide. "Um … Dagny. That's the seamstress—"

His chuckles interrupt me. "I think everyone in the castle knows Dagny, for better or worse."

"And Sabrina has been kind to me."

He flinches at the mention of his tributary's name. "Yes, she is special."

Is. None in the household has seen her since last night, but she's still alive, at least. "She watches over my daughter often." I hesitate. "Lilou was asking after her this morning. She hopes she will come play with her again soon."

The king opens his mouth, but stalls. Whatever he's thinking, he doesn't say it. "It is good to find a few trusted friends, and keep them close."

"Do *you* have any of those?"

"My two captains. We've fought together for many years. I trust them with my life."

"I'm happy to hear that." *Especially if you're marrying that monster from Kettling.*

The king leads me to a pavilion draped with vines of bold fuchsia and sapphire flowers, some the size of my palm.

"These are beautiful." I reach up to rub one of the petals between my fingertips. "They feel soft, like velvet." Lady Danthrin had a blue velvet dress. That's the only time I've ever felt fabric like that.

"They were my mother's favorite." Plucking a smaller bloom off its stem, the king saunters over and tucks it in my braid, his fingertips grazing my temple in the process, sending a tremble through my core. His eyes drift over my face, lingering on my mouth.

My cheeks flush at the attention. He is a natural flirt, that much is obvious.

The king hops down from the dais and dives behind a thick and sturdy bush. He frowns with disappointment. "Your son might be smarter than I was at his age."

"There doesn't seem to be a secret passage or trap door he can't find," I admit.

His gaze wanders the library. "What's his name again?"

"Mika."

"Mika!" he bellows, his deep voice carrying through the library. "This is your king. Your mother and I are looking for you, and we need you to come out now."

Silence answers.

"Maybe he's not here, after all." Fates knows where he might be, then.

The king bites his lip in thought. "I heard Corrin mention something about apple fritters," he says loudly.

A metal clatter sounds, followed by a thump, and then footfalls as someone runs along an aisle. Mika suddenly appears.

The king bellows with laughter. "I am glad to see you have your priorities right."

"Mika, you know you aren't allowed in here!" I admonish, beckoning him to come to me with my outreached arm.

"I was bored." He wanders over sullenly. "Are there actually fritters?"

"You'll need to ask the baker." The king drops his voice to a mock whisper to add, "But I hope so. They're my favorite."

Mika's eyes light up. "Mine too!"

"Anything sweet is your favorite, my dear child." I push my hand through his brown mop of curls. Both of my older children inherited my unruly hair. It's yet to be determined if Suri will be blessed or cursed with it too.

Mika reaches upward, aiming to stick a hand inside the sling to disturb the sleeping baby.

"Don't you dare." I grab hold of his little fingers before he has a chance. "Thank you for your help, Your Highness. I will try to keep Mika out of here."

"Not on my account, I hope. I should be thanking him." The intense gaze he levels me with makes my cheeks flush again.

"Well, surely, you have matters you must attend to, so we won't keep you."

Shaking his head as if snapping out of his thoughts, he says,

"Books are meant to be read, not to collect dust on shelves. You are welcome to borrow one. Though I doubt you'll find such stories as Hania's." He winks, then moves his focus to Mika, leaving me with my mouth hanging in shock over the generous offer. "And you, stop giving your mother such a hard time."

"Yes, Your Highness." Mika bows in response like Corrin has been trying to teach him, but with the exaggerated flourish of a court jester and the balance of a newborn foal.

With a chuckle, the king strolls away.

I watch his back until he's gone, in a daze over this morning's turn of events.

"Look what I found, Mama!" Mika whispers excitedly, stuffing a hand deep into his pocket.

"It had better not be another mouse." He's always bringing things back from his adventures. A feather, a rock. That day's live loot was an unpleasant find.

"Do you think it's a magic potion?" He peers up at me, holding out his hand. Inside his sweaty palm is a tiny glass vial with a dark liquid in it.

I gasp, snatching it from him. Doing a cursory glance around us to make sure no one is watching, I whisper, "Where did you find this?" It's so small. I can see now why they were searching everyone so thoroughly.

Mika points behind him, his eyes wide at my reaction.

"*Here*, in the library?"

His head bobs. "Is it a magic potion?"

"No. Tell me *exactly* where you found it and do not dare lie to me."

He's not used to hearing my sharp tongue, despite the many times he's earned the right to it. His bottom lip starts wobbling. "I heard someone comin' so I hid. The lady put it behind the shiny books."

The shiny books?

"Show me." My stomach spasms with dread as he leads me down an aisle to the very far end, through an archway, to a smaller section where the tomes are all bound and encased in gold.

The books on the royal family.

The gold book in Lady Saoirse's possession was exactly like these.

"What did this lady look like?"

Mika shrugs, studying his feet.

"You *must* tell me, son. The truth. It's very important."

"She had black hair."

"Down to here?" I gesture to my shoulders.

Mika bobs his head.

"Dear fates." I squeeze my eyes against the truth. "She did not see you hiding, did she?"

He shakes his head. "I was over there." He points to the coat of arms standing sentry.

The vial burns within my palm. If I get caught with this in my possession, it's an instant execution. The smart thing to do would be to set it back where Mika found it and mind my own business. There *must* be a reason for the future queen to have a vial of this poison in her possession.

But in the back of my mind, the answer is there. Her reason is to hurt people. That is the *only* reason.

What if she uses it to harm the king?

To kill him?

My fist clamps around it. "Come, Mika, we must go now. And you are *never* to speak of this again."

14
ROMERIA

"The desire for blood is *gone*?" Kienen asks, doubtful.

"Within Ulysede, yes. There is no urge. Not even an ability," Elisaf explains, as if this is a normal conversation between two old friends and not mortal enemies standing across a map in the castle war room.

"But once you step outside the walls, past the gates …" Kienen's focus shifts to Jarek, who has played my shadow since we came back inside, no more than two feet from my side, his attention homed in on the Ybarisan. From this proximity, it's impossible to miss his dark mood. It radiates from his massive frame as he waits for Kienen to react to my admitting I'm no longer loyal to Neilina.

He's looking for an excuse to sever the Ybarisan's head from his body.

But so far, Kienen has hidden his views behind a masterful poker face. He must know his life depends on every word that comes out of his mouth.

"Romeria should not have come to me like that." Jarek's molars clench. "Tainted or not, her blood was impossible to resist."

"Because you have not built up an endurance outside," Abarrane scolds.

"I have been busy *in*side the walls."

Kienen's head bobs back and forth between the two as they bicker. "But in here, right *now*, you have *no* desire at all."

"I have desires." Abarrane circles around the Ybarisan, one hand toying with a braid while the other plays with the dagger at her hip. "The desire to kill my enemies is still *very* strong."

Kienen watches her for a moment, before deciding something —likely that she's all noise, at least for now—and shifts his attention back to Jarek. "You lunged for Her Highness but sailed through the air as if thrown by an invisible hand. Was that—"

"*We* will ask the questions." Zander leans over the map, his arms splayed. His favorite pose.

I avoid meeting Kienen's curious gaze. He may have seen the way my eyes glowed like a caster's, but there's no way he could guess the truth. How long will we be able to hide it from him, though?

"Radomir!" Zander barks, losing patience. "There is an army of a thousand Islorian soldiers marching here to kill us, and we have much to discuss before they arrive."

The sapling's head snaps back from the view out the window, where the sun has climbed past the horizon, its morning rays casting purple and pink hues over the river. "I apologize. My thoughts are scattered."

"That's understandable." I offer him a smile, still in awe of how such a hideous creature could morph into this handsome man.

Radomir dips his head in deference, though he still looks dazed as he returns to the table. He's been subdued since the transformation, all traces of his previous arrogance gone.

"When did Queen Neilina seek you out?" Zander asks him.

"I cannot say, exactly. Decades ago. Twenty years. *More* than twenty."

Zander looks to me, and I'm sure our thoughts match. More

like twenty-five. As soon as Princess Romeria was born and King Barris had a daughter to barter. "And she wanted information on what?"

"*Everything* Islor. On the royal family, on its cities, on your allies, and those who would unseat the king if given the chance."

And there it is. The answer of who within Islor has been working with Ybaris all this time, feeding them intel.

Zander frowns. "How did you gather all of this knowledge from your stronghold high in the mountains, avoiding the daylight?"

"Moving in shadows is easier than you might think, even for my kind. We have a lot of practice at it. It took time but there are many of us. We have forged alliances of our own, through both threats and promises."

"Which was Lord Isembert of Norcaster?"

"A little of both." If Radomir feels at all guilty for his decades-long treason against Islor's crown, he doesn't show it.

Zander studies the map. "And Neilina promised to reverse the saplings' curse in exchange for this help."

Radomir nods. "She said her daughter would marry the future king of Islor one day, and when that day came, Ybaris would cross the rift and claim the throne, and she would bring casters to free us."

Zander folds his arms over his chest and paces. Another favorite position. "So, Neilina used the saplings to gather information and then sent her children across the rift for a wedding with wagons of poison." His gaze lands on the Ybarisan warrior. "And you moved them up to the mountains at night from Cirilea, while camped outside the walls?"

Kienen looks to me, and I can practically hear his thoughts out loud. *Haven't you already filled him in?*

Zander sees it too. "I want *your* version."

"Call it a test," Abarrane adds. "If you lie, we will know, and the outcome will not be pretty."

Kienen falters. "We didn't travel to Cirilea with it. We were here"—he points to a spot on the map, just outside Lyndel —"when Prince Tyree became concerned that some of our wagons would not make it south, so he negotiated with Prince Atticus that Lyndel send fresh ones to replace them. We left the ones in disrepair where they stood."

"It was a ruse. The wagons were sturdy. We gathered them and brought them through the pass with the help of a dozen Ybarisans who remained behind," Radomir confirms.

Zander's eyebrows arch. "Atticus left Ybarisan soldiers behind without an escort?"

"He was unaware. They left camp one night on a scouting mission, by Prince Tyree's orders," Kienen confirms, but spears a glare toward Radomir as if annoyed by his honesty.

"And the Islorians did not notice *twelve* soldiers escape in the night?"

"Both sides preferred to keep their distance, Your Highness. Ybarisans, because of the blood lust, and Islorians, because of our connection to our affinities. It was not difficult to leave unnoticed."

Zander shakes his head, his thoughts keeping him quiet for a moment. After all these months of speculation about Ybaris's plans, we're finally getting real answers. "And the vials were in those wagons."

"Yes, Your Highness."

"And you've dispersed them using Islor's trade routes."

Again, Kienen looks to me. "When Prince Tyree left to seek out tributaries to the nobles in the major cities, he placed me in charge. It would be impossible for so many Ybarisans to move around Islor unnoticed, so he told me to form alliances with the mortals in the northern villages, find those unsympathetic to the throne, and utilize the routes south to shuttle the rest in time to reach Cirilea for the city fair."

"And it sounds like you've been successful."

"We have nothing left," Kienen says solemnly, without a hint of arrogance.

A muscle in Zander's jaw ticks. "Have you ever witnessed an Islorian die by this poison? It is an agonizing death."

"We were following orders, Your Highness." Kienen's face remains unreadable.

"The elven aren't the only ones suffering. There are mortals caged and others executed in squares." Abarrane steps in close, glaring up at him. "Children being hanged." If I didn't know better, I'd think she genuinely cared.

Finally, Kienen's stoic face breaks, his jaw tensing as if her words sting him. "If it is any consolation, we did not know what we were carrying into Islor at the time."

Zander frowns with doubt. "*Who* didn't know?"

"*I* didn't. The soldiers who remained outside Cirilea's wall with me did not even know Islor's king and queen had died until much later. I can't say if those closest to Her Highness had any clue of these plans." There's a hint of something hard in his voice. Gesine said Kienen was Tyree's closest advisor, and yet Tyree didn't trust him with the true plan? Princess Romeria's lady maid was found with a vial in her pocket, and her guards knew enough to condemn her when they were questioned. So, is Kienen telling the truth now or attempting to save himself? I suppose how much they all knew and when doesn't matter. They were following orders.

"And on the day of the attack, where were you?" Zander watches him closely, weighing his words for honesty.

"We fled with Prince Tyree as soon as the alarms sounded. He told us Islor had turned on us, and that we needed to head north to shelter in the mountains because we would not be able to return to Ybaris. There, he received a letter from the queen, announcing that King Barris had been murdered by an Islorian assassin—"

"We had nothing to do with that. *She* killed him," Zander growls. "By her hand or her commander's."

Kienen's eyes flash to mine.

I see suspicion in them, but not shock. "You already knew that."

Kienen shakes his head. "I wondered how an Islorian would find their way across the rift, into the jeweled castle and the king's chamber without notice, but I did not ask."

"Queen Neilina killed King Barris, and Tyree knew she was going to do it." He told me as much from his dungeon cell. "He supported it. He didn't want an alliance either. He wanted to kill every last Islorian. So does Neilina. That's been their plan all along."

Anger glints in Kienen's face, at them for deceiving him or at me for saying such things, I can't tell. He opens his mouth to speak, but then stalls.

"What is it?" Zander asks. "Speak your mind."

"When the prince revealed these vials of poison in the mountains, he said the queen had been afraid of Islor betraying the alliance, but King Barris would not listen to reason. So she enlisted the help of Mordain's chemists to create the poison. It was meant to be a fallback, to punish the Islorians as needed." He falters. "Is this true?"

Zander makes a strangled sound, his anger rolling toward its boiling point. It does every time someone questions his or his father's nobility. "Islor had *every* intention of honoring the arrangement. *Ybaris* is the one who betrayed the alliance by poisoning the king and queen. They had plans to kill my entire family. Fortunately, those plans were foiled."

Kienen's eyes flip to me, as if looking for confirmation.

"The poison was never a fallback, Kienen. It's always been the point. Queen Neilina's plan has always been to destroy Islor so she can claim it for herself. It just didn't go as expected."

Kienen's sigh is soft, but I catch it all the same. "It seems the prince did not see the need to entrust me with much."

"You were very close to Tyree, so why do you think that is?" I think I already know the answer to that. I hope I'm right.

His jaw tenses. "Because I would not agree with these plans."

"And yet you had no trouble sending all that poison into my lands." Zander glares at him.

"I was following orders from my prince, at the behest of the queen. I believed we were at war. And I believed Tyree when he said you had betrayed us."

Because, beyond prince and soldier, they were friends. "And now?"

"Now … I *know* we are at war, but I no longer know which side I am to fight for." His eyes flitter around the room. "I assume I'll die no matter the choice."

Abarrane harrumphs but doesn't say anything. Perhaps his frank honesty has scored some points with her.

"How many vials of poison were there?" Zander asks.

"I do not know exactly—"

"Guess!"

"Thousands. At least. We did not count."

I swear under my breath, peering at the spiderweb of tiny, blue-tinged veins in my wrists. Thousands of vials, with plenty of doses in each. Not enough to taint every mortal, but plenty to spark paralyzing fear. How long did it take to collect that much?

No wonder Kienen hasn't openly questioned the story that Mordain created the poison. Even if he heard rumors about my blood, how could he believe such a thing? How could anyone?

I *could* correct him. I could explain how Queen Neilina forced Ianca to summon Aoife. It would shine a brighter light on her corruption. But it could also open other doors to things we're not ready to admit to yet, like who—and what—I really am.

"King Barris's alliance with my father would have given Ybaris desperate access to fertile soil so your population would not starve each winter. Queen Neilina murdered him for it, and now wages a war that will cost countless lives. What more do you need to hear to believe your queen's treason against your own people?" Zander asks, trying to steer the conversation away from me and my secrets. "She wants power, she wants my lands. She wants to tear Islor apart from within and then cross the rift with an army emboldened by lies and deceit and claim it. She doesn't care who dies, only that she wins."

Silence lingers in the war room.

Until finally Kienen asks, "Forgive me for asking, Your Highness, but how are *you* standing here now? After all this treachery, why have the Islorians left you to live?"

Because I'm a key caster.

Because Zander is in love with me.

If Kienen truly has no clue about the summons to Aoife—which it seems he doesn't—then he doesn't know about the second part of the summoning, the one that makes Zander unable to resist the princess. Not that that seems to be an issue any longer. Zander loves *me*—Romy Watts of New York City. "Let's just say I've seen the error of my ways, and Zander knows he needs me in order to win the war against my mother."

"We have far bigger issues to discuss than Romeria's treachery." Zander flashes me a look of warning, refocusing on the map, moving stones into position. "Telor's men will arrive outside these gates soon, and we need to convince them that I am not a traitor to Islor."

Kienen bites his bottom lip. "And you think having an army of Ybarisans and saplings will prove that?"

"No, I think it will do exactly the opposite until I have a chance to speak with Lord Telor," Zander admits. "I do not want a battle with them. But if we are drawn into one, we will win. I can promise you that." The confidence in Zander's voice brokers no argument.

"Queen Neilina used you and those soldiers outside to help kill innocent people. This is your chance to help us fix that. I'm banking on the hope that Kienen is a soldier with a conscience.

Kienen's chest heaves with a sigh. "The men outside these gates will not take commands from an Islorian king, exiled or current. But they have pledged their allegiance to the royal family. They will follow their princess's orders."

"Even at the rift?"

His expression hardens. "King Barris was beloved by many. If they were to learn the truth of his death and that Queen Neilina leads us into an unnecessary war, they will not be so eager to aid her cause."

Abarrane's hand releases its white-knuckled grip of her pommel. Beside me, Jarek's tense frame seems to relax.

One down. I release a slow sigh as I turn to Radomir. "And the saplings … how many of you are there?"

"At last count, there were three hundred within the stronghold," he confirms. "Those are the ones who follow my lead."

"And will they follow *my* lead? Zander's lead?"

He hesitates. "You said this power only works within Ulysede's walls?"

"For now, yes. But my goal is to end the blood curse everywhere." If I can figure out a way that won't bring death and destruction to all. "I want *everyone* to be free of it. And then this poison Ybaris brought will no longer be an issue."

"I would ask how you plan on accomplishing such a feat, but given what I've already seen, I do not need an explanation. Only faith." Radomir's gaze shifts out the window, toward the brilliant morning sun. "My companions who traveled with me will have sought shelter in nearby caves for the day. Allow them the chance to feel what *I* have felt." His hazel eyes blaze with purpose as he meets mine again. "Allow this, and you will have our strength, for whatever it is worth."

I purse my lips to hide the stupid grin that wants to form. We have an army. A small army, where more than half the soldiers can only fight at night, but five hundred and seventy is a far cry better than the fifteen we started with.

Zander sets a white stone on the map, marking the new player on the board. The corner of his mouth twitches, the only crack in his stony expression that says he knows how happy—how relieved—I am.

"How will you convince Lord Telor and his approaching army to join your cause, Your Highness?" Kienen asks.

"That is between myself and my trusted advisors. You may return to your men outside Ulysede's gate. Radomir, we can offer you an escorted walk through Ulysede until the sun is down."

A clear line drawn in the sand, one that says Zander only trusts the Ybarisan and sapling so far. I can't blame him. It's one thing to declare loyalty, but Zander's been burned too many times to take it at face value. He'll need to see proof in action. It's how I won him over, eventually, and that took months.

Kienen's lips flatten, but he nods. "I would feel remiss not to warn you that Prince Tyree met with a group from Lyndel. Mostly mortals, but there was an elven."

"Who?"

"I do not know, and I did not hear their conversation, but we delivered a crate of the vials to them. They were soldiers wearing Lyndel's crest."

"It can only be the mortal army," Abarrane says.

"Lyndel has a *mortal* army?" I've only heard of mortals as servants, not trained soldiers.

"Yes. They've been fierce and loyal fighters for Telor and the crown for decades, fighting alongside our kind." Zander turns to Radomir. "What do you know of this?"

"I cannot confirm or deny it. The city's guards are far more aware and vigilant of my kind entering their walls than most. I do know they are not without cases of poisonings."

"I doubt there is a village in all of Islor that can claim otherwise." Zander seems to mull that over. "So Lyndel's army may be divided. That is important to know. Thank you, Kienen," he adds with reluctance.

"Your Highness."

"A moment, Zander?" I jerk my head.

With a nod, he follows me to a corner, out of earshot.

"Three hundred saplings plus two hundred and fifty-four Ybarisans. Not bad for a morning's work."

"I thought you were mad, bringing them in here. But you've done the very thing I thought impossible."

"Yeah, I thought I was crazy, too, for a second," I admit with a breathy laugh.

His attention flitters over his shoulder toward where Elisaf, Kienen, and Radomir discuss something on the map. "It's a tepid union at best. The sapling will attempt to seize Ulysede out from under you if you do not deliver on your promise, but we will use him to our advantage until we can't."

Leave it to Zander to focus already on all the ways we can be betrayed. "Give them a chance to prove themselves." But this isn't why I called him over here. I collect his hand, reveling in its strength. "We need to tell Atticus."

Zander's attention snaps back to me. "Tell him what?"

"About Neilina's plans for Hudem, about how much poison there actually is out there." For weeks, we assumed it was a few vials here, a few there. We didn't grasp the magnitude of it. "He's going to hear about Ulysede as soon as Telor sends a message. At least we can tell him what it does for your kind, what it did for Radomir."

Zander shakes his head. "Atticus will not listen to anything we have to say. He is bullheaded."

"Does he care about Islor?"

"He would die for it." In that declaration, Zander's voice doesn't waver.

"Then we need to tell him. He already wants me dead, so how much worse can it get?"

"If he finds out what you are, he could ignore the threat to the rift and send every Islorian soldier to our gates instead, allowing Neilina open passage through."

"Okay, that would be worse. But like it or not, he is the king right now, and he orders the armies. He should know what's coming, if he doesn't already. And remember, he has Wendeline." If he didn't execute her. "She might have already told him about me."

"No." Zander shakes his head. "If she had divulged that information, we would have heard about it."

"Either way, Neilina is the bigger threat to him than we are right now. If you want to prove that you are still loyal to Islor, tell him what we know. We can't save it on our own. If she succeeds, there won't be a throne for you to take back."

My words seem to sink into Zander's head. "That taillok … is it here?" he calls out to Kienen.

"Yes, Your Highness. With the men, outside the gate."

Zander bites his bottom lip in thought. "We need Gesine."

"Instead of scolding me, why don't you be useful?"

"How about I tie you down? Is *that* useful enough for you?"

Jarek and I share a smirk as we stroll into the library to the sound of Gesine and Zorya bickering.

"I don't have time for your games. We *must* find Lucretia's book."

Pan sees Jarek and me and trots toward us. "Hey, Romy. Thank fates you're here."

"What's going on?" I ask.

He scratches at his head of curly brown hair. Sometimes I forget the mortal from Bellcross is only a few years younger than me. "Dunno. I just got here, but it sounds like they're looking for somethin' important, and Gesine seems really upset and Zorya wants her to rest after healing Drakon and …" He peers over his shoulder warily and drops his voice to a whisper. "I think Zorya might actually tie her down. She brought rope with her."

With a sigh, I march to where the caster and the warrior argue, a stack of books between them. "This sounds like fun."

If looks could kill, I'd be a corpse the moment Zorya's single eye hits me. Pan wasn't kidding—she has a cord of rope looped and dangling from her hip, like Indiana Jones.

"Lucretia? Who's that?"

"The all-knowing key to *everything*, according to the witch," Zorya mutters sarcastically, before stalking off down an aisle.

Gesine sags in her chair, her eyes red from exerting her healing powers. Zorya's not wrong—she needs to rest, even for a few hours. "An oracle for the nymphs and immensely knowledgeable. I've stumbled across several books now that mention her. I didn't think too much of it until I found this one that mentions you—"

"*Me*?" I lean in to study the page where she points, but it's indecipherable, the foreign language a mess of strange letters.

"It says here that the oracle's lessons will have the answers the Queen for All must seek." She drags a fingertip over the line. "We *must* find this book, Romeria. But this place is too vast." A tinge of hysteria laces her voice.

Guilt slides down my spine. Gesine has been killing herself in here day and night, looking for anything that might help me, and all she faces is grief and suspicion and accusations from every angle. "What are we looking for?"

"Her name, I suspect?" She points to a jumble of letters.

"Okay. Write it out and I'll help look. *Somewhere*." Where the hell do I begin?

"You do not have time for this," Jarek says, suddenly behind me.

"I can make time. So can you, seeing as Gesine made time to heal Drakon." I flash him a knowing glare.

His jaw clenches, but then he nods.

Pan leans in. "What's that?" He points to an illustration on the opposite page—a smaller circle within a larger one, and nymph scrawl filling the space between the two.

"I would assume it has something to do with this. Why?"

"'Cause I've seen it."

Her face fills with hope as she looks up at Pan. "Here? In a book?"

He shakes his head. "No, but in the castle."

"*Where*, Pan?" I push.

He hesitates. "So, I know you told me to stay away from your throne and I've *mostly* listened, but I just happened to be going near it the other day. I didn't sit on it this time, I swear—"

"Pan!" Gesine barks, a rare display of temper for his incessant babbling.

"Okay! Yeah, I've seen this symbol." He holds up his hands in surrender. "Come, I'll show you."

The outdoor court that serves as Ulysede's throne room is as breathtaking now as it was the first day we discovered it. The grand trees shelter the area with their weeping branches. Gnarly roots and rose vines crawl everywhere, coating the ground, the castle walls, the black stone of the pavilion, giving it an ancient and overgrown quality.

"Like I said, I was checking things out, but I *did not* sit down, and I noticed this." Pan trots toward my throne—a treacherous seat of polished metals and white branches, its back ten feet tall—and squats in front of it. He pushes aside leafy vines that have crawled over the ground, forming a green natural carpet. "See? Here. This looks like it, right?"

Jarek drops to his knee and yanks at the vines, tearing them free. A large carved symbol in the stone matches the illustration in the book.

Gesine holds the book in front of her. "That is it."

Jarek looks up at Pan in disbelief. "How did you find this?"

Pan shrugs. "I saw a leaf with a funny shape, not like the others, you know? And I thought that was neat, maybe it's good luck, and maybe Eden would like it, so I tugged at it and—"

"Fuck. Forget I asked." Jarek shakes his head. "Nitwit."

I dismiss them both, dropping to the ground to trace the scrolling lines with my fingertip. High-pitched giggles sound in my ears that no one else hears. "This is definitely something."

"Look here." Gesine brushes aside the last few branches to uncover a small space where a hand could fit.

I groan. "This again. Great." The last time I did this, I lost at least a pint of blood. But it opened up Ulysede to us.

What will this open?

She peers at me in earnest. "The book with Lucretia's lessons must be hidden in here. This is important."

"We should notify the king," Jarek says.

I shake my head. "He's busy. And we need answers. *I* need answers."

With a sigh of reluctance, Jarek nods.

"Back up, everyone. Clear the circle."

Jarek grabs Pan by the scruff of his shirt and hauls him away like he's a little boy who can't be trusted.

I fit my hand into the space and wince at the bite from the jagged stone shards that cut into my flesh. Despite the pain, I watch with fascination as my blood trails along the scrawling lines, just like it did on the exterior wall.

A loud rumble sounds, stone scraping against stone. Gesine and I share a look of trepidation and then suddenly, the entire circle sinks, releasing my hand in the process.

A steep, circular set of stairs waits for us, the burning torches that line the walls beckoning us to descend into the darkness.

I peer over the edge. "Well … I guess … shall we?" I can't see the bottom.

Jarek draws two swords. "Pan, stay here. If there's any sign of trouble, you find the king." The warrior spares a steely look for the mortal. "And if you are not standing in that exact spot when we come back, you and I will have a very long and *painful* discussion."

Pan swallows hard. "Don't move. Got it."

Jarek leads us down the uneven, winding steps, pausing several times for me to find my balance against the dizziness. Finally, we reach the bottom, ending in a circular stone chamber no more than twenty feet in diameter, dark save for the burning torches.

Four stone nymphs sit perched on pedestals around the circle, all facing inward. Beyond them, it's empty.

"I don't see this book anywhere."

"Neither do I," Gesine whispers, as she takes in the gargoyle version, much like the one that looms in the grand hall.

"Look at this, though." I wander over to the wall, where nymph scrawl is carved into stone. It's a tall rectangle, a hard, etched line defining the shape. "What is this?"

"I do not know, but there are more like it here." Gesine points out two other rectangles with engravings.

"There are more around the room," Jarek confirms.

I draw a fingertip over a line in the one nearest me, expecting that familiar childish laughter, only nothing responds. It's as if my link is cut off. "It's not answering me. Maybe it's not from the nymphs?"

"I have seen something much like this before, deep within Mordain. What it means, though, what it is for … I have no idea. The seers have not seen the answer."

"But it must be something important." Why else have it hidden and protected within this vault?

I catch the faintest sound at my right, a second before my peripheral vision spots movement, and then it's suddenly four feet away from me—a snake the color of midnight, rising up … up … up … until it towers, its citron eyes boring into mine.

Jarek dives between us before I can even scream, his blade angling for a sweeping blow just as Gesine shrieks, "No!"

But his blade never reaches the snake's body before striking an invisible barrier, the metal vibrating from the force of impact.

Jarek grits his teeth against the painful jolt to his arms. "Was that you, witch?"

"It was *not* me," Gesine says calmly, her focus locked on the creature. "But you must stay your blade. I think this is Lucretia."

The snake's forked tongue slips out, waggling at him, and it seems a tease.

Jarek ushers me backward with an arm across my chest as the long, scaled body folds into itself and turns, over and over again, melding until its scales disappear and it no longer resembles a snake. When it unfolds again, its form is veiled behind sheer fabric that offers no coverage for the feminine curves beneath.

"Clever sorceress," the humanlike creature purrs, her voice throaty and seductive, as is the way she moves.

"What are you?" Jarek growls, his swords still gripped in his fists.

"What do you wish me to be?"

"Dead, if you intend harm."

She answers with a smile. Everything about her looks human —or immortal—except for the same vertical pupils cutting through citron-colored irises as her previous form. Even with those, she is beautiful. "What am I, Sorceress?"

"A *sylx*." Gesine's eyes flare with emerald light as she arms herself. "Be careful, Romeria. They are said to be powerful and treacherous creatures."

"More treacherous than your kind?" The female's head falls back with a raucous laugh, a curtain of deep auburn hair reaching halfway down her sculpted back. She doesn't seem fazed by the caster. Where Gesine has found any shred of affinity after healing Drakon, I can't imagine, but she obviously feels we need it. "Besides, I would not harm my queen."

"You won't harm *any* of us," I reach for my own affinities.

"Is that a command from Her Highness?" Her lips curl, as if my demand is funny.

"Yes."

"Then no harm will come of your servants by my will. There is no need to arm yourself so." She circles Jarek, her rapt attention on him. "I have pined for this moment for many millennia."

"How long have you been in here?" Trapped in this dark hole in the ground, with nothing but cold stone, firelight, and carvings.

"For as long as the gates of Ulysede have been sealed." She keeps moving, that graceful stride as she slips around us. Much like a snake might move, winding around its prey before closing in, squeezing.

It sets the hairs along the back of my neck, but I release my grip on my affinities, allowing them to slink back.

"In service to the nymphs?" Gesine asks.

Lucretia narrows her eyes. "Why do your servants feel they can speak to me freely?"

Something tells me arguing that I don't have servants won't win me points with this creature. "They're my advisors. Answer her question."

"Your Highness." She dips her head. "I have been tasked to serve as my masters' voice between the worlds until their return."

"You are the oracle that the tomes speak of, yes?" Gesine asks.

"That is one name for me."

"Gesine found books that say you have all the answers."

Lucretia grins. "And *you* have all the questions."

"I have *so* many questions," I admit.

"Then you need only ask. I know much, about what was and what will be."

"Lucretia's lessons," Gesine says. "It is not a book. It is her. She is your guide, your teacher."

A wave of exhilaration overwhelms me. Where do I even begin? "What is Ulysede?"

"It is your kingdom." Lucretia's beautiful face twists with mocking. "I would think that obvious, given you've claimed the throne."

"Right. And the nymphs built it for me?"

"No, they sealed it for you. This was always their home."

"And what made the fates banish the nymphs in the first place?"

Her musical laughter rings. "Who says the fates banished the nymphs?"

My eyes flip to Gesine.

"Everything we know about the nymphs has come from interpretations of seers' visions and sparse details from ancient scripture found in Shadowhelm," she admits. "The seers saw great strife between the nymphs and fates, and it was assumed—"

"*Assumed*. Yes, these wielders of the elements are all alike, are they not?" Lucretia sneers. "The mystics of days past thought themselves so clever as well. Cobbling together crumbs until they could call it cake. Their type always *assume* they are right."

"Perhaps if every text on the matter wasn't locked up in Ulysede, we would know more," Gesine snaps.

Lucretia only laughs in response, but in her eyes, challenge burns.

I hold up a hand to calm Gesine. "What are you saying?"

Lucretia circles Jarek again, slowing, stepping in close, her head tipped as she surveys his face, his mouth. "My masters are exactly where they chose to be."

He glowers at her. "And where is that?"

She smiles. "Very close, and eagerly awaiting their return."

I school my expression. What would the nymphs do if they knew I have no plans to release them? "Tell me everything I want to know."

After another moment staring at Jarek's mouth, she shifts away. "*You* must tell me what you wish to know."

"'The oracle's lessons will have the answers the Queen for All must seek,'" Gesine recites in a whisper. "That is what the text said."

Lucretia will tell me only what I ask. But what if I don't know what to ask? I heave a sigh of frustration. "Okay. Why does Malachi want me to open the nymphaeum door?"

"Because, for the fates to walk this plane, so must the nymphs." She shifts toward Gesine, cocking her head to appraise her form.

"And he wants to be king again." We've suspected as much.

"I could assume so, but I have not spoken to him personally, and I do not peddle *assumptions* as others do." She traces a finger over Gesine's gold collar. "You will have to ask him that. You have a sanctum above us, do you not?"

I catch her meaning. "I am not *summoning* him." Just the thought makes me shudder.

Lucretia shrugs. "Then you will not have your answer to that question until it comes to pass." She veers around, approaching me. "You are far too worried about the past, my queen. You should focus on your future." From this proximity, the yellow in her irises gives way to a ring of red around her pupil.

"What does that look like?"

"As Queen for All? My Highness, the possibilities are endless for you. The power contained in Ulysede will spread, healing the lands of its impurities."

"What about the blood curse?"

"Gifted by Malachi." She dips her head once. "It has already begun, has it not? Outside these gates, where the land suffers, does it not show signs of new life?"

"The grass," I whisper. Is that what's happening?

"An unfortunate scar upon the land when Ulysede was sealed, but my masters will repair what damage they have caused."

If the nymphs can fix broken land … "And the rift? Will that close?"

"I am afraid even my masters' connection to this world cannot reverse some damage. And some, they would not wish to fix." Lucretia moves along the wall, skimming the engraving with her fingertips. It's as if she can't stay still.

"What is all that scripture on the wall for? What does it do?"

"Not much anymore. The fates have caused great havoc since my masters were here last."

"What *was* it for?"

"For finding answers. I will show you when the time is right."

"Aren't *you* supposed to answer all of my questions?"

"You are not asking the right ones." Lucretia strolls past Jarek, reaching up to toy with one of his braids. "I would very much like to keep this one for a while."

His body stiffens. I see nothing but murder in his gaze as it meets hers.

I grit my teeth with frustration. Okay, fine. She wants the right questions? "What happens if I don't open the nymphaeum door, don't release the nymphs?"

Lucretia freezes, his braid slipping from her fingertips. "Whatever do you mean, Your Highness?" Her head cocks; she looks genuinely confused.

"Exactly what I said. What if Zander and I don't take the stone on Hudem and the nymphs remain wherever they are?"

Realization dawns on her face. "That is what you believe must happen?"

"Isn't it?"

"Though, of course, I suppose it is not your fault. Even Malachi was misinformed once, with disastrous results. Though I thought they would have figured it out, as Malachi since has. But these wielders and their assumptions ..." She tsks.

Wariness slips down my spine as I steal a look toward Gesine to find her eyes squeezed shut. "What are you saying, Lucretia?"

She closes in on me, studying my features intently. "That it is already begun, Your Highness. It began the moment you unsealed the door to Ulysede."

15
ROMERIA

I've already unsealed the door.

I feel the blood drain from my face as I replay her words in my head. "No, that's … not possible."

"And yet it is. You have done what you came here to do."

"*That's* what Malachi meant? That I open Ulysede?" My words are hoarse, barely audible, as I search through my memories and the words I clung to for weeks while locked up in my wallpapered prison. "But Sofie said to *retrieve* a *stone*." Which seemed straightforward until I saw the nymphaeum. Then it was a matter of interpreting words.

And that's how I interpreted it.

But it's also what Wendeline thought would have to happen for a key caster to open the door.

"Retrieve a stone. I do not know this Sofie or what tales she spun to coerce you. She might not even understand it herself. She is a wielder of the elements, yes? Treacherous creatures, they are." Lucretia glares at Gesine. "If I were to make *assumptions,* I would *assume* she told you what she thought you needed to hear. That's what they do," she purrs. "But your kingdom is set in stone, and you did retrieve it from its sleep, did you not? Or rather, you claimed it with a crown upon your head."

My mind works furiously, but nothing adds up. "She said it was guarded by soldiers." *Soldiers of a sort* were her exact words. "And surrounded by a garden. There's no garden out there!" I throw a hand haphazardly toward the stairs. "The land outside the gates is dead!"

"Dead now, yes. But once, long ago, the path to this kingdom was lush with an entrance fit for a queen. You should have seen it. You *will* see it. And as for Ulysede's guards"—she glides toward me, smiling as she leans in—"do not assume that which you can't see isn't *all* around you, watching."

I shudder at the feel of her breath against my ear, still not willing to accept her words as truth. "Malachi wanted me to open the nymphaeum in Cirilea, just like he had Farren try."

"And how did that work out for him?" Musical, mocking laughter rings out through the cave. "My dear queen, you will soon see that it is all connected. Malachi had the right idea and also the wrong one. But he persevered, and now here we are. He has given my masters what they sought, and this will allow him what he longs for."

"What did your masters want?"

"A Queen for All. *You*." Her pretty face furrows. "Why do I sense such distress from Her Highness?"

How is someone so full of knowledge also so obtuse? "Because Malachi is a cruel god, and he wants to be king!"

"He is not our favorite, that is true, and yet there is no life without him."

"There will be plenty of death with him. He releases daaknars for fun." If this secret book from Shadowhelm that Gesine talks about is true, people suffered at his hands.

"Yes, he is powerful, and yes, he is cruel, but he must forgo some of that strength in order to walk this plane. Besides, *you* are also powerful. And while you are not cruel, you have an army who can behave as terribly as needed."

"Islor is divided, and no one follows me. I have five hundred soldiers who will probably turn on me the second they find out about this." Only an hour ago, I was beaming with triumph.

She waves off my words. "Not that army. They are useless. No … the one that awaits your call. The one that has been waiting in the void for two thousand years."

Two thousand years. "You mean the Nulling." I was so focused on how this could have happened, I forgot about what will happen next. "It will open." Of course it will.

Jarek curses.

Lucretia cocks her head, as if confused by our reactions. "Why are you not pleased?"

"How could she be?" Gesine asks before I can. "The creatures from the Nulling serve no one but chaos."

"Do they not?" Lucretia's patronizing laugh makes me want to choke her. "Is that what your seers have told you?"

"No, that is what history tells us!" Gesine's calm is wearing thin as well. "King Ailill and Caster Farren, under the guidance of Malachi, tore the barrier into the Nulling. It took fifty years and untold deaths to cleanse these lands from that mistake."

"Because my masters were not here to help rein them in. But now my masters are coming, and they have found their queen." She frowns curiously between Gesine and me. "Surely, the few that remain in this realm have sought you out by now."

"Yeah. If 'sought me out' means tried to kill me." First the nethertaur, then the grif.

Lucretia shrugs. "I did not say they weren't without problems."

Gesine's brow furrows, as if she's rifling through a catalog in her mind to compare Lucretia's cryptic words with what she knows. Or thought she knew.

"Romeria!" Zander's booming voice echoes with his footfalls down the winding stairwell. He comes to the base with a skid before taking in the secret vault with a cautious gaze. "Pan said you were down here. What is this place?"

"It's where Lucretia has been waiting. She's—" I turn back to find the sylx vanished. Not even the snake remains. I weave around the stone statues, but there's no hint of her. "Where did she go?" There's no way out except the stairs Zander just descended.

"It seems she's unwilling to reveal herself for the moment," Gesine says, also searching the shadows.

Zander slides a hand over the engraving in the stone wall. "What is this place?"

"Gesine found a book about an oracle named Lucretia who would have answers for me." And she does. They're just none that I expected.

And one that I dread.

It dawns on me then. "You knew, didn't you? That's what you've been searching for in the library, isn't it? You kept saying we were running out of time. It wasn't because of the change though, was it?"

The pained look in Gesine's eyes answers me. "I suspected. I *feared*. And then when Elisaf mentioned the land outside the gates, the new blades of grass, the plants—"

"You *suspected*, but you didn't say *anything*?" My shrill voice cracks over my anger.

"Because I did not want to alarm you needlessly." She swallows. "I did not want to say anything until I knew for certain."

"Knew *what* for certain?" Zander steps between us, alarm splashed across his face. "Would *someone* please enlighten me?"

Oh God. Zander ... I press my hand against my roiling stomach. All this time, I've insisted I would never give Malachi what he wanted, I would never put Zander's people in harm's way, and yet I've done it, anyway. Stupidly, cluelessly. "We had it all wrong."

"What do you mean?" He turns to Gesine. "What does she mean?"

"They've opened the nymphaeum door," Jarek answers for us, his deep voice amplified in our hollow.

Zander stares at me like he's been slapped.

"Ulysede," I whisper.

He swings his focus to Gesine and rage contorts his face. "Is this true?"

"I warned you that taking the stone on Hudem might not be the only way, did I not?" Her voice is a husky whisper. "That *all* paths may lead to opening it?"

"Including the path *you* chose?" He roars, and the torches along the wall flare to three times their size. "Your insistence that we come to Stonekeep, that there was … what did you call it—a token of the nymphs' loyalty waiting for us?" His laugh is bitter. "Suddenly sharing caves with hundreds of saplings does not sound so foreboding."

"I did not suspect it would lead to this. But it seems we have been wrong in many things. The nymphs successfully hid what they did not wish us to see." Gesine's shoulders sag with a sigh. "Prophecy will always find a way."

Silence lingers in the cave as everyone absorbs the shock.

"You should have told me. You had no right to keep me in the dark about this." Guilt battles with anger to overwhelm my emotions.

"I was only trying to protect you. You need to focus on your training, and on uniting with Telor—"

"Fuck Telor!" I burst. "He's the least of our problems now."

Zander sighs, pinching the bridge of his nose. "And yet he is our most immediate one. His men are arriving."

"*Already*?" I thought we'd have another day.

"The first riders have been spotted." He surveys the statues. "Wherever this Lucretia is, she will have to wait. Tell no one of this discovery, or what is coming." He meets each of our eyes in turn. "*No one.*"

"So, that's what a thousand soldiers look like?" From my vantage point within Ulysede's tunnel entrance, the men are little more than specks in the distance as they set up camp. Smoke curls in the air where cook fires burn.

The Ybarisans stand in formation to the left of our gate. They're more at ease now that Kienen has returned to them. If they're curious to see what's on the other side of this tunnel, none seem interested to mix with the Islorians to scratch that itch.

"I imagine they rode hard to get here and are now perplexed by what they see." A tiny smile curls Zander's lips. He always likes having the advantage.

But how can he care about that? How can he care about *anything* else right now? I did the one thing I swore I wouldn't do.

I've opened the nymphaeum door.

Over and over, that reality has slammed into me since we left Lucretia's crypt, and each time, a wave of panic follows. Is it true? Have I given Malachi and Sofie what they wanted? Are so many more people going to die because of me? Not Princess Romeria … I can't blame her for this one.

I swallow against these thoughts. A queen can't crumble, not here in front of everyone. Maybe tonight, behind the safety of my bedroom door, I can let the full weight of this crush me. *If* there is even time to sleep. "How long do we have?" My voice sounds hollow.

Zander looks up at the waning sun. "If I know Telor, he will approach tonight, with an ultimatum to surrender by morning. Where it leads from there, I cannot say. We may be in battle at dawn."

I've already seen my share of death since I arrived in Islor, and the last thing I want is to witness war, let alone be a part of one.

"My men will return as soon as the sun drops past the horizon," Radomir calls out from within the depths of the tunnel. "What should I expect when I cross that threshold to see them?"

"The first time the blood curse takes hold of us, it is overwhelming," Zander warns. "I assume it will be the same for you. When it is time, we will have our caster provide aid to you, in case your transition is more difficult than expected and you turn on us. You may speak to your men then, share the news of our alliance."

"And send them to fetch my legionary," Abarrane demands. "I want him back before daybreak."

God … Abarrane. What will she do when she finds out what I've done?

Radomir nods, his hand smoothing over his cheek, as if trying to memorize this face before it's taken from him again.

Zander peers at the letter in his hand, at the black wax seal, the silver flecking it like stars in a night sky. We argued for an hour about how much to tell Atticus before we put ink to paper. "I fear we are putting too much faith in my brother to do the right thing."

"If he doesn't, that's on him."

"If he doesn't, we will all pay the price. Gesine!" Zander bellows, making me jump.

"Right here, Your Highness," she calls out calmly from behind him.

Zander's gaze hardens on her. After this, I don't know that he'll ever see her as anything but traitorous Mordain. I'm beginning to understand why. "The taillok?"

"I have respelled it. It will carry your message to Cirilea." She gestures to a sizable cage draped in oilcloth nearby, nodding toward Kienen.

He draws the cover off.

Murmured voices rise among the legionaries as they appraise it.

"This *thing* has delivered messages to Cirilea?" Jarek peers at it with amazement.

"A handful of times, especially closer to the wedding," Zander says.

"How did I miss that in flight?"

"It is far stealthier than its size would portray," Kienen confirms.

The taillok stands three feet tall, with two spindly legs capped by clawed feet. Hawkish black eyes lined with humanlike eyelashes and surrounded by a vibrant orange mask watch us as if cataloging our every twitch. Its feathers are an iridescent white, save for a dozen wispy gold ones standing on end around its head, shaped to look like a crown.

"You said this came from the Nulling?" Doubt steeps in my voice. "But it's ... beautiful."

It answers with a piercing screech that makes us all wince.

Gesine smiles. "Not all creatures that come through the Nulling are as terrifying as the grif. Some, you would never suspect."

Like Sofie's husband, I suppose, if he ever makes it through.

This messenger bird may be stunning but no doubt it's deadly if it wants to be. That hooked beak looks like it could tear chunks of flesh from my body with little effort.

Zander hands her the letter. "How long will this take to arrive?"

"It should be there by the morning. The caster who spells the bird shares its line of sight, so I will see when it lands in Cirilea's hands."

"You mean, you can see what it sees right now?"

Gesine dips her head once in answer. "All the time, Your Highness."

A worrying thought strikes me. I turn to Kienen. "Was that cloth over it this entire time?"

"Most of the time. The prince's instructions were to keep it covered when it returned with communication from the queen so as not to tax the caster linked to it. We were to uncover it once each morning or if something important should happen, so the caster could relay our whereabouts to the queen."

Important, like an unimaginable kingdom within the deeps of Islor? "What about when you arrived here last night?"

Kienen inhales. "The caster will have seen the gates of Ulysede, yes. And you, standing within it."

I curse.

"I apologize, Your Highness. I did not know the depths of the queen's betrayal to Ybaris."

"No, it's not your fault. You were just following orders." So Mother Dearest will know I'm alive and that I'm with Zander, and the Ybarisan army is with us. A darker thought strikes me and panic stirs. "Wait. What *exactly* did the taillok see?"

16
AGATHA

A knock sounds on my door, followed by a creak.

"I told you not to bother me this afternoon," I admonish, not breaking my gaze from the old text I'm studying.

"Still as fixated on your work as ever."

My head jerks up to find Lorel standing in my office doorway. "Prime?" It's another few beats before I remember myself. Setting down my magnifying glass, I ease out of my seat as quickly as my body can move. "I apologize. I was not expecting you." It's been decades since a much younger version ventured to my office. I assumed she wouldn't remember her way here. "Can I help you with something?"

"I hope so." She pushes the door shut and saunters in, her heels clicking on the uneven stone floor. "You know more about matters of the ambiguous than anyone else in Nyos. In all your years of studying the seers' foretelling, have you ever come across a gate in the Venhorn Mountains?"

"A *gate*, Prime?" Wariness creeps in, mention of the very mountains that Gesine was heading to too coincidental. "No, I do not recall mention of any *gates*." A token from the nymphs, the seers have seen. Something vague but of great value, meant to be found one day, by those in Islor who need it most. "What sort of gate?"

"One you would find at the entrance to a city." She sighs. "Queen Neilina has just sent word. Her taillok remained with the Ybarisan soldiers in the Venhorn Mountains since the queen's last letter to the prince. Last night it showed an image to Caster Yesenia of Princess Romeria standing within a set of gates. The exiled king was with her."

"And you believe the answer to this lies within *prophecy*? My, my ... how interesting." I can't keep the incredulity from my voice, the mocking smile from curling my lips. The Prime has never been a supporter. She's gone as far as to suggest the seers are a burden, better off put out of their misery the moment the change takes hold, their ramblings useless and a waste of effort to document.

Lorel's cheeks flush with anger. "I will give you some leeway because you were the first face I remember in Nyos, but do not forget to whom you are speaking," she warns sharply. "I do not know if any of this has to do with prophecy, but I do recall there is a wall of nymph scripture within those same mountains."

Lorel wasn't *completely* dismissive of her early learnings. "A stone wall with no answers that no one can explain. Not even the seers."

"Yes, well, Her Highness expects an answer, and there is no one else in all of Nyos who has such a grasp of these things as you. That is why I've come now."

I temper my self-righteous glee, for I will be of little use to anyone from a dungeon cell. "Did the taillok see anything else of note?" What I would do to have that messenger for my own devices. My letter to Gesine is on its way via Allegra's skills, but fates knows when it will arrive.

Lorel falters. "This is, of course, confidential. I do not feel it necessary to share beyond this room."

Which means she has no plans on enlightening her Seconds. "Of course."

She paces. "There were saplings among the Ybarisans. They had an Islorian prisoner, and it looked like they were surrendering him. One of the warriors exited the gate to collect his comrade and immediately crumbled for some unknown cause, and when the princess reached out to grant him support, he turned on her, fangs and all!" Horror splays across her face. "Savages, all of them."

My eyebrows arch. "The warrior fed on the princess?" But that should have killed him.

"No." Lorel frowns. "He was assaulted before he had the chance. With an affinity powerful enough to send him flying back in a split second. Yesenia could not pin the source, though."

Could not, or *would* not? The elemental caster was a dear friend of Ianca and Gesine's and, if I had to guess who helped facilitate their escape, I would bet on Yesenia's involvement. "And where is the taillok now?"

Lorel's expression turns dark. "That is part of the issue. The connection was severed earlier today, and there is only one way that could happen."

"A powerful caster has claimed it for their use."

She nods. "I believe Caster Gesine and Caster Ianca have found their way to the princess. That would explain this, as well as what happened to that warrior."

"It certainly would." I feign ignorance. "For what purpose, though? Are you saying they ran from the queen, only to join forces with her daughter, who shares her mother's ambitions?"

Her lips twist. "Yes, it does not make much sense, I agree. But more and more, I am sensing a growing plot within our ranks."

"*Here,* in Mordain?" I keep my voice light. So, she isn't as oblivious as I thought. "To what end?"

She shoots me a patronizing look. "For the coveted position of Prime, naturally."

Stupid, stupid caster. She would believe that is the only possible motivation. Lorel always was power hungry, though, even as a child.

"Master Scribe, I have those—" Cahill stops in my doorway abruptly when he sees I have company, his arms laden with books.

My inhale is sharp—too sharp, for a simple interruption. Of all the times for him to barge into my office!

Lorel sizes up the boy, stalling on his face a few beats. Cahill is growing into a strapping and handsome young man. I've noted more than one young caster in Nyos spying on him. Thankfully he is too shy to engage in conversations and any other sort of mischief.

Cahill doesn't have the first clue what lingers beneath his skin, waiting to manifest, but all it would take is an assessment by a tester to find it. That or a glimpse of the dull silver medallion hanging from a chain around his neck to stir suspicion. I never told anyone of the token an elderly journeyman handed me on my trip to Shadowhelm so many years ago. He said it suppressed caster abilities, and that he had no use for it in Skatrana, but perhaps Mordain might find a use one day.

Years later, I did. Caster Elica came to me in the middle of the night with a baby boy elemental tucked within her arms, unable to deliver the death sentence required. I couldn't bring myself to either. So we branded him a weak caster and assigned him to scribe duty, where we have hidden him his entire life, molding him to live a life in servitude to prophecy.

Finally, Lorel dismisses Cahill.

And I let out a soft sigh. Ignoring Cahill—it's best everyone does—I smile at the Prime. "I will begin my search of the tomes that we believe tie to Islor."

"That would be helpful, Master Scribe."

"I must warn you, there are far too many to count. It will take weeks, months even."

"Hopefully, Neilina's war will shift her attention elsewhere soon enough."

Her war, with Mordain as her soldiers. "Yes. Hopefully."

I count to ten after Lorel departs before I open my desk drawer, running my fingertips over the book that speaks to this token for the people of Islor.

Ulysede is a city.

A great nymph city.

17
GRACEN

"Are your hands soaked in something?"

I stall. "Pardon me? I don't understand."

"You won't stop wringing them. All day, since you got back from fetching that troublemaker"—Corrin aims her peeling knife toward Mika, who sits on the floor in a corner playing checkers with himself—"you've been wringing and pacing. You know who else paced like that? Princess Romeria. And fates knows the trouble she got up to." She steals a glance at the two guards stationed at the door—a new addition since the attempt on the king's life—as if wary of being caught even saying that name.

"I do not know what leaves me so restless." I shoot Mika a warning look. I told him they'd send us back to Freywich if anyone discovered what he'd found in the library and who he saw put it there. That seemed even worse than telling him the truth—that the only place we'd be going is the execution square. "Perhaps I'm overwhelmed by the work left ahead of the wedding." Hudem is in less than a week!

"There is still much to do," Corrin agrees, her curiosity over my behavior appeased. She shifts her focus back to the enormous pot to finish the potatoes—a task for the scullery staff but one she does regularly, claiming it's therapeutic. I think it's because she's a queen's maid without a queen and can't stand idle hands. Lady Saoirse brought her own servants with her—not that Corrin would be eager to serve that one.

A medley of aromas blend in the kitchen tonight—roasted boar with sage and honey, parsnips and squash, an earthy mushroom soup—that promises a delicious meal. We never ate so well in Freywich, relegated to stale bread and broth while the keepers filled their bellies. Here, there is always more than enough to feed both the castle's inhabitants and frequent guests, and the household staff eat well.

I set to work mixing batter, but my mind is on the vial of poison in Mika's little palm. Between leaving the library and getting back to our room, I decided there was no good reason to keep it and plenty of reason to be rid of it. So I tossed it into the latrine, praying the king's guard is above sifting through feces. Even if they aren't, they would be hard pressed to tie that back to me.

But it doesn't solve the problem.

Lady—soon to be queen—Saoirse was in possession of this poison. If she wasn't the one who tainted Sabrina's blood, it means there is more of it within the castle. If she *is* guilty of tainting Sabrina's blood, why would she wish to cause her future husband harm?

And if she succeeds—if she finds another vial—I'll *never* forgive myself.

But what am I to do?

"That doesn't look like pie pastry." Corrin's voice cuts into my thoughts.

"Uh, no. It's not. I'm making fritters today."

Her face pinches. "Again? But they just had them yesterday."

Mika perks up. "Just like the king said you would!"

"The king." Corrin stops her peeling to stare at me. *"He* asked you to make fritters?"

"Not exactly. I ran into him in the library, and he mentioned that they were his favorite." That could have been simply conversation. "He helped me in my search for Mika, so I thought I would make them again as a thank-you," I explain as casually as possible, even as my cheeks heat.

Corrin sets her potato and her knife down, brushing her hands over her apron. "Mika, make yourself useful and fetch more apples from the cellar."

He scrambles to his feet and trots toward the door.

"And if you so much as *breathe* past that pantry door, I will make you sit and watch me eat every last one of these." She gives him her most severe glare.

He laughs. "You don't even like apples!"

"You're right! But I'll enjoy them enough to torment you. Now never you mind. Go!" She shoos him away.

He picks up speed, scurrying out the door.

With him out of the way, Corrin ventures over to collect the last of the fruit from a bushel basket in the corner. "You've had a lot of encounters with the king lately."

"Coincidence has our paths crossing more than one should expect it to," I admit.

"First the assembly, then in the servants' quarters, now in the library." Corrin closes the distance. "Coincidence or not, it would seem you have captured His Highness's attention."

"He pities me is all." But my heart skips several beats with excitement at the possibility that she is right.

Corrin snorts, taking her peeling knife to an apple. "I have served this family since my own Presenting Day, as Queen Esma's servant for almost as long. She saw *many* things in her youngest son, but the capacity for pity was not one of them. Neither is following the rules." She watches me closely. "Be careful, my girl. Those who find themselves catching His Highness's gaze usually find themselves in his chambers not long after. Especially now that his tributary cannot perform her duties. For whatever reason, he has not called in another, but eventually, he will be looking for someone new, possibly someone in secret. I did not think that was a role you wished to play again. Being *used* like that?"

"It isn't." I prayed my days of giving my vein were over for good, but with the issue of this poison, everything is changing. "But if my blood *is* what the king is intent on, I cannot refuse, so there is no point worrying about it." Though, I could think of far worse situations. I like what I know of him so far. I'm certainly attracted to him, and I've never been attracted to *any* of the Islorian males I've been forced to serve. It's not that some weren't pleasing to look at. Even Lord Danthrin could be considered handsome, until you saw the demon hiding beneath his skin.

But the king hasn't hinted of any monsters lurking. Every time his eyes touch me, I feel them as readily as if his hands were on my body, and I don't dislike it. "At least he does not seem the type to want a breeding mare."

"No, he is not interested in the outcome of the act. But the act itself, he is *very* fond of." She gives me a knowing look. "If you are marked as the king's tributary, you become a target for this poison. Look at Sabrina."

Mention of her stirs a pang of sorrow inside me. "Have you heard anything—"

"No. Other than her body hasn't been collected from the execution square yet, so she must still be alive. For how much longer, I cannot say. I doubt long."

The poor, young girl. She doesn't deserve to die. But it's a stark reminder that Corrin's worries are valid. I don't want the same fate.

"I suggest you make yourself scarce. And stop baking the king's favorite for him."

I look at the bowl's contents. "But the batter is already made. That would be wasteful."

"Oh, well, we wouldn't want that," Corrin mutters wryly, coring the apple before moving to the next one. "As I said, be careful. There are many dangers within these walls, too close, and they all revolve around His Highness."

Don't I know it. I hesitate, keeping my focus on my task as I lower my voice. "If you knew something that the king would want to know, but revealing it would likely put you and those you love in danger, what would you do?"

Her eyes narrow. "I would tell my trusted friend, Corrin, and she would help me determine if this is in fact something the king should know."

I knew she'd say that. I considered telling Corrin earlier but decided that her knowing would only put her in danger. Maybe I could get an anonymous note to His Highness, to warn him? But how do I admit what we found in the library without outing myself? It wouldn't take much thought to make the connection.

"Is this enough apples?" Mika hollers, dragging a bushel basket across the stone floor toward us.

"Za'hala! How many fritters do you suppose your mother is going to make for you, child!" Corrin exclaims with exasperation. "And how did you even get that up the stairs?"

"A guard helped me!" His giggles push away the dark cloud hanging over my head for the meantime.

But it doesn't go far, and by the time I've slid the last batch of fritters into the kiln, I know I must find a way to send a message to the king, to warn him.

My arms strain beneath the silver platter as I slip into the dining hall through the staff entrance door. I've never been in here, never had a reason for it. It's as splendid as the rumors claimed, the ceiling reaching high above us, with curved windows around the top to give a glimpse into the night sky. Candelabras dangle from the main beam, countless flames flickering from each to cast light down over the expanse of tables, where more candles burn.

A collection of string instruments play an upbeat song from the dais across the room, and jovial laughter carries, the tables full of the nobility staying in Cirilea ahead of the wedding. No one would guess someone tried to kill the king not twenty-four hours ago.

I seek out the king and find him instantly, seated at a long banquet table at the far end of the room. Lady Saoirse sits next to him, laughing at something he said.

My anger flares, but doubt chases quickly. They look so at ease around each other. Is there another reason why the future queen of Islor was hiding poison in the library? Maybe the king knows, and I'm stressing over nothing?

No ... the way he behaved toward her, what he said to me, I don't believe that. He is a showman, and this is an act for the crowd. He is doing what he thinks he must for the sake of Islor, and that honorable cause will likely get him killed.

Meanwhile, she will be queen of Islor—for centuries, possibly—all because of the family and station she was born into.

Seated on the other side of the king is an Islorian with olive skin, a trim beard, and long hair pulled back off his face. He wears the leathers of a fighter. Could this be one of the king's few trusted friends? The man's gaze drifts about the dining hall while a female beside him—a stunning blond with long, smooth ringlets that cascade down her back—prattles in his ear. Whatever she's saying, her pinched face smacks of displeasure.

That lord from the day of the assembly, the one who suggested the king could not honor Princess Romeria's bargains and that I should go back to Freywich, sits beside Lady Saoirse, his goblet held high, silently demanding more wine. With them side by side, I see a familial resemblance. He must be important if he sits next to her. Maybe her father?

I need to pay more attention to the household gossip. I am clueless in here.

And this was a terrible mistake. Though I served Lord Danthrin and his guests plenty over the years, this is the castle. There are routines and protocols, and my place is in the kitchen, not scuttling into the dining hall with fritters and a harebrained scheme of slipping a note into the king's pocket. I shouldn't have come.

"Gracen." Fikar slows and grins, at the fritters or me, I can't tell. The lanky servant's a terrible flirt. "What are you doing in here?"

"Fikar!" I hold up the platter. "Can you take this to the head table for me?"

"Uh … Sure. Let me just …" He glances around, searching for a place to cast the empty silver wine pitcher in his grasp. There isn't anywhere. "Give me a minute to refill this, and then I'll be back." He's gone before I can stop him, leaving me standing there, raucous laughter and conversations all around me.

"My, haven't you grown comfortable in Cirilea's castle."

I nearly lose my grip of the silver tray at Lord Danthrin's crisp voice in my ear. *Fates*, of course he's here. I'd like to say I thought he'd left for Freywich to be with his pregnant wife and their charred orchard, but I simply didn't think, too focused on the king and this poison.

And now I feel cornered in the middle of a room. "They've welcomed me." I clear the shake from my voice as I edge away from his looming presence before daring to meet his gaze. He's as polished as usual but the veneer doesn't hide the stains beneath, at least not for me. "Joining the household has been a blessing for us."

He steps closer, erasing the space I created. "You have a glow about you." His cold eyes scour my face before sliding down my neckline, over my swollen chest, aching with the need to nurse.

My skin crawls, remembering all the times he's looked at me like that, and what it always led to. "It's called being fed." I don't know where these brazen words come from. I never had the nerve to speak to him with such acrimony before.

Rage flashes across his face, the likes of which I've seen many times, though I've never rightfully deserved. I brace myself for a backhand across my cheek, dreading the aftermath of the attention it will bring as I'm sprawled out on the floor, my afternoon's work edible for no one but the swine anymore.

But Lord Danthrin seems to catch himself, stealing a glance toward the head table.

I follow suit, and my breath hitches.

The king watches us, his arms propped at the elbows, his lips pressed against his folded hands, hiding his expression from view.

"You are fortunate to have won His Highness's favor, though I am not surprised. You do have more compelling *skills* than one might expect, buried beneath the flour and sugar and lard."

I push away the images he's conjuring in my mind, the tears threatening to spill along with the wave of revulsion.

"How are my children doing?" Lord Danthrin smooths his hand over his lapel. "Are you taking good care of them for me?"

I grit my teeth. "They are *not* your children." Where is Fikar? He should be back by now. I glance frantically around, my focus landing on the king again.

He's leaning over to say something in the male's ear sitting next to him.

"Come now, Gracen." Danthrin's responding smile is vicious as he pulls my attention back. "Every one of those little bastards that sucks on your teats is breathing because of me. Because *I* found a mortal willing to spill his seed into you until you succeeded in bearing fruit. They would not exist otherwise. And it cost me dearly."

"I never asked for *any* of it." If he paid anything, it was to those mortal men's keepers, and the mortal men he brought forth weren't particularly kind or gentle about their tasks.

"What you asked for or wanted is of no consequence. Do not get caught up in foolish thoughts like that. Then again, that is not your fault, given what you're surrounded with. They've filled your head with nonsense, I can see. No bother, it will all be undone soon enough." Glee sparkles in his wicked eyes. "Those offspring are mine, and once the wind changes direction around here"—his gaze wanders around the lords and ladies—"I will come back to claim them."

Paralyzing fear seizes my heart. "I will *never* allow it."

Deep laughter sails from his thin lips. "You will have no

choice. As for what I should do with my dear, talented baker … You're getting old and weathered. I haven't decided if you've outlived your usefulness." His fingers clamp over my chin, squeezing as they shift my face this way and that, as if sizing up my features. "Maybe I'll let you beg me to take you back, or maybe I'll tie you to a tree and leave you there, so you can imagine the ways I punish those children for your betrayal while you slowly die—"

"Danthrin, you've stalled the dessert from reaching the head table," a deep voice interrupts. It's the bearded male who sat beside the king only moments ago, receiving his whispers.

Lord Danthrin's lips press together as he decides how polite he needs to be. A gaze toward the head table says he recognizes the man as seated at the king's right hand, literally. "Surely, you've learned to address noblemen by their proper title, soldier?"

"Captain." The male pulls an apple fritter off my platter and takes a bite. He mumbles around his mouthful, "Seems I missed that day in school."

I decide I like him, whoever he is.

Fikar returns then, out of breath. "I got hung up." With a curt nod toward the two men, he collects the platter from my grasp and whisks it away, leaving me empty-handed and itching to run from my previous keeper and his threats.

The captain scowls at Fikar's back. "If I'd known he was going to do that, I would have grabbed more."

"They are waiting for you at your seat." Danthrin gestures toward it—an attempt to dismiss him.

"They'll have to wait until I return from escorting the baker to the kitchen. Shall we?" He angles his arm for me to collect.

I hesitate, sneaking another glance. The king is in deep conversation with the blond, no longer paying attention to me. But he must have sent his friend to my rescue; there's no other reason for it.

"Come, before they eat them all." The captain nudges me with his elbow.

Tension courses through my body as my fingers curl around his powerful biceps.

"I'll see you again soon," Lord Danthrin calls out as I'm led away, his threat fading into the noise.

"Thank you," I manage as we head toward the servants' entrance.

"Thank the king. He noticed you needing an escape," the captain says, his smile crooked. "I would have to say I agree. I believe I heard something about being tied to a tree?"

A part of me is disappointed that the king didn't rescue me himself, but that would be silly to wish for. He is *the king*. "Lord Danthrin used to be my keeper before I came here, and he seems determined to be my keeper again."

"Fortune has favored you, then. *Gracen*."

I falter. Why does my name on his tongue sound like a warning?

"I'm Kazimir. The king entrusts me to know everyone and everything that goes on within these city walls as it relates to him. I'm a *very* important person. Surely, he's mentioned me to you."

"Uh …" I can't tell if he's joking. "No, but we've spoken little. Barely at all."

The smirk on his face suggests otherwise.

The servants' door is ahead. "Thank you, again, for your aid, and please, pass my gratitude on to the king—"

"What are you doing in here, Gracen?" All pretenses at humor and ease have evaporated. His arm tightens around my hand, trapping it against him.

"I'm sorry?"

"We have servants to run food and drink. You had no need to come here tonight, and you've never been here before." He surveys the faces around us as we walk, lowering his voice. "You see, I not only keep tabs on goings-on, I am also very interested in identifying and removing *all* threats to my good friend. Even the most unsuspecting. You've heard by now the recent attempt on his life?"

I nod dumbly, wondering whether I've left one demon only to face another.

"So I would like to know *why* you would risk coming into the dining hall and subjecting yourself to the wrath of your previous keeper? Is it to catch a glimpse of the king?"

"No," I sputter. That's not why, though seeing his handsome face was not a hardship.

"Are you sure? I've heard you've grown quite smitten with him."

My cheeks flush at his insinuation, as true as it may be. And where did Kazimir hear such a thing? From the king himself? "I … I was hoping to speak to him, privately." I wasn't planning on admitting to that, but something about the way Kazimir speaks—quickly, softly, and with precision—pulls the confession out of me.

"The mortal baker wants a private audience with Islor's king?" The captain's mouth curves into an amused smile. "For what reason?"

"My reason is important, I assure you, but"—I glance around—"it is of a sensitive nature, meant for the king's ears only."

Kazimir swings me into a corner, bracketing my body between his and the wall. "The reason will then drift to my ears to be dealt with, I assure you." He studies my face, his gaze lingering on my nose and, likely, the smattering of freckles. "It would need to be an exceptional reason, or you will find no friend here, and you do not want me as your foe."

Brilliant. Kazimir now suspects I am here to either moon over the king or kill him. While I'd like to steer him toward the former, as embarrassing as that is, it won't help the king any.

"I am the only one here who will go out of his way to arrange a private audience for you, Gracen. Consider that."

There's no use sitting on this information. I do another scan for nearby ears, but I doubt anyone would even know I'm here, hidden behind this warrior's frame. "I think I know who tried to poison the king."

He stares down at me. He's waiting for me to elaborate.

I swallow. "The future queen."

His expression turns hard, but no shock touches it, I note. "That is exceptional, and quite the accusation, one that could end your life. Do you have proof?"

"Yes … no? … Honestly, I don't know what I have." The confession of an impish little boy. "But I do know she had a vial of the poison."

"And where is it now?"

"In the latrine."

Pulling himself to his full height, he smooths his thumb over the pommel of his sword as he steps back and does a cursory glance around. The captain has six weapons on him that I can count, and who knows how many more hidden. "Go about your evening as you would, and I will seek you out when it's time. And Gracen?" He levels me with a hard gaze. "Speak about this at your own peril."

By the time I reach the kitchen, my hands are shaking.

18
ATTICUS

"Why would Saoirse try to poison me *before* the wedding?" From the balcony of my chamber, I study a couple strolling into the castle's lush gardens. "After? I fully expect it and will plan accordingly, but if I'm dead before, she does not become queen. Not without a fierce battle, anyway. Do you think the mortal speaks the truth?"

"I do." Kazimir leans against the stone rail next to me, sharing my view. "And to answer your other question, to strike fear."

"Say more."

"Adley came to you in the sparring court, looking to move up the wedding and Presenting Day. He used the recent attack on you as an excuse, but I don't think he was merely seizing an opportunity. I think he orchestrated it. He knew you would never feed without a guard sampling your tributary first, so the risk would be worth it."

"*Never* is a strong word." If that guard hadn't been so stoic to his duty—or fearful of Boaz's reprimand—he might have allowed me to brush him aside. "Perhaps you are right."

"I told you already, I've caught whispers. Of lords and ladies who wish for a change of rule beyond the boundaries of your bloodline."

"Yes, I expect as much. They've always been there, even when my father was king." They've been circling like vultures since my parents were murdered.

"Those whispers come with urgency now. They suspect you did not plan for this ascension to the throne, and they do not want to give you too much time to gain a stronghold. Adley is not blind or deaf to these schemes. If I were him, I would try to control the outcome before he can't."

"How?"

"By courting the usurpers with the might of Kettling in his pocket while ensuring he gains the throne for his daughter."

Kazimir can be cynical at times and turn an innocent exchange into a multifaceted conspiracy theory. But he's always right when it matters most. "So you're saying I seized my brother's crown to keep the kingdom out of enemy hands, and yet I might have made it easier for new ones to claim it."

"You've proven it can be done. The throne has not been taken since King Rhionn executed his father for tempting Malachi. It's been two thousand years."

I pinch the bridge of my nose, this lingering headache unwilling to abate. If anything, it's worse.

Kazimir sighs. "You aren't trained to suffer through withdrawal for weeks, Atticus. You are not a legionary."

"I knew my gluttony would come back to haunt me one day."

"You *are* a greedy pig," he mocks, but his tone shifts to seriousness. "You need to feed. You are long past due."

"And what? Ask another guard to risk their life for me?" I can't shake the bloodcurdling screams that echoed in my chamber when the Islorian fell to the floor in agonizing pain, as Sabrina realized she was the source.

The staff did a commendable job, scrubbing the blood from the carpet where I speared him with my blade, putting him out of his misery, and yet every time I look at that spot, I still see a fresh pool of crimson. It doesn't make sense. I've battled, I've bled, I've killed. Why does this weigh so heavily on me now?

"I will do it—"

"*No.*" I glare at Kazimir. "You are far too valuable to me to risk."

"You're right, I am. So then pick someone you don't like. That day guard of Princess Romeria's. What was his name?"

I snort. "It seems a cruel punishment to anyone, friend or foe. I must assume any tributary I seek will be poisoned, ultimately."

His lips twist with thought. "So you risk one guard once and then have her sequestered here. The queen's lady maid can bring her wine, to ensure it isn't tainted. You trust her well enough to do that, right?"

"Corrin would not actively scheme against me." But I wouldn't be shocked if she buried the truth for those she cares about. "You're suggesting I keep a prisoner in my bedchamber?"

"Let's call her a long-term guest who gets to fuck the king nightly." He smiles wryly. "You have many admirers. I doubt any of them would see it as a punishment."

"Saoirse would not be pleased."

"That alone would be worth it."

It *would* be. "I do not think there is a tributary in this castle that I could tolerate living within my space."

"No? Not even the baker?" His tone rings of teasing.

"That's just it. She's a baker, not a tributary. The royal family has always followed tradition when it comes to that." A virtuous position, but one my parents felt set the right example for the realm.

"You seized your brother's throne and exiled him. I didn't think tradition would stop you."

I glare at Kazimir. "Sometimes you go too far."

He holds up his hands in surrender. "I'm only pointing out that these are different times, and you will have to bend more than one rule."

I sigh. He's not wrong. "She has three children. What am I to do with them?"

"Give her the queen's quarters. There is plenty of room for all of them there."

My head tips back as I bellow with laughter, imagining Saoirse's rage. "You have an answer for everything, don't you?"

"That is why you begged me to stay." Kazimir watches a group of four down below, the females giggling as they head toward the cedar labyrinth. The cool evening air won't stop whatever depraved acts they plan on participating in within the thicket. I would know—I've joined in plenty myself over the years. Gracen claimed my kind is far less modest than mortals, and she isn't wrong.

"I do not know what it is about her." I often wander the castle library when I want to clear my head. It's peaceful in there. Running into Gracen was a welcome surprise, and while I may have been digging for information to find a deeper connection to Romeria, all I found was a comfortable, albeit nervous, companion.

I was equally startled to see her in the dining hall, her arms laden with a tray of my favorite sweet—something I'd admitted to earlier today—her face a mixture of trepidation and excitement. I noticed her before she realized it, but with Saoirse prattling in my ear, I had to keep up appearances and pretend not to.

And then her previous keeper pounced on her, and it took all of me to not intervene. The king siding with a mortal—the same one, again—would draw attention to her, and little of it would be good. I sent Kazimir in my stead, while feigning that I wasn't glued to every second of the exchange.

"Right. You have *no* idea ... You mean, besides that face and breasts that strain against her dress?"

"She's nursing, you idiot." None of my tributaries have ever had children, let alone newborns. For all my experience, I haven't the first clue how that process even works.

And here I am, already thinking about her as if she's my tributary.

"Nursing or not, I am more than willing to risk my life as your tester on that one. And if *you* don't want her—"

"Don't even think about it. Stick with your women down on Port Street," I warn him.

He grins, as if he's just proven a point.

"Why are you pushing me toward her now? You were suspicious of her motives earlier. According to you, she could be plotting my downfall as we speak."

Kazimir chuckles. "You and I both know that mortal is no more plotting you harm than your horse is, but please continue to shovel shit at me as you stall. I love it."

"How did you leave things with her?"

"I told her to go back to her room and shut her mouth if she valued her family's lives."

"You have such a way with words," I drawl. "Seriously, what instructions did you give?"

"I said I would seek her out when it is time. Is it that time? Would you like me to fetch her so you can *question* her more thoroughly? Or shall we continue this 'should I or shouldn't I' dance?"

"The hour is late."

"That mortal was consumed by worry. She will be waiting for my call. And if what she says is true, no hour is too late."

I'm interested to learn what Gracen witnessed, but I'm more interested simply to see her again. "I think it would be wise to hear what she has to say."

"Yes, a *very* wise choice indeed." He pulls himself up and strolls toward the door, as if happy to be given the task.

"And Kaz?"

He spins, still walking, his eyebrow arched in question.

"Don't be a prick."

He bows with a flourish. "I will try my best, Your Highn-*ass*."

A two-knuckle rap sounds on my door.

"Enter." From my perch on the settee in my seating area, I watch the door open with a creak and Kazimir stroll in. Behind him, Gracen trails.

She looks like she's been dragged from bed, her white nightgown veiled by a gray wool cloak she hastily threw over. Her hair is loose, the wild curls flowing around her delicate face.

My pulse speeds up at the sight of her, surprising me. When was the last time I reacted this way to a female rather than to what I was getting from her?

Oh, yes ... of course. Princess Romeria, as I escorted her south to Cirilea, and she charmed me for her nefarious purposes. *Look how that turned out,* I remind myself bitterly.

"As you requested, Your Highness. I will be outside *if you need me.*" With a dramatic gesture toward Gracen—for my benefit, something he knows I'll ridicule later—Kazimir strolls back out, pulling the door shut behind him. I don't have to see his face to know he's wearing an obnoxious smirk.

Gracen lingers where she stands, her hands wringing, her curious eyes searching all the fineries of my chamber. Even in the shadows of candlelight, the intricate moldings and vaulted ceilings are something to behold, especially compared to the damp staff quarters she calls home.

Suddenly, Kazimir's joke to put her and her family in the queen's chamber doesn't seem so out of the question. I feel the urge to rescue her from that squalor.

But an even more compelling urge to have access to her whenever I wish.

That will subside as soon as my cravings are satisfied.

"Being king has its perks, doesn't it?" I smile. "You're welcome to sit."

She jumps as if startled out of a daze and rushes forward. "Yes, Your Highness." There is plenty of space beside me on the settee, but she chooses the single wing chair across. My disappointment flares. I could order her to move closer to me and she would comply, but I'd rather she do it of her own volition than be forced.

I see what Kazimir meant when he said Gracen was drenched in worry at the dining hall. Even without my elven traits, I'd be able to read the mortal. I sense it in her rushed, shallow breathing, in the stiff way she moves. She was not like this in the library, earlier today, when I found Saoirse accosting her. Then, she was also riddled with fear, but that melted as we walked through the library in search of her son, her anxiety replaced by an appealing mixture of wonder and ease, coupled with a flush of lust that I haven't been able to stop thinking about all afternoon.

Whatever Gracen discovered, it must have been after I left her, and now she is apprehensive again.

"Your children are asleep?" I ask casually, hoping to ease her nerves.

"Yes, Your Highness." She sits primly, her hands folded in her lap. Uncomfortable around me, which is the last thing I wish for her.

"Atticus, when we're alone." I won't lie, I've enjoyed the title and the reverence these last weeks. Yet, I don't think I enjoy it on her plump lips. It's a formal address, and I crave something far more intimate with Gracen.

What is it about this mortal that intrigues me so? She seems so … timid and helpless, two qualities that don't appeal to me. But there's a quiet strength as well. She would do anything for her children. I believe she would have dropped to her knees and groveled that day in the assembly, had she felt it would make a difference. And yet earlier, I saw her show hints of defiance in the face of that lowly lord who terrifies her, who likely still haunts her.

"Yes … Atticus," she says, testing it out, her eyes widening at my name, as if she's shocked she said it out loud.

It's so endearing, I can't help but chuckle.

Her pretty face breaks with a smile. She's even more beautiful. How is this divine creature mortal?

"Must you rush back?" I clear the sudden huskiness from my voice. "Or can you stay?"

"Suri normally feeds at midnight, so I have *some* time."

But not a lot. I expect the clock tower to toll soon. My discontent flows.

Speaking of feeding ... My focus dips to her delicate neck and the skin where it meets her shoulder. The buttons on her nightshirt are fastened this time, not allowing me a glimpse of the delicious swell of flesh beneath. Just the memory of it hardens my cock.

There are privileges to being both king and keeper. I could demand Gracen undress for me. I could demand she lie down and offer herself, give me her vein.

What would she think of me if I did?

I would never do it, but I *could*. Many others of my kind *would*.

This train of thought will do nothing but torture me. Besides, I much prefer my conquests willing.

"Kazimir said you had a startling discovery to share with me."

She swallows. "Yes, Your ...yes. After you left us in the library."

"Go on, then," I prompt.

That delightful smile is gone, and she's nervous again, her fingers fumbling together within her lap. "My son, he likes to collect things when he's about the castle. Little things that he stumbles upon, nothing of value. Usually, a feather or stone. Once, a mouse." She grimaces.

I chuckle. "Alive or dead?"

"Very much alive. It was a gift for Gladys. One of the cats," she adds when she sees me frown in question. "But this afternoon, he was excited to have found a magic potion in the library."

"A magic potion." I imagine the little boy with the curly mop of hair announce that. Children don't normally interest me, and yet that one has grabbed my attention more than once. He has a brazen and impish quality I can relate to.

"Yes, in a tiny glass vial." She peers at me as if checking my reaction.

I hold my expression even as all humor fades. "And where did he find this *magic potion*?"

"He said he was looking at a suit of arms when he heard someone coming, so he hid behind it, knowing he wasn't supposed to be there. He watched a female with shiny black hair tuck the vial behind a book. When I asked him to show me where, he led me to the section of the library with the gold-bound books."

"Master Sicily's editions," I finish for her. Saoirse had been there today, had taken the volume about me. A false pretense, I see now.

She nods. "It's hard to mistake them for anything else."

"Impossible, one might say." Saoirse should have chosen something less memorable.

Gracen's brow pinches. "You don't seem shocked by this news."

"As I've said, this marriage is one of need, not want. It's for the good of the kingdom."

She opens her mouth to speak, but then stalls.

"Go on ..."

"I mustn't." Her brow pinches as if pained.

The fire crackles in the growing, tense silence.

I sigh. "Since I've become king, I have been surrounded by people who lie and scheme and guard their words." Aside from Kazimir, and even he acquiesces a little too often for my liking. "I could use a reprieve from that. You will not be punished for anything you say, Gracen, as long as it's honest. So, please, speak freely, or do not speak at all."

She flushes. "I'm sorry. I'm not used to anyone wanting to hear my thoughts."

"Such is the plight of any mortal, I imagine." Though Zander never seemed interested in hearing my thoughts either. He certainly never took my advice.

She nods, her focus settling on the coffee table between us as if gathering her thoughts. "It seems to me that a queen who schemes to murder her king will not prove to be good for the kingdom."

It's not at all funny and yet my head falls back with a bellow of laughter. "Oh, the irony of it all."

A tiny, confused smile touches her lips. "I don't understand?"

"It's as if history is repeating itself, is it not?"

Realization dawns on her. "You mean King Zander and Princess Romeria."

"Yes. That is what I mean."

"But I thought … given they ran and are presumably in hiding together, is it even true?"

"That Princess Romeria of Ybaris poisoned my parents? Oh, that's very true. That she had my last tributary tainted? Also true. That her soldiers tried to kill me? I have the scar to prove that one." I yank up my tunic. Even Wendeline's magic can never erase the mar of that merth arrow.

Gracen's eyes flare as they land first on the scar, before dragging downward over my torso, taking in my bare flesh.

I'll admit, I enjoy the rapt attention. I only wish she were closer to me.

She drops her gaze to her hands, but I don't miss the way her cheeks flush and her lips press together, as if to stifle a smile. "I apologize if I sound like I doubted it. It's just shocking to me, that the same person who saved me that day in the market would conspire so cruelly against you."

"Not just me, my entire family." I release my shirt, letting it fall. "But I do not know that she *is* the same person." I've dwelled on this but never spoken about it, not since the day Zander confided to his inner circle about her supposed amnesia. That I'm willing to share it now so freely with a mortal is foolish and reckless, but I want to gauge her reaction. "Princess Romeria died the night of the attack, of that there is no doubt. Captain Boaz put a merth bolt through her chest in the rose garden. He saw her corpse. I trust Boaz to recognize one."

"But then … how …" Gracen's words drift.

"Did you hear of the daaknar unleashed on Cirilea that night?"

"I *heard*, but I never know what to believe. That wasn't just rumor?"

I shake my head. "High Priestess Margrethe summoned Malachi that same night, and the next thing we know, Princess Romeria is alive again."

Her eyebrows pop. "And you think Malachi brought her back to life?"

He brought *someone* back to life. Who, though, I am no longer certain. "When she woke up, she didn't remember who she was or what she'd done. A complete loss of memory."

"She could have been lying to save her skin."

"That's what I assumed at first. But the princess in the castle after the attack is not the same one I escorted south from the rift before her wedding to my brother. That one was sweet and seductive, and said all the right things to manipulate those around her. This one?" I smile as I think of the day Zander foolishly put her on the dais. "She's brash and clever and funny, and she seems to care genuinely for mortals. *And* she loves my brother."

Gracen seems to absorb this, her anxiety from earlier no longer consuming her. "So then perhaps Malachi gifted us a better version?"

"Perhaps." But Malachi granted new life to her, and he would not give that without expecting something in return. The fates will blind you with a shiny coin before they cleave off a pound of your flesh, my father always claimed.

"Do you think this version of Princess Romeria means Islor harm?"

"Not explicitly, no, but it does not matter because the guidance she offers my brother will cause damage all the same, and he does not see it. He is infatuated with her. Besides, there is only one version of her that people care about, and that one *has* caused us harm. Irreparably so. Her close association with my brother, the choices he was making for Islor's future … too many of Islor's lords and ladies would never have accepted her on the throne, even before they learned of the poison. And now that it is filtering through every corner of the realm, poison that is the very blood that runs through her veins, her intentions mean *nothing*."

Gracen bites her bottom lip in thought. "The night of the tournament, when you … were appointed king …" She chooses her words carefully.

"When I used my brother's army to seize the throne, you mean." I know how I'll be remembered by history, if Master Sicily chooses to capture it accurately. I hope he also captures my reasons, which were never anything but with Islor's best interests at heart.

"Would you have executed Princess Romeria had you caught her?"

"Yes."

Gracen flinches, and a part of me regrets being so frank.

"Either her amnesia is real, or she is an even better manipulator than her predecessor. Regardless, it doesn't matter. The poison that plagues us flows through her veins. There can be no future for Islor if Princess Romeria lives. Whoever she may be now."

Gracen studies her hands a moment. "There is much gossip within the castle. I don't know what's true and so I pay attention to little. But I heard Caster Wendeline helped with the princess's scheming."

"Wendeline played her part, but she has revealed nothing of use upon questioning. I doubt she ever will." The only thing the caster cared to admit was that Zander had no clue about her deception.

"She's still alive?" Gracen's eyes light up. With relief, I realize.

"She is, for now. I haven't decided if she can be of use to me yet. Why, do you know her?"

She shakes her head. "I mean, I met her the day we joined the royal household. Princess Romeria took us to see her in the sanctum. She fixed Mika's hand."

"I noticed his scars. Burns, right?"

"Yes, he ate an apple without permission, and Lord Danthrin punished him for it. He didn't have much use of his hand after that and suffered from constant pain."

My teeth grind. It's a good thing I didn't know this that day in assembly. No wonder the children cried.

"But Caster Wendeline erased all that as if it had never existed." Gracen smiles, and then catches herself and smooths her expression. "I am grateful to her. But I don't know her."

There is something so pure and honest about Gracen, despite all the hardships she has faced—some I probably can't guess at, some I wouldn't want to. "I do miss having her healing touch, I will admit that much." I sigh. I didn't bring Gracen here to talk about the previous queen-to-be's betrayals. "So you threw the vial into the latrine?"

"I was afraid the guards would search us again, and I didn't want to risk being caught with it in my pocket or anywhere in my room. I knew what that might look like." She sounds apologetic.

"You did the right thing. Nobody would have believed you. But *I* know you're not conspiring against me." I lean forward, resting my elbows on my knees as I watch her steadily. "At least I hope not."

She shakes her head, holding my gaze. "I would not, I swear." After a moment, she adds a breathy "Atticus."

I love the sound of my name on her tongue.

I would love to hear it in her moans too.

The bell tower gongs, signaling the midnight hour. "You must go." My insides sink with disappointment. I could talk to Gracen for hours and I doubt I'd get bored.

"Yes, I suppose I must. As young as Suri is, she's already on a clock. Mika and Lilou will sleep through much but not a baby's cries." Yet she lingers. With her own reluctance?

"I'll escort you to the door." I rise from my seat, and she

follows suit instantly. My hand grazes the small of her back and she stiffens, like she did earlier in the library. I don't like that much. I'm certainly not used to it. Is it my touch, or *any* male's touch? She can't be entirely unfamiliar to the latter, given the three children she's produced. So what did that prick Danthrin put her through?

The question is on the tip of my tongue when she peers up at me, and asks, "What will you do? About your future wife who means to kill you?"

"Don't allow her to succeed?" I chuckle.

Her brow remains furrowed as we walk.

"Thank you for being brave enough to seek me out."

"I feared telling you," she admits. "Not for my own sake, but for my son's. He's a little boy. A little *mortal* boy, accusing the future queen of conspiracy and treason."

"And you are afraid I will name him a witness to such a thing."

"Yes."

"But you came forward, anyway."

"I couldn't ignore it. Especially not after the kindness you've shown us."

"So you felt that you owed me."

"Yes. I mean, no ... it felt like the right thing to do."

It was, and yet not many servants would. "Practically, Mika is what, four?"

"Five."

"*Only five*. He cannot be named a witness against the future queen. The court would not accept it, and I would be considered a fool for doing so. Regardless, naming him would put him and you in danger from those lords and ladies plotting against me as we speak. And that, I would never do."

Her throat bobs with a hard swallow. "Thank you, Atticus."

Fates, her voice is like a soft melody in my ear, singing me to sleep.

And that racing pulse in her throat? The euphoria its contents promise to bring? I feel the burn against my gums, where my incisors beg to emerge. It's been too long. If I keep her here any longer, I'm liable to take something she hasn't offered and risk my life in the process.

This time when I place my hand on her back and keep it there, she doesn't stiffen. "By the way, how were you planning on sharing this disturbing news in the dining hall?"

"Oh." She smiles sheepishly. "With a note."

"A *note.* What, tucked inside a fritter?"

"That is actually not a bad idea," she admits with a laugh. "No, it was in my pocket. Foolish, I know. Even more so when I saw you sitting beside *her*." Her jaw tenses with that word.

"You really do not like her. Why?"

"Because she is cruel to the servants, and she means to kill you." She hesitates, then bows her head to add, "Lady Saoirse doesn't deserve you or Islor's crown. I would not want to see her with either."

Is it her hatred for Saoirse the reason she came to warn me? Or her personal fondness for me? "It's a good thing you saw the risk and stayed away. I would rather Saoirse think you are just the baker."

Gracen's heart races—with trepidation or excitement? I can't tell. "But I *am* just the baker."

A stray hair hangs over her forehead. I reach up to push it back, letting my fingers graze through her unruly curls. The strands are deceptively soft, and my fingers don't tangle.

"I don't normally invite kitchen staff to my chambers to whisper about conspiracies." Doing so would be considered beneath a king. And yet now that I have her here, I accept Kazimir is right—I couldn't care less about traditions surrounding royal tributaries. I want her as mine, and not simply for what's in her veins. I want to feel the warmth of her flesh, the taste of her skin, the sound of her coming apart beneath me.

Her eyes wander back to where we came from, beyond, to the doorway where my bed waits, as if she realizes where my thoughts are heading. She hesitates before asking, "Is Sabrina still alive?"

Mention of my last tributary's current predicament is a bucket of cold water on the explicit thoughts racing through my mind. "For the moment, yes."

She nods but doesn't ask more. She doesn't have to; I sense her fear taking over. What would happen to Gracen if I took her as tributary and then her blood became tainted?

What about her three children?

They don't deserve to be motherless.

"Do not mention our talk to anyone, not even Corrin. And do not ever repeat what I've told you tonight."

"I wouldn't."

I reach for the door handle.

"Wait. One more thing?" she says suddenly.

"Yes?" I stall, hovering precariously close to her. Her breath skates across my skin, where my tunic gapes at the collar.

"Tonight, when Lord Danthrin cornered me, he said something." She frowns as if trying to decipher it. "About the wind changing direction around here and that he'd be back to reclaim me when it does."

The fool clearly thinks there is a change of rule coming soon. Perhaps the minor lord's grand aspirations have made him allies I wouldn't have expected. He is cunning, after all, having successfully escaped his tithe.

"Listen to me, Gracen." *You are mine now.* I bite back the urge to claim her so boldly. "You and your family are under my care, as your keeper and king. You will *never* return to him. That is a promise I can make."

Her shoulders slump. "Okay. Thank you."

"Any time you wish to speak to me, find Kazimir and he will arrange it. But do not risk coming into the dining hall." Because if Lord Danthrin accosts her again, I'm liable to kill him where he stands, and that may not win me favor. On impulse, I lean in, allowing my lips to graze across her cheek.

Her sharp inhale is nearly my undoing.

"Sleep well." I open the door, stepping back, away from her.

Kazimir waits outside, a frown on his face at Gracen beside me. "Do you need me ... for anything?"

"Yes, please escort Gracen back to her room."

His sigh is soft but noticeable. He really thought I was going to satisfy my needs with her tonight. "Yes, Your Highness."

"And find Rhodes." It's time we learn what Freywich's lord has been up to.

19
ZANDER

Romeria is a lone, silent figure, standing at the mouth of the tunnel, her cloak swaying in the cool breeze, her attention outward toward the glowing fires in the distance and the army that will either be our allies or dead by dawn.

Dusk has settled and an odd somberness clings to her, veiling the panic that I know still thrives in her thoughts. I don't have to ask what has caused it. Guilt claws at her heart. She blames herself for what is coming, what she promised—me, Abarrane, Elisaf, anyone who knows her secret—she would never be party to.

Romeria has opened the nymphaeum door, and we have only chaos to look forward to.

That is, if this Lucretia is telling the truth, and not some perverted fabrication of it. But it makes sense given all that we've done to get to this place. We should have seen it.

I should have seen it.

"She will come to terms with it."

My jaw clenches at Gesine's voice in my ear. "Is that what unleashing a waiting army of monsters and battling with a fate for rule of my land is? *Coming to terms with it*? Do you realize the weight you've placed on her shoulders?"

"I only mean that there is no blame to be laid. There is no other path but one, and we would be fooling ourselves to think it. This was written for you both long ago, and we must move forward as prophecy dictates."

"The blame does not lay at Romeria's feet." Or even mine, but I can find plenty for the caster standing next to me, who seems to be shirking all responsibility. "Tell me, *High Priestess,* if prophecy declared that I was to take an arrow to the chest, would you hand my enemy the bow?"

"That is not how prophecy works—"

"But if it did?"

Her brow furrows, as if to consider her answer to that question.

"Your Highness, a banner flies," Loth calls out, his sights on the distance.

"We will continue this conversation later." I stroll toward the exit. Romeria moves to join me, but I hold up my hand to stop her. "I am stronger, but that does not mean I trust myself around you." I've crossed this threshold and battled the curse's craving a handful of times today and, each time, the need's assault grew weaker. Still … "Give me a moment."

She nods and waits as I step out. The Ybarisans watch from a safe distance, no doubt equal parts curious and wary about the exiled king whose knees buckle every time he steps outside the secret city. Earlier, when Radomir drew his cloak and stepped out —and crumbled under the weight of the curse, turning him back into his sapling form—they wore masks of horror, but followed Kienen's lead, remaining in place.

This time, the need is nothing more than a nuisance—thankfully—and it vanishes in seconds.

Far ahead in the evening dusk, four silhouettes canter forward on horseback. They're nothing but tiny specks that even my eyes can't decipher, the navy blue and white Lyndel banner waving high above them. But Telor will be among them. He's never been one to send a messenger to negotiate a surrender or launch a battle. He has too much pride for that. "My horse."

I expect Abarrane to answer the call, but it's Romeria who rides out, leading my black stallion by its reins next to her chocolate-brown one. Whatever doubts the Ybarisans have of this alliance with Islor, they seem to stand taller at the sight of her. The truth about King Barris's assassination has penetrated the ranks and, as Kienen expected, their anger is potent. No one has opposed following Ybaris's heir to the throne.

Yet, that little voice screams.

But each day forward will only bring more danger, more dark truths. Too many bad actors with access, too many easy mistakes to be had.

If I were to lose her, I think I might burn this entire realm.

I climb into my saddle. "It's amazing how proficient a rider you've become." I still remember that first day, riding through the streets of Cirilea with her ramrod back and her obscenely poofy dress.

"Jarek's a good teacher." Her beautiful, clear blue eyes squint as she tries to make out the figures ahead. "Do you think Telor's already sent a message to Atticus about us being here?"

"Yes, but it won't get there before the taillok does." Gesine confirmed the bird would arrive in Cirilea by sunrise, its wings capable of speed like nothing we've ever seen before. "Are you sure you want to do this?" I nod toward the enemy line.

"What do you mean? I *love* meeting people who want me dead," she mutters wryly. But the humor slips as she adds, "At least now they have a good reason. I can't blame Princess Romeria for what *I've* done."

I want to collect her face in my palms, kiss her worries away. But now is not the time for that. Maybe my words will offer her some comfort. "You have been a tool all along, for the fates, for prophecy, for politics. The blame does not sit on your shoulders, and I will quiet *anyone* who suggests otherwise."

"I don't know if I believe that, but thank you for saying it."

Others ride up to our flanks then, our commanders taking their rightful places by our sides, Elisaf and Kienen next to them. Gesine holds tight to Zorya on their horse, and Radomir hides within his deep cowl.

"On your lead, Your Highness." Abarrane's horse prances in anticipation.

We begin forward in two lines.

I ignite each bonfire as we pass it, creating a blazing path. If nothing else, it should serve as a warning to anyone with nefarious ideas. Lord Telor, I do not worry about. He is too principled.

Abarrane's glance over her shoulder at the soldiers behind us says she's thinking the same thing. "What parlor tricks should we expect from you, *Ybarisan*?" she asks Kienen. "What do you hide in your little pocket?"

"A big blade, *Islorian*," Kienen retorts.

"I'm sure it won't impress me."

I've seen the way Abarrane prowls around him, and I know my commander well. She's enjoying baiting him more than usual, which usually means she has plans to have him on his back to perform for her before too long. That won't keep her from putting a blade through him after, though.

"Twenty gold coins, I'll wager," Elisaf whispers, and I stifle the urge to laugh. His thoughts are along the same as mine.

"What *is* your affinity to, Kienen?" Romeria asks.

His eyebrow arches. It's a subtle tell, but one all the same. Would Princess Romeria know Kienen well enough to have that answer already?

I sense her heart rate spiking with her mistake, but she recovers quickly. "Aminadav, right?"

"Yes, Your Highness. Though I do not rely on it often."

Romeria's pulse radiates with a wave of relief, her blind guess a lucky one.

But Kienen's gaze on her remains curious, and I can't be sure it's worked.

I hate that she must play this role again, but if the Ybarisan knew the person inside this body was not the heir to the throne, would she still have his loyalty?

"True warriors do not rely on it at all," Jarek pipes up, either because he's read the situation as well, or simply to throw a shot across the bow at Kienen.

I smile. "You know, Jarek, it would not hurt you to learn how to use yours. It's another viable weapon to wield in your role to protect Ulysede's queen."

"Aye, I will be sure to take your advice, Your Highness, as soon as my corpse is rotting in the ground."

A deafening screech in the distance pulls everyone's attention to the north.

"Maybe those bonfires aren't the best idea," Elisaf says. "They're like beacons in the night."

"You won't be saying that when another hag springs out from the shadows," I retort, though there are far worse things than that creature. It, at least, is easy enough to kill with fire.

"The number of Nulling beasts crawling out of their nests is increasing each day," Kienen notes mildly. "Has anyone else observed this?"

"There have been more than expected as of late." I steal a glance Romeria's way, to see her jaw tensing, her wary attention on the dusky sky as if something might swoop down at any moment. "Let's hope this one keeps its distance. Hold the line here." We've passed the last bonfire, and my connection to the flame is weakening.

We stop and watch as the forms ahead take a clearer shape. I can make out Telor's silver-white hair at the center. The other riders wear their helms, obscuring their faces, though I imagine his son, Braylon, is among them. He has always been brash and would not miss his chance to see me ahead of a battle.

Telor raises a single hand and they stop their approach. He guides his horse forward.

As I expected, he wants a private parley. "Remain here. I will meet with him alone first—"

"I do not think that's wise," Jarek interrupts. "Lord Telor is following Atticus's order, and if what the Ybarisan says is true, there are compromised soldiers within his ranks."

"I will meet with Telor first alone," I repeat with bite in my voice. Abarrane may be surly, but at least she doesn't question me in front of others. "I trust Telor as I do Rengard. He is noble. He follows the rules of engagement and will not attempt anything untoward during parley, regardless of what he thinks of me. We are like-minded in what we stand for." And I have things hidden deep within my chest of knowledge that I can use to remind him of that. "The issues with his ranks, we will deal with later. Remain here."

"Have you decided how much you're going to tell him yet?" Romeria asks, worry furrowing her brow.

"No, but I figured I'd follow your lead for once and wait for the answer to come to me."

"Good luck with that." She reaches out to squeeze my forearm.

With a deep breath, I guide my horse forward, across the craggy ground. Fighting a battle on such uneven terrain will be unpleasant, but hopefully we will not have to fight one at all.

"You are full of surprises as of late, Zander Ascelin, First of His Name," Telor calls out, he and his white stallion cloaked in matching navy blue coats. They stall, forcing me to move in farther, putting me farther from reach of my flame.

"It has been forever since I heard that address."

"It has been forever since I uttered it. Frankly, I do not know how to address a banished king."

"How about an old friend?" Telor was Lyndel's lord long before Hudem's moon ever granted me life.

"That is the only reason I am standing alone before you now. My son fought me in coming here at night and alone to parley. He said I couldn't trust you."

"My advisors were equally uncomfortable with the idea."

He smiles sadly. "I wish we were meeting under better circumstances."

Silence lingers, and he seems to be struggling with how to proceed.

"Tell me, Ailis, how does dear Erwynn fair these days?"

Telor swallows, the reminder of his one glaring indiscretion now placed clearly between us. He'd been unlucky in love for centuries and had all but given up when he fell for a mortal from Kier and, unwilling to lose her, infected her. It's a secret I've kept for him, rather than bring him forward to my father and ensure he was punished. For a man so intent on following the rule of law, I'm sure that's never far from the forefront of his thoughts. "She is well."

"I am glad to hear that. I've always thought she was good for you."

He clears his throat. "Would you prefer I recite the king's declaration?"

"That I'm a traitor to my realm? No, I've caught the gist of it."

"Yes, well … I have been ordered to capture you and the princess Romeria and bring you both to Cirilea for judgment before the king."

"And kill my legionaries, I gather."

"What's left of them, yes. And whoever else you've allied with."

The Ybarisans standing outside the gate, he means. "I imagine you appreciate the destruction I alone could cause your army." I've spent my life hiding the true strength of my affinity from others, saving it for when it would serve me best. Still, few have seen my full power. Lady Danthrin, for one, and I'm sure that news has traveled to Cirilea by now.

"His Highness has warned me, yes. But he believes you will be too honorable to incinerate your own kind in such a devastating way. That you would rather die in an honest battle."

"I assumed my brother would have too much honor to steal my crown. So, what have assumptions about honor taught us?" My laughter is a hollow sound in the night.

Lord Telor's gaze veers behind me, toward Ulysede. Even in

the dark, his awe is visible. "My scouts informed me of a magnificent gate where Stonekeep used to exist. I accused them of imbibing in hallucinogens and put them on latrine duty. I suppose I shall apologize at some point."

Now my laugh is genuine. "I can assure you, the gates are real and the city behind them, even more so."

"Is this to be your new home then?"

"Islor is my home, and though it may seem within our borders, *that* is not Islor."

"I cannot begin to understand what that means."

"No, you cannot. I fear there is much you have heard, Ailis, but much more you have not. I would beg you to stay your judgment and your choices until you have given me a chance to speak."

"*Beg*." Telor's eyebrow arches. "When has the great and powerful Zander ever *begged*?"

"Never, I will admit. I am far too arrogant. But in this instance, yes, I would plead with my once-loyal allies and those who share a genuine love of our realm. Islor is in great peril."

"Yes, both mortals and immortals are dying every day because of this Ybarisan plague that *you* allowed to take hold."

I could claim that I didn't know about the poison until I'm without breath, but I know that's pointless. "It goes far deeper than that, and the poison may be the least of our issues soon. But to explain it would require faith in me that I have not forsaken Islor, that I am working to save it from ruin. In all the years we've known each other, as you look upon me now and listen to my words, do you truly doubt this?"

His lips twist. "I'm listening."

Behind him, Braylon and others shift in their saddles, restless, as if they think I might lash out at their lord, that I have no respect. My anger spikes at the nerve, but I squash it, keeping my focus. "You and I have sat across the table, late into the night, more times than I can count, fantasizing about a world where we no longer had to survive off the blood of mortals."

"I recall those nights and that fantasy." He smiles fondly, before it slips away. "I dare say you and your princess have taken it in a far darker direction than the one I dreamt of."

"That is Queen Neilina's dream coming to reality. Not mine, and not the princess who rides at my side. We are playing both pawn and scapegoat."

Telor surveys my line of companions in the distance. "And your brother the king would claim you are still playing the love-struck fool."

"I would say the same if I knew as little as he did. But he is wasting your time, having you chase after me when he should be gathering Islor's forces at the rift."

"We are aware of the growing army on the Ybarisan side. I have soldiers there."

"Not enough. Did you know you have traitors among your ranks? The mortals, certainly, but also elven."

"I did not. How do *you* know this?"

"Because Prince Tyree delivered crates of poison himself. His right-hand man, who is with us now, witnessed it."

"Lies to sow discord."

"Possibly," I agree. "But I would lean toward caution."

Telor's brow furrows as he glances over his shoulder at Braylon. No doubt he'll be tasking him with ferreting out the truth as soon as we're done here. "What do you know about what to expect?"

Far more than I care to share right now. "Neilina plans to claim our lands for herself, once and for all. A vast army is gathering from all over Ybaris, fueled by lies of King Barris's assassination and their children's murders. They will cross on Hudem. Soldiers and casters. She is drawing heavily from Mordain. Their elementals, all of their strongest."

"And you know this how?"

"A letter from Neilina, delivered by the Ybarisans to Romeria. I have read it myself. It is true."

He curses. "Does the king know this?"

"I've written to inform him. Whether he acts is another story."

Telor curses again, his horse shifting to and fro with his growing agitation. "Armies have scattered across Islor, chasing after this poison. His Highness's focus is on keeping Cirilea and binding Kettling. They will never be able to gather and make it to the rift in time."

"No, likely not. Atticus cannot do much but rule from the throne. That leaves your army, ours, and anyone we can gather along the way. I've already written to Bellcross, pleading for Rengard's aid." Fortunately among the generous supplies Theon granted us were several messenger pigeons, trained to reach him.

The corner of Telor's mouth quirks. "You wish to bring the Ybarisans to the rift to fight the Ybarisans."

"Yes. As well as an army of saplings."

His bellow of laughter carries. "You really have gone mad, my friend."

"You do not know the half of it." I waver over the urge to hold tight to what I know, protect Romeria a little longer. But I relied on secrecy and lies to rule before, and it ended up not serving me well. Besides, we won't be able to keep this to ourselves much longer. Not when the Nulling opens on Hudem, and untold creatures crawl out. "What if I told you that, after two thousand years, the end to the blood curse is upon us, and the answers lie within the kingdom you see before you and the queen who rules it? One who wants peace for all."

A slow breath slips from his lips. "I would very much like to meet this queen."

"I can arrange that."

Behind Telor, Braylon and his two riders approach. "Your son has grown too impatient to wait, I see."

"Hold your ground. We are not finished yet!" Lord Telor demands without glancing behind him, but the riders keep moving in at a steady trot.

Behind me, hooves pound, moving more urgently. Rushing to catch up to their counterparts.

Telor scowls. "This generation ... they do not show proper respect to decorum or rank."

I chuckle, listening to Telor complain about his son a nostalgic song in my ear for all the times I've heard him say similar things in the past.

But the comfort evaporates as Braylon and his men draw their weapons.

20
ROMERIA

"What's going on?" Only a moment ago, I heard a man's laugh. Now the three soldiers who accompanied Telor are closing in. It's difficult for me to see in the growing darkness, but I didn't notice Telor beckoning them.

"Pups who do not follow orders," Jarek says.

"We should go in, too, then."

"He would signal us if he were concerned." But Abarrane's horse dances in place.

Zander is alone, too far from a flame. Still, he hasn't drawn his weapon or hinted that anything's off. Maybe Abarrane is right, but I don't like the ratio. "Can you place a shield on him, Gesine?"

"Not from this distance. Especially not when I have this bird in my head. It is distracting."

I forgot. She shares the taillok's vision, and it's in flight. We should have waited to send the message to Atticus. She's virtually useless to us when we need her most.

"I don't like this. Something feels off."

"Who is that male?" Kienen asks. "The one leading."

"Lord Braylon Telor," Jarek answers. "Telor's son."

"Why?" I ask.

Kienen meets my gaze, assessing me as if I'm a puzzle he can't solve.

"What is it?" I snap.

He pulls his horse up, filling the space Zander once took. "The elven who met with Tyree was wearing that helm."

"The one with the horns. Are you sure?"

"I am positive."

Alarm bells ring. I kick my heels into my horse's flanks, launching it forward. Behind me, hooves thump, but I can only focus ahead, my heart walloping inside my chest.

Is Braylon working against his father?

Or *with* him?

Neither scenario plays out well for our cause.

For weeks now, Zander has held out hope that he could sway Lord Telor, that Lyndel is the start to winning back loyalty and his throne, one house at a time.

All four affinities crackle under my skin, waiting to be unleashed on these traitors. I will scorch the earth where they stand if anything happens to Zander.

I've closed half the distance when the approaching soldiers draw weapons. My fear surges. I launch an air shield in front of Zander a split second before an arrow flies toward him. It strikes the invisible wall and ricochets away.

Metal rings as Zander draws his blade.

But it's Lord Telor who roars. "What is the meaning of this!" He spins his horse, rearing on his men. "Stay your—"

My jaw drops as Braylon Telor drives his sword deep under his father's arm where the armor has an opening before dragging it clean.

"No!" Zander yells as his longtime friend and ally topples off his horse to land on the hard ground.

Braylon and the others are already charging back toward their camp. "They've killed Lord Telor!" a frantic voice calls out in the night. They're too far for their shouts to be heard, but it won't be long before that lie catches ears and spreads. No one from their camp will have seen Braylon's attack unfurl from this distance, in the dark, to disbelieve his claim.

"Telor must not die! Save him!" Zander urges his horse forward. It rears on its hind legs, kicking at the shield. I release my hold on my affinity and Zander rushes away, Abarrane, Elisaf, Kienen, and Radomir on his heels moments later.

Jarek stops at my side. "That was a merth blade. He will not survive a wound like that."

I drop from my horse and stumble to where Lord Telor's limp body lies, blood pouring freely from the gash in his side. "Let me worry about that. Help them." When Jarek falters, I scream, "That's an order!"

He spurs his horse into a gallop without another word.

Zorya slows long enough for Gesine to scramble from their horse before speeding off with the others. "Does he have a pulse?"

I press my fingers against his neck. "Yes."

"Then it is not too late."

"Fix him!" I plead with the caster.

Gesine hovers a hand over the wound. "It is deep. I will have to release my hold of the taillok, and we will lose it."

"I don't care. Telor can't die."

"Then *you* must do this, Romeria."

"I can't!"

She guides my hand and places it on Telor's failing body. "You have done it before when it mattered. It matters now."

Right. Elisaf. Adrenaline pounds in my ears. "I'll try. But if I can't, forget the stupid bird and save him."

She nods. "Focus on what is at stake."

I close my eyes, reaching for those soothing, cool strands of Aoife's power. If Lord Telor dies and Braylon's lies reach his men …

Zander's right. Telor *must* survive.

With fear firmly in place, I let my affinity flow.

Somewhere nearby, the ground rumbles.

21
ZANDER

"They've slain my father! Prepare for battle!" Braylon's hoarse shouts carry. But do they carry enough? No one will have seen him skewer his father in the middle of the open, dark plain, but they will believe him without question. Telor said he argued with his son about this parley, about going out at dusk. Now I can see it was all part of the plan, and surely, he spoke these words in front of others.

If Telor dies, it will be another false crime to hang on my shoulders, followed by one I commit when I'm forced to kill every one of those men in that camp. And then where does that leave Islor but weakened even further?

Rage fills me. The camp's flames are still too far away. My reach will likely find them just as Braylon's shouts do.

Suddenly, my horse rears, the ground beneath its hooves tremoring. Kienen speeds past, his focus on the males ahead.

I watch with a mixture of awe and horror as all three drop into the earth.

Jarek slows down at my side long enough for me to catch his "What the fuck?" before he urges his horse forward.

The rest of us close in as Kienen hops off his mount, sword in hand. There is nothing to combust in this arid deadland, but thankfully, our elven vision does not need light to make out the crater in the earth, deep and wide enough to fit three fallen horses and the riders trapped beneath them, groaning from the immense weight and their injuries.

"A shame to lose such animals," Elisaf says, his voice sincere. He has always been soft for the breed.

It is, but all I can feel right now is relief that we stopped them, however temporary it may be.

"That one is still alive." Zorya points to the horse pinning down Braylon. "Maybe the witch can heal it."

"Both its front legs are broken, and Gesine has more important things to focus on," I counter as Jarek, Abarrane, and Elisaf jump into the pit.

"This one's mortal." Elisaf crouches to test his pulse. "And dead."

"These other two will wish they were soon enough." Jarek grabs hold of Braylon's arms and yanks him out from beneath the horse, earning the beast's distress and Braylon's screams.

The third soldier fights Abarrane, but her merth blade against his throat stills him. "Another mortal."

"That's Lev." I met him once, two decades ago when I last traveled to Lyndel. He was barely more than a boy, with a few spare hairs growing on his upper lip.

I steal another glance at the camp ahead. The lookouts still haven't raised any alarms, which means they're blind to how far things have gone awry. But soon, they will wonder what is taking so long, and a group will ride out. "Let's get them back before Telor's men decide to be brave."

With help from Radomir and Kienen, we drag the injured soldiers up. Elisaf and Zorya each haul one onto their horse, keeping blades at their necks.

Kienen quietly climbs back into his saddle.

"That was you?" I point to the pit, though it's not really a question.

He nods.

"Seems your *pocket* isn't as small as Abarrane thought."

"That remains to be seen." With a sly smile, Abarrane takes off at a gallop.

He smirks. "I recognized that one's helm—" He nods to Braylon. "He is the elven who was there to collect the vials that day."

"If you had suggested that earlier, I never would have believed you."

"I had no idea, and Tyree never told me." He shrugs. "Clearly, he was working against his father, but to what end beyond shuttling poison, I could not tell you."

"My guess would be power," Radomir offers. "Lord Telor has been keeper of Lyndel and the rift's guard for centuries and showed no signs of stepping down. What better way to get rid of your father than to blame it on the current king's enemy?"

"And *you*, with all of your connections and web of information, were truly not aware of this?" I can't help the accusation in my tone.

The sapling pushes his hood off to meet my gaze, as if I can read the truth in those black eyes. "I was not, Your Highness."

I want to believe him. "We have a mess to clean up, and it seems I owe you my thanks, Ybarisan." I hold out my hand. A peace offering.

Kienen looks at it. "If it's all the same, I would prefer your honesty."

"In what regard?"

He looks back to where Romeria and Gesine kneel, attempting to save Telor's life. "Who is this person who plays the princess of Ybaris?"

22
ROMERIA

A feeble hand grips my forearm, breaking my hold of my affinity.

"What are you doing to me?" Lord Telor croaks.

My spirits surge. He's conscious and speaking. "Trying to save your life. Stay still and let me focus."

"But you're ... Ybarisan." I can only make out shadows of his face in the darkness, but his Islorian eyes are stronger and can surely make out every feature of mine.

"I'm a lot of things, actually, but it's a long story for another time."

Horses close in, Elisaf and Zorya racing past, each with a bound figure held at dagger point. Zander jumps from his saddle and drops to his knees beside me. "How is he?"

"Conscious. I closed the wound but just barely. There's still a lot of work to be done inside." I could feel the threads knitting, but they're too loose.

"Braylon ..." Telor whispers.

"Alive for now, but seeing as he tried to kill you, I have questions for him." Zander collects his hand. "Gesine should be the one—"

"She can't. If she breaks her hold on the taillok, we'll lose it." I set my jaw. "I *can* do this, but you have to let me concentrate."

A piercing screech—the same one as earlier—cuts through the quiet night, setting my neck hairs on end. I scour the inky sky for its source. High up, among the smattering of clouds that pass the waxing moon, a large, dark shadow circles. "What is that?" I hiss.

"Nothing good." Zander must have seen it too.

"She is drawing it in," Gesine whispers, as if the beast can hear her. "It is not safe for us out here."

"All right. We need to get you inside the gates, my friend. Do you think you can ride?" Zander asks.

"Ride?" Telor lets out a weak chuckle. "How am I even breathing?"

Together with Jarek, Zander hauls Telor off the ground, earning the injured lord's groans of protest. They hoist him onto Abarrane's horse. "Get him inside the gate now. We're right behind you."

Abarrane takes off as we clamber onto our horses, Kienen helping Gesine onto his.

I'm reaching for my reins when the ground shudders. Eros rears, catching me off guard. I tumble backward and hit the dirt, the impact knocking the breath from my lungs.

"Romeria!" Zander is kneeling next to me in a split second, his hands gripping my shoulders.

"I'm fine," I croak, though I'm not sure I am. What made the earth rattle and Eros react?

"Fates," Zander whispers, tension coursing through his touch. "You must get up, Romeria. You must get up *now*." He hauls me to my feet as if I'm a small child, fallen. Together we back up slowly, his body blocking mine. I can't make out anything ahead, the darkness swallowing all.

My view of the camp across the plain—all the little campfire lights—is just … gone.

"What is it?" The horses shuffle back and forth, their riders struggling to keep them in place.

No one answers me.

Gesine's orb materializes and floats outward, rising above us, swelling as it climbs, illuminating an enormous, scaly body.

"Oh my God." My fingers grip Zander's arm with terror as I take in the beast that sits no more than thirty feet away from us. It's at least five times the size of the grif, and ten times as menacing, jagged horns protruding from its forehead like a crown, its bat-like wings held high in the air.

"Have you ever seen anything so big?" Kienen whispers.

I have … in movies, in fantasy, never in real life. Can it breathe fire? Will it char us where we stand with a single puff?

"We cannot fight that," Zander says.

"We cannot outrun it either." In Jarek's voice, I hear defeat, something I thought impossible.

It lifts its head and its nostrils flare, much like the other Nulling beasts did.

"It's here for me." A strange calm washes over my body, knowing this is finally the end.

Why is it not attacking, though? It sits there watching us through shrewd dark eyes that seem too small for its massive frame. I'm sure it can see every twitch.

"Even you cannot defeat this," Gesine whispers, suddenly standing next to me. I didn't even notice her climb down from Kienen's horse. "Get on Eros, and ride hard, back to the gate. You should be safe within Ulysede." Her gaze flares with emerald light.

I realize what she's about to do. "If I can't fight this, you definitely can't!"

"No, I cannot," she agrees solemnly. "But I can buy you a little time. The Queen for All must survive, at all costs."

"She is right." Zander tugs on my arm.

"No!" I pull free. "I need you. *We* need you." Despite all the ways Zander is convinced Gesine has betrayed us, we never would have gotten this far without her. "We still have so far to go."

"You will find your path." She smiles. "It has been an honor to serve you. Now you *must* go." Her hands stretch out to her sides, her eyes turning an electrified green, like they did the night we escaped Cirilea.

This thing will eat her whole.

Zander seizes my arm. "Romeria—"

"No." I plant my feet and beckon my affinities—*all* of them. They answer instantly, surging through my limbs, coiling around each other, vibrating with energy. If by some miracle we survive this, I'll have nothing left for Lord Telor.

He sighs. "Then I suppose we will all meet our end together."

Metal rings in the night as the others draw their swords. Behind us, the bonfires flare with Zander's affinity.

The beast claws at the ground in challenge and then stretches its neck, revealing black scales that glitter against the firelight. It releases a deafening roar that rattles my teeth.

I'm preparing to hurl everything I have inside me when it suddenly rushes several steps away from us and launches itself upward, the ground shaking in its wake. I watch with a mix of awe and horror as its powerful wings carry it high into the sky, Braylon's fallen horses dangling from its claws. They look like tiny toys within its grasp.

No one utters a word for a moment.

"Everyone, ride now before it changes its mind and returns," Zander commands.

I don't hesitate, scrambling into my saddle, trusting in Eros's sense of direction as we race toward the gate. I feel each second in my chest—dragging, achingly long seconds—as I cling to my affinities, refusing to let them go in case that thing decides it would rather chase its kill.

The Ybarisans meet us halfway, their swords drawn and faces astonished, countless questions on their tongues about whatever it was they must have seen landing. But I keep riding, only allowing myself a breath when we've made it past the gate.

"I have lived in these mountains for too many years to not

have seen evidence of such a creature before now," Radomir declares, closing in behind us.

"It must have been hiding deep within the rift." Even Zander seems mystified. "Has Mordain heard of such a beast before?"

"The seers have seen *all* kinds, though I can't say on which plane they reside. Ones that can deafen with their shriek, others that can blind you just by meeting your gaze. If I recall, there was a great winged beast that was said to devour herds of cattle and burn villages with the fire they breathed from their mouths."

"You mean, a dragon?" Because that's what that thing looked like.

"I do not recall any name for it. Only that it ruled the skies in long-lost times." She casts a knowing look my way. In the long-lost time of the nymphs, she's saying.

"It seemed to be there for the fallen horses rather than us," Zander says.

But it sensed me all the same.

He searches the dark sky, but it's impossible to see anything. "Let us hope it has no interest in trying to breach these gates for more."

"I doubt it would even fit." Jarek observes the grand tunnel. "Not that I want to test that out."

"Come, we have more vital things to focus on, like making sure Telor survives and Braylon tells us what we want to know."

Our company moves farther into the tunnel.

But Kienen hangs back. "I will remain outside with my soldiers if you permit it, Your Highness."

"So you can be carried off in its claws?" The Ybarisans were riding out to help us. To die with us if need be. "No, you're coming inside. You're *all* coming inside." Both Kienen and Radomir drew their blades to fight alongside us in a battle that could only end in our deaths.

Kienen's wary gaze flitters to Zander.

"The queen of Ulysede demands it, and so that is how it shall be." He sets his jaw with determination. "You are our allies. You should have the safety of our city." He surveys the few remaining saplings who also rode out. "*All* of you."

23
GRACEN

"Go on, then! If you're gonna accuse me, check the pockets, will ya!" Dagny shoves the ball of material into the guard's hands, indignation lacing her flustered tone.

He flips the garments this way and that, shaking them before tossing them back at the seamstress. "Just following the king's orders."

"And I prefer to keep my flat feet on the ground instead of danglin' at the end of a noose, just so ya know." She marches through the kitchen toward me, her scowl replaced with a beaming smile. I can't help but counter. She's the friendliest soul I've met since arriving in Cirilea. "What are you doing here, Dagny?"

"I thought you might need a new dress, now that ya've popped out that wee one. Where is she? Oh! Look at you!" She bends at her waist to take a closer look at the sleeping baby. "She's like a doll! I can't remember my Dagnar ever being that little. 'Course, he wasn't. Came out the size of a mule. Nearly tore me in half. Couldn't walk for weeks."

I chuckle. There isn't much Dagny keeps to herself. "How is the wedding dress coming along?"

"Oh, *dreadful*." She steals a glance over her shoulder at the guards, to make sure they're not listening, but drops her voice to a whisper anyway. "She insisted I make the exact same dress as the one I made for Princess Romeria to wear on tournament day. Oh, you should've seen her, Gracen. Her Highness was ..." Dagny's words fade, her clasped hands pressed against her ample chest. Then she sighs. "So, I made the exact same one, and brought it to Lady Saoirse, and she started screaming that I'm dim-witted, that she can't wear the same dress as what Her Highness wore! So now I have to add some things and take away some other things and hope she doesn't have me executed on her first day as queen. As it was, I thought I was gonna catch on fire the way she glared at me." She shudders for effect.

"I know that look." It's the same one she leveled me with in the library, when she accused me of being Princess Romeria's spy. "But the wedding's almost here, Dagny."

"Don't I know it! The *Silver Mage* just came back to port, and I can't even check if there's some new bolts come in because we're not allowed outside these walls. King's orders! Suppose I could use some of the stock I picked up when Odier came for the fair. I hate to waste any of that fine material on Lady Saoirse when it was meant for the princess."

There's never been any doubt in my mind that Dagny is still a fan of Princess Romeria, despite all the rumors and accusations. Maybe that's part of the reason I like her so much.

"Oh! And then you know what she told me? While I was pinning the hem?" Her eyes widen. "She said the king is moving Presenting Day up to this Hudem."

"*This* one coming up?"

She nods. "And youngins will be sold."

"*What*?" I gasp.

"It's true. She said the king'll be announcing it at next assembly."

He never mentioned that last night. "How young?"

"She didn't say an age. She said 'children.' I suppose given this terrible poison, they're trying to protect what they can. Still, it seems terrible, to be rippin' wee ones from their mother's arms." She shakes her head. "Dagnar just came of age. He was gonna be gone next Hudem, anyway, but I thought I'd have a few more months with him."

"Can't he join the castle staff?"

Her brow furrows. "Like I said, my boy's a mule and about as smart as one. The royal family seems to prefer daintier and refined tributaries, usually female." She shrugs. "But, with all that's been going on, maybe they won't be so picky. Princess Annika might like him?"

I assumed my kids would be taken in by the castle when the time came, but perhaps that was foolish thinking.

Why didn't Atticus mention anything about this last night?

Because he knew it would distress me, likely.

"But enough of that nonsense. How 'bout this one on you?" She holds up a simple gray wool dress. "Will it fit?"

"I think so, but …" My hands are caked with flour and lard, or I'd hold it up against myself. "You're the seamstress. You tell me."

"I think it'll fit ya just right. And here, I scrounged up these for that scrawny boy of yours, now that it's getting colder." She shuffles through the clothing tucked under her arm, holding up a pair of brown breeches and a wool tunic, followed by a yellow smock. "And this is for your little angel."

"She'll love it. Thank you, Dagny."

"Oh, it's no trouble." She waves me off. "If I can get my hands on some fabric, I'll sew something nicer for ya next time."

The kitchen door swings open, and Corrin plows through, her eyes finding me. "Where is that boy?"

"In the cellar, sorting potatoes."

"He most certainly is not! I was just in the cellar, waiting for him."

"He went down after first meal!" I should have known not to trust him to make it there. "I don't have time to hunt for him."

Corrin casts a furtive glance at the guards before lifting her chin to pass them. "What's goin' on in here?"

"Dagny brought me some new clothes."

Corrin saunters over to inspect them. "Anything extra sewn into them that I should know about?" Her eyes widen knowingly as she begins folding Lilou's dress.

"Well, best I get back to my work." Dagny sets the other pieces down on the table and, with a smile at Suri, she marches away.

"What was that about?" It's not the first time Corrin has made a snipe to Dagny sewing things into things.

"Nothing to worry you with. But whatever she gets herself caught up in, don't you get involved." Corrin sets Lilou's dress down and collects mine. "Dagny's full of gossip and empty of sense."

Speaking of gossip … "She told me she heard they're moving up Presenting Day to this Hudem and auctioning off children. Lady Saoirse confirmed it."

Corrin's hands falter before she continues, creating a tidy stack of folded clothes. "I suppose it'll be what it'll be.

"But what does that mean?" I peer down at my sleeping baby, a fresh wave of panic surging. "Are they going to take my children from me? Will Mika be auctioned off?"

"Never you mind that. We'll make sure to warn anyone who so much as bats an eye at him how much trouble he causes."

"Missing a child?" a male voice calls out. Kazimir lingers by the kitchen's entrance.

Finding the king's friend at my door last night was a surprise, but it turned out to be a welcome one. "Yes. Would you know where he is?"

He waggles a finger, beckoning me. "You are going to love this."

"Oh, child, what have you gotten yourself into now." With a heavy sigh, I scrub the pastry off my fingers in a bucket of soapy water and trail him out.

"Tell me he didn't discover that cedar labyrinth." Ahead, the cobblestone paths disappear into a magnificent array of trees, manicured hedges, and flower gardens. I've never seen the royal gardens myself before, but Sabrina said a person could easily get lost in its enormity.

Kazimir chuckles. "If he had, I doubt we would have found him for days. This way." He leads me to the right, toward the sounds of metal swords clanging. "We were working through our morning routine in the sparring square when we discovered a spectator, hiding in the bush. A guard nearly put an arrow through him."

I gasp.

"Don't worry, he is unharmed. The king stopped it before it could happen."

My heart was already racing with fear for my son. Mention of Atticus has it racing for another reason. He sent me off to another sleepless night, my mind turning his words over, looking for meaning within them.

I would rather Saoirse think you are just the baker.

What am I if not the baker? I ask myself this now, though I know the answer. At least I know what he's intending.

Is the king still here? I wasn't expecting to see him this morning, and I don't need a mirror to know I'm a mess. I comb my fingers through the loose strands of my hair to try to calm it. "I hope you gave Mika a little scare. Otherwise, I can't promise you won't find him in the bushes again, now that he knows where the soldiers practice." He's always been fascinated with swordplay.

"He's promised His Highness he'll sit on the wall next time when he wishes to watch." Kazimir gestures to the square.

My heart skips a beat at the sight.

Atticus is down on one knee in front of Mika, guiding his fist around a wooden sword to teach him how to hold it properly. "There. Like that. Ready?" He stands and takes a step back, wielding his own wooden sword. He's in a tunic and breeches, though the air is chilly. "You need to be able to move. Match my stance."

Mika's brow furrows as he studies Atticus's boots intently, before shifting his feet to match.

"Good. Now I'm going to take one step forward and lunge with my sword, and you are going to parry. Do you know what that means?"

Mika notices me watching, and his face splits with a grin, his concentration lost. "Look, Mama! I'm learning how to fight!"

"I see that. And not with just any teacher." I bow. "Your Highness."

Atticus smiles, showing off deep dimples.

"I hope this was worth you sneaking off. Corrin is looking for you, and she is *not* happy."

His grin falls, earning Atticus's chuckle.

"Trust me, you do not want Corrin angry with you. She'll put extra salt in your stew. Go now, little man."

"Can I come back later?" He peers up at Atticus, his blue eyes filled with awe.

"You can, but remember the rule." The king points a finger at him, his expression suddenly stern.

"No more hiding in bushes!" Mika drops his wooden sword with a clatter and takes off running.

"Mika! Come back here and … put away your sword." He's already gone. I rush forward to clean up after my son, but Atticus is there, bending to collect the child's practice weapon, his tunic hanging to reveal the muscular torso he showed off last night.

I thought I was going to pass out from the fluster it stirred.

"I am so sorry. He was supposed to be sorting potatoes in the cellar, but he is impossible to manage sometimes."

"No need to apologize for a child's spirit. It's refreshing to be around." Together we watch a guard open the door. Mika runs through. "Honestly, I do not know how he's held on to it, given all that he's seen. But I think that is a testament to the unconditional love he gets from his mother."

I'm acutely aware of how close the king stands to me. "All children should have that, shouldn't they?" I tip my head back to meet his eyes.

They roam my face before he smiles. "You have a little something …" Reaching up, he brushes his thumb across my cheek, pulling away to show off the streak of flour.

My cheeks flush with embarrassment, even as my body heats from his touch. "I was busy in the kitchen when the captain came to find me."

"And what are you making today?"

"Bread."

His smile sours. "That's not very exciting, is it?"

His boyish reaction makes me laugh. "Why do I think my son isn't the only one with an incorrigible sweet tooth around here?"

He leans in to mock whisper in my ear, "Don't tell anyone."

A shudder runs through my core as his breath skates across my skin.

The playful smirk on his lips as he pulls away tells me he knows what his little touches and whispers do to me. He knows, and he intentionally seeks out my reaction.

On the other side of the court, metal swords clang, as guards hone their skills. It reminds me where we are. I clear my throat, not trusting my voice. "I'm sorry if Mika interrupted your time here."

"It's fine. He's already showing more promise than Kaz as far as his swordsmanship goes."

"I heard that!" Kazimir hollers from his spot, his back to us, his elbows on the square's perimeter wall—a stone structure no more than three feet tall that separates the fighting space from the beauty of the grounds beyond.

In the distance, I spot two willowy figures strolling along the path. One, I recognize instantly, her jet-black curtain of hair impossible to mistake. Look at her, all but caught with this poison and yet still free to enjoy the garden. Meanwhile, had I been found with that same vial in my possession, I would no longer be breathing.

"What distresses you?" Atticus asks.

Only then do I realize my teeth are clenched. "I do not understand politics, is all." Or perhaps I understand them too well. Dagny's words from earlier linger, of Lady Saoirse's grim news. I hesitate. "Is it true you are moving up Presenting Day and including children in the auction?"

His easy charm slips. "Where did you hear that?" he demands, his voice suddenly hard.

"It's what Lady Saoirse is telling the servants," I stammer, shrinking away. I don't want to name Dagny and get her in trouble.

His eyes thin on his future bride as she vanishes into the garden. "My betrothed is speaking out of turn." He seems to notice my reaction and steps closer. "I'm not angry with *you*, Gracen."

I swallow my fear. "So it isn't true, then?"

Seconds pass without his answer, and my hope fades.

"I haven't decided yet," he admits, finally. "But I may not have any other choice. Our current situation is dire. Within the castle, our options for tributaries have dwindled. And outside of these walls … it is far worse."

"The mortals keep taking the poison, despite the executions?"

"More each day."

That should tell him something. That should tell them *all* something—that many mortals would rather die than suffer under the current way of things.

He sighs. "I will have to decide soon."

I know I should bite my tongue, be thankful he's granted me the answers to the questions I've asked, but I can't help myself, now that I have his ear. "And who decides which mortals the castle shall take as tributary?"

"Normally, the king and queen. It is a grand affair of sorts, and an honor for the mortals to be selected by the royal family. Given the wedding, I may assign the task to my sister." He frowns. "Why?"

"If my children are to be auctioned off—"

"Your children will not be taken from you. I can promise you that."

A wave of relief washes over me, though I'm not without worry. If Saoirse is queen, my family and I still have plenty to fear within these walls. At least we'll be together. It sounds like not all families will be as fortunate. "What about the seamstress, Dagny?"

His frown turns curious. "What about her?"

"Her son has just come of age, and I know she would be thrilled if there was a way to keep him within the castle's employ, even if he is not a fit tributary."

A slow, teasing smile stretches across Atticus's lips. "Are you trying to wield your power and influence over me, Gracen?"

"Your Highness?" I stammer. "I do not have either of those things over you."

He steps closer, tossing the wooden swords, his hands seizing my waist. "Don't you?" He leans in and for a moment, I'm sure he's going to kiss me out here in the middle of the sparring square. But he stops short, mere inches away, and studies me, his eyes dark with want.

For me?

For my blood?

For all of it?

The heat from his grip sears my skin through my dress. Every nerve ending in my body thrums with heady anticipation as I hold my breath and my lips part, and I wait for him to do *something. Anything.*

I don't think I'd mind whatever he chose.

"Your Highness! Will you be joining us in the war room?"

Captain Boaz's gruff voice seems to break the spell that hangs between us.

Atticus releases his grip and steps away, his breathing uneven. "Your timing is impeccable, but, yes, I suppose I should get to work." He sighs and adds quietly, only for my ears, "Before things get out of hand here. Until next time." Casting a lazy salute, he turns and strolls off.

And I release a lungful of air, wondering myself what the next encounter with Atticus will bring.

Kazimir closes in to collect the wooden swords. He holds one out. "Care to go a few rounds with me?"

I'm so flustered by the last few moments, I can only stare at the hilt.

"I promise, I am not as unskilled as the king would suggest." He winks.

Something tells me Kazimir isn't talking about swordplay.

I clear my throat. "I'm sorry, I have work I should return to." And a baby to feed.

And my sanity to regain.

I back away.

He throws his hands in the air. "Why does no one want to spar with me?"

"If you're looking for a playmate, I'm sure my son will oblige," I throw over my shoulder as I move away.

24
ATTICUS

"Is this a joke?" I inspect the black-and-silver-flecked wax seal more closely, and the emblem branded into it. "Did my brother claim a cave and name it for a kingdom?"

"That is from Zander?" Boaz's voice marks his shock.

"Or someone with identical handwriting." After decades of messages from my brother while dealing with one skirmish or another around the realm, I easily recognize my name in his scrawl. But it's the intersecting crescent moons branded into the hard wax, the same symbol that Wendeline marked those mortals with the night of the royal repast, that is most jarring.

"What does it say?"

I shake my head, not having read past the first line of address. "'Dear Atticus, I know we are presently at odds"—I snort—"but for the sake of Islor, I share my knowledge and pray you heed my guidance. Much has happened since we saw each other last. Hopefully, there will be time for harsh words later. But now, you and I must unite in the face of the coming trouble, some of which you cannot begin to fathom …'" My voice fades as I read the rest of the sobering words quietly. There are two different hands writing to me on this page, the top one Zander's, the bottom with a feminine touch.

Romeria's.

The tension in my limbs grows as I read each line.

Is this another one of my brother's ploys? A scheme he has spun to win favor and control the narrative for his means?

Not fifteen minutes ago, I was standing around this map, scouring my mind for what reason Zander could have to go into those mountains. Now it's all laid out for me in black ink, by his hand, and I could not have imagined it had I tried.

"Anything vital I should be aware of, Your Highness?" Boaz is practically dancing from impatience.

I'm not sure yet. I clear the worry from my throat. "Zander and Romeria are deep in the Venhorn Mountains, at Stonekeep."

"Stonekeep." Boaz shakes his head. "What kind of protection your brother thinks to find within those deadlands, I cannot fathom."

"It is curious." I reread Romeria's alarming words at the bottom. "You've been alive longer than most, Boaz. What do you know of that place?"

"Only that it is not a place. It is a nymph relic far older than I. Older than anyone alive, I hazard. Nothing more than a stone wall with scripture."

"The *nymphaeum* is a stone wall with scripture, and yet you and I breathe because of it," I remind him.

Boaz's brow furrows. "Why do you ask this?"

"Because Zander claims they have found a hidden city there, with the help of the caster."

"A city that no other caster has known about for thousands of years?" He shakes his head. "An attempt to lure you there to see for yourself."

"Perhaps." The rest of his claims about this place, I will keep to myself. Boaz will think I've gone mad for even uttering the word *prophecy*. "They also claim that Queen Neilina has amassed a powerful army of Ybarisans and Mordain's strongest and intends to cross the rift on Hudem, to take our lands while Islor is in turmoil. It has always been her plan."

"Reports from the rift have said as much."

Tyree attempted to steer me from this idea. "Zander wants me to send Telor and his men back to the rift, along with as many soldiers as can reach it before Hudem."

"So he and his Ybarisan traitor can attack Cirilea while it is unguarded?" He scoffs.

"From all reports, he has only a few legionaries remaining, so I don't know how effective he would be. Though he has found the Ybarisans stationed in the mountains. According to this, he plans on marching to the rift alongside Telor."

Boaz's eyebrows arch. "*With the Ybarisans*?"

"It does sound doubtful." Legionaries would rather lie with a daaknar than fight alongside a Ybarisan. "But desperate times call for desperate alliances."

"This is a ruse, Your Highness. A tactic to turn our focus north and weaken our city's defenses."

"Our defenses are already weak."

"And this would make them weaker. What else does the letter say?"

"That the Ybarisans used our trade routes to move the vials of poison, with instructions for the mortals to wait until Hudem to ingest it."

"Clearly, the mortals have not heeded that," he mutters.

"*Some* have not. The poison will have circulated to all corners of Islor by now, and he says there is far too much of it. He wants me to declare this coming Hudem a day of abstinence rather than celebration." My hand cramps with the thought of all the letters I would have to write to even attempt that.

"Impossible. Hudem is next week! Mere days away!"

Boaz is right, I can't so easily stop two millennia of ritual. Yet, I know his counsel is laced with hatred for Zander, which is fueled by guilt for his own shortcomings, losing one king to poison and another to treason against the crown. He's no longer capable of seeing what we both know—that despite my brother's mistakes, his words should never be disregarded.

"Let's hope everyone's apprehension to the poison will make them think twice about following tradition, regardless of whatever declarations I may or may not make."

"Some are already planning to abstain, I'm sure. And then there are those who will refuse to be held hostage by fear."

"Then they make their own beds."

"And of your betrothal to the Lady Saoirse? Is he aware of that?"

"He is." I imagine Rengard informed him. "He says I've made a poor choice for a queen, and I must renege immediately." I can practically hear my brother's voice in my head, chastising me for the coming centuries of misery. *If* I survive even a week.

Boaz harrumphs. "That is rich coming from him. I would not trust *any* of his claims, Your Highness. After all, they arrived by the Ybarisan queen's messenger."

"The taillok?" That fierce-looking iridescent thing? It delivered messages to Princess Romeria several times on our trek south from the rift. I swore I'd put an arrow through it if I ever saw it again.

"Exactly. And guided by the casters, I've heard. Mother and daughter are likely scheming together against you."

"No, Zander would castrate himself before joining leagues with Neilina. This caster of theirs must have captured it somehow."

"I would have said the same once, not long ago, about him joining leagues with Princess Romeria after her crimes."

"She has certainly won him over," I agree. My brother is hopelessly in love with her.

"Anything else of value in the letter, Your Highness?"

My eyes graze the feminine writing at the bottom of the page. She is determined to end the blood curse. That is *impossible.*

Isn't it?

Suddenly, I wish I'd paid more attention to my studies as a child.

There is someone who might be able to answer that question.

So far she has been unwilling to speak, but maybe seeing Romeria's own words will inspire her to share what she knows. They became close in those weeks after the attack.

"Nothing but fairy tales and lies." I fold the letter and tuck it into my vest for safekeeping. I don't need to seek Boaz's counsel on the rest of it. I can already hear his words.

Deceptions.

Treachery.

Disregard.

He may even decide I'm unfit to wear the crown should it appear I am taking a Ybarisan's advice to heart.

"How do you wish to respond?"

"You handed me this letter five minutes ago, Boaz. I need more than that to consider my options."

"Of course. The taillok waits on a roost. For how long, I cannot say."

"It will wait there as long as it's been instructed to. A minute or a lifetime." At least that's what Romeria told me once, when I asked that very question, eyeing the odd thing as it sat idle on top of a wagon. "But time is something we don't have, if Neilina is on her way." I move for my desk, collecting paper and quill. How do I respond to such wild claims and requests?

"Do you think the marriage proposal between Tyree and Annika will sway her decision? Change her course at the rift?"

"I doubt it has reached her yet, and even when it does, how is she to swiftly respond, now that we have her carrier?"

"I'm sure she can find other methods of communication. She has a tower full of those elementals, after all." Boaz's lips curl with distaste.

"Perhaps. In the meantime, I must do a better job selling the idea to Annika." She's currently somewhere in the castle, spitting my name onto the stone floor. "Have Tyree brought to the same rooms where his sister was once imprisoned. Bring him clothes and food he can eat without convulsing. Station three guards at his door and triple the ones below the balcony. Arm them all with merth bolts."

A knock sounds on the door.

"What now?" I shout.

The door creaks open, and a guard escorts Corrin in.

I chuckle. This is a first.

"A lady's maid does not seek an audience with the king!" Boaz barks.

I wave him off. "It's fine. Thank you. I will bring a letter for the taillok shortly."

"Your Highness." His jaw tightens at the dismissal, his steel boots heavy as he marches out.

I lean back in my chair, smiling. "This should be interesting."

"Your Highness," Corrin begins, her voice crisp, her chin lifted. What this mortal lacks in size—she reaches my chest in stature—she makes up for in attitude. My mother always valued and trusted her. "I do not know what your intentions are with the baker—"

"Nor should you. She's my subject, and I am the king to do with her what I wish," I say evenly.

"Yes, of course you are. I would never suggest otherwise." She pauses to choose her words. Or perhaps to bite back the salty ones she wishes she could utter. "I merely want to make sure you are aware of what sort of keeper she faced before she arrived here."

"A lying, thieving, conspiring one?"

Her brow furrows. "Yes, perhaps he is all of those things as well, but I mean what he did to *her*."

My smug smile slips off. "Continue."

"When Gracen and her children came to the castle, they were skin and bone. I doubt those children had had a proper meal in their entire lives. And Gracen … I helped her into the bath once and"—she flinches—"there were marks *all* over her body. Bruises and bites, worse than anything I'd ever seen. So many of them."

"A tributary should not wear those." Not if their keeper is treating them correctly. Even the teeth marks should fade quickly.

"She should not even have been a tributary!" Corrin's voice fills with indignation. "She was carrying a child. A *third* one, that he forced her to bear, with some stranger she'd never met before! The law states—"

"I know what the law states. Thank you, though." My anger simmers as I hear these new facts.

She purses her lips. "Not only was he still feeding off her regularly as she reached term, but he would invite other keepers over to feed off her and use her in *other* ways. He liked an audience." She gives me a knowing look.

My fist closes over my quill, snapping it in half.

A knock sounds.

"Fates, grant me an hour to myself." There has been a parade of people all morning. "Is there anything else you feel you need to share, Corrin?"

She clears her throat. "When Princess Romeria rescued her from that dreadful situation, Gracen believed her days of serving as tributary were over, and she was *very* relieved about that."

So that's why Corrin is here. She's noticed my interest in Gracen and has put two and two together. I shouldn't be surprised. "Sometimes things change. In case you didn't know, I'm running out of tributaries." And yet her words spark my disappointment.

"It is a dangerous position to hold in the castle as of late," she agrees. "Very dangerous for anyone, but especially a mother of three, who might find herself in a dungeon or execution square through no fault of her own."

Corrin would never dare come outright and tell me I can't have Gracen as my tributary, but she may as well have. Her defiant expression says as much.

"I think we are done here. You may enter!" I holler to whoever waits outside.

Rhodes strolls in. The lithe warrior's smooth, umber skin glows as if he ran hard all the way here. Kazimir is behind him. "Your Highness," they echo each other.

"Thank you, Corrin. You may go."

"Your Highness." She bows and strolls out, ignoring the captains as if they don't exist.

"Are you sure she's not the one trying to poison you?" Kazimir says the moment the door shuts.

"That would be beneath Corrin. What have you found out, Rhodes?"

"I followed Lord Danthrin to Port Street last night, as requested, Your Highness."

"And?"

"He spent an hour at Jadelight."

One of the pricier brothels in the area. "Drowning the sorrow of his recent losses between a mortal's legs? He doesn't spend like an impoverished lord."

"From what I hear, he has been there every night this week."

"And did you find out who the unlucky lady is?" After what Corrin told me, she certainly is unlucky.

Rhodes's deep brown eyes crinkle with his smile. "Not yet, but I will. Afterward, he made his way across the street to the Goat's Knoll."

"A step down, if he was looking for another vein." The tavern is a seedy meeting place for ale and sex and blood—or all three.

"He did not partake."

"And how much time did Bexley grant him?" Why else would he be there?

"He did not meet with her. She was not even there. At least not in the main room."

"That is a rare occurrence." I don't think I've ever shown up there and found its owner absent. "Who was Danthrin there for, then?"

"He shared a drink and a laugh with Lord Spire first."

I rub my chin in thought. Fernhoth and Freywich are leagues apart. What business would one have with the other?

"A drink is not proof of anything. Perhaps it was friendly chatter," Kazimir offers.

"There's nothing friendly about Spire. Did he meet with anyone else?"

"Some males I have not seen before. From Kier, I think."

"They are a long way from home. What are they doing in my city?" And my realm, for that matter.

"I asked around and several sources named them mercenaries."

"Loyal to whom?"

"To whoever has gold, is my guess. But they spend much time in Kettling."

"And so the plot thickens." *What are you up to, Danthrin?* And who could he be working with? Adley, maybe? Was my future father-in-law's efforts to help Danthrin reclaim Gracen and her children a way to show power by swaying my decision, or an offer of help to this lowly lord in exchange for something? Still, there will be others involved. That much I know. "Keep an eye on our rabbit. See where else he hops. And I think I'll pay Bexley a visit. Without a guard."

"Your Highness." Rhodes dips his head.

"*Now*?" Kazimir cocks his head. "This early in the day?"

He's right. I normally wait until after dark to skulk about the city. "She's always open for me." In more ways than one.

He chuckles. "And how do you plan on avoiding Boaz's notice?"

"I have a few pressing tasks for him." Between moving Tyree and sending this letter, it should give me enough time to slip out. I study the blank page sitting before me on the desk. What am I to make of Romeria and her wild claims? The end of the blood curse in Islor?

Would that news even be welcomed? Surely, it would be for the mortals, but what about my kind?

What would happen to our way of life?

Romeria betrayed me once already. There's no reason to believe she wouldn't again. Of course, I then betrayed her, or some version of her. Are we even now, or will this be a game of trading tainted favor for favor until one of us dies?

I can't trust her.

Dipping a new quill into the ink, I jot down my message and seal it.

25
ZANDER

"I apologize for dragging you from your rest, but I thought it important they see you, know you are alive and our guest rather than our prisoner." A two-hundred-soldier contingent arrived at dawn, demanding answers and threatening to bring the whole of Islor's army for an attack. They saw the great beast swoop in and accused our caster of sending it to kill Lord Telor and their men.

Telor's face is sallow and full of sleep as he rides next to me through Ulysede's tunnel toward Islor and the coming dawn. For as long as Romeria worked on him last night, it's clear he hasn't recovered yet. If Gesine were free of the taillok, I would ask her to finish. "No, you were right to do so. They have already concocted a story that does not bode well for our union. Paisley is a good soldier, but not a true leader. I do not want him doing something foolish."

The portcullis ahead is closed. "I would highly advise against you passing that threshold. You are still weak, and when the blood curse takes hold of you for the first time, it can be overwhelming. I am not sure what it will do to you in your condition, and I would not want you keeling over dead after all of Romeria's efforts to keep you alive."

Telor shakes his head. "I have *so* many questions."

I chuckle. "And I told you I will answer them in due time."

We reach the outer gates. The soldier who delivered his earlier threats dips his head. "My lord, it is good to see you. We thought you had perished."

"If not for His Highness and Princess Romeria—*Queen* Romeria now, it seems—I would have."

The soldier—Paisley, I presume—frowns, his eyes flashing to me. "My lord?"

"Have the army decamp and ride for these gates. I will be back within the hour to address everyone." He guides his horse back around and rides away without another word, his mood somber.

Abarrane holds one end of the rope that binds Braylon Telor's wrists as she leads him toward the outer gate. He has barely a scratch on him. His accomplice took the brunt of her questioning, and Abarrane made Braylon watch every minute of it until he was sobbing, begging through his tears to end his friend's suffering and singing the names of those who conspired with him.

Abarrane granted his request by slashing the male's throat.

There is nothing more important to Telor than loyalty and honor. Braylon must realize he is walking to his execution. I would pity the Islorian, had he not tried to kill his father, a noble male and my friend.

Telor rides on the other side of the line of legionaries, his gaze avoiding his only son.

Horik pulls the lever and the portcullis draws upward. Beyond it, a thousand men wait in formation for their lord.

"Are they gathered?" Telor stands firm just inside the gate line. He has no interest in appearing weak before his men.

"Yes, my lord. All seven names on the list they gave us." Paisley nods to the right, where seven soldiers—a mix of mortals and elven—have been stripped of their armor and their weapons. They wait on their knees.

Abarrane leads Braylon out by the rope and hoofs the backs of his legs. He buckles and joins the others.

Whispers carry as a row of legionaries find their places behind the men.

Telor's throat bobs with a hard swallow.

"Would it help if I gave the order?" I offer in a whisper.

"No. They will fault you for this, rather than hold those who deserve it accountable. I must be the one." Telor heaves a sigh and then bellows for all to hear, "For the crimes of conspiracy, treason, and attempted murder of their lord and Islor's fourth king, I sentence those kneeling before you to death." He hesitates, long enough to take a slow, deep breath, and then gives the signal.

The legionaries' blades move swiftly and without remorse.

26
ROMERIA

I open my bedroom door and frown at the regal figure standing next to Jarek. "Gesine?" She's swapped her plain beige dress for an emerald silk gown, and her raven-black hair is as sleek and smooth as when I first met her. "I thought you'd be back to your books by now."

"Good morning, Romeria." She dips her head in greeting. "Or, closer to good afternoon. And yes, I'll be back to the library shortly, but I wanted to see you first. How do you feel?"

"Like I got hit by a truck." Once we were within the safety of Ulysede, I went back to work on Lord Telor's wound, trying to repair the damage his son's blade had done. By the time it felt firmly knitted, Zander had to carry me to bed, my energy sapped.

But already, that familiar and comforting buzz deep within my core has returned, my well of power replenished.

"A truck? What is that?"

I chuckle. "Something you sit in that gets you places. Never mind. How is Telor?"

"A little worse for wear, but he will recover." She smiles. "You did as well as I could have."

"I'm not sure about that, but … thanks."

Jarek leans against the wall, arms folded, ankles crossed.

"What have I missed?" I ask.

"Let's see." The warrior leads us down the hall. "We executed Braylon and his conspirators at dawn, outside the gate. Telor gave the order."

What must that be like? Probably as painful as having your son try to kill you, I guess.

"And Iago is back."

My posture relaxes with that news. "How is he?"

"He'll live. Resting now. He could use your healing, though, since *that one* still has a bird in her head." He juts his chin toward Gesine.

"You didn't lose your connection?"

She shakes her head. "Almost, but no."

"And did the saplings come inside?"

"Yes. They are probably still sitting on the bridge, staring at the sun."

I smile. I wish I'd been there to see their reactions as it rose. "And the Ybarisans?"

"We gave them an area near the orchards, and the last I saw, they were eating all our fruit like a bunch of locusts."

"They've been hiding in the mountains for months. What *have* they been eating?"

"What all you Ybarisans eat … twigs and berries." Jarek casts a smirk over his shoulder at me.

"Has the dragon been back?"

"No. They're waiting for you in the war room. There is much to discuss that they need you for." Jarek picks up his pace, but he seems to be giving us space to speak.

"The taillok has reached Cirilea and delivered your message. It awaits a response," Gesine says.

To think I once lived in a world where I could send a message to a place thousands of miles away in an instant by clicking a button. Now we need magically fueled bird beasts from the Nulling. The thought brings a fleeting smile to my lips. "Do you think Atticus will respond?"

"That would be customary, but Atticus has not shown regard for customs."

"No, I guess he hasn't." Sleeps with his brother's fiancée and then hijacks the king's army and steals his crown in front of an arena full of Islorians? No one's going to give Atticus a gold star for following protocol.

"I hope he does send one, though, and that it is soon." She gives her head a shake. "I can truly appreciate Yesenia's plight now. She must be relieved to be spared this constant double vision."

"That would drive me insane." But a bird is not what's on my mind. "Listen, about last night and that dragon … beast … *thing*." I bolted awake this morning in a cold sweat, the memory of those few moments, of believing that was truly the end for me, a vivid nightmare. It took me long minutes to shake the discomfort and fear. "I appreciate what you were willing to do for me." For *all* of us. I saw how quickly it moved, how powerfully it launched itself into the air. Had I agreed to run and it attacked, I doubt we could have reached the gate in time, but there is no doubt Gesine would not be walking beside me now. There'd be nothing left of her.

She was willing to give her life for *a slim chance* to save mine.

Gesine's lips part, but she stalls to choose her words. "Despite what you and the king may believe, my only motive has ever been to provide you guidance in your journey to fulfilling prophecy."

"I believe you. I just wish you'd start trusting us with the truth up front, rather than hiding it from us."

"Sometimes the only way to move forward is with good intentions and without permission."

Because she knows we'd never agree. "Well, it sounds like prophecy is already fulfilled. The nymphs and Malachi don't need me anymore, so don't go sacrificing yourself on my account."

"I do not believe that to be true. The Queen for All will bring peace to the lands, but she cannot do that from the belly of a beast."

"I suppose not." I shudder at the thought of being swallowed whole. "But how I'm supposed to bring peace when, apparently, I've invited an army of monsters and Malachi through the Nulling, I would love to know. So, if you're holding back any more thoughts or worries, now would be a good time to share them."

"There is still much to learn within these walls. If I discover anything, you will be the first to know. I promise."

We reach the great hall. Zorya waits, her hands on her hips, the irritated look painted across her face harsher than the nymph gargoyle she stands next to.

"I suppose I should be off to find what I can about this dragon beast *thing*, and any other creatures we might face in the coming days." Gesine purses her lips. "I would guess the conversation you are about to walk into will require more openness than you had previously hoped."

Zander already warned me that Kienen named me an impostor and has demanded the truth. Telor knows firsthand of my healing abilities, something elven are not capable of. "We knew it was only a matter of time."

"Remember that you are a queen, and *you* decide what they need to know."

"I can't lie to everyone forever." It's too hard to keep up.

"I did not suggest lying, only that some details are better left unsaid, allowing others to focus on what will aid the cause, which is an honorable one."

"That's what you do, Gesine. And it doesn't feel good." She withholds details that might distract us, might sway our choices another way. Then again, here we are, standing in a city where the blood curse is gone, so maybe she has a point.

Or maybe it's time to stop hiding.

"Prophecy will always find a way." She hesitates. "I know I have stressed the importance of your paths moving forward together, and I still believe this to be true, but while His Highness's focus must shift to uniting Islor at the rift, I would urge you to use this invaluable time to gain knowledge."

"You mean, stay in Ulysede while Zander goes out there? Gesine, I can't—"

"*Please*, listen to me in this, I implore you." Gesine grips my forearm, her brow furrowed. "Lucretia is the single-most valuable being at the moment. Far more valuable than I am. Her knowledge may prove vital in decisions you both must make soon enough."

That means going back down to the crypt with that serpentine creature. "*If* she'll speak to me."

"You are her queen. It is *only* you she will speak to. There is still much to learn, things that she has hinted at but not explained. What of this Nulling army? She alluded to the possibility of them fighting *for* you."

"All they've done is try to kill us so far."

"The beast last night did not, and it knew what you were. Can you imagine if you had the might of it *with* you?" Her green eyes widen.

I don't know what the rift passage even looks like, but having that massive body sitting in the middle of it would have to be a deterrent. "Neilina would think twice."

"*All* would think twice. You must explore this. I will search for what I can within the pages, but I believe Lucretia will be our better source. And remember, those soldiers and lords waiting in that room for you? They do not have the depth of knowledge into caster affinities and fates. They do not know that the end of the blood curse goes hand in hand with opening the nymphaeum door. They do not know what the nymphs are capable of, both good and bad."

"Neither do we."

"And that is what you must find out. You are the only one who can do this, and you can't if you are at the rift." With a gentle squeeze of my wrist, Gesine glides down the steps, pausing to offer Zorya a pleasant smile—as if the warrior isn't scowling—before they leave together, side by side.

"The witch's bravery last night was commendable, I will give her that," Jarek grumbles, falling back in line beside me as we climb the stairs toward the war room, where untold confessions await.

I hesitate, the weight of the coming conversation settling on my shoulders. "Listen, Jarek, there are some things we've never talked about, things you're likely going to hear very soon, and I'd rather you hear them from me first. You're my commander, after all." I add after a beat. "And my friend."

He sighs heavily. "Tell me, Romeria, do I look like a simpleton?"

An urge to crack a joke stirs, but I squash it. Now's not the time for deflecting serious topics with humor. Not when I'm so nervous about his reaction.

He peers over his shoulder at me. "Do you think I haven't noticed things?"

"Like what?"

"Like how you healed a fatal merth sword wound that no one should have walked away from. How you crumbled a cave's worth of stone to save that mortal imbecile. How you ignited a ring of fire to protect mortals in an execution square in Norcaster. My favorite, though, how you launched me in the air without laying a hand on me." He lists all the ways I've demonstrated my caster affinities as if he's been cataloging them.

I don't miss that each example is of a different affinity.

Four, to be exact.

"Or how about how your blood unlocked a kingdom sealed for tens of thousands of years, and now, according to that crypt snake, you've released the nymphs?" A grim chuckle sails from Jarek's lips as he stalls at the landing to meet my wary gaze, dark humor glinting in his.

"So, you aren't just a pretty face and a good time, is what you're saying."

"Give me some credit, Romeria. I have pieced together enough. I may not know the how or the why, but when the fates are involved, that hardly matters."

"And you're still here." I bite my lip. "Why *are* you still here?" Jarek despises Ybarisans and Mordain in equal amounts, which I'm both, and he would do anything to protect Islor, which I've now endangered. And yet he's stood by my side for weeks, saying nothing.

His jaw grits as he yanks the door open.

I guess we'll finish that conversation later.

"… no reason to doubt my claim, after Braylon's actions last night," Kienen says, heat in his tone. "If the princess would only—"

The discussion cuts off as I step into the war room to meet the circle of stony faces. My heart pounds in my throat, but I lift my chin. "I'm sorry if I'm late. I needed a little extra rest."

"No need to apologize." Zander's expression yields nothing.

"That's a first," I tease dryly.

That earns the smallest twitch at the corner of his lips.

Lord Telor stands at the far end of the map. His sallow complexion leaves me wondering if I've done enough for him.

Zander once told me to offer Lyndel's lord as genuine a smile as I could fake, but there's no need to fake it now. I'm relieved that I was able to save his life, even if he was here to take mine. "I heard you're up."

"Thanks to you, it would seem." His responding smile is tight-lipped, but I can't expect him to kiss my feet. I was enemy number one up until last night. Maybe I still am. Or maybe he's more focused on how his own son tried to kill him.

Beside Telor and Kienen are Radomir and Elisaf. "Where's Abarrane?" She's not a friendly face, but she's a female one. Now, I'm surrounded by men.

"Resting after a long night with the prisoners," Zander says.

Telor's jaw tenses. "The Ybarisan says my son has been working with you and your people. Is this true?"

And the Princess Romeria charade begins anew. "Kienen warned me of your son's betrayal only moments before the attack.

If not for him, you would be dead. Zander, too, likely. If he says it's true, then I believe him."

"Are you maintaining that you were not aware of whatever arrangement was made between my son and your brother?" Telor's tone is sharp. "I find that hard to believe."

Not so hard if you knew the truth.

"The Princess Romeria who crossed the rift was well aware of Neilina's scheming and the key players involved, but the princess who stands before you was completely unaware of it," Zander answers for me.

"Is this the 'memory loss' we've been hearing about? Atticus said you might claim innocence based on it."

I meet Kienen's gaze. It's the same calculating one he wore when I asked him what his affinity was to. I've seen it more than once now. He doubts who I am, and yet he spoke up when it mattered last night. He joined the fray and helped stop Braylon from getting away. He stood shoulder to shoulder when that dragon landed, even as he mistrusted me.

I see why Tyree had lies readily available to feed Kienen. Lies that Kienen could stomach, because he knew the soldier wouldn't stomach the truth of what the Ybarisan crown was tasking them to do.

I'm not asking him to keep going down that path. I'm asking him to help me fix what Ybaris has done. Do we really need to feed him *more* lies to get him to do that? Besides, it's too late for that. He's too smart; he's seen too much. Eventually, he'll decide that Ybaris's ruling family no longer deserves his loyalty.

I wish I had more time to feel him out, but we don't, and we can't risk losing him or the Ybarisans. They might only be two hundred and fifty-four out of an entire nation, but they're a start.

"Yes. And no." Gesine's counsel rings in my mind, but I can't keep up this charade anymore. "What I am about to tell you, I haven't openly admitted to anyone—"

"Romeria." Fear floods Zander's voice as he warns me off.

But I know in my heart what I have to do. "We can't keep

going around in circles, expecting people to trust us with their lives if we can't trust them with the truth."

He grits his teeth as I step forward to the head of the table, but he doesn't argue. "Twenty-five years ago, Queen Neilina forced an elemental caster to summon Aoife and create a weapon against Islor. That weapon was an elven princess whose blood was toxic to Islorians and who the future king of Islor would not be able to resist." I watch Kienen closely for any hint that he might have been lying before, that he might have known this. "The poison in those vials is not something the elementals made. It's my blood."

His brow furrows. "We heard rumors of this in recent weeks and dismissed them as lies spun to villainize Ybaris more. I have watched the queen execute lords for suggesting we summon the fates to help heal our lands. It didn't seem possible that Her Highness would tempt the fates so recklessly."

"Do you deny her hatred for us?" Zander asks. "Your lands are dying, and she is desperate, but she would rather seek war and untold consequences than an alliance."

Kienen studies the map intently. I can't get a read on where his head is at.

"The daaknar who tried to feed off me learned about my blood the hard way." I yank the collar of my tunic down. "I don't recommend meeting one of those things. They're not friendly."

His lips twitch with the hint of a smile. "And yet you survived."

"Thanks to a healer."

"The same who foiled this plan of Queen Neilina's."

"Wendeline. Yes. She and Margrethe were working with Gesine, Ianca, and a small faction of Mordain." I hope she's still alive.

"Against Ybaris?"

"Not so much against Ybaris as for prophecy."

"What does all this have to do with you and your memory loss?" Telor interrupts impatiently.

"Watch your tone. You are speaking to a *queen*, one who saved your life," Jarek warns, his hand shifting to his dagger.

I wave him off. "It's okay. It's a fair question, and I'll get to it." I smile. "The queen also enlisted the saplings to gather as much information as they could on Islor. By the time Princess Romeria crossed the rift, they knew everything there was to know about the royal family's allies and enemies, Islor's weakest spots, the best ways to attack. Radomir can vouch for that."

Telor glares at the sapling. "Why would your kind agree to help Ybaris?"

"Because Queen Neilina promised that Mordain would help lift this curse that plagues us, keeping us in the dark," Radomir says matter-of-factly. "And we believed her."

"Princess Romeria came to Cirilea with plans to kill the entire royal family on Hudem, poison as many Islorians as she could, and bring the Ybarisan armies across the rift to take Islor's lands. But Ybaris's plans backfired on Hudem, thanks to the casters, and Princess Romeria was shot by a merth bolt. She died that night."

"And yet she stands before us now." Kienen's eyes flitter over me before dropping, almost as if in apology.

"That's because Gesine and the others believed Princess Romeria needed to live for prophecy to be fulfilled. So, Margrethe summoned Malachi and resurrected Princess Romeria. Hence, the daaknar." If nothing else, that demon serves as proof. "Only, instead of her, they got me."

"And who are you?" Telor asks, his brow furrowed.

"I'm also Romeria. That was the name my mother gave me." She once told me it came to her in a dream. Maybe it did, but now I have to wonder if Malachi was somehow whispering in her ear. Or, more likely, Sofie. "But I've never plotted to kill anyone, and I don't hate the Islorians." In fact, I love one with everything I am. "Consider us two separate people. The old princess is dead, and I have no idea what she was planning, but I will do everything in my power to stop it."

Silence falls like a heavy stage curtain over the room.

"The old princess could not heal fatal sword wounds and launch commanders through the air," Kienen says quietly. "Her eyes did not glow silver."

Gesine said Kienen was respectful to the elementals—unlike the others—so he must value them. That, or have a healthy fear of them. Either way, he isn't ignorant to what they are and aren't capable of.

"Yeah, I come with a few extra skills." That I'm still learning how to use, but they don't need to know that yet.

"Why would Malachi do this?" Radomir asks.

"The fates do not explain themselves," Zander cuts in, silently pleading with me. I can practically hear his warning in my mind. *It's too dangerous.*

For weeks, Wendeline hid the truth from me about what I was, and when she revealed it, it was with a stark warning that I would be executed if anyone found out. Then I hid it from Zander, afraid he would kill me as she feared he might, until I couldn't anymore.

He didn't kill me, but he warned me that others would without question or remorse.

Since then, Jarek has figured it out on his own, and he hasn't killed me.

Abarrane *would* have killed me, had she been given the chance in that tent in Eldred Wood, but she seems to have accepted me too.

For months, it's been one lie and secret after another, to hide what I am.

To protect me.

But there is great value in what I am. Zander saw it, even when he was holding me at arm's length.

I have to hope these elven will see it as well.

I offer Zander a reassuring smile, one that I hope says *It's time to stop hiding.* "To answer your question, Radomir, Malachi brought me here because he needed a key caster in order to open the nymphaeum door."

Kienen curses.

Telor's face—already sallow—pales even more. "Are you saying that *you* are a key caster?"

I take a deep breath. "That's exactly what I'm saying."

Behind me, I sense Jarek shifting, ready to defend me against attack.

But Telor only leans against the map table as if for support as he digests this news.

"This is why all these Nulling creatures have come out of hiding," Kienen muses. "They're drawn to you."

"To *all* casters, but me especially."

"And you knew this about her?" Telor stares at Zander, his tone filled with accusation. *You knew what she was and yet you didn't kill her when you had the chance?*

Zander shakes his head. "Not until we were running from Cirilea. It was a shock to me, at first."

"And now?"

"Now ..." Zander's smile is soft. "I know Romeria's heart. I know she speaks only the truth when she says she wants to undo all that Ybaris has done to us."

Can he sense the relief that's swelling inside me?

One secret is out, and no one's drawn their sword ... yet.

"Where did he find you?" Radomir asks.

I laugh. "That is a question for another time. Trust me."

"But how? How does one rid us of this terrible poison that is tearing apart Islor, murdering its people every day?" Telor looks to me. "I will admit, I do not know much of caster affinities or what a key caster is capable of, but I assume if you *were* capable, you would have done it already."

He might not know about caster affinities, but he's wise and his words are sharp. And they offer a new clarity. "You're right, I can't do it. Not on my own. I need help."

"From whom? Mordain?"

"No. From the nymphs."

Telor's eyes widen, but he remains quiet.

"They built Ulysede. Their power is at its pulse. You've been inside the city for hours now. You've felt the difference, haven't you? You've seen what it can do?" I gesture toward Radomir.

Telor studies the sapling. "I did not see this transformation that Zander claims, no. But I do feel the difference in myself."

"That's because the blood curse is gone. That's what the nymphs' power is capable of—reversing the fates' summonings. Their power can take away the blood curse, making the poison not matter."

"That is in here. What about out *there,* beyond these great gates, where people are dying? How do we help them?" Telor pushes.

The answer is right there in front of me. It's been there all along. "By opening the nymphaeum door and releasing the nymphs. It's the only way forward." I look to Zander. "It's *always been* the only way forward. We just didn't want to see it."

He nods slowly, my words finding purchase.

Telor's eyes are wide as he shifts between the two of us. "You can't be serious about opening the nymphaeum door!"

I swallow my nerves. No more lies. "We already have. We didn't know it at the time, but when we unlocked Ulysede, we started the process. The nymphs will return on Hudem, and their power will rid Islor of the blood curse. It's what prophecy has foretold." And what Lucretia has promised.

Elisaf's hand smooths over his mouth, but the move doesn't hide his shock.

Zander drops a hand on his friend's shoulder—a silent apology for not telling him sooner. "Romeria is right. As much as I have not wanted to admit it, as much as we have fought the idea of it, through the fire is the only way to get to the other side in this. Queen Neilina's summoning started a chain reaction that has now forced our hand. The nymphaeum door had to be opened, whether we meant to or not. Things are now in motion that we cannot stop, so we must focus on what we can. One enemy at a time."

Kienen frowns. "But will the Nulling—"

"Yes. It will open, and untold creatures will emerge." Zander nods. "But that is an enemy we can see, that we can slay with our blades." His jaw is set with determination. "We did it once before, and we will do it again, if we join forces."

Will Malachi be so easy to slay once he has taken over Elijah's body and his feet touch Islor? Gesine is right. There are *some* truths better left unsaid.

"At least her casters will have something *else* to focus on when the Nulling opens," Elisaf notes.

"Do you think Queen Neilina will abandon her aim to invade Islor?" Kienen asks.

"I do not," Zander admits. "And I would never trust any alliance with her."

"What about an alliance with the heir to the Ybarisan throne?" Radomir asks. "It seems to me the easiest way to solve the problem of Ybaris would be to kill Queen Neilina. The throne would go to Romeria."

"Me?" I already have one throne I didn't want, and now he's suggesting a second?

Zander smirks. He knows what I'm thinking. "The thought has crossed my mind, and it is true that we will never see peace while Queen Neilina breathes. But she will not join the battle. She will not even cross the rift until she can declare victory."

"And she will travel with a circle of Shadows and elemental casters," Kienen adds. "No one will be able to spit on her, let alone kill her."

No one except perhaps her daughter.

"Unless our odds change, our main strategy *must* be to keep Ybaris from crossing the rift pass." Zander slides the stone that represents our various bands toward the rift on the map. "The king's army is scattered across Islor, trying to contain this poison. I have written Atticus to inform him of what we know, but I imagine he is too occupied with protecting Cirilea from Kettling's aspirations to risk focus on the north. That leaves *us* to hold Islor. I hope, with forces from Lyndel"—he holds up a navy blue stone to represent the city, and then another stone, this one purple—"and Bellcross, we might present a viable defense. Whatever happens, they cannot cross the rift. In that, we must be united." Zander turns to Telor. "Will you march with us and face this threat *together?*" It's a tentative rallying cry.

But Telor's face tightens with doubt. "Hudem is in three days. It takes a week to move an army down through this mountain range and then up to the rift. We will not make it in time."

"We will if we go through Soldor." Zander taps the map.

"Where?" When did they come up with that plan? It must have been while I was sleeping.

"An old mining city, riddled with Nulling beasts, parts of it likely fallen right into the rift. The eastern entrance was barricaded centuries ago." Telor shakes his head. "No one has gone there, for good reason."

"I have," Radomir counters. "It's not as bad as you describe. Only two spots that open into the rift. There's even a water source."

"How delightful." Elisaf is no more thrilled about this plan than Telor is, but he hasn't been happy since the name Venhorn was first spoken.

Radomir shrugs. "The creatures in there are on the small side and easy enough to kill, though they tend not to bother my kind. They don't have a taste for us."

"And what about *our* kind?" Telor glares at Zander. "You cannot seriously be considering this? What about our horses?"

"I've ridden through on horseback many times," Radomir answers.

"And we have swords for the creatures," Zander says evenly. "Radomir knows the passage well and says we can be through within thirty-six hours, placing us at the rift's pass. But we must move as soon as possible."

"My stronghold of three hundred will be trekking through caves and underground passages. They should emerge here"—

Radomir taps on the map, on a spot north of us—"by nightfall. If we meet them there, we can march to Soldor together."

"Traveling through the night?" Telor sounds doubtful.

"If it's any consolation, it's always night in Soldor." Radomir chuckles.

"We use this passage, we do not stop, and after the second sunrise, we will be at the rift and ready to lead whoever is there. The saplings can wait until nightfall of Hudem to emerge." Zander nods, as if the plan is coming together.

But he doesn't have Lord Telor's agreement yet, and by the deep frown across the lord's face, I don't know if he'll get it. "The rift soldiers will see Ybarisans ride out and they will attack before I can reach them."

An idea strikes me. "What if they don't see Ybarisans. What if they see Ulysede's soldiers?"

"The armory." A slow smile stretches across Zander's lips. "There is more than enough to outfit them with helms, shields, and weaponry. It should buy us enough time with confusion. Good idea. Will they agree to this, Kienen?"

Kienen's lips press. "If Her Highness orders it, so it shall be done."

Zander turns to Telor. "What say you? Are you with us? Will you help us save Islor?"

Finally, he sighs. "If there is a battle to be fought at the rift, you know I will be there."

27
ATTICUS

I can't recall the last time I was in the Goat's Knoll this early. It's filled with shadows, empty save for two couples in booths across the room. The air reeks of last night's ale, making this dull ache in my head all the more potent.

"Where might I find the owner?"

"At this hour? You may *not* find her." The hostess manning the door keeps her focus on the green leaves she hand-stitches into a corset.

"That is some talent you have there." I set three gold coins on the wooden counter.

She blinks at them, but then returns to her work. "My lady does not wish to be disturbed before she comes down for the evening."

I can sense her heartbeat racing with want. Bexley treats her mortals well, but this pretty young blond could sew a hundred gowns and never receive such payment. *"Your lady."* So, Bexley is upstairs in her apartment. Perfect. I lean over the counter on my elbows, dropping my voice. "I don't recall granting Bexley land or title in my realm, and my father and brother certainly did not." How Bexley ever secured a prime business establishment like this one on Port Street, I've never cared to ask. I know little about the tavern owner, besides what I've had my mouth and hands on from time to time. Those parts, I know *very* well.

Finally, the servant's eyes flip to mine and widen. And then widen more. "I … Your Highness?" She moves to put her work down, but I set my hand atop hers.

"No need for formalities. In fact, I'd prefer discretion." It's why I used the passageways behind the walls to leave the castle, why I donned my leathers and hid within my deep cowl.

Her head bobs, her breath shaky.

"It's been a while." I can't recall her name, or how she tasted, but I do remember her pale green irises. "How are you?"

"I didn't know you were … *you* that night." Her cheeks flush a scarlet red.

"I wasn't *me* that night." I wasn't the prince or the commander either. I was just an elven male looking for a release after my parents had been murdered and I had been duped. "Thank you for the information. I will ensure she does not punish you." I set another two coins on the others. "And this is to ensure my visit here is never confirmed, nor discussed."

She nods furtively.

I stroll past and up the creaky stairs.

The hall is narrow and dark and smells of rose petals, much like Bexley's skin often does. I skip the doors to the left and right—an office and storage, and rooms for her most prized servants—and aim for the wooden door straight ahead, rapping my knuckles against it.

There's a lengthy pause and then a sharp, "Who disturbs me?"

"Your favorite king."

Another pause and then, "Enter."

The inside of Bexley's suite is as dark as the tavern below it, even with windows that reach to the ceilings. It's all one room in moody grays and deep greens and hints of gold, with a sitting area in the center and her bed to the right. There's no kitchen to speak of, but I imagine there's one in the back downstairs. Bexley isn't the type to stir a pot herself.

A gilded mirror on the wall casts my reflection as I approach the cast iron bathtub that faces a window overlooking the street below. Bexley rests within it, her back to me, her strawberry-blond hair pinned on top of her head. A curl of smoke rises from the pipe within her grip. "The king himself in my suite. What *ever* could you be looking for?"

I settle into the velvet green chaise beside the bath, giving me a clear look at her naked body that she does not attempt to cover.

She's as beautiful and tempting as ever, her sleek limbs and ample feminine curves on display. But the dark circles under her eyes betray her calm. Bexley is tired, a rare sight, and one that suggests she hasn't been feeding either.

She brings the pipe to her full lips and sucks on the end.

I inhale. "Sage and lavender." Common herbs for sore joints. I wonder if it would help with my headache. "What ails you?"

"Life," she croaks between an exhale, her red lips parting. "And all these fools at my doorstep as of late, issuing thin threats and empty promises in exchange for information."

I adopt a lazy posture, my arm slung over the back of the chair, my thighs splayed, as if I'm unbothered. So she's figured out why I'm here. I would expect no less. "And tell me again, which fools have visited you? Lord Spire of Fernhoth, you mentioned? Lord Danthrin of Freywich, Lord Adley …"

Her eyes narrow as she regards me, their violet color a richer shade than normal. "I would never meet with someone as insignificant as Danthrin."

But Spire, she's met, Rhodes already confirmed. Adley was a guess that she hasn't denied, and that's not a slip. Bexley never gives up information accidentally. She wants me to know.

"My skin felt oily after five minutes with that Kettling lord. Reminded me why I left that city in the first place."

"You know, I was just thinking the other day … how well do we know each other?"

She bends her legs and lets her thighs fall apart. "Well enough that I can already feel the shudder you will make as you come."

I smile at the taunt. "I realized how little *else* I know of you. For example, when did you live in Kettling?"

"*Now* you ask these things, after all this time." She brings her pipe to her mouth again. A stall tactic to decide how to answer. "Many years ago."

"And how long have you lived in Cirilea?"

"Too many years," she says between a puff, her legs sliding back into a more discreet position. "How fare the wedding preparations?"

Steering the conversation away. I'll allow it for now. "Dreadful."

Her throaty laughter fills her apartment. "I thought you were smarter than to put Lady Saoirse on the throne beside you."

"It's almost as stupid as allowing her into my bed," I drawl.

"And you believe this union will give you an advantage?"

"I believe it will give me my *only* advantage," I admit. "I'm doing what I can to keep Islor together."

She studies me through a shrewd gaze for several long moments. "The only one with the advantage here is Adley. You must not go through with the engagement, Atticus."

"I will lose the east's support if I don't."

"You do not have it, even with the union."

"Is that a fact?" This is the first time Bexley has ever warned me so brazenly about anything. I have to assume she knows something.

"I never offer facts. And do not suggest bringing me forward to name names in your silly little court."

"I would not dare. Who am I, but *the king*?" I mock.

"I will deny everything." She lifts an eyebrow as if to challenge me.

I sigh. So this is the game we're playing. "We both know I could have thrown you in a dungeon cell for treason many times over. But have I ever used my power or position against you?"

"Much is changing and quickly. These are desperate times."

"You are right. I am desperate. Islor is falling apart all around us because of Ybaris's treachery. I cannot allow them to tear us apart from within too. So give me *something* to work with, Bexley, please. Do I need to kneel before you? Should I beg?"

She hesitates, then draws on her pipe. It takes everything in me to keep my patience while she studies the ceiling, weighing her urge to hold her power over her willingness to help a friend. "Ybaris's deceit has raised the stakes, yes, but Islor was doomed the moment two kings across borders exchanged letters, daring to seek an alliance. There are those who no longer feel Islor's ruling family knows what's best for Islor's people, no matter which of you sits on the throne."

"Tell me something I don't know."

"Those same people aim to redraw lines and allegiances, and they grow restless."

"*Redraw* the lines of Islor?" I curse, though I'm not shocked. As Kettling's lord has grown more powerful and bold, so have the leaders of other cities. "Adley leads this?"

"Adley plays both hands, but I would imagine he leans toward the one where his daughter sits on Cirilea's throne and he sits on Kettling's."

Her claim feels like a slap. "Are you saying he sits at my dining table and yet means to declare himself *king* of the east?" That is far bolder than I expected, even from him.

"These slippery eels *never* stick to only one path to reach their means, you should know that," she chastises.

"How does he plan to do this? The eastern army is camped outside my gate." That was part of the deal in this union. Cirilea needs the protection.

"*Half* their army."

"And the other half is scouring their lands for this poison."

"Is *that* what they are doing?" Bexley smiles, but it doesn't reach her eyes. "To me it looks like they're preparing to claim territory."

My nostrils flare. "Are you telling me there is an army gathering at the Sanguine?" The river has always lent itself well as a border between our side and the smaller, eastern arm of Islor that connects us with Kier. It is wide and tumultuous to cross, with only one bridge.

"*West* of the river, according to a source."

"*West.* But that is in the Plains of Aminadav. They do not have enough men to claim that much land."

"The Kierish army that moves toward them will change that."

Her words are like a punch to my stomach. Adley has always been friendly with King Cheral, an ambitious mortal king with four wives and a hatred for Cirilea. What has Adley promised for that level of support?

Bexley is well connected, but how does she know this? I've heard nothing. "Who is this source of yours?"

"I cannot tell you that, but I can promise they are reliable, and they have seen it with their own eyes."

"Impossible." My anger flares. "I need a name."

"I don't have one to give you." Abruptly, she stands and steps out of the tub, the water sluicing off her body and onto the hardwood floor as she makes a slow point of drying herself off with her towel in front of me.

In the past, even our quarrels have ended in ripped clothes and gyrating bodies, but I didn't come here for that and have no desire for that now. "Who can I trust?"

"No one. Well, perhaps those lurkers you've sent to tail the lords."

I cannot believe the east is attempting this. And if Bexley's source is accurate, they might succeed.

She tosses her towel to the floor, collects her pipe, and strolls over to lie on her bed. "You wanted to be king, Atticus. What did you expect would happen when you seized your brother's crown? That everyone would simply bow in your presence? That all the growing tension would fade? That these cunning *dignitaries*"—she snorts derisively, as if the very title is an affront—"and their lofty ambitions for power would evaporate?"

"No, I'm not a fool. But I did not expect their scheming to be so blatant."

"Even in the time of King Ailill, a far more intimidating ruler than you with his caster affinities, they plotted against him." Her naked body relaxes within the silken bedding. She's the picture of seduction—her creamy skin unmarred and flushed from her bath, her nipples pert. "It is the nature of holding such power. Why should anything change now?"

"I suppose you're right." I pause. "And I did not seek this role. I felt obliged to take it."

"There comes a time when we are all bound by obligation." She puffs on her pipe, her thoughts seemingly elsewhere. "What do you know of your brother and the Ybarisan princess?"

The letter tucked inside my leather vest feels heavy, the truth inside it even heavier. What would lords and ladies say if they knew that Romeria has claimed some secret kingdom within Islor's lands? They'd declare me an even less effective ruler.

"The last I heard, they were hiding in the Venhorn Mountains." Bexley's knowledge is firmly rooted in the whispers of elven and mortals, not of nymphs and prophecy. I doubt she'd know anything of use. She can't be trusted with that information, as much as she would love to wield it for her own benefit.

"Hmm … Yes, I've heard the same. Send up the girl at the desk on your way out."

A dismissal if I've ever heard one. It is almost laughable, how I am king and yet with Bexley, she acts like the ruler. But there's nothing more I'll get from her at this point, anyway. I rise from my seat. "You should be careful. There is more poison circulating than we originally thought, and it is too easy to become a victim." I know firsthand.

"Do not concern yourself with *my* safety. Focus on your own. Your city is overflowing with strangers from all over Islor ahead of this reckless wedding. Mortals are disappearing every day, into kennels and cages or running off into the wilds. Your lords conspire against you, and you do nothing but spy on them." She draws a long drag. "You have already lost. You just haven't realized it yet."

"It is usually a pleasure. I cannot say the same this time." My anger boils. If anyone could hear her speak to me like this, I'd be forced to punish her.

"What do you expect?" she snaps. "You've disturbed my peace and made me choose sides."

"I didn't make you do *anything*, Bexley. You just realized how much you love giving advice to a king."

Her lips curl into a sneer. "If you want my advice, *Your Highness* ... Do not become another king who wastes time playing games for allegiances you will never win. Give them a reason to fear you, or hand over your crown now."

Clouds promising rain obscure the sun by the time I emerge from the darkness of the tavern. I peer up at the window Bexley bathed in front of. Her harsh words claw at my mind. I was a commander, leading an army of soldiers, loyal to me because of my swift action. These last few weeks have been suffocating as I navigate the politics that come with the throne, trying to behave as a king would. And yet lords—even pathetic ones like Danthrin—plot right under my nose. That should be my first sign that I'm failing miserably.

The only advantage I have right now is that they think I'm blind to what's happening in the east. But will I be able to play the ignorant king through tonight's assembly?

"At least your brother had the decency to wait until dark to lurk in squalor," Boaz hisses, suddenly behind me.

Fuck, he's like a homing pigeon.

I pull my cowl forward to hide deeper. "I'm not in the mood." My voice carries enough bite to warn Boaz.

"Yes, Your Highness." He dips his head, his words curt. "I've dispatched your message with the taillok, and Prince Tyree has been moved to new quarters."

"Thank you." I take in Port Street in the afternoon. Plenty of people mill about—some visiting the shops, others lingering outside the brothels, while the rest share quiet words within small groups. It's as busy as usual, though the air is thick with apprehension. That likely has to do with the Cirilean soldiers roaming the streets. That, or the rotting corpse hanging from a light post on the corner. The *Silver Mage* arrived this morning, and the Seacadorians who arrived with it can't seem to look away.

Zander's letter said the Ybarisans used the trade routes that led here, and that there was too much poison to control. How many of these mortals have come across it already? How many already have tainted blood? Several of them could be carrying poison within their pockets as I stand here, or they could have hidden it beneath a rock. There are too many rocks in this city to look under them all.

If I were to corner each one, I'm sure their pulses would race. But how much would that be from guilt rather than fear of being questioned by the king?

At least *they* fear me.

Bexley is right, I've wasted too much time playing by the rules when no one else seems to be.

"I need you to seal the gates and port immediately, but *quietly*. Stall anyone trying to leave and let no one in. No messengers are to leave unless their letters bear my seal. Any letters that arrive are to be seized and brought to me. And if *anyone* attempts to wield their positions to contradict these orders, punish them accordingly."

"But people arrive every day ahead of the wedding and Hudem—"

"No one enters. No one leaves."

Boaz dips his head. "Your Highness."

"Also, gather your thirty most trustworthy and skilled of the guard—discreetly—and have them meet in the main stables in an hour. I must pay a visit to the soldiers outside the gate." Fates, I wish I had the Legion at my disposal. Their skill was like no other.

Boaz bows. "As you wish, Your Highness. But may I ask what this is about?"

"Reminding everyone that I am king, and this is *my* family's realm." I march for my horse.

It always smells of piss and shit down here.

My nose curls as I march along the narrow hall of the dungeon, rodents scurrying from my steady pace. Normally, a wave of pity hits me for the guards stationed in this hole, but now I feel only determination as we stop before the solid door.

"Open it and leave us," I command of the guard. "And bring a light in for her."

"Your Highness." He rattles the key in the lock and then pushes the door. It swings open with a creak. Peering in first and, I assume, satisfied by what he sees, he hangs a lantern on a hook before moving out of the way.

His heavy footfalls echo down the hall.

Wendeline sits in the corner, on her pallet. Her white-and-gold garb is gone, replaced by a torn and soiled shift. She's lost weight, her exposed arms and legs spindly. Gray-threaded hair that was normally combed neatly now hangs oily and limp. In the opposite corner, where a plate of bread and broth sit, two mice dine.

They make me think of Mika and his pocket of treasure for the castle cat.

"Was it worth it?" The weeks in the dungeon have not been kind, that much anyone can see.

Wendeline peers up at me with vacant eyes. I remember when news first reached us, of a caster arriving by ship, a baby in her arms. My father sent the guards at once to fetch them and bring them before him. He wanted to assess her intentions.

We learned of her plight—to save the elemental baby with an

affinity to Malachi. A death sentence in Ybaris. My parents welcomed them both, offered them safe haven, and positions of importance within the kingdom.

How could she knowingly lead my parents to their deaths?

My anger roils with the thought. "Would you do it again?"

"Would you like the truth or a lie?" Her voice is raspy, weak.

"I'll take that as a yes." Burn marks mar the bottoms of her feet, and a stained bandage wraps where her pinky finger is missing. Boaz said his men had only begun their work when I ordered them to stop, betting time might serve me better than dismemberment. "You did not heal yourself."

"That is not possible."

I sigh, wandering farther in. "Are you willing to talk now?"

"As I have already told your men since the first day, His Highness was innocent of all conspiracy."

"That's old news." I lean against the stone wall. "Tell me about the end of the blood curse."

Her eyes flare, but she remains quiet.

I slide out the letter, opening it, feigning to read the message already emblazoned in my mind. "Romeria and Zander have found a secret city in the Venhorn Mountains. Zander's need for blood is all but gone within it."

"Is that from Romeria?"

"And my brother." I hesitate. "Do you wish to see for yourself?"

She clears her throat. "Very much so, yes."

Maybe some goodwill will work better for me than torture. I pass it to her.

Her hands tremble as she reads, her lips moving softly over the words. "Stonekeep … Fates."

"You did not know about this."

"No." She emphasizes that with a headshake. Wendeline was always adept at veiling her feelings behind an impenetrable wall of caster ability. But now that wall is gone, revealing the turmoil within her—of surprise, hope, relief.

Of dread.

"How is it that this elemental caster they are with does?"

"Gesine spent years studying scripture. She knows more about prophecy than anyone, save for perhaps the Master Scribe herself."

"And is this *Gesine* working with Queen Neilina?"

Wendeline shakes her head. "She and Ianca escaped Neilina with the help of casters."

"Gesine *and* Ianca. There are *two* casters with them?" Fucking Tyree.

"One caster and one seer, by the time they arrived in Cirilea. I do not know what became of the seer."

"And they are working with Mordain?"

"No. Not as a whole, anyway. The guild does not even know Neilina summoned the fates for her daughter. At least, they didn't. I do not know what truths have reached them now."

"Not enough, seeing as they have joined forces with Ybaris to march south. That or they do not care, so long as Islor suffers."

Wendeline shakes her head. "Mordain is bound to Ybaris by need, not by loyalty. It has always been the way. It will continue to be the way as long as Neilina sits on that throne."

Interesting. But not important now. "What does it mean that this secret city is tied to the nymphs?"

"I do not know."

"But you fear it."

"I fear much these days, Your Highness." She trembles. Maybe from the cold, but Wendeline always did seem on edge. "Has the poison truly reached Cirilea so abundantly?"

"The corpses of mortals I've had to punish would suggest so, yes. How does it feel to know *you* had a hand in so many deaths?"

She flinches. "I did not see another way."

"And sacrificing the lives of your fellow sisters in the sanctum?"

"I told Boaz they were innocent—"

"They're all dead. The sanctum sits empty now." A decision I abhorred, but one I had to make all the same. Perhaps that also fuels my anger toward this caster.

A tear rolls down her cheek. "They had no part in this," she whispers.

"You left me no choice." I nod toward the letter. "But perhaps you see a new choice in front of you. One that will offer some shred of redemption for all your treachery."

Wendeline's focus shifts to the bottom of the page. "Will you spare them? The tainted mortals?"

"Why? Because *Romeria* has asked it of me? Zander acquiesced to her requests and look where that got him." I will not make his same mistakes. But I will also not be too big a fool not to use this caster to my benefit. "Can you mark the mortals in the way she suggested?"

"It should not cause me difficulty."

"Then it seems keeping you alive might serve a purpose after all."

She looks up and in her eyes is a tiny spark of hope. "Yes, I would be happy to. Thank you for allowing me the opportunity to serve Islor again."

I push aside any twinge of regret for what she must have gone through under Boaz's blade. She truly believes her actions were necessary. "In exchange for that service, I will have you moved somewhere more comfortable. But you will not move freely."

"I would never expect that much leniency, Your Highness."

"Good. And listen to me very carefully, Wendeline …" I move in, crouching to her level. "If you do not mark every single mortal accordingly, if you do *anything* that suggests betrayal, it will be the mortals who accept punishment on your behalf. *Any* mortal. I will make you watch, and you will beg for your own death by the time we are finished." My easy smile clashes with my promise. I will not make the same mistake as my brother did.

Her throat bobs with a hard swallow as she passes the letter back, her hand trembling. "I have never wished you or your family harm."

"And yet your actions have told an entirely different story." I move away, turning to leave.

"She is not Princess Romeria."

I falter. "Who is she, then?"

"A pawn, as we all have become. But she is someone who does not wish to see Islor fall, and who loves your brother dearly."

"Neither of those things matter." I move swiftly from her cell. "Take her to the east wing. Have the servants clean her up. Do not leave her unguarded for even a second."

"Your Highness."

A single cough sounds, somewhere in the depths of this misery. "How many prisoners do we currently hold?"

"A dozen."

"Have them loaded into a wagon and readied for travel to front lines where they may be of more use." We will need these cells soon.

"And the tainted tributary? Should I send her to the block?"

Yes. I know that's the right order, the only one that should suffice. But Gracen's request fills my thoughts. Between that and Romeria's claims—however wild they may be—I cannot utter it. "Bring me to her cell."

28
GRACEN

"You are drunk, little one." I chuckle as my nipple slips free of Suri's mouth, her eyes rolled back in her head as she drifts off, sated. I place her into her basket to sleep and set to washing my skin at the basin with a cloth and soap. The smell of sour milk—however faint—always curls my stomach.

A gentle knock sounds on my door as I've just finished up. "Come in," I call out, expecting one of the staff girls or Corrin.

I turn to find Kazimir standing in my doorway, his attention locked on where my fingers work at my buttons.

After a moment of stupor, he clears his throat, drops his gaze to study his boots.

"Why are you here?" My cheeks blaze as I quickly finish.

"Why else? The king wants you."

"Excuse me?"

Kazimir's lips curl with a devious smile. "He wants you to be tested."

"*Tested*. How?"

The smile slips off. "You follow the king's orders. You don't question them."

"Of course. I wasn't questioning him. I just …" I let my excuses fade.

"Bring the baby. Where are your other children?" He looks around as if they're hiding somewhere in our tiny room.

"In the cellar, helping sort for the winter." With trepidation, I collect the basket and follow Kazimir out.

"I wish I could sleep like that."

"I'm sure you did once, long ago."

I feel his gaze on me, but I ignore it, my cheeks burning again at the thought of what he saw of me. Kazimir is attractive, there's no denying that. But if I'm going to pine secretly for any Islorian male, it's not him.

A guard stands in front of the servant dining hall.

"These two," Kazimir announces, and the guard opens the door. "Go on." He goads me forward.

Sitting at one of the long tables is a face I was not expecting to see ever again.

"Priestess!" I exclaim, a mixture of relief and shock mixed in with my voice.

She smiles. A sad one, but it seems genuine. "The baker with the little boy whose hand was burned. I'm so glad to know that you and your baby are safe."

I move in and take the seat she pats next to her.

"What was your name again?"

"Gracen."

"That's right." She's so much thinner than the day I saw her in the sanctum, her cheeks hollowed, her skin pale. And her hand … it's wrapped in bandages. She seems nervous.

"Are you well?"

"Much better now, thank you for asking. And who is this beautiful new child?"

"Her name is Suri."

"Lovely choice." She tips her head to regard Suri's still form, an odd peace passing over her.

"You have much work to do, Priestess," Kazimir stands at the door, waiting.

"Yes. Of course. Your hand?" She holds hers out, palm up.

I slide mine into it.

"You must remain still for me, please. This will sting a little but only for a moment." She holds her injured hand over mine and closes her eyes.

Heat seers into my flesh, my jaw clenching from the burn. But it's gone as quickly as it came.

"There." She releases my hand. "Now you are marked."

A dull brown symbol fills the fleshy part of my thumb—a circle with two interlocked crescent moons. I'd heard about this. "Wait, does this mean—" Panic stirs inside me as I look from it to her. "Have I been—"

"No." She smiles reassuringly. "But if you were to be infected, it would glow and that would serve as a warning not to take your vein."

My shoulders sink.

"Do the baby too," Kazimir says. "You said your other two were in the cellars?"

"Yes."

A frown flitters across Wendeline's face. "I hate to wake a sleeping baby."

And she certainly will. "Wait. Can she mark the other two first? Suri will be screaming after this, and if they see that … It will make things easier for all of us if they go first."

Kazimir sighs heavily. "Wait here." He ducks out, sending the guard in to watch over us. As if a baker, a newborn, and a tortured priestess are intent to conspire.

A tense energy lingers in the room.

Wendeline swallows. "How was the childbirth?"

"How it *always* is. Difficult."

"I cannot imagine. Will you allow me to offer you aid?" She reaches out but then freezes, checking for my reaction. "Only if you would like it."

"Of course. I'm on the mend, but speeding it up would be great."

She sets her healing hand over my abdomen. Almost instantly, a calm floods my body, soothing dull aches and twinges of discomfort. "There … that should have sped things along nicely."

"Thank you."

"I did not realize how much I missed using my gift for others. So thank *you*."

I remember the day in the sanctum, when the priestess settled her hand on my swollen belly and confirmed the baby inside was progressing well. "Could you tell me … I mean, she *seems* to be fine, but you never do know, do you?" There are plenty of stories of healthy babies who go to sleep in their cradles and never wake up. If there is something to be seen, perhaps the caster could fix it?

"The baby? Oh, certainly." Wendeline sets a hand over Suri's chest and closes her eyes again.

I watch her serene face as I did all those weeks ago.

Suddenly, her eyes flash open, shock in them.

"What is it? Is something wrong with her?"

"*No.*" She punctuates that with a headshake, schooling her expression. "She is perfectly fine. Healthy and strong. And *perfect*." She peers down at Suri. "Tell me, when was she born?"

"Uh … it's not even been a fortnight yet."

"A fortnight," she echoes, and her thoughts seem to drift.

"Why?"

"Oh, no reason, I was merely curious—"

The door flies open.

"What need do you have of them?" Corrin demands to know as Kazimir leads Mika and Lilou in, the lady's maid on their heels.

"King's orders," he throws over his shoulder before disregarding her. "I know this one's yours. What about this other one?"

"Priestess!" Mika exclaims, his face lighting up as he rushes forward. "I haven't seen you in so long!"

"It has been awhile." Wendeline laughs, taking him in. "And how is that hand of yours?"

He holds it up and flexes it open and closed in proof. "Can't even tell no more. I can climb trees again."

"And trellises up the castle wall," Corrin adds, accusation in her tone.

"That is wonderful news. Can I see it more closely for a moment?" Wendeline holds out her palm.

He readily agrees, slapping his hand into hers.

"See? It's almost as good as new!"

"*Almost*. I'm here to make it *even* better. Now, I must add something to your hand, and you must remain very still, okay?"

"Add something?" His face scrunches up. "Like another finger?"

"What need is there for this when I'm not a tributary and they are *far* too young?" Corrin scowls at the dull mark on her hand, her words obscured by Suri's shrill screams. Beside Corrin, Lilou sobs. Mika is the only one unbothered by the momentary burn, holding his hand out in front of him to admire his new brand. Gesine placed it over his scar, partially hiding it.

"All mortals within the castle are to see the priestess for their test today, without exception," Kazimir says with forced patience. "Take the kids back to sorting in the cellar. Gracen, the king seeks an audience with you."

"Again?" I only just saw him this morning, not that I'm going to complain. But why? My heart races with a mixture of excitement and trepidation.

"Yes. *Again*." He scowls at the baby in my arms. "Can you make it go back to sleep now?"

Corrin shakes her head at him. "Here. I will take her."

"Please. Allow me," a voice calls out.

As one, we turn, a round of exclamations escaping us as Sabrina approaches along the hall, smiling sheepishly. Gone is the finery she wore as the king's tributary. Now, she dons a modest dove-gray dress—typical household garb. On her hand is the same symbol as ours, but it glows a brilliant silver, impossible to miss.

"When did they let you out?" I burst.

"Not long ago." She collects a wailing Suri from my arms. "Shh ..." She croons, rocking her. "It's okay. I know what it's like to be scared. I was so scared too." She peers up at me with glossy blue eyes. "The king came to visit me in my cell. He said you spoke on my behalf."

"I did, but ..." I didn't think it would matter. Atticus listened to me?

"Come on, the king does not wait for anyone," Kazimir urges.

"I'll get her settled again." A tear rolls down her cheek. "Thank you, Gracen."

With a squeeze of her forearm and a warning to my other two to be good, I follow the captain down the hall and up the stairs, smoothing my hands over my dress as best I can, wishing I'd had time to fix myself.

Kazimir leads me down the same great hall he did last night, only where before it was vacant, now lords and ladies and a few tributaries linger. They pay no attention to me as we pass, which I'm thankful for.

The two guards at the bottom of the grand staircase that leads to Atticus's chambers don't question us, don't even flinch, as we pass.

"How is the king?"

"He's been better. There is a lot going on in the kingdom, and none of it is good. Plus, as you well know, his last tributary was tainted, so he suffers. Headaches, weakness, and the like."

"Why has he not taken a new one yet?" I've heard there are still a few in the castle to choose from.

"He would not risk another guard's life, so he has abstained. Now, thanks to the priestess's help, he no longer needs a sampler."

I look at the dull brand on my hand. *The king wants you.* That was what Kazimir said earlier. I knew this was coming. Atticus hinted last night. A wild mix of emotions hits me—of fear stirred by long nights and painful memories, of nervousness that in the end, I will not please him.

What will it be like to be the king's tributary?

"Is it really such a bad thing?" Kazimir asks. He must sense the swirl of anxiety.

"From my experience? Yes."

"You seem like an intelligent mortal, Gracen." Kazimir's leather boots scuff the stone steps. "I think you can tell by now that Atticus is not like that other keeper of yours."

But what if he is? that little voice inside my head asks. What if it's all been an act up until now? I've seen these Islorians, with their impeccable manners and serene personas, turn into something entirely different.

I've seen it *many* times.

Just the thought of Atticus turning into one of them, after charming me so thoroughly ... my chest tightens.

Kazimir knocks on the door but doesn't wait for a response before opening it. "You know your way." With a wink, he pulls the door closed behind me.

My heart pounds in my throat as I pass through the living area, as opulent and grand in daylight as it was by candlelight. "Hello?" I call out, my voice wavering.

There is no answer, so I continue on, through the open doors to his bedchamber—a fancy room of mostly black but with hints of gilt, mainly on the trim and molding along the walls. An enormous feather bed centered along one wall. A fireplace in the corner sits cold, the smell of soot lingering in the air.

The room is empty.

A solemn figure stands on the terrace, his back to me, his hands braced on either side of the stone wall. Atticus has changed into his king's finery, his tailored black jacket fitted to his powerful frame, his sword at his hip.

His gold crown dangling from a finger, as if nothing more than a trinket.

This is not what I was expecting. Sabrina described a *very* different scenario when he called on her.

I step out, wrapping my arms around my chest to ward off the cold. Heavy cloud has rolled in, and the rain will surely start soon. "You wanted to see me, Your Highness?" My pulse races.

"I remember being in awe of this view as a child." His voice doesn't carry the same usual lilt of humor that I've come to recognize, that it held earlier today when he was flirting mercilessly with me in the square.

I edge over, taking up a place beside him. My breath catches at the expanse of land. "It is a spectacular view." I saw the royal garden for the first time this morning, and now I see it from above, the meandering paths disappearing into lush foliage and flowers. It is stunning, but it is nothing compared to the sight beyond Cirilea's towering wall, of rolling hills as far as one can see.

"You traveled through these lands to get here, did you not?"

"Yes, but I didn't see any of it. We sat in a covered wagon with the barrels of mead."

"I am afraid there will be a day very soon when I shall not be able to see it from this perch anymore."

I steal a glance at his profile. There isn't an angle of him that isn't handsome. "Kazimir said you are weighed down by dark thoughts."

"Dark thoughts." He chuckles. "That is one way to describe what sits in my mind."

"About the future queen?" *And the fact that she tried to kill you?*

"Saoirse is the least of my worries. She is not as smart as she thinks she is."

But clearly, he has many worries. I hesitate. "It can help to talk about it. Sometimes, solutions reveal themselves when you lay out your problems." My mother always used to tell me that. I wonder if she's still alive. I've heard of tributaries keeping in touch with their families, but Lord Danthrin never allowed it.

Atticus turns to give me his full attention. "*You* wish to help solve my problems for me?" A sly, crooked smile curves his lips.

My cheeks flush from embarrassment. "I mean, not *me*, of course. I don't know anything of politics and kingly duties. I'm merely a mortal baker—"

"The eastern lords are plotting to divide Islor and claim those lands as their own," he says, cutting off my stammering. "Lord Adley of Kettling aims to establish himself as the new ruler."

"New ruler." My jaw drops. "But that is treason! And why, when you are already marrying his daughter? She will be queen of Islor." Fates help us.

"I would hazard Adley knows the plans of the east are too far gone to be stalled. He would rather rule both halves than only one, and he is feeling the pressure to ensure that happens."

"How can he do that? *You* are the king. *You* command the armies."

"Armies with soldiers who seemed keen to follow me when I was on a horse in front of them. Now that I'm a spectator over the lands, they follow others." Atticus studies the onyx stone in his crown. "I can see now why my father named me, his son, commander and sent me out there to lead. Unfortunately, I do not have a son of my own to send, to trust," he says, more to himself. "Lord Adley is adept at spinning stories. Who knows what sorts of lies have infected the ranks of the eastern soldiers, about the future of Islor with this poison circulating."

"What can be done to stop this?"

"Things that my father and brother were unwilling to do. Things that may add to the turmoil gripping Islor at a time when we cannot afford more."

I can't fathom what he may mean, but I doubt it bodes well for these eastern lords. "And if this Lord Adley answers for his crimes, I imagine someone else will quickly take his place."

"See? You do know something of politics." Atticus flashes a

dimpled smile that makes my heart jump, despite the topic. "And you are already lightening those dark thoughts of mine, just by being here. Come, the rain is about to fall." He guides me into his bedchamber with a hand on the small of my back.

My heart races under his touch.

"How was your visit with the priestess?"

I study the mark on my hand. "I was glad to see her. *Surprised,* but glad."

"Did she say anything of interest?"

"Just that she was happy to be of use again." It's what she didn't say that struck me. I can't shake the look on her face when she checked Suri for ailments. She was hiding something from me. I don't know what, but I don't want to cause her unnecessary problems by mentioning that to Atticus. "I was even more glad to see Sabrina."

"Yes, I'm sure I will hear about my decision to release her before long." He tosses his crown onto a side chair as if it's a common hat. "But she was tainted because she was *my* tributary. How could I execute her for it?"

"You're the king. You *could* have, very easily." He has time and time again. I haven't been outside the castle walls since I arrived, but I've heard the terrible rumors, of the corpses that hang in warning to all. "If it means anything, I am so happy you showed her mercy." I hesitate. "Thank you, Atticus."

"If I'm being honest, it was a selfish decision on my part. Now you have someone to help mind those children of yours when you are otherwise indisposed. Especially that mischievous boy."

"He will have her running through the entire castle before long," I joke, but his words catch. When I'm otherwise indisposed.

He closes in with measured steps, to collect my hand and study the mark. "It is not as obtrusive as I thought it might be."

My pulse races. "No, though I imagine it will take some getting used to."

His thumb strokes over the lines. "Why are you so troubled, Gracen?"

Of course he can read my anxiety. I focus on his lapel. "Because I know why you've summoned me here."

"And you do not wish to give it to me." It's a statement, rather than a question.

"It's not that, it's just …" My words drift.

"Corrin paid me a visit."

My eyes widen. "She did?"

He chuckles, but the sound falls off with a serious look. "She told me a few things about your previous keeper. About what he did to you. What he made you do."

I sigh, feeling my cheeks flush. "I shared those in confidence."

"She didn't go into too much detail. But enough. He was cruel."

"Yes." A tremble courses through my body. "Danthrin was never gentle, and he always took too much." Of everything. Of me. "I can't say how many times I blacked out afterward and was punished for it. The other men he let feed off me were even less gentle." Silence meets my confession. I dare peer up into those blue eyes, lined with a heavy fringe, to see fury.

"If I had known this before, he never would have walked free." He reaches up to stroke my cheek with the soft pad of his thumb, pulling away to reveal a dusting of white powder.

I laugh. That's the second time today I've met the king with flour on my cheek. My dress has smears of lard on it. Who knows what the rest of me looks like. Certainly not a groomed and delicate king's tributary. "Why me?"

His hand finds the underside of my chin and lifts it until I meet his gaze again. "I can feel your pulse, Gracen." He steps in closer until we are a hair-width apart. "When I stand this close to you, I can feel how your body reacts to me."

Another wave of embarrassment hits, even as my desire stirs. "Surely you would find that same reaction in *any* mortal you approach." Especially any female.

"Yes, most." His breath skates over my face with his chuckle. "But I don't want *any* mortal. You are my choice."

His blunt declaration stirs every nerve ending in my body. But quickly chasing it is a wave of fear. He's the king, and he's been kind to me. If I deny him, will he punish me? But if I say yes, the same worry stirs: Will he change into someone else? Someone to loathe?

I may be his choice, but *I* have no choice in the matter. I'm fooling myself if I think otherwise. I reach up to unbutton the top of my dress and push the linen past my shoulder. Cool air grazes my bare skin, stirring gooseflesh, as I grant him access.

He takes it immediately, his grip seizing my nape, guiding my head back, exposing my neck to his mouth. His soft lips graze my flesh where my pulse pounds like an invitation, and I brace myself for the sharp pain.

Only it doesn't come, his featherlight kisses continuing up, along my jawline, over my cheek, until his mouth meets mine. Shivers skitter down my spine as he angles my head, deepening the kiss. I let my lips fall open and his tongue is there in an instant, sliding over mine with teasing strokes that pull a moan from my throat and coax me closer to him, my fingers trailing over his biceps for purchase, the gold threads of his king's finery lingering beneath my touch.

I've never been kissed by *anyone* like this.

"You may go," he whispers against my mouth before releasing me and stepping away, his breathing ragged.

"What? But …" My hand fumbles toward my dress, only to discover he already adjusted the collar and refastened the buttons without my notice, while I was so deeply entranced by his mouth. "Have I done something to upset you?"

"No, you've done nothing wrong, Gracen." He punctuates that with a headshake, reaching up to stroke my cheek with his thumb. "But I know you were relieved to not serve as tributary anymore, and I will not take something from you that you do not wish to give."

Knuckles rap on the outer door, and Kazimir steps in. "I apologize, Your Highness, but the assembly is gathered and growing anxious."

"Perfect timing." Atticus presses his fingers against his temple. He is suffering, Kazimir had said.

Is he feeling weak? Atticus can't afford to be weak now, not with all he told me.

"A guard will escort you back to the servants' hall." He offers me a bland, tired smile. "You should go now."

"Yes, Your Highness." I rush out, passing a sulking Kazimir.

My head spins with a medley of emotions I don't understand, and none of them are relief.

29
ROMERIA

"Should I put my face on it?"

Zander pauses in his search to give me his attention. "Should you put your face on *what*?"

I hold up a gold coin. It has Ulysede's emblem on one side and the nymph's swirling scrawl on the other. "Where I come from, when they mint money, they put the faces of rulers on their coins. Some countries have king and queens. Mine has dead presidents."

Zander chuckles, shaking his head as he continues his search. "For someone who did not want to be queen, you are readily embracing the role."

"Does the vault in Cirilea have this much wealth in it too?"

"Why? You want to rob me, thief?"

"This one's got jokes today." I toss the coin at his back. It bounces off him and lands with a clunk on the stone floor. "As if I need more." There are countless chests full of coin within the long and narrow room beneath the castle, along with gilded weapons and household wares—goblets and platters and candlesticks—and solid gold busts of people Zander doesn't recognize sitting on stands around the outskirts. An enormous, gilded mirror leans against the wall across from me.

And then there are the jewels. Crates of rubies and emeralds and sapphires—some cast in gaudy rings and elaborate necklaces, others raw. I inspect one—a ruby that has to be at least twenty-five carats. My old pawnshop dealer, Skully, would drool over this. "It seems ironic, doesn't it? The nymphs could have made my crown out of anything and yet they made it out of what looks like silver bones." Sharp enough to draw blood.

"Perhaps the nymphs don't value gold and jewels."

"Why have this vault full of it, then?"

"Currency, for those who do value it."

"Yeah, I guess that makes sense." I sidle up beside him. "What are you looking for, anyway?"

"I hoped there might be a token from the fates here. Something that could be of use to us in Soldor. But there is nothing." He tosses a gold dagger back into the crate, his shoulders sinking with disappointment. "I should prepare. We need to leave soon if we are to meet Radomir's men."

The knot in my stomach that's been present since this morning coils tighter. "I don't like this."

"What don't you like?"

"You, going into that mountain for thirty-six hours with soldiers who were our enemies only days ago … us being apart. You fighting at the rift. Take your pick."

"You are the one who forged this alliance. You keep telling me I do not trust enough."

"I don't trust anyone with you. You're my heart."

He reaches up to stroke a strand of hair off my forehead. "There comes a time when you either trust those who stand beside you or you do not. There is no in-between anymore, no wavering at a line. We are heading into war, and we all must have faith in each other now."

I sigh. "You're right."

"But the Legion will be with me, and you can be sure Abarrane will be watching my back." Zander's hands settle onto my shoulders with a gentle touch. "And you cannot go through Soldor with me. We will be as close to the rift as we can get without being inside it. You would draw in every beast around and put us at far greater risk."

"I know." I hate it, but I know. "I wish you didn't have to leave, but I understand why you have to."

"And I wish you didn't have to stay, but I understand why you have to." His thumbs stroke my shoulders. "Gesine is right. You need to learn whatever you can from Lucretia."

"What if she's gone?" Zander and I went down to the crypt together earlier, but the sylx didn't show herself, even after Zander's taunts and my royal demand as her queen.

It felt so empty in there.

"She's not gone. She's playing games, for whatever reason. When she does return, don't let her leave until she's answered every question you have about the nymphs. And don't go alone. Bring Jarek with you."

"Good idea. She *likes* him. Maybe he can draw her out." I sink into his chest, inhaling his scent. "And then Gesine can teach me how to fly so I can come to you."

He chuckles, folding his arms around me, cocooning me in his warmth. "I do not know if casters can actually fly, but if anyone can figure it out, it will be you."

I revel in the silence and privacy, even as panic surges inside.

Somewhere above us, two hundred and fifty-four Ybarisans, now dressed in armor with two intersecting crescent moons on their chests, prepare to hold the rift beside us.

You hope, that little voice inside my head reminds me.

They strap extra weapons and shields and helms to their horses, enough for three hundred saplings to wear as they prepare to go to battle with us.

You hope.

They will all ride alongside a thousand Islorians, who will accept this alliance and Zander as the true king of Islor.

You hope.

And what if all that happens, and yet it still doesn't matter?

Hudem is in three days. On that night, what we've done—what I've done—will be obvious to all, for better or worse.

What if this is the last time we hold each other like this?

"Come back to me," I whisper, a tear slipping free. "I can't live in this world without you."

He releases me, only to lean in, pressing his forehead against mine. "I know the feeling." His voice has turned hoarse.

I stare through the sheen, into his light hazel irises, struggling to pick out the flecks of gold, afraid I'm about to crumble. Once, not that long ago, those same eyes were full of hatred when they landed on me. It seems impossible now. "Remember when you wanted me dead?"

A muscle in his jaw ticks. "No." The faintest touch of humor laces that single word.

"Oh, come on, remember? In the tower that night, when you had me up against the wall—"

Zander moves so quickly, the next thing I know, there's stone against my back and his hard body is pressed against my front. His hand cradles my head. "I have no idea what you're talking about." His lips catch mine, coaxing them open, his tongue slipping in to bait with expert strokes. It's the kind of kiss that *always* leads to more.

I break free long enough to whisper, "Really? You tried to take away my ring—"

He cuts me off with a deeper kiss, and I abandon my teasing, tipping my head to give him better access.

If this is the last time ...

No. I won't think like that.

His fingers curl around a fistful of my hair, his affection turning urgent. I respond in kind, seizing his bottom lip between my teeth, sucking on it, earning his guttural groan.

His hands grip my hips, pulling them against his, allowing me to feel the hard length of him against my belly.

"Now." The single word is all I can manage, as I claw at his tunic, yanking it out from its safety within his breeches, uncovering the hard expanse of muscle over his torso. We break free long enough for him to help me pull it over his head and toss it to the floor, and then his mouth is crashing into mine again, both our fingers fumbling with buttons and buckles, unable to unfasten things fast enough. Sword belts tumble and boots are kicked off, and then he's lying me down on the pile of clothes. The stone beneath us is jagged and hard, but all I feel is Zander's breath skating along my skin as his lips find my neck, my collarbone, my breasts. I arch my back into his mouth as his teeth scrape against a nipple.

"I promise you, we will see each other again," he whispers, settling his delicious weight onto my waiting body. The ache building inside me is too much, and I cry out as he sinks into me, my fingernails dragging across the expanse of muscle over his back, pulling him closer to me.

"There is no queen …" His hand slips beneath my head to cradle it, protecting it from the stone. "Or fate …" His hips begin to thrust. "Or army who can keep me from you." Raw desire burns in his eyes as they lock with mine, holding them. Our bodies move in sync, the only sound within this vault of riches beneath the castle the tangle of our breaths, and for a few last moments, all my fear and worries about what comes next fade away.

The two lines move parallel to one another across the arid soil toward the valley, but the gap between them yawns.

"Have we made a mistake?" We've dressed the Ybarisans in Ulysede's armor, the polished golden metal gleaming in the waning sun. But they are still Ybarisans. I know it, they know it, and Telor's men certainly know it.

"Even if it is, this is our best hope." Zander looks on from beside me at the gate, his horse readied for him to join shortly. The legionaries sit on their horses, waiting.

"How much longer, Gesine?" Zander asks. "I cannot wait here all night."

"It is almost here." Her gaze scours the sky as she shares the taillok's vision.

I search above as well, but not for the messenger bird. "Any sign of the dragon?" It would be hard for a creature that size to hide.

Horik shakes his head. "No one has seen a hint of it since last night."

"It has likely flown back into the rift." Zander smooths a hand over my shoulder. "Either way, you should be safe in here."

"I'm not worried about me."

"There!" Gesine points at a shimmering body sailing through the air, before abruptly diving. With a single warning screech that makes us all cringe, the taillok lands at her feet. It stands still as Gesine unfastens the letter attached to its leg. She hands it to Zander.

Zander stares at the seal—*his* seal—a long moment before snapping it open. His jaw tenses as he reads it.

"What does it say?"

He hands it to me without a word.

Looking forward to our next game of draughts. Atticus.

"What the hell does that mean?"

"That he will never trust anything you say."

I grit my teeth. "There's a war coming. We're trying to help him, and he's still hung up on that?" I wave the letter, anger flaring. "And *I* did not sleep with him!"

Horik's bushy eyebrows pop.

I sigh, trying to calm my frustration. "Your brother is an idiot."

Zander's mouth twitches. "Yes, he is. But we have honored Islor with our attempt to aid him. Now, his mistakes are his own."

Gesine guides the taillok into its cage and pulls the cloth over, then sighs heavily. "Thank the fates that is over for now." She rubs her temple as if a headache pains her.

"I expect the taillok to find me at the second dawn with an

update from Romeria," Zander declares, "and I will swiftly send a message in return."

"I will ensure it arrives safely to you. Now, I have found an entire section in the library on mythical beasts, so if you have no other need for me, I will bid you farewell, Your Highness." She bows and then meets Zander's eyes. "Stay safe, and perhaps we will meet again."

He watches the caster as she glides away, but I can't read that look. She's been at our side every day since we met her in the apothecary, and he's expressed every emotion for her from open hostility to tepid alliance, but never trust. Given her connection to Mordain, that may be forever a lost cause.

"The queen will be safe within these gates. On my honor," Jarek promises, offering Zander a curt bow before stepping away. Horik, Zorya, and Loth follow his lead, giving us space to say our goodbyes.

The painful knot in my throat flares as I reach for Zander's hand, squeezing it. "The taillok will be there in two mornings. Promise you will be too."

"With everything in my power, I will be there." He pulls my body into his in a rare show of public affection. "If you learn of anything from Lucretia, however insignificant it may seem, share it with me."

"I will."

He leans down until our foreheads touch, his jaw clenching. "You dwell not only in my every waking thought but also in my dreams. And we will see each other again, soon."

Tears slip and I don't bother to wipe them away. Let Abarrane mock me if she dares. "You *will* see me again. In, like, three days, when I learn how to fly."

His chuckles break the tense moment, and then his mouth crashes into mine, abandoning all his kingly decorum to kiss me deeply.

I cling to his shoulders and savor the taste and feel of his tongue against mine for as long as I can, until he tears his mouth free and pulls away, stepping back.

Our fingertips are the last to touch.

And then he's in his saddle and his horse is cantering away to join the others.

My tears flow freely as I watch the small company ride off, Elisaf and Abarrane at Zander's flanks, and I feel like part of my heart is riding off with them. The part that keeps me alive.

A dull whack against the back of my knees has me howling and spinning around, fury twisting my features. "What?"

"Come on." Jarek twirls his blade. "Time to train."

30
AGATHA

"A secret city in Islor's mountains." Allegra repeats my words.

"Yes. That is what the taillok saw."

Her eyes flare, but she tempers her shocked expression, glancing around to ensure no one is listening. We're high in the parapets, with a bird's-eye view of Nyos and the port below, where the ships prepare passage of our casters to join Ybaris's war. "Okay, tell me what Yesenia saw."

"What did she *actually* see? Or what did she tell the queen she saw?" I relay Lorel's words. "Yesenia and Gesine are friends. I will wager she helped with the escape."

"So she might hold back details."

"If they could prove harmful to our cause, yes." Namely, that the Princess Romeria at the gates is no longer her daughter.

That she is a key caster.

"I am sure it must be this Ulysede." My whisper is full of excitement. That single word scrawled in a rush on the bottom of Gesine's letter. It all makes sense.

"Do not sound so thrilled, Agatha!" Allegra hisses, her panic rising. "Stonekeep was a wall of nymph scripture and now it is a city, and we must assume the *key caster* opened it. Can you appreciate what this means?"

"Far more than anyone else in Nyos." An edge lines my tone. "The nymphs will walk these lands again in the time of the casters. It is prophecy."

"And what else might walk alongside them?" The Second paces. "We cannot wait for a response from Gesine any longer."

"And what would you recommend we do, then? Go to the council with this?"

"Fates, no." She scoffs. "Lorel will run to the queen and blame us. The queen will execute us for treason and use the elementals to summon the fates again. No, that is not a choice we can consider." She shakes her head to emphasize her words, her gaze narrowed on the ships below. "There is no other choice. We must go to this Ulysede ourselves." She spins, her finger pointed. "*You* must go."

"*Me*?" I laugh. She *must* be joking. "I cannot leave Nyos."

"Why not? You have gone on excursions, all across Ybaris and Skatrana. You were even in Seacadore once."

"Yes, *many* years ago. Besides, the Prime has assigned me a task of sifting through prophecy for answers."

"Which you have no plans to give her, anyway."

"But if I leave, she will grow suspicious."

"This is a task she has given to you in secrecy, yes? I am not supposed to know about it."

"Yes."

Allegra bites her bottom lip in thought, and my fear swells. What web is her deceptive little mind weaving? "As a Second, I order you to escort my two elementals to Argon. The Prime cannot counter that without an explanation, one she will not wish to give. There, you will find Yesenia, glean what more you can from her, and then, instead of returning to Nyos, you will make your way to the rift with the caravan. When they cross, you go west."

"But … but …" I sputter. "I am eight decades old, Allegra! I am no longer built for traipsing across the realms, especially not in the middle of a war!"

"Exactly. An old scribe. No one will find threat in you. And you are not as feeble as you paint yourself to be." Allegra closes in, her face earnest. "There is no one else who knows more about prophecy than you. Mordain needs a bridge to Ulysede."

"Gesine is that bridge."

"No, Gesine is an elemental caster who could go through the change at any time."

"Yes, and *I* could go through the change of old age at any time. From breathing to *not*!" It takes hours for my joints to unstiffen in the mornings. How long before my body decides it's had enough?

She scoffs. "You are as healthy as an ox. *You* are the bridge. You have been since the day Mordain learned of Neilina's breach. All of this was possible because of you." Her lips twist. "Or you can spend the rest of your days in Nyos, dwelling in dusty books, reading about prophecy instead of witnessing it unfold."

The prospect of seeing this nymph kingdom, of meeting this key caster, *is* enticing. *If* I can make it there. "This is not how I expected my day to turn."

She sets a hand on my shoulder. "The ship leaves in an hour for Argon. You must pack."

"Protect our scribes at all costs." I wrap the tome in parchment to safeguard it from the elements, and stuff it into my rucksack with three others—the only books in all of Nyos that hint of the Queen for All and the nymphs' token. I know it is wrong to remove these from our libraries, but for now, the safest place for them is with me. "When the Prime begins to suspect the truth and questions you, you must tell her that I have acted alone in this."

"Yes, Master Scribe." Zaleria dips her head.

"*You* are Master Scribe now, by my wishes if not Lorel's appointment soon enough." The caster was a gangly prepubescent when I was already collecting information from my first seer, but decades later, we've formed a loyal bond—part mentor-mentee, but mostly in our devotion to prophecy. Zaleria was the first I approached when news of Ianca's summoning reached my ears.

"Until your return."

I take in my office one last time, my haven for so many years. I will not likely see these walls again, but this is to be my path.

A knock sounds at the door. Cahill hovers. "Are you goin' somewhere, Master Scribe?"

A sting pricks my chest. I've left Nyos on adventures before and come back to caster children who were grown by years. This time is different. This is likely goodbye. I wish I had more time, but perhaps it's for the best. "Just to Argon, to escort the elementals. I must leave now if I am to catch the ship." I heave my bag onto my shoulders. My old bones scream with protest as I make my way to the door, pausing long enough to collect Cahill's hands in mine. "You shall listen to what Caster Zaleria tells you to do. Her above anyone else, do you hear me?"

His pale green eyes shift to the slight caster with olive skin and gray threaded through her black hair. "Yes, Master Scribe."

"And the pendant I gave you … it remains where it is, out of sight, always."

He nods, his face splitting with a wide grin that shows off his dimples. "I know, Master Scribe."

"Good boy."

I meet Zaleria's gaze and she nods. I don't have to say the words out loud for her to hear them.

Protect him.

And when it's time, guide him.

31
ATTICUS

"Let me understand this. She offered her vein, and you *refused* it?" Kazimir's whisper is harsh, his pace steady with mine as we march toward my throne room.

"She offered it because she felt she had to, not because she wanted to."

"You are the king. Did you expect her to refuse?"

"No. I expected ... I don't know what I expected." A filthy little fantasy has been lingering in my thoughts since the night in her servants' quarter, of the demure mortal pushing me backward onto my bed and claiming me. But that's likely all that will ever be—a fantasy. Despite all the pressing matters that weigh on me, I haven't been able to shake Corrin's warning words from earlier, of all the ways Lord Danthrin defiled and abused Gracen.

It's a wonder she can even stand to be in a room with me, her keeper.

But that kiss we just shared ... that was *something*. Intoxicating and urgent. The conflicting stir inside her says she felt it too.

"They cannot all be like Sabrina. And fates knows what that last keeper did to her. I told you what I overheard."

"No, you did *not*." I glare at Kazimir. "What did he say—"

"Nothing you need to hear right now." Kazimir shakes his head. "Remember, he is our rabbit. We need him hopping."

"I haven't forgotten." Yes, hopping all the way to his co-conspirators. Adley and Spire think they can use a lowly lord from the west to scheme in plain sight and no one will be the wiser? We shall see about that.

"I know you. Do not so much as glance at Danthrin in there," Kazimir warns, his finger in the air. "Otherwise you will tip him off, and then where will we be?"

With a heavy sigh, I nod. He's right. I'm liable to murder Danthrin a thousand times with just a look.

"But you *should* have taken her vein. You would be calmer now. Stronger."

"I was so close," I admit. I had my mouth on her neck, the taste of her sweet skin and the scent of her even sweeter blood engulfing my senses. "I could not bring myself to do it."

"After this assembly, I will find a tributary—"

"No."

Kazimir's mouth gapes. "No?"

"I don't want someone else." I can't explain it. It's never happened to me before. Gracen lurks in my thoughts day and night, far more than any mortal should. Taking from someone else doesn't appeal to me.

I want her.

All of her.

He sighs, shakes his head. "I didn't take you for a masochist, but we'll deal with that later. Are you ready for *this*?" Kazimir nods toward the heavy doors ahead, where Boaz and a handful of guards wait. Beyond it, voices buzz, none the wiser. "It could get ugly. Many are angry about the gates being shut."

"Why? Where else do they have to go that's so important?" I drawl, but my humor fades instantly. "It must be done."

Boaz charges forward to meet us. "Your Highness."

"How goes Wendeline's work?"

"All mortals within the castle have been marked. None *appear* to be tainted." He emphasizes the word *appear*, to highlight the fact that he doesn't trust Wendeline and is convinced she's still trying to kill us all.

"Good. After the assembly, have her begin branding the city's mortals. She should not stop until every last one is marked. Take her door to door and bring any tainted ones to the arena." I hesitate, though I know what must be done, as distasteful as it may be. "Also, collect all children and bring them to the castle."

"*All*, Your Highness?" Boaz falters as if he might have misheard me. "Where should we put them?"

"In the west wing ballroom. They are to remain there until after Hudem."

He dips his head. "By your order."

"Now, let us take care of *this* business." I steel my spine and lift my chin.

"Be alert, stay vigilant, and act without hesitation," Boaz commands his guards as the soldiers manning the doors heave them open. The buzz inside cuts off instantly. "All rise for King Atticus Ascelin, Fifth Ruler of Islor!" he bellows, leading the entourage.

We stroll down the aisle, the only sound within the throne room the pounding of metal boots against the marble. Boaz stops front and center, grip firmly on his pommel. His hand-selected guards fan out, following suit. The assembly never has this many soldiers present, and based on the wary expressions, it's left everyone unsettled about what's going on.

Or perhaps that's their guilt revealing itself. How many are involved in this scheming?

My sword weighs on my hip. I feel the urge to draw it.

Annika sits in one of two chairs set at the bottom step, facing the rows, her eyes spitting daggers at me.

I see the news I delivered this morning about her betrothal still irks her. "Remind me not to leave my sister alone with her future husband when they meet. She's likely to slit his throat."

Kazimir snorts.

"Annika." I nod as I pass her.

"*Your Highness,*" she pushes out through gritted teeth.

With a smirk, I start to climb the steps, but then decide I should be at eye level for this. "Thank you for gathering," I begin with a fake cordial tone. But my head pounds. I'm in no mood for dancing with politics anymore. "Queen Neilina plans to cross the rift on Hudem with a great army of Ybarisans and casters, to claim Islor's lands."

A rush of voices fills the throne room as panic explodes.

"Silence!" Boaz bellows and the noise dies down.

"Your Highness, if I may." Adley steps forward, and my molars gnash. "How did you receive such concerning news?" I hear what he doesn't ask—why is he hearing about this with the general assembly and not before? As if he's entitled to private updates.

"From Queen Neilina herself," I lie without flinching, knowing that admitting the truth of my source is not an option. "Did you not see the taillok that arrived this morning?"

His expression hardens. The news that I had all day to enlighten him and I didn't will grate on his nerves.

That is the least of his worries.

"We knew this was likely coming, and we cannot ignore this threat. I have already dispatched orders to Bellcross to move for the rift immediately." Regardless of where Rengard's allegiances hang between my brother and me, he will respond to this, I know it. "As well, I have ordered Lord Telor to relocate his soldiers there."

"But Telor is hunting the exiled king and princess!" Someone in the crowd exclaims. I can't find its owner, the stir of voices drowning out anything intelligible.

I expect Boaz to bark for order again, but it is Saoirse who steps out from her place in the front row, holding her hands up for quiet. "Princess Romeria has already done all the damage she can," she hollers over the noise. The crowd quiets as they wait curiously to hear their future queen speak. "Those traitors hide in the mountains, powerless. They do not present further threat to Islor."

I wouldn't be so sure of that. What will all these lords and ladies do if one day they wake and their fangs don't drop, if the laws this realm has abided by for two thousand years no longer apply, the structure for power over mortals crumbles? They are greedy nobility, comfortable in their way of life. Will they consider this a blessing or a new curse?

I'm not even sure what *I* think about it, but I would expect rebellion—first from the mortals, and then from my kind.

"His Highness's decision to send all available soldiers north is a wise call. We must not ignore real threats from our Ybarisan enemies." She dips her head to acknowledge me and smiles.

Bravo. I resist the urge to clap at her performance. "Surely, we must not ignore real threats, Lady Saoirse. They are all around us now."

Her smile wavers.

"Yes, certainly," Adley speaks up, finding his tongue again. "The east's army stationed outside Cirilea's walls will prepare to march. I will speak to them at once, Your Highness, if you'll inform the guards at the gate to allow me passage out."

Another move I anticipated. "No need. I gave them the order several hours ago, and they have already begun their march north." Before Adley had a chance to counter my plans by doing something as foolish as sending them east to shore up defenses there.

Kettling's commander seemed startled when I rode out to greet him, the king's guard at my side. Why wasn't Adley delivering this message? He dared ask, confirming all I needed to know about where his loyalties lie. I removed him from the ranks and kept removing officers until I found one I was confident had no connection or clue as to what Adley was planning. He was quick to rally them.

Adley's eyes flare with shock and rage—at being outmaneuvered—but he smooths that over. "Wonderful news. And will you be following with Cirilea's army in the morn?"

To leave my city unguarded? "My army and I will leave as soon as justice has been served, and we will march east, to deal with Islor's other enemies. Guards." The command is soft, calm.

But they move as one, securing their targets and hauling them before me.

"What is the meaning of this!" Adley jerks against the two soldiers who secure either side of him, bringing him in line with Lords Stoll and Spire, and their respective wives.

A single drop of water would reverberate in this room right now, as the assembly looks on in various stages of shock. Saoirse's face is as white as freshly fallen snow.

I step down until I am on even footing with them. "Did you honestly think I would not learn of your treason?" I raise my voice so everyone can hear. "These eastern lords have been plotting to seize the rich lands east of the plains and establish a new realm. Lord Adley fancies himself a king."

Gasps sound.

"That is preposterous!" he exclaims. "Why would I seek this when my daughter is to be queen?"

"I asked myself that same question. But tell me something, Adley ... what did you offer King Cheral in exchange for the troops that now move through my lands?"

"How did—" He catches himself, but it's too late. He's tipped his hand too far.

Bexley's source was right. I owe her my thanks.

"Do not worry. I've made plenty of room in the dungeons for you all. Get them out of my sight."

The guards drag them away.

No one else moves. No one utters a sound.

Saoirse stands alone in the front row now. When my attention lands on her, she rushes forward, reaching for my forearm. "Atticus, I did not know of their deceit." She shakes her head, her long, sleek locks shifting like a curtain. "*Truly*. I would never be a party to dividing a country I am to rule with you."

"It wouldn't make much sense, would it." I step forward, drawing a fingertip along her chin. "By the way, how is that book?" I whisper, as if we have a secret.

She blinks.

"Master Sicily's account?"

"Oh!" Her face lights up with understanding. "Enthralling."

I swallow my disgust and move in closer. "Did you enjoy the chapter on the battle in the plains, when the Kier raiders sailed in to attempt a raid of our harvest?"

"Oh, yes." She hums, stealing a furtive glance around to see everyone watching. This is what she's always wanted—for us to stand in front of the assembly and fawn over each other as Zander and Romeria once did. "You were so brave."

I slide the pad of my thumb across her lip. "How so?"

She shrugs. "Just in your command."

"I did not command in that battle. I was not even there."

She falters. "I must have been mistaken, then. You've fought in so many battles."

"Or you have not even cracked the spine on that book. But perhaps there was another reason for you to visit that section of the library that day."

Her mouth gapes.

Not that I had any doubt about what Gracen told me, but there is my answer.

I step away from her and the charade. "Let it be known that Lady Saoirse of Kettling was behind the tainting of my tributary, in an attempt to influence me to move our nuptials forward and secure her position on the throne before I could discover what the east has been plotting. A *very* reliable witness came forward to inform me of her crime. I can only imagine what else she planned for me." I nod toward the guards. "Put her in the tower."

"But … but … you cannot do this!" she shrieks. "I am your betrothed!"

"I don't think it's going to work out between us." Relief overwhelms me the moment our engagement is officially ended.

Saoirse looks around as the guards drag her away, as if searching for someone to speak up on her behalf.

But no one wants to draw any attention to themselves.

"As I am sure you all can appreciate, these times are perilous, and Cirilea must be protected at all costs. Therefore, the gates have been sealed until further notice. I will not be granting anyone access to the nymphaeum on Hudem. All celebration is canceled, and I strongly suggest you refrain from taking a vein until your tributary can be tested and marked."

Quiet murmurs sound, but no one dares counter me.

I should leave now. I should end this assembly and walk out, feeling successful.

But I can't bring myself to ignore the sour face in the crowd. "Lord Danthrin of Freywich! Please, come forward for a moment."

"Atticus," Kazimir whispers in warning.

I ignore him as I watch Danthrin plaster on a glossy expression to hide his apprehension. "Your Highness." He steps ahead with a flourish and then bows deeply. "How may I be of service to the king?"

This prick abused Gracen and her children. He passed her around like a bowl of confectionaries, to be shared among friends. "I would like you to repeat for me exactly what you said to my servant in the dining hall."

His eyebrows arch. "Your Highness? Which servant are you referring—"

"You know which one."

Wariness flickers, his eyes darting to Kazimir. "I told her how much I missed her culinary skills."

"Her *culinary* skills." He lies so smoothly I can't help but be impressed.

But he lies.

"She is unmatched in all Islor. That is why the traitor princess took her from me in the first place."

He takes any chance he can to mention Romeria's involvement, as if that might win him points, turn the attention away from his wrongdoing.

"Is that true, Captain? Was Lord Danthrin of Freywich complimenting my servant?"

Kazimir sighs reluctantly. "If a compliment includes threatening to torture her children while she dies slowly, tied to a tree."

Audible gasps sound as my rage ignites. If he would say such things to her in the middle of a crowded dining hall, I can only imagine the sorts of things he said—and did—to her in the privacy of his home.

Danthrin lifts his hands to pat the air in a sign of surrender. "I assure His Highness that the captain grossly misheard—"

I've drawn my sword and swung before he finishes his sentence.

Screams sound as his head sails across the throne room floor, landing many feet away as his body collapses. A spray of blood leaves a trail to be cleaned.

My adrenaline races. There hasn't been an execution in the throne room since the days of King Rhionn. But I don't feel the least bit of regret. No matter what happens to me, Lord Danthrin will never utter a single word, cruel or otherwise, to Gracen. "In case it wasn't clear, any threat against my household is a threat against the throne, and it will be dealt with accordingly." With that, I spin on my heels, marching toward the war room, blood dripping from my blade.

Kazimir closes in behind me. "What was that?"

"I want them to know I was serious," I drawl. "And apparently, he liked an audience."

"You just chopped off our rabbit's head."

"Don't worry. We'll have others to chase soon enough. Put tails on them all and see which holes they run down." We will follow until we've caught every last treasonous one.

32
ROMERIA

"Romeria ... Romeria."

"Hmm?" I crack my eyes at the sound of my name. It takes a moment to register that I'm alone in my bedchamber and I must be dreaming. Or wishing that Zander was lying next to me again. But he is already within Soldor, facing God only knows what without me.

A hollow ache yawns inside me from his absence.

Beyond the gauzy curtains that frame the doors to my terrace, two moons glow, both nearly full.

Hudem will be here in a blink.

What will happen to Islor then?

My chest tightens as it does every time I acknowledge what I've done by opening the gates to this city, what I've invited. *We have no other choice, anyway,* I remind myself. Releasing the nymphs and accepting their magic is the *only* way to save Islor from what Princess Romeria did. What comes next ... Zander is right. We'll fight it together.

But if anything happens to him, I'm afraid I'll burn this world to the ground.

"Romeria."

The hairs on the back of my neck spike at the sound of Lucretia's voice. I didn't dream it after all. I bolt out of bed, my affinities rising instantly, crackling beneath my skin like static currents as I search the shadows of my room. "Show yourself." I half expect the snake to slither out from beneath my bed, but no one appears —neither reptile nor seductive female form.

Jarek and I visited the crypt together after Zander left, hoping to draw her out, but she didn't appear then either.

"Romeria." Again, she calls, my name like a breathy whisper on a breeze. A taunt.

I have a feeling I know where she'll be. Throwing a cloak over my gown, I drop the ward on my door. The hallway outside my chambers is empty. Jarek must be seizing a few well-earned hours of sleep.

I move for his room down the hall—another requirement of accepting the position of commander was that he be stationed close to me. This is the first time I've actually seen him use it. I lift my hand to knock, but falter as a soft, muffled sound of a female's moan touches my ear.

Eden must be with him tonight.

I back away and continue on, leaving them to it.

The halls of the castle crawl with shadows, my footfalls echoing. I'm never walking alone anymore, and especially not this late. It's eerie, and suddenly, I regret not grabbing a dagger on my way out.

But I'm far from defenseless, I remind myself with a chuckle.

And maybe I'm never truly alone. I steal a glance up at the nymph statues that play silent sentry as I pass, wondering what will happen on Hudem, when Lucretia's masters arrive. What do these nymphs look like? How many are there?

Ulysede is their gift, but what if there is a curse to go along with it? Gesine said they were known to cause great chaos and barter in lives, but everything Mordain knows about the nymphs so far seems either wrong or distorted.

"Romeria."

"I'm *coming*!" Luckily for me, the legionaries are at the gate and all the mortals are in their beds. No one is around to hear me growling into an empty grand hall.

But I know someone who likely isn't asleep.

I aim for the library and, not surprisingly, find the door ajar. With a headshake, I slink through the gap, moving quietly. The table Gesine always occupies has a stack of books waiting and a lantern burning, but she's not there.

Her name is just about to leave my lips when I spot her at the end of a lengthy aisle, but she's not alone. Zorya hovers close, her fingers tangled in the caster's hair, their bodies pressed against each other, their mouths lost in a deep kiss.

I duck away before they notice me there, a smile touching my lips.

At least Zorya doesn't want to kill her anymore.

With that happy thought, I head to Lucretia's crypt alone.

The sylx is already waiting when my feet hit the stone floor. "You came."

"You called." Was she in my head or in my ear? "How did you do that, anyway?"

"Because we are in Ulysede." Her serpentine yellow eyes drift to the stairs. "Where is your servant? The one I like?"

There can be only one she means. "Occupied." Maybe I shouldn't have admitted that so freely. "He'll be here soon," I add.

"Hmm." She hums like she doesn't believe me, and I catch a hint of disappointment—for my lie or his absence, I can't tell.

"Is that who you've dressed for?" I nod toward her gown—a shimmering silver this time, and more revealing than the last. It's cold down here, and yet it doesn't seem to faze her.

"Your king has left you all alone in Ulysede," she says instead, gliding toward me.

"I'm far from alone." I tug my cloak closer. I wish I'd grabbed a dagger. Though I doubt a blade would stop this creature. "He had to go. There's war coming."

"There is always war coming. That is the nature of their kind. They bring it upon themselves with their lust for power."

"Why didn't you show yourself when Zander and I were here earlier? Or when Jarek and I were here?"

She brushes up along my arm as she passes. "Because I do not answer the questions they ask."

I keep her in my peripheral. All her constant moving makes me uneasy, and I'm sure that's the goal. "But I'm seeking the same answers."

"Then all you need to do is ask." Her laughter is both musical and mocking.

Fine. "Can I reverse what I've done? Can I reseal Ulysede? Put that stone wall back up and no one will be the wiser?"

"What is done cannot be undone."

A wave of déjà vu hits me. Gesine said that to me once, the first night we met, when she confirmed my fears—this was my new life, my new body, and there was no going back.

Lucretia frowns. "You do not wish to do that. My masters arrive soon, and when they do, the lands will be healed, the blood curse ended."

"And Malachi will come out of the Nulling along with a bunch of monsters."

She tsks. "You fear too much."

My annoyance flares. "And you don't fear anything because you hide down here in your little crypt, vanishing when you don't want to come out. If *you* had to go out there and face off with that giant fucking dragon or whatever you guys call it—"

"Has Caindra come to visit?" Genuine excitement laces Lucretia's voice.

"It has a name?"

"*She* does. And she has seen much."

"Did she come through the Nulling?"

"Caindra has been here for *many* years."

Not an answer. Gesine alluded to the dragon's long life the other day, when she was talking of seers' visions. "Since the last time the nymphs were here."

Lucretia smiles. "I wondered when she would return."

Is that supposed to be a yes? "Return from where?"

"From hiding."

Getting answers out of the sylx is like pulling teeth. "And where does a thing like that hide for thousands of years where no one ever sees her?" Even if it was deep in the rift, she'd have to come out to eat every so often. Radomir, who has lived within these mountains for centuries, has never seen her.

"They have seen her. They just didn't realize it."

"Why does it seem like you're avoiding answers rather than giving them?"

"Some things are better left unsaid, Your Highness."

My frustration flares. I didn't stay in Ulysede to deal with this. "No, they're not!"

In the next breath, Lucretia is gone.

Vanished.

"Fuck," I hiss, my curse hollow in the empty vault. She doesn't like being shouted at. Noted. But how long before she comes back? I don't have time for this. Loose stones scrape beneath the boots I hastily threw on as I stroll around the ominous statues, studying each in turn. "Hello?"

Nothing.

I sigh. "Lucretia, I'm sor—"

"Who is the blond mortal?"

I startle at the sylx's voice suddenly in my ear. "What?"

She reappears beside me, her breath washing over my face like a puff of ice-cold air on a bitter January day. "The blond mortal who lies with your warrior servant?"

It takes me a moment to clue in. "You mean, Eden?"

"Eden," Lucretia repeats, continuing on with her serpentine walk as if she was never gone. "A lovely name for a sweet girl. I wouldn't think she was the warrior's type. She seems quite smitten. Though I can see why, the way he moves inside her." Her creepy eyes blaze with heat.

Wait. "Did you just go into Jarek's room and *watch* them?"

Her responding grin doesn't show a hint of shame. "You are right, he *is* occupied."

A shudder skitters along my spine. If she can float around Ulysede unseen … "Who else have you been spying on?"

"My masters wish to understand Ulysede's occupants."

"From their bedrooms?" My anger flares a second time. She must have been in my room tonight, calling me here. My ward didn't keep her out. That's a concern. But has she been in there before?

Has she spied on Zander and me?

I'm pretty sure I know the answer to that. But forget what she's seen; what has she *heard* of our conversations? Of how much we don't trust the nymphs and don't want to release them.

I take deep, calming breaths as Lucretia weaves the statues. If I yell at her, she might vanish again. "Caindra was outside the gates last night, and she *didn't* kill us."

"I presumed not, given you are still alive."

"You're a pervert *and* a smart-ass," I mutter. "Is she on our side?"

"She does not choose sides."

"Will she fight for us?"

"If she feels like it."

I shake my head in frustration. "But you said I could use the creatures from the Nulling to help me fight this war."

"Caindra is not a creature from the Nulling."

"Fine. How do I get her to *feel like* fighting for us?"

"That is for you to discover. I do not have a view into her mind or control over her will." Lucretia's fingertips skate over the hand of the daintiest, childlike nymph statue. "You are not looking at this the right way, Your Highness. Islor will be free of the blood curse. Everyone will have a common enemy. The two elven halves and your spell wielders will have no choice but to unite. It will be as it once was."

"We're just trading one war for another."

"As I've said, their kind cannot seem to escape that path."

"And the nymphs? What will they do?"

She tips her head back to admire the gargoyle statue. "They will exist as they always have, as a check and balance. Only now, they have a Daughter of Many and a Queen for All. Never before have they had that."

"And why does that matter to them?" What do they get out of it?

Her perfectly symmetrical eyebrows arch. "Because you are powerful, and you are now bound to them as they are to you."

"Because of Ulysede."

She smiles.

"If I'm their queen, can I order them to not open the Nulling?" That would end the blood curse and yet stop Malachi and untold monsters from flooding this world.

"That is impossible."

"Why?"

"Because it is all connected. The Nulling shall open, my masters will return, and their power will heal the lands."

"Are you saying the nymphs are in the Nulling?"

"It is all connected."

I still don't understand. "But Farren was a key caster too. How did she open the Nulling and not the nymphaeum door?"

"She did not open the Nulling, she tore into it. She did not hold the right key. My masters did not return." Lucretia drags a nail along my forearm, tracing one of the blue lines.

"You mean, my blood."

"The blood of the Daughter of Many and Queen for All." She pauses to study me before moving off again. "Caster Farren tore a hole into the Nulling by channeling her affinity through one of the stones, yes. But without my masters here, the fates cannot pass through."

Lucretia's words strike a chord. "One of the stones. How many are there?"

She waves a hand around the room toward the nymph scripture on the wall.

It dawns on me. "These are *all* nymphaeum stones? Like the one in Cirilea?"

"They are all connected." She strolls over to a rectangular engraving across from me. "Go ahead."

I follow her and run my finger across the script. Childish laughter rings in my ears. "That didn't work before."

"Others no longer work. This one does. Channel your affinity into it and see for yourself," she coaxes.

"Which affinity?"

Lucretia's laughter is taunting, as if I should be ashamed that I don't know the answer. "The Daughter of Many does not choose one over the other. Let them merge until they are as one, and you will know power like none other."

"That's not what Gesine taught me."

"Your wielder servant?" More laughter. "What little she knows of the Queen for All's abilities."

Gesine did insist I learn what I can from Lucretia.

With a deep but wary breath, I follow her instructions, tugging on the threads that rise from my core, coaxing them to wind together. The power thrums inside me, growing in intensity by the second, until it vibrates with a level that feels almost overwhelming, like it might tear me apart.

It reminds me of that moment before I killed the grif.

"Good." She applauds, as if she can see what I'm doing.

"What can I do with this?"

"What *can't* you do with it?" She nods toward the stone. "Send it there. Gently. Not too much. Just a little tap."

I release the bound thread, and it reaches toward the scripture on the wall like a long, tentative finger. The second it touches, the stone changes shape. It's no longer just an engraving in a wall. Now it's a tall rectangular stone.

My breath catches.

I've seen this one before … in Cirilea's nymphaeum.

My mouth gapes as I take in the soaring trees and feel the cool air. I'm literally standing in Cirilea again.

This is what Lucretia meant when she said they're all connected. They're doors.

A smile stretches across my face as I turn, seeing the familiar pillars again, the stone altar …

The two forms mere feet away from me.

33
GRACEN

Fikar strolls into the kitchens, his arms loaded with silver wine jugs. "Did ya hear? The king executed a lord in the middle of the assembly! Just cut off his head with a swing of his sword!"

The bowl in my hands slips with his outburst, clattering against the stone floor, shattering.

Atticus *executed* a *lord*? Himself?

I settle on my knees to collect the shattered clay and bits of pastry dough. He did allude to doing something drastic at that assembly. Something that his father and brother were not willing to do.

"And he threw all the eastern lords into the dungeons, accusing them of a plot to overthrow him. They say he has gone mad."

He has *not* gone mad! They *have* been plotting. Lady Saoirse herself is a part of it! But I bite my tongue against the urge to defend him. Everything Atticus told me, he told me in confidence.

"Do ya know who it was?" one of the scullery workers asks. Now that the servants have been marked by Wendeline, the guards aren't hovering in the kitchens and people feel free to chatter again.

"No one too important, from the sounds of it." Fikar dumps the jugs into the washbasin. "*And* he's thrown the Lady Saoirse in the gray tower."

"*What*?" This gossip, I welcome. "Does that mean he is not marrying her anymore?"

"I would think not, but after the last king ran off with his family's murderess, who knows."

A bubble of elation swells inside me. It would be best for *everyone* if that marriage agreement was no more. Islor wouldn't have a cruel queen seated on the throne. Atticus wouldn't have a wife who wants him dead. And if he wants *me* as his tributary, as he has all but declared … I wouldn't have to share him with *her*.

I slide my teeth along my bottom lip. I haven't stopped thinking about that kiss since I walked out of Atticus's chamber—I can still feel his mouth against mine. Nor have I been able to shake his words. He said he wouldn't take something from me that I wasn't willing to give. He must have read it in my pulse, the fear of reliving the worst nights of my past.

He is the king of Islor. No one denies him anything. But he is also Atticus, and he is nothing like the terrible keepers I've known. Every encounter I have with him, the more confident I am of that.

The less apprehension I feel.

The more excitement.

Was I a fool earlier? I didn't reject him, but I might as well have, my thoughts reeking of hesitation. Atticus has been nothing but kind to me when he could easily have not been. Today, he needed me.

He still needs me.

I look up to find Corrin studying me intently. She always seems to know what's spinning in my mind. "What about all the cakes for the wedding?" I blurt, as if that's my only concern.

"They will get eaten. Never mind all the cakes. And *you* never mind all your gossip and exaggerating." Corrin claps her hands at Fikar. "Get to work."

"It's not gossip if it's the truth!" He sets to hanging the clean silver jugs from the hooks on the ceiling. He's the only one who can reach them. "Ask Manfred. He had to haul the headless body out."

Gasps sound as servants steal looks to see others' reactions.

"Whoever it was, surely they deserved it," I mumble.

Too loud, it seems. As one, they gawk at me, as if they had all assumed my tongue didn't work up until now. I've never joined in any of the chatter before.

But none of them know why Atticus did what he did. *I* know why. The king himself divulged his secrets to me. A warm glow spreads in my chest with that knowledge.

How long before I can see him again?

A darker thought stirs.

What if I can't? What if he thinks I've made my choice and he's already in search of someone willing to serve him?

Jealousy burns inside with that thought.

Fates, I was such a fool.

"You shouldn't be on your knees," Corrin scolds, bringing a broom over. "You'll cut yourself."

"I won't. And stop mothering me. I'm fine." I'm *more* than fine. All those aches and twinges after birthing Suri have vanished since Wendeline's healing touch. The residual bleeding has ended. Even my stomach feels taut. Aside from my ability to nurse, my body feels like my own again.

And I'm irritated with Corrin. "You went to him?" I whisper with accusation, not wanting anyone to hear.

Her jaw sets with indignation. "Of course I did. On your behalf."

"Why?"

She crouches alongside me, picking at bits of pastry with her stubby fingers. "Because he needs to know that you have no interest in being a tributary again. Is that not true?"

I swallow. It *was* true, but that was before I met the king.

Now ... I don't know what I want, except that if I get another chance, I might do things differently.

Corrin's stare is severe. "Remember your place, Gracen. You are a mortal in a kingdom where we serve, and nothing more. Do not get swept up in fantasy and charm." She shakes her head and sighs. "These relationships between tributary and keeper are not always like what you faced, but they can be equally dangerous."

The only relationship I've ever experienced was one of abuse and neglect, and all the keepers in Freywich were the same, so I have nothing to compare it to. But I've heard tales of mortals who fall in love with their keepers, who are utterly devoted to them. "I don't know if I would call it dangerous."

"That is because you have not picked up the pieces of their hearts for them. I promise you, it's much like *this*." She casts a hand over the bits on the floor. "I have seen more than one young woman fall victim to foolishness, caught up in a crown. Look at Sabrina! She was his tributary for mere weeks and already fawning over him."

"She was," I admit.

"And the moment she was no longer of use, he cast her into the dungeon."

"That is different, Corrin, you know that. And he didn't execute her." He couldn't bring himself to punish her for serving him. He told me so.

Corrin harrumphs as if that's not proof of anything. "The royal family's tributaries are highly sought-after positions. The mortals who serve can do so for decades if they prove their loyalty and form a bond. I assure you, Sabrina had lofty dreams about her life. I'm sure she dreamed of being his *only* tributary." She snorts. "And what kind of life do you think she'll dream of now, wearing that mark and playing the baker's nursemaid?"

As if mentioning her name summons her, Sabrina strolls into the kitchen with Lilou in her arms, Mika trailing beside. Her mark glows like a beacon, and people step back and steal wary glances, as if they can catch her disease.

She lifts her chin to feign bravery as she makes her way to me. "Suri is fast asleep, and these two wish to say good night."

I climb to my feet. "Do you have everything you need?"

"Dagnar put a pallet in the corner of the room for me. It's a bit cramped in there. I hope you don't mind that they've put me with you."

"I don't mind at all." Though she might. Her new home is a far cry from her tributary quarters.

Her demeanor is subdued as compared to the Sabrina of the past. Maybe she needs a good night's sleep after spending days awaiting a noose. Or maybe Corrin is right and her heart was left in pieces on the dungeon floor.

"Thank you, Sabrina."

She nods solemnly and smiles, but I see the sadness where earlier, tears of appreciation masked it.

I give my kids each a kiss. "Good night, my loves. You be good."

"Why can't my mark glow like Sabrina's?" Mika exclaims, holding up his hand.

Sabrina and I share a wide-eyed look before she swiftly escorts him out. "You do not want it to, Mika, trust me …" she hisses as they vanish out the door.

Corrin sighs and climbs to her feet, the last of my mess collected. "That *was* kind of His Highness to spare Sabrina's life," she admits begrudgingly.

"Yes, it was." But I already know he can be kind. "Is it true what they're saying? That the king has arrested the eastern noblemen?"

"From what sparse things I've heard, it seems to be."

"How will Kettling react?" I've never been to the city in the east, but I've heard plenty about it. Most of it unpleasant. Rumors that they don't honor Presenting Day traditions or the law. They barter in children as readily as adults.

"It depends when they hear about it. The gate is sealed, and no messengers can pass through to carry the news."

"That was shrewd."

"His Highness is not foolish when it comes to battle, and I would wager he has launched himself into one intentionally. What the fallout might be, I suppose we will soon learn."

Motion at the door catches my eye. Kazimir strolls in, towering over everyone in all his leather and weaponry. He moves for the counter of leftovers. The scullery staff scoot away from him as he reaches for a cake and stuffs it into his mouth. In a covert move that is not so covert, he meets my gaze, jerks his head toward the door, and then strolls out.

"I think I have been beckoned." My heart stirs with a mixture of excitement and worry as I brush my floured hands against my apron and unfasten it. Is this good or bad?

"Yes. It would seem so."

I make to move, but Corrin grabs my wrist.

"Please be careful. The king may have stifled some of his enemies, but I am sure there are plenty more still loose within Cirilea's walls. Those nearest him will be the first targets."

I nod, tossing my apron on my table.

Kazimir waits outside the kitchen door, chewing.

"You can't pass by a platter of sweets without eating one, can you?" I tease.

He swallows his mouthful and throws back, "*You* can't go a day without flour on your cheek, can you?"

"A hazard of the job." I brush my palms across them, my face flushing.

He chuckles and, slipping the charcoal cloak from his arm, places it on my shoulders far gentler than he seems capable. "You'll need that. It's cold outside."

"Thank you." I fasten the clasp at the collar as I fall into step beside him. "Don't tell me Mika has snuck out to the sparring square again." I'm only half joking. There were mere minutes between saying good night to my son and Kazimir's arrival in the kitchen, but Mika has astonished me more than once with how quickly he can slip away.

"No." Kazimir's eyes skitter over my face. "Atticus waits for you there, and apparently, I'm his errand boy."

Atticus waits for me. My heart skips several beats at the prospect of seeing him again so soon, after worrying I might not see him at all.

And why does Kazimir so freely use the king's first name with me?

The captain grins. I hate that my kind is so easy to read.

I test the cloak's material between my fingertips as we take the stairs up into the main castle hall. It's soft and new, and the gold threading in it smacks of finery. "There have been many rumors today."

"I am sure there have been. Much is afoot." His smile is bitter. "Did you hear the one about the headless lord?"

"Yes, there was mention of that." I hesitate. "I assume whoever it was deserved it?"

"I would say so, though it wasn't a wise move on the king's part."

"Why not?"

"Because keeping him alive would have led us to enemies far more dangerous." Kazimir holds a door open for me.

I falter. It's not often that an immortal soldier shows such courtesy to a mortal. "So then what happened?"

"Atticus's anger got the better of him."

"And so he just chopped off the lord's head. Because he was angry?"

"One clean swipe."

"Does he do that often?"

Kazimir chuckles. "I have to say this was a first. But he seems to be experiencing many firsts as of late. For example, he will not take a vein from any of the remaining tributaries, even though they are now marked."

Relief that I *shouldn't* feel over this news stirs. "Perhaps he does not trust what the caster did?"

"That is not it."

"Then what is it?"

"I haven't the foggiest idea." But he looks at me as if he knows *exactly* why Atticus is resisting. "But he needs to, and very soon, for his own safety. If you could convince him of that, I would greatly appreciate it."

How on earth am *I* supposed to convince a king to take a vein?

There is only one way of that: to give it to him.

Kazimir was not exaggerating about the cold night air. I tug the cloak around my body to ward off the chill against my skin, as excitement and nervousness fuel the heat coursing through my limbs.

"I imagine you have never walked the royal gardens before."

My pulse doubles in speed at the sound of that deep, melodious voice, like freshly poured syrup. I quickly locate Atticus, leaning against the stone wall. He's still wearing his formal king's attire from earlier, but the crown is missing and the top buttons of his jacket are unfastened, showing off a columnar neck and jutting Adam's apple.

Dark circles line his eyes.

I remember myself and bow. "No, Your Highness. I have not had the pleasure."

He pushes off from the wall and swaggers over to me as if he didn't just imprison the most powerful lords in Islor and decapitate a minor one. "Care to accompany me?" He offers me his elbow, his deep dimples only highlighting the full lips in between, that I struggle to peel my focus away from, remembering the feel of them against mine.

"Certainly, Your Highness. Whatever you wish." I curl my arm through his, reveling in the strength of it. He smells of leather and an earthy spice, the same scent that lingers in his rooms.

He leads me past a dozen heavily armed guards. Are there always so many out here at night? They weren't stationed every ten steps this morning.

"The royal garden is closed for tonight," he orders the last one in the row before we turn down a stone path. "Don't you have some rabbits to chase, Kaz?"

"Gladly," comes the raspy voice behind me.

Something tells me rabbits are not actually rabbits, but I'm content not to know what those two are up to.

An odd calm envelops me as we move past an ivy-covered archway and deeper into the garden. Many of the showy blooms that thrive in the summer's heat have withered, giving way to subtle flowers and greenery that can withstand the cooler temperatures. Here and there, a lantern glows with firelight, but many more sit cold and dark.

"We used to rely on the casters to light them each night," Atticus explains, as if tracking my focus.

"But not anymore?"

"Casters no longer have a place within Islor. They've proven they cannot be trusted."

I peer down at my hand. But one caster—supposedly the worst one—was trusted to do this.

Not trusted. *Needed*. Out of desperation.

"How was the rest of your day?" Atticus asks.

"I burned a batch of bread pudding." My thoughts were stuck in daydreams about Atticus. "And Mika is pestering me to bring him back to the priestess so she may give him more markings."

Atticus's laughter carries through the night.

I smile. "Otherwise, it was uneventful." I hesitate. "Less so than yours, from the sound of it."

His delight peters off with a sigh. "And what have you heard about the rest of *my* day?"

Fikar's words sit heavy on my tongue.

"Speak freely. I will not punish you or anyone else for it. I am curious what is fact and what is fabrication. They think me mad, don't they?"

"That may have been uttered once or twice," I admit.

"Good," he murmurs.

"Good?"

"Yes. A mad king is an especially dangerous one, and they need to see me as such right now. Fear breeds caution."

"They say you've imprisoned the eastern lords and ladies."

"Not *all* of them. Only the ones from Kettling, Fernhoth, and Hawkrest."

"So *only* the largest cities in the east."

"A mortal who knows something of Islor's geography," he teases, pulling me closer. "I am impressed."

I cling to his arm, the feel of his body against mine makes my heart hammer. "Master Cordin traveled often. He had a picture on the wall—a hand-drawn sketch of Islor, with all its cities. He used to talk about them a lot."

"I would like to meet this old keeper of yours one day."

"I would love to see him again, but I do not know how he fares, if he is even alive. If my parents and younger siblings are alive." I feel Atticus's gaze on my profile, but I keep it ahead. I don't want to see pity there.

"I can make that happen, Gracen."

Because he is king of Islor. And for some daft reason, he seems set on me.

"What else are the servants saying?" he asks.

"That your betrothal to Lady Saoirse is no more?" It comes out as a question, one I desperately want an answer to.

"I can't imagine she's sitting in the tower, still planning our wedding." He smiles wryly.

"So, it's true. There is to be no wedding on Hudem." I hold my breath.

"There will be no celebration of *any* kind on Hudem."

I could float away, that news lifting a weight from me.

"That makes you happy." It's not a question; he can read my glee.

"Relieved. She would not make a good queen." And Atticus will remain an untethered king, at least for now. Which of those two stirs more elation? I know what the answer *should* be, but I don't think it would be the truth, even as Corrin's warning rings in my ear. The king will marry eventually, and I will remain a means to serve his needs, until he finds another.

I know this, and yet I can feel myself getting swept up in his very presence—in each look that touches me, each smile I garner. Corrin said royal tributaries could remain in service for *decades* if they formed a bond. I used to pray every day of service with Danthrin would be my last, that he would tire of me, leave me to the kitchen and forget me. But decades with this Islorian male? Imagine the kind of life I might give my children.

"No, she would not. But we no longer have to worry about that." The path ahead forks. Atticus steers us to the right, as if he has a specific destination in mind.

"They also said you executed someone in the throne room." Kazimir has already confirmed it, but I like hearing Atticus's own words.

"I did. It wasn't ideal, but Lord Danthrin deserved it."

"Lord … You mean …" Shock buckles my knees.

Atticus moves quickly, shifting to face me, his hands seizing my waist. A deep frown mars his handsome face. "Does that news bother you?"

"No." I grip his forearms as I take a few minutes to collect myself, absorbing the heat radiating from his body. "It's just … he's gone? Truly gone?" Lord Danthrin has played the starring role in my living nightmares for years. Within our little world of Freywich, he was so powerful, unstoppable. He drew so many tears—of pain, of fear, of anguish—and stirred so many sleepless nights.

That he is simply *gone* now seems impossible.

"Truly. Not even a fate could bring him back." Atticus adds quietly, "And if they do, I will kill him again." He returns to his place beside me, only this time, his arm is secured around my back. We continue along the path, through a tunnel shrouded in thick ivy. It's pitch-dark and I can't see, but Atticus guides us with ease.

"What did he do to earn that punishment?" Besides make Atticus angry.

"Beyond his lies to avoid paying the tithe? We believe he was conspiring with the eastern lords. He has been meeting with several of them nightly, under the cover of Port Street brothels."

Those poor mortals. No amount they earned would have been enough for his tastes.

Atticus shifts us off the path. The grass is cold and damp against my soft leather shoes. They'll likely be soaked for days. But I wouldn't trade dry shoes for this experience. I savor Atticus's tight grip, his heat searing through my cloak, through my dress, warming my skin. "And what will happen now?"

"Any supporters within these walls are panicking, afraid of ending up like their prominent lords. They cannot flee. I've closed the gate and sealed the port. So they will either abandon all scheming for the moment while they wait to see if there is an execution, or they will seek advice from their fellow conspirators on what to do. If the latter, my men will be waiting."

"And will you? Execute them?"

"In time. It's better they remain alive for now, to keep those wishing to step into their shoes at bay, even if temporarily. In the meantime, I must ride east with my men to battle this traitor army."

A battle? My fear flares. "When?"

"Not tonight." He releases my waist and collects my hand. He guides me into a stone pavilion, a lantern glowing on each corner. I recognize the four pillars. Lady Danthrin forced all the servants to attend the sanctum service weekly in Freywich, so we could pray for a fruitful harvest that year. "There's a sanctum in the garden?"

"This is the nymphaeum."

I take in the space with new understanding. "You mean ..." I'd heard about this holy location even as a child, where Islor's immortals could appeal to the king and queen for access four nights a year as a means to have a child. Lady and Lord Danthrin themselves were here for that reason, and now her belly swells with the result.

This is the most sacred space in all of Islor, brimming with otherworldly powers on Hudem.

Mortals aren't allowed here.

Atticus smooths a hand over the stone block in the center. "My sister and I were conceived right here, as was my brother the exiled king, and all the immortals of Islor."

"Right there." I take in the dark and open space around us. "For some reason, I thought it would be, I don't know, grander and more … enclosed."

He chuckles, leaning against the stone, his arms crossed at his chest. "You did accuse us of having no modesty, didn't you?"

"Couldn't you at least put up a curtain?"

"I suppose we could. But the blessing is a miracle of sorts. No one wishes to hide it."

A stone wall behind the altar catches my attention. I wander over to study it, enthralled. "What does this mean?"

Atticus's powerful form closes in behind me. "Something from the time of the nymphs. No one knows, or no one has told us."

"It looks like it was carved only yesterday."

"One of many mysteries."

I reach toward it, but then freeze.

"Go ahead. You can touch it. It won't bite."

I trace my fingertip over the ancient scripture. "It's beautiful."

"So are you."

My pulse flutters with his words as strong hands settle on my hips, turning me around to face him. The clouds from earlier are breaking apart, allowing a glimpse of the waxing moon. It's nearly full. In days, a second one will hang below it, as if appearing out of thin air, not there the night before, and gone the next, but its brilliant power is enough to create new life.

"What I said earlier, about Lord Danthrin, about why I punished him …" Atticus reaches up to unfasten a tie in my hair, then another. His deft fingers weave through my braids, unraveling them with efficiency. "It wasn't entirely true."

My unruly hair tumbles down around my face. "You mean, he wasn't conspiring with the others?"

"I am certain he was." Atticus's chuckle is dark as he strokes a strand off my cheek. "If he'd stayed alive long enough, he would have proved it. That *was* the plan."

I shut my eyes against his gentle caress, the sensation stirring desire in me that I know he can sense. "Then what happened?"

"I thought about what he's done to you, to your family, what he would do if he ever got his hands on you again, and I could not leave him alive for one more second." His breath skates across my lips.

And his words sink in. "You executed him for *me*." The king chopped off a lord's head in the middle of an assembly for me? I swallow against that truth. "That's … sweet?"

His deep chuckle vibrates in my chest.

Finally, I dare open my eyes to find his trained intently on my lips.

"Should something happen to me, at least he cannot harm you."

"Nothing will happen to you."

He smirks. "Let us consider the history of Islorian kings for a moment, shall we? King Ailill was executed by his own son, my father was poisoned by his future daughter-in-law, my brother was betrayed by me, his brother. The only king who died peacefully of old age was Rhionn, and even he faced countless assassination attempts. So, yes, Gracen, something will likely happen to me, but at least you and your family will be safe from whatever sick obsession that keeper had with you." He cups my cheeks with his palms. "Though I think I am beginning to understand it." His hands slide back, falling to my neck, his thumbs stroking the sensitive skin behind my ears. "Because you are in my thoughts far too often to be healthy."

"As you are in mine," I admit brazenly, my pulse pounding in my eardrums. Before I can talk myself out of it, I lift onto my toes to press my lips against his in a tentative and soft kiss.

His eyes blaze with hunger as he breaks away, a mixture of surprise and raw heat in them, and something I can't easily decipher.

I don't have a chance to try before his mouth is on mine, parting my lips and sliding his tongue in, his fingers tangling through the untamed curls he just released.

This is … even better than the earlier kiss, his grip tight against my body, sandwiching us together as his tongue delves in with a skill I didn't know possible. I've never kissed anyone like this before, but I'm learning fast, meeting each stroke with one of my own. On impulse, I graze his top teeth with the tip of my tongue. There's nothing sharp there to prick me.

"Gracen." My name is a groan on his lips. His hands slip under my cloak to fist the material of my dress, as if he'd like to tear it off right here. But he doesn't. He only grips my waist tight and kisses me harder, his lips never leaving mine as our tongues and teeth and breaths tangle with increasing abandon.

Is this what it's like to be the king's tributary? If so, no wonder Sabrina danced around the castle the mornings after and moped with longing on the days he didn't call.

Strange new sensations are igniting in my body—heat between my thighs, an ache in my lower belly. Feelings I've heard others whisper of but never experienced myself, and all stirred by a kiss from this Islorian male.

I barely notice when Atticus hoists me and sets me down on the altar, the stone cold and hard against my backside. Our mouths are still frantic against each other as he slides his hands over my thighs, and the hemline of my dress begins to hike.

"Wait!" I manage between kisses, my hands finding his chest. "Wait."

He peels away, his breathing ragged. "What is it?"

My own breathing is also uneven. "This is the nymphaeum. Is this okay? I mean, *nothing* will happen?" I look to him knowingly.

A grin slowly emerges. It's downright devilish. "I know I'm good, Gracen, but I'm not *that* good. It's not Hudem. *And* you're mortal. And this is just a kiss." He leans in to trace my bottom lip with his tongue.

"It is not just a kiss," I whisper against his mouth. It's utterly euphoric and addictive, and a thousand times more intimate than anything I have ever experienced with a male before.

"No?" His eyes are wild with lust as they search my face. "What is it, then?"

I don't know how to describe it except … "Hope." That my past will not taint everything for my future.

That a kind king might lead Islor to a better place.

That my children might not be relegated to a life of misery.

A strange look flickers across Atticus's face. "You didn't have any hope before?"

"Not until …" *Princess Romeria saved me.* "… I came here." I smooth a hand over his chest. "And now I've met you, and no one has ever made me feel like this before."

"Like what?" His voice has turned husky.

"Like I matter. Like what I want matters."

His fingers are gentle as he strokes strands of hair off my cheek. "And what *do* you want, Gracen?"

I hesitate, but only for a moment, to trace his square jawline with my fingertip, letting it skate over his lips. "Choice." I've never had one before. Even my two older children were named by Lord Danthrin, as he sat by the fire with his wife, sipping glasses of wine and discussing options, like they were naming the newest pet.

Atticus said he wouldn't take anything I wasn't willing to give. The promise was so simple and yet so profound, because the only thing these keepers have ever done is take from me.

His throat bobs with a hard swallow, before sliding his hand through my hair to grip my nape. "If you do not want me—"

"I do," I blurt, my cheeks flushing. "Fates, you must be able to feel how much I want you."

The corner of his mouth kicks up in a sexy smile. He leans in to trap my mouth in his once again, this time the kiss slower, more sensual than before.

And more intoxicating, as emotion seems to bleed into every stroke of his tongue.

The ache inside me grows more urgent.

I need him closer.

But his hands stay put—one tangled in my hair, the other against my hip, and his lips never leave mine, as if he can't get enough of my mouth, or he doesn't trust them elsewhere.

He hasn't taken a vein, I remind myself. He's had plenty of chances. He could have gone to someone else tonight, but he didn't. Wouldn't. With a shaky hand, I unfasten my cloak, letting it tumble off my shoulders. My buttons come next, just enough to loosen the collar of my dress for him.

"What are you doing?"

Slipping a hand around to the back of his head, my fingers toying with strands of his hair for just a moment, I break away and guide his mouth to my neck.

His voice is ragged in my ear. "You do *not* have to do this, Gracen."

"I know I don't." But Atticus does, and the thought of his mouth on someone else makes my chest ache with jealousy and regret. "I have a choice, and I choose this." I don't want him going to anyone else for it.

A long, soft sigh sails from his lips, sending shivers down my spine. "I will not hurt you," he promises.

I close my eyes in anticipation as his tongue traces the length of my neck from my collarbone to my ear and back again, before his lips replace it, his breath hot against my skin.

I feel the sharp prick against my throat, one I've felt countless times before, and I brace myself for the pain that comes with each draw. Only it doesn't come. Atticus is so very gentle as he takes what he needs from me, slowly, his palm smoothing back and forth over my hip while his other hand cradles my head.

My blood flows freely.

Willing.

Maybe because, for once, *I am* willing, to give Atticus what he needs to survive, to remain strong. And if we were in his warm chamber, in his bed, I wouldn't hesitate to give him *every*thing he might want.

Eagerly.

My eyes crack open, my vision hazy with desire.

Through the blurriness, I see a cloaked form standing behind him.

34
ROMERIA

Gracen looks so small and fragile, perched on the stone altar, as a hulking form leans over her.

Feeds off her.

Wait a minute. I *know* those short wisps of blond hair, those broad shoulders, that muscular frame.

Atticus is feeding off Gracen.

And any second he's going to catch a scent of my Ybarisan blood, discover I'm standing behind him, and then what? I need to get out of here immediately.

I rush to thread my affinities together as Lucretia taught me.

Gracen's eyelids crack open. She blinks to focus.

Panicked, I channel into the nymphaeum stone, and in the next instant, I'm back in Lucretia's crypt.

"Holy shit." I release a lungful of air. "Oh my God."

Lucretia grins. "See? They are connected."

"Oh, I *saw*." Irritation settles over me. "You can't just send me through wormholes like that."

She frowns. "There are no worms in the stones."

I shake my head. "I almost got caught by Zander's brother!"

"But you did not."

I couldn't have been there for more than a few seconds. It all happened so fast. Too fast, I hope, for anything to register in Gracen's mind. How Atticus didn't sense me there, didn't catch the sweet neroli oil scent of my blood, I can't explain. Then again, he was preoccupied with his fucking fangs in Gracen's neck. I grit my teeth.

"Her Highness seems troubled."

"Yeah, because I saw something troubling." Why is Atticus feeding off Gracen? She's a baker, not a tributary. I rescued her from that lecher Danthrin so she and her family would be safe, *not* so she could be used as a blood bag again.

At least she's still alive. I was afraid Atticus would have sent her back to Freywich—or worse, execute her—to punish me. But maybe this is his way of punishing me?

My anger flares at the thought of him using the poor woman like that. She's been through enough. Now to be used by Atticus? I have to get her out of there. If only I could bring her and her family here to Ulysede, within the safety of these walls. Or at least out of Cirilea, away from Atticus. Was she still pregnant? I couldn't tell, with Atticus hovering over her. But she must have had her baby by now.

I hit pause on that train of thought as I study the other rectangles of scripture with a new understanding. "Where do these all lead?"

"Most lead nowhere anymore. Once, to key cities within the lands. What you call Nyos and Argon and Shadowhelm. But their connections were severed by Aminadav when he broke the lands in two. They are no longer viable."

"Will they ever be again?" If I could walk in and out of these places without the need to ride across country on a horse, the possibilities would be endless.

I could reach Queen Neilina, and end her dreadful reign.

"We shall see. Maybe they will heal when my masters return. But for now, this one offers you safe passage between Ulysede and Cirilea, where you can get the answers you seek."

That's what she said these were for: getting answers. I wish we'd known about it when Zander was here. "This is helpful, Lucretia, but I can't walk around in Cirilea like this." I gesture at myself. "The guards all know my face. I mean, I guess I could hide myself like I've done before." The way I escaped the legionaries notice in the camp outside Norcaster, the way I used to steal diamond necklaces from unsuspecting marks. "I don't know for how long I can keep that up." Minutes, maybe?

"But no one knows *this* face." A silver object materializes in her hand out of thin air, and she hands it to me.

I study the plain mask, featherlight, its silver gleaming in the nearby lantern's flame. "This is a fates' token, isn't it?" Like the gold from my engagement ring was from Aoife, and the smooth ebony from the cuffs that trapped my elven abilities was from Malachi. "From Vin'nyla?"

"Forged from her wings," Lucretia confirms. "It is quite old. As are all tokens I guard." She waves a hand and the wall before me is no longer solid but a display case of sorts, with a dozen hollowed-out nooks within the stone.

Zander was scouring the vault for these. "Of course you were hoarding them all."

"Not hoarding. Safeguarding for my masters."

The chests of gold and jewels, the nymphs don't care for. These, they value. "How do you have so many?" I count eight nooks, and in all but two, an object gleams.

"My masters negotiate well," she answers cryptically.

What exactly did they negotiate with the fates for? A question for another time. I focus on the silver token in my hand. "How does this work?"

"Like any mask. You put it on."

"Just put it on."

"Yes."

"And you don't think a person walking around the castle wearing this will raise alarms?"

She laughs. "They will not see the mask. They will see the face you wish them to see."

Her meaning sinks in. "I can change my face with this."

"That is its power."

"To any face I want?"

"To anyone you can picture." She cocks her head. "Who would you like to be?"

I smile.

35
ATTICUS

It's a careful balance, between taking what I need and not more than Gracen can give. I already feel my strength returning, the ache in my head dissipating, the gnawing hunger abating. And yet my need for her only grows. I could easily lose myself in this delicate mortal body and all its feminine and supple curves. She's pliable, willing. I could part her thighs right here and show her how I thank my tributaries for their gift.

Suddenly, Gracen stiffens.

I pull away in an instant, letting my incisors slip back to their hiding spot. "What's wrong?" She seemed to be enjoying it, but something changed.

She studies the empty space behind me. "Nothing. I thought I saw someone standing there."

"Where?"

"Right there."

I glance over my shoulder, at the empty space between us and the stone wall. "My senses are usually quite strong, and I didn't notice anyone." Though feeding does temporarily dull them.

She shakes her head. "I was obviously seeing things. In a haze, I guess. I'm sorry. Do you still need to … I mean, do you need more?"

I graze her cheek with the back of my knuckles. She's so soft, so delicate. I can't get enough of touching her. "No."

"Are you sure?"

"I am sure." Sure that I don't regret killing Danthrin. Sure that I want to slaughter every male who's ever harmed her and would be riding to Freywich tomorrow to do so, had Zander not beat me to it.

A tiny line of blood trails down her neck from a puncture wound. I lean in to catch it with my tongue, lapping at her skin before kissing the tiny marks. I was extra careful. They should be gone by tomorrow.

Her body shudders.

"That wasn't so bad, was it?" I whisper against her ear.

She turns in, nuzzling her nose against my jaw. "It wasn't bad at all." She smiles sheepishly, tugging her collar up.

"Allow me." I fasten each button, wishing I was working in reverse instead, and pulling every last bit of clothing off her body so I could lay her down and take everything I want from her. But it's cold out here, and she will need to get back to her infant.

Her fingers test the fabric of the cloak. "This is very fine. I've never felt anything like it before."

"It's yours now." As is anything else she might want. I'll have to look for better quarters for her and her family as soon as we've gotten a handle on the poison within Cirilea and the risk to her is diminished.

Will there even be a need to, though? What if what Romeria said is true, and Hudem brings the end of the blood curse? The entire tributary system will come crashing down in days, and then what will Gracen be, besides the castle baker and a mortal I can't shake from my thoughts?

I think I will still want her.

"Come. I'll walk you back." I help her down off the altar and lead her through the quiet, empty gardens, reveling in the feel of her clinging to my forearms and the quiet contentment that seems to surround us. With Gracen, there is no scheming, there are no lies. It is a relief.

The clock tower gongs the midnight hour as I spot the first of many guards.

And I know I am not ready to say good night. "Come to my chamber after you've fed your baby." I didn't mean for it to sound like a command, so I add softly, "Only if you want to."

She gazes up at me, and I sense her mortal heart begin to pound with excitement. "I want to."

36
AGATHA

It is midnight by the time our ship eases into Argon's port, the docks lit by countless lanterns. Only the outline of the grand castle shows. "Wait until you see it in the daylight, girls. The jewels will wink at you from a thousand angles."

Beatrix and Cressida peer out from beneath their deep cowls at their new home, their gazes wide with a mixture of excitement and apprehension.

"We're not ready, Master Scribe," Cressida whispers, her hand smoothing over her forearm, where the emblems of Aoife and Aminadav glow—badges she does not deserve, since she has not yet mastered the affinities—after the Prime insisted on sending her off with them.

"It will inspire her," Lorel had claimed. *Fool.*

I pat the girl's shoulder, offering her what I hope is a motherly smile on my wrinkled face. "Do not worry. Your elemental sisters will guide you where your trainers have not had the opportunity. Learn, practice, and—most important—uphold the guild's laws, and you will do fine."

Their heads bob in unison.

"Disembark!" the ship's captain hollers into the night.

As one, the Shadows step forward in strict formation, Solange in the lead. They look fierce within their armor, truly like their namesake. Unseen.

Brigitta's healers are like startled doe by comparison, huddled as they follow. They are not here to appear fierce and fight, though. They are here to keep those fighting alive.

The hour is late, but Allegra warned me not to dally. "Come, ladies. The queen is anxious to meet her newest elementals."

And I am anxious to find answers.

The guards draw open the doors to Argon's throne room without a word to us.

"… And you do not feel you owe this to your murdered king?" Queen Neilina asks, her reedy voice quiet but cutting.

The man kneeling at the dais trembles. "My three sons have marched to the rift. I wanted to but, you see, my wife is very sick, and someone needs to remain behind to care for her and our livestock."

"And why did you not request the services of a healer?"

"We did, Your Highness, but the healer said the sickness came from the Ill-Gotten River, and it was beyond her skill."

Mordain has heard rumors of this lately—both mortals and elven alike afflicted by disease from these waters south of the Dead Wood. The mortals perish quickly, but the immortals suffer for years, withering away as their elven body fights whatever plagues it.

"Perhaps it is. But that was not for you to decide."

The elven male keels over, his hands clawing at his throat.

Beside me, Beatrix gasps.

"Do not make a sound," I warn in a hiss. The queen will consider it a flaw in her elementals.

We stand quietly and watch as Queen Neilina strips the air from the male's lungs with her powerful affinity to Vin'nyla. Her connection is said to be unparalleled. A divine blessing. A mortal would last mere seconds, but it seems like forever before he stills, his face turning shades from pink to red to purple, his body convulsing as it struggles.

"And now your wife will suffer alone, anyway," Queen Neilina purrs to the corpse. "Get him out of here."

Two guards move in and, collecting a leg each, drag the man out.

Now it's our turn.

"Come forward."

I lead the two elementals down the aisle of the stately throne room, brimming with decadence—pristine white marble woven with gold, jeweled mosaic windows depicting three of the fates, Malachi conspicuously absent—and empty of life at this hour.

Queen Neilina's ice-blue gaze feels heavier now than it did the last time I bowed before her in this very spot, almost fifty years ago. "The years have not been kind to you, Caster Agatha."

Master Scribe Agatha. It's a wonder she remembers who I am. Does she know Gesine was my mentee? I push that fear aside. I would already be clutching my throat for air, if she had any idea. "Such is the plight of a simple caster, Your Highness."

Queen Neilina hasn't aged a day. Maybe there is a small crease here, a single gray hair there, but it would be too minute to pick out. She is still devastatingly beautiful, with cheekbones that should cut through skin, and irises as icy as the waters high in the mountains of Skatrana, a stunning contrast to her inky-black hair and creamy, pale skin. Normally gold would not complement such a complexion, and yet her shimmering dress flatters her, as does the gleaming gold chunk of antler fastened around her neck—the largest token anyone in Mordain has ever laid eyes upon. It appeared there one day with a vague explanation about a gift from a Udralian emperor, and she has worn it devotedly ever since, in its raw form. What its purpose is, no one knows. If Neilina does, she has never shared it with anyone. Perhaps we should have paid closer attention to the fact that it materialized around the same time Neilina announced a coming heir.

The throne beside Neilina sits empty, glaringly so.

I liked King Barris. I heard him address Ybaris and Mordain on several occasions. He was soft-spoken—unexpectedly so for a king—and yet he carried himself with such grace, all would stop to listen.

Standing at Queen Neilina's side is Commander Caedmon Tiberius, a handsome and fierce-looking immortal. It's a blessing to the queen that her daughter inherited all of her fine looks and none of her father's. It would have been much harder to hide Princess Romeria's true lineage had the girl been born with the commander's blond locks.

"Bring my new elementals forward," she commands.

I urge Beatrix and Cressida forward with a nod. They glide toward the bottom of the dais, to kneel as they were taught.

Queen Neilina rises from her throne and strolls down the steps, her shimmering gold gown dragging behind her willowy frame. "Stand and show me your arms."

They do as asked, pulling their sleeves up to reveal the glowing symbols.

"Aoife and Aminadav. *Both* of them." Her voice rings with displeasure.

"They are the only two elementals in Nyos who are remotely ready." And even they are far too young.

She sniffs. "I suppose they will do." She sizes them both up and then calls out, "Collar, now."

A servant comes forth, a pillow balanced within his grasp as if presenting a crown.

"You. Come forth." Queen Neilina's attention is locked on Beatrix, who takes a shaky step forward and lifts her chin.

The queen secures the gold collar around her slender neck and pushes the two ends together. The click is loud and ominous. "There. You may go to your room now."

Wait a minute. "Your Highness, Caster Cressida requires a collar as well."

"Do you have one handy?" she asks crisply. "Because I do not. Two were *stolen* from me. Now I must endure the risk of an uncollared elemental caster in my midst. I do hope your guild trained her better than they did those other two."

Yes, a young and impressionable elemental, perhaps easier to break. I would hazard that using her last collar on the older of the two was not a coincidence.

"You have nothing to fear of Cressida, Your Highness. She knows her place is here in Argon. No amount of manipulating will persuade her to break her sacred oath. She would rather forfeit her own life."

The queen's eyes narrow, and for a moment, I'm afraid I've admitted to knowing too much. "Thank you for your escort, Caster. I shall retire now. I suggest you two do as well. We leave for the rift at dawn."

Fates. "You do not mean to bring *them* to war, do you?"

"Are you questioning my judgment?" she snaps.

I will not survive the hour if I don't get a handle on my tongue. "I am simply wondering if remaining in the tower would be more beneficial for their adjustment period. They are still young and inexperienced."

Her smile is wicked. "Do not worry. From what I've heard of Islor's current state, I do not expect much of a resistance."

"Your Highness." I bow again as she strolls away, her clicking heels an echo.

She didn't mention her missing children even once.

"Come, girls. Let us get you settled in." Though there doesn't seem much point.

My lungs are puffing by the time we reach the floor where the young elementals will be staying.

"This will be yours." Caster Elowen presents the small, windowless room with two cots adorned by white cotton sheets. A lantern burns on the nightstand between them, and another on the small four-drawer dresser. The only thing to distinguish it from a prison cell is the solid oak door rather than bars, but it can lock from the outside as needed, all the same.

Beatrix smooths a fingertip over a tiny vertical line scratched into the stone wall. There are dozens, as if a person was keeping count of something. "Whose room was this?"

"Caster Gesine and Ianca were the last to occupy this room," Elowen confirms with pursed lips. What she thinks of the two escaped elementals, I can only guess. She was once a pupil of Nyos and possibly even of mine, but if she was, I do not recall her face.

The two young girls share an uneasy glance. Even with a channel between land, I'm sure whispers have reached all corners of Mordain by now.

I clap my hands, trying to remain upbeat while foreboding hangs thick in the air. These girls were babes when they were taken from their parents. Nyos is all they've known. Now, they will remain in Argon's elemental caster tower until the change takes them. Maybe they'll make it back to Mordain one day, but I will be long gone from the realm of the living by then. "Casters, let me help get you settled in, then." I wave a hand at the servants, and they drop the crate that holds the girls' meager belongings before departing.

"I would normally give you the tour, but it is very late, and we are all leaving in the morning. It doesn't seem to make sense, does it?" Elowen gestures out the door. "The latrine is down the hall and to your left. The tower's dining room is on the ground floor. Morning meal will be served two hours before dawn. I would dress appropriately for our travels, with layers. It is normally three days' journey to the rift from here, but we can plan to arrive in half that time if we do not stop."

I stifle my complaints. I have yet to secure passage for this grueling adventure.

"Master Scribe, may I show you to your bed for the night?"

"I would very much like that, but first, allow me a moment to bid my farewells."

"Of course."

The moment Elowen is out of sight, Beatrix grabs my forearm. "War? They're sending us to war?" Of the two of them, she is the more skilled, but the weaker in connection to her affinities.

"You heard Her Highness. She is not concerned." Because life is only as valuable to her as she can expend it, I want to say. That will do no one any good to hear. "You will be fine. Your elemental sisters will take care of you."

Cressida's fingers skate across her naked neck. "We haven't learned about summoning yet."

"You have learned all the reasons why it has been banned." The actual process, though, that is the last lesson before their training is complete—more a warning of what *not* to do. Summoning is as much about intent as skill, and an elemental only needs the former to succeed. "Just stay away from any sanctum, and you need not worry about inadvertently summoning *anyone*."

"Yes, Master Scribe." But her furrowed brow belies her worry.

"Do not fret, sweet girl." I collect her hands in mine. "I remember you in diapers like it was only yesterday. I have watched you grow into a lovely, fine caster. You will do splendidly." Giving them each a hug and looking away before they can see my tears, I stiffen my spine and enter the hall where Elowen waits, pulling the girls' door shut behind me.

"The descent should be easier, but would you like a moment to catch your breath before we tackle the stairs again?"

I've already caught it, but I may as well take advantage of Elowen's consideration. "Yes, that would be a good idea. Is Yesenia's room on this floor, perhaps? I know it is late, but I wish to stop by to see her for a moment, if possible. It's been so long, and she was a favorite of mine."

"It is! And certainly. I doubt anyone is managing sleep tonight, ahead of tomorrow's departure." She falls into step beside me. "Tell me, how does Nyos fare these days?"

"Oh, the same as always. *Busy*. Students accidentally setting fire to bushes and such."

Elowen smiles. "And what of Caster Gesine and Ianca? Any news about them?"

"I believe someone said they saw them in Skatrana, but I haven't paid much attention. Why do you ask?" I know Gesine had help within this tower, but aside from Yesenia, I can't be sure of where anyone stands.

She shrugs. "I was just wondering. Their departure caused quite the stir. This is Yesenia's room." She knocks on the door.

A moment later, the petite, chestnut brown-haired caster answers. "Master Scribe!" She throws her arms around my neck, nearly knocking me over in the process.

I laugh as I return the gesture. She has aged so much in the decade since I last saw her, but her little upturned nose and smattering of freckles remain the same. "I thought, why not come and see my most troublesome pupil." To Elowen, I say, "Did you know that Yesenia had a habit of sneaking litters of kittens into my library? It wasn't until the third that I caught her doing it."

Yesenia flings her arms up in dismay. "That was twenty years ago. When are you going to stop holding that over my head?"

"Never. Holding things over my pupils' heads is one of the few joys this old woman has left." I stroll into her room without an invitation, hoping it's clear that I need to speak with her. Alone.

"I can bring her down to the guest quarters?" she offers.

Elowen nods, only too happy to shirk the responsibility of playing host and tour guide.

"It is so good to see you doing well here," I say with exaggerated cheerfulness, hoping those are the last words that catch Elowen's ears as Yesenia shuts her door.

"You are here about the taillok."

"I am." It's true that Yesenia was one of Nyos's most troublesome caster students, but she was also one of the brightest.

She moves for her dresser to continue folding laundered clothes. "I must admit, it is a blessing to have that blasted thing out of my head."

"I can only imagine. The Prime told me what you relayed to the queen, about what you saw last through its vision."

"The princess and Islorian king standing within a gate in Venhorn? Yes, that was unexpected, as much for Her Highness as for me. It looked quite grand." She tucks a stack of undergarments into her rucksack. "There was nothing there before, I'm sure of it. The taillok flew over those deadlands many times, and it was nothing but cracked earth and mountains."

"That is not entirely true. There was also a wall of ancient nymph script that has been there for longer than anyone can explain. I believe Caster Gesine figured out how to open it." The book buried in the bottom of my rucksack almost guarantees it.

Yesenia's eyes widen. "How?"

"She studied."

"I wish I'd paid more attention to these things." She sighs. "Gesine and Ianca have obviously made it, then? They're the only two who could've broken my link with the taillok."

Not the only two. A key caster could shred that link, I'm sure. "Gesine has. Unfortunately, Ianca went through the change on the way."

Sadness morphs Yesenia's pretty face, but it flitters off just as quickly. It is a distressing end these elementals must face, and most try not to dwell on it. "You've heard from Gesine? What did she say? About this gate and what's beyond? What is it like being surrounded by Islorians?"

"I've received word of Ianca, but beyond that, I haven't heard. We sent a letter, but who knows when it will arrive." I will no longer get the response. I suppose I will have to hear it in person, if I survive the journey. "The Prime said you saw an Islorian warrior attack Princess Romeria and fly backward, as if hit by Vin'nyla?"

She hesitates. "Yes, that's right."

"What *didn't* you tell the queen?"

She bites her bottom lip, her gaze shifting cautiously to the door. "I'm almost positive it was the princess herself who sent the warrior flying. Her eyes … they glowed *silver*. That's *impossible*, isn't it?"

"Silver." The mark of a key caster. "Have you told anyone else—"

"No." She shakes her head. "I didn't even dare tell Her Highness! I was afraid she'd accuse me of lying and have me executed."

"I would not put that past her." But more than likely, Neilina would look for ways to use that to her advantage. "Listen to me carefully, Yesenia, do not speak of what you have seen to anyone. There are things at play now that cannot be stopped. It is best we do not hinder them."

"Like this war we are heading to against the Islorians?"

I sigh. "Yes, well, this new version of the princess may be our only hope to stop it." If that is indeed her plan.

"What are we to do?"

"*You*? You are to do nothing. You stay alive. That is what all of you must do. I am leaving with you for the rift in the morning, to find a way across."

Yesenia's brow furrows with worry. "The Prime sent you on this journey?"

"No, the Prime thinks I'm below the castle, which is probably where I should be. She will not be happy when she discovers that I've gone, but it will be far too late for her to do anything about it." It's best I secure a spot in the wagon with the healers. The last thing I want to earn is Queen Neilina's notice. I will not be able to lie away my presence, for what use does a scribe have in her war? "Now, come, lead an old woman to her room, and let us pray that I wake up in the morning."

37
GRACEN

The dim glow of a candle and a baby's cries greet me as I step into my room.

"She stirred only moments ago," Sabrina whispers, Suri in her arms.

"Yes, she has an uncanny clock built inside." I slip off my new cloak and hang it on a nail by the door, and then unfasten my dress, hoping to silence her before her fussing wakes Mika and Lilou.

Sabrina brings her over to where I've settled in the wooden chair in the corner, handing her off to me. "Why are your hands so cold?"

"I was outside." I offer Suri a nipple and she latches on. My body responds instantly, the milk flowing into her greedy, toothless mouth. Not unlike my body's response to Atticus, though he is far from toothless, and it was not milk he wanted. But when I compare the two, are they all that different? Both offer vital nourishment for those in need.

They are nothing *alike,* I scold myself, stifling a laugh. This is a motherly, nurturing act.

What I'd like to do with Atticus is entirely different.

"I had one like this." Sabrina is by the door, my new cloak in her fingertips. Her glowing mark is a beacon in the darkness. "It was given to me on Presenting Day, when I became a royal tributary." Sadness laces her words. She may be relieved to have avoided the execution square, but she misses her role.

And the way she's looking at me now hints at her suspicions, that I have taken her place. But of course, the pieces fit easily. She knows I'm the one who spoke to the king on her behalf. How would I even have his ear otherwise?

"Kazimir handed it to me on my way out. I guess he had an extra?" I'm sure it's a lie, but I offer it to lessen the sting.

"Who?"

"The captain. Atticus's bearded friend?"

"*Atticus*?" Even in the candle's shadowy light, I can make out the shock painted across her face. "He lets you call him Atticus?"

I falter over my answer. Don't all his tributaries do this?

She swallows. "It's okay. I know His Highness must be desperate for a vein. It is actually smart during times like these, to choose a nontraditional route. No one would suspect you."

Yes, smart. Because why else would the king charm the baker so?

Sabrina slips into her pallet in the corner without another word.

It's only minutes before my ears catch the first of her soft sobs. She tries to stifle them, but they carry on, weighing on my heart as Suri feeds, depleting one breast's supply and moving to the next.

Finally, my nipple slips free of her gaping mouth and she sleeps soundly again. More than anything, I want to tuck her tiny body into her basket, clean myself up, and sneak off to Atticus's bedchamber as he requested. But Sabrina will guess where I'm going, and that seems unnecessarily cruel, especially on her first night out of the dungeon.

I can't, in good conscience, leave her like this, and so I sit on the edge of her pallet, smoothing a hand over her shoulder as guilt riddles me. "I am sorry, Sabrina."

"It's not your fault," she manages after a moment. "I

remember when I first came here after Presenting Day, before all this business with poison. In the beginning, the new royal tributaries are meant to serve the nobility as needed, and some of the ranking soldiers, the legionaries. But I saw His Highness walking through the castle one day. The other tributaries were fawning over his brother, but not me. I've always only ever wanted to serve him. I prayed he would choose me before his brother did. They never liked to share." She giggles through her tears. "Unlike the others, His Highness is known for changing tributaries often, and so I patiently waited *months* for my turn, hoping he would select me. When Genevieve went to him, I was *so* jealous of her. I wished something would happen to her so that maybe it could be my turn next." She says that quietly, like it's a secret. "And then something *did* happen. Something terrible. And I got her place. But I can't help but think that I wished this on myself." Her words fade into fresh sobs.

"No, you didn't. This is not your fault." Sabrina is only a few years younger than me, and yet she seems so young by comparison. Maybe it's that we've lived different lives since our Presenting Days, mine laden with brutality and worry. Hers, focused on fancy dresses and which prince might choose her.

"You're right. It's that terrible Princess Romeria's fault," she whispers bitterly.

I bite my tongue against the urge to defend the princess. I already know where Atticus stands. "The Lady Saoirse is the one responsible for your tainted blood." Either by her own hand or by someone else's.

She sniffles. "I heard Fikar saying that the priestess has been going door to door through the city to mark all the mortals, and the king's guard has been bringing the infected ones to the arena."

There's only one reason to do that. "Are there many?"

"Dozens so far, according to him. Most aren't tributaries."

"That is Fikar. He is known to exaggerate."

"He also said that the king gave orders to mark and take *all* the children from the households, even if they're not infected."

Take them. I was just with him and he never mentioned anything about that. "Where?"

"He didn't say." Sabrina rolls over, curling up against me, her tears soaking into my linen skirt. "Those poor children. They must be terrified."

My gaze wanders toward my bed where my children sleep soundly, imagining them taken from me by orders of the king. My chest pangs with sorrow. "None of this seems fair." But would Atticus do something so callous as take children from their mothers?

According to Sabrina and Fikar, he *is* doing it. Worse, he gave the order and then took me on a stroll through the royal garden, charming me as if nothing was wrong.

I stroke my fingers through Sabrina's blond locks until her sobs quiet and her breathing grows shallow. But my thoughts are hooked on her words. How could I possibly carry on tonight with him, knowing there are innocent mortals collecting in the cold arena, waiting for death? Children being ripped from their homes?

All I want to do is hold my children close, and pray for those who can't do the same. He gave me a choice, not an order. I will use the late hour as my excuse to not attend, should Atticus question me.

With that decision made, I climb in next to a sweaty little Mika, holding him tight, afraid that one day, I, too, will know the pain that so many of my mortal kin feel tonight.

38
ZANDER

"Welcome to Soldor!" Radomir bellows, he and his horse framed by the gaping mouth of the mine behind him, the helm bearing Ulysede's mark hiding his bulbous forehead and sunken cheekbones. But it cannot hide his black eyes.

"Still intact after so many thousands of years." Telor tips his head back to marvel at the gate that has existed since the earliest of any tomes, and who knows how long before. "Had I known there was another opening in the east, I would have destroyed it years ago."

"It is a good thing you did not know, then, isn't it, my friend? Because we would not have a hope in Azo'dem of reaching the rift in time." I take in three separate lines of soldiers beneath the cast of the moon's light—Islorian, Ybarisan, and the saplings we refuse to claim as our own. Tension has gripped our company since we left Ulysede to meet them, and then only amplified when the band of murderers and thieves emerged from their cave system, cords of merth dangling from their belts.

For all his scheming and aid to Neilina, Radomir was wise in bringing several of his most trusted into the gates to experience the nymphs' power firsthand. Once they heard that Princess

Romeria would honor Neilina's promise, that they need only suffer within their sapling skin until Hudem's moon, they agreed to shed the merth cord and accept Ulysede's helms and shields instead.

But I did not miss the way Radomir has marveled at Ulysede's splendor.

"What happens when Hudem's moon rises and they get what they want?" Elisaf whispers in my ear, as if reading my mind. "Do you really believe they will wear that armor and proudly serve Romeria for the rest of their days?"

"They will wear the armor to get themselves through the gates. They may even bow before her. But eventually, they will attempt to claim Ulysede for themselves." Radomir has led within these mountains for fates only knows how long. He all but declared himself the king of Venhorn.

He may have melted into a weepy puddle and professed his undying loyalty to Romeria, but there is no honor in these beings. There wasn't when they were the Islorians of their past—that is how they ended up in their predicament. Thieves and murderers, even then. One would be a fool to believe Radomir isn't already scheming. He won't be the only one, I'm sure. "They will not be allowed back inside the gates." There may only be three hundred of them, but that would be enough to overwhelm an empty city.

"Drakon and Iago will not forget." Elisaf nods to the two legionaries who sit on their horses, murder in their eyes. "I'm not sure even Abarrane's order to stand down will control them."

"It *must*. At least for now."

"Over twelve hundred soldiers on horseback through this mine, led by saplings who would betray their kin for their own gain in a heartbeat." Telor looks to me. "Are you sure, Zander?"

"That we must get to the rift and hold off Neilina until the Hudem moon? Of that, I have no doubt."

He peers back at his force. I see the same guarded faces he does. They follow orders as their lord marches alongside an exiled king. Earlier, they watched their lord order legionaries to execute seven Islorians alongside his own son, on charges of conspiring with the very Ybarisans who ride alongside us now.

The Islorians do not understand, and yet they follow.

The Ybarisans do not understand, and yet they follow.

The saplings have seen an end to their plight, and so they follow … for now.

"Let us lead by example."

Telor dips his head. "Your Highness."

Together we march toward the opening where Radomir waits, the legionaries riding in formation around me. Kienen joins us.

I look up at the moon and say a silent prayer that I see it again.

39
ATTICUS

The black spiral staircase creaks, announcing intruders.

"Is there nowhere in this kingdom I can hide and not be bothered?" I call out in a lazy drawl.

Kazimir and Rhodes stroll down the aisle of the library's fourth floor toward me.

"And at this hour too." The early-morning sun peeks through the window.

"No one in the city sleeps these days. The army is preparing to march for the east. Boaz has been banging on doors with the priestess in tow all night. She's marking everyone. Tributaries, regular household, the children."

Because that was my order. "Have they found any tainted?"

"They have. Too many to hang on the streets."

My stomach tenses. Will the city have any mortals left by the time Hudem arrives?

Kazimir slips a book off the shelf, feigning interest. "I always was fond of my theology teacher."

"And why is that?" I fan through the book in my hand before setting it back on the shelf. I've rifled through nearly every volume on old world speculation, but I have yet to uncover something about the nymphs or Stonekeep.

"She taught me much. Nothing about the fates, though." His tone is thick with lewd implications.

I inhale deeply. "Why do you smell like sex and ale?"

"Because you told me to chase rabbits, and they led me to Port Street."

"And into the loving arms of a mortal?"

Kazimir grins. "Sometimes questioning requires a certain finesse."

Beside him, Rhodes chuckles, a rare sound.

"I'm sure." At least someone enjoyed company last night. "And what has your *questioning* turned up?"

"Rumors run rampant. Everything from Adley and Spires being in a dungeon cell to burning on a pyre, Presenting Day moving up to this Hudem, His Highness stealing children from their keepers—"

"I'm not *stealing* them." I'm safeguarding them.

"Some believe they are to be sold to Kettling's underground child market as part of the bargain struck with Adley."

"They honestly believe I would ..." My voice drifts with a grunt of disgust. "Well, there's no use for that bargain, anyway. The wedding is no more. Saoirse is in the tower."

"Some believe she will be released and back in your arms, just as the Ybarisan princess was."

I scowl. "Saoirse has never been in my arms."

"People are afraid." Rhodes's deep voice grates in the quiet library.

I sigh. "That was the plan." Though a dangerous one. Fear breeds desperation, followed quickly by recklessness and rebellion. I need it to hold off until Hudem. If Romeria's claim about the end of the blood curse is true, I will release every child. "Anything else?"

"Now that the wedding is no more and the nymphaeum is closed, most of the nobility are desperate to return home. Several have been caught trying to bribe their way out. Boaz has punished them accordingly."

"With strong words?" I jest, but I know better. He'll have divested them of their gold and publicly flogged them to make a point. They'll never be loyal to me now. I'll have to strip them of their lordships and remind them that I could have stripped them of their heads. "And the port?"

"The captain of the *Silver Mage* made a fuss at the docks because we wouldn't let him board to sleep in his cabin. Claims you'll be hearing from Empress Roshmira if his ship isn't released soon."

"Likely, but not for another week or two." Hudem will be long past by then. Pissing off Seacadore's ruler is not in my game plan. We need her for vital trade.

And we have more pressing matters ahead of us than spying and collecting gossip. "The king's guard will hold the city while the Cirilean army rides for the east. Rhodes, you will lead them. Kaz and I will follow in a day's time and find you before you reach the plains." A handful of soldiers move much faster than an entire company of them.

"Your Highness." Rhodes bows and strolls away to relay the order.

I flip through the last book on the shelf, disheartened. "All these volumes, and not one gives me what I need."

"Seriously, what are you looking for?"

"Answers to questions that likely do not matter." I slide it back where it belongs.

Kazimir frowns. "The eastern lords are in the dungeon, you are riding to war, and it appears you took a vein. I was expecting you to be in a better mood."

"One would think." He's right. My adrenaline should be surging in anticipation. I've always preferred the battlefield to these castle walls. "Tell me, what was your read on Gracen last night?" Did I somehow misunderstand everything?

Kazimir studies me a moment. "She gave you her vein willingly?"

"Of course." I glare at him. "And she was supposed to come to my chamber after tending to her baby's needs, but she did not."

"You ordered her?"

"I *requested*, and she seemed eager." And then I lay in an empty bed, waiting for her. I toyed with the idea of sending someone to bring her to me, and then I almost found my own way there, worried something might have happened to her. In the end, I decided against it, telling myself that her baby must not have settled and she was needed.

That is what my ego needed to hear.

I came to the library, as much to distract myself over my silly and inexplicable pining over a mortal as to find vital answers about the possible fate of my realm.

A knowing look fills Kazimir's face. "So go to the Goat's Knoll to satisfy your other needs."

I snort. "After our last exchange, I'm not entirely certain Bexley wouldn't bite my cock off." I hesitate. "And I have no interest in her." Or anyone else.

His eyebrows arch. "I have known you for how long? Fought beside you how many times? Seen you fuck your way through how many tributaries?"

"Too many to count," I admit.

"You change them more often than I sharpen my blades. So, what is it about this one that has you so enamored?"

"I don't know. Honestly." I smirk. "Maybe she has me under a spell, like Romeria has trapped Zander." That was the only reasonable explanation anyone could find for my brother's relentless weakness.

Kazimir goes quiet, and I know what he's thinking. *You were under that same spell, Atticus.* He watched me slip out of her tent just before daybreak. He knew what we'd done. "Or maybe you are subconsciously looking for a suitable queen to sit next to you, someone to share the burden of the throne. It is applaudable. *Shocking,* given it's you ... but applaudable."

I roll my eyes. "Maybe I am."

"Good. But Gracen has no aspirations for that role, nor is she suited to it."

I know this, and yet my thoughts and my wants keep gravitating toward her.

Kazimir smooths a hand over his beard. "What do you plan to do with her? Make her immortal?"

"*No.*" The answer comes without thought.

He folds his arms over his chest in challenge. "You *could*. You are the king. You could break Islor's most sacred of laws."

"She wouldn't want that," I murmur, more to myself. Would she?

"No," he agrees. "She is a simple baker from Freywich."

"Baymeadow, actually. In the plains. She had a keeper named Cordin. He was kind to her. Taught her how to read."

Kazimir blinks. "And tell me, where did Sabrina grow up?"

I falter on the answer, seeing his point. Have I ever known this much about any of my other tributaries?

The look on my captain's face answers that for me.

"Gracen is a mortal mother with three young children, whom she will want to grow old with. And you are an immortal king who is taking children from their parents and executing her kind every day."

My anger flares. "As if I have a choice!"

He raises his hands in surrender. "My read on her, Atticus, since you asked ... is that she may be smitten with you, but she is not a fool, and she will do anything to keep herself and her children alive. As for why she did not come last night, perhaps she's heard rumors of the children Boaz is prying from mothers' arms and storing for you and isn't so smitten anymore."

"I'm only trying to protect them."

"You see that, and I see that, but mortals may see it differently, and they are the ones out there ingesting poison and rebelling against the elven rule."

I sigh. I've been so focused on what the lords and ladies and Boaz think of my decisions, I haven't given any thought to what the mortals think. Another of my brother's strengths, which is clearly a flaw for me.

I released Sabrina by Gracen's request. It was the right thing to do, anyway, and the decision eased my weighted conscience, but it was because she asked that I did it at all.

What would she want me to do with these mortals?

And what can I do that will not make me look as ill-fitted to rule as my brother did by the end?

"I think it's time I paid a visit to the arena."

"For what, may I ask?"

"To ensure Boaz isn't handling this situation in a way I may one day regret." I haven't told Kazimir about Romeria's wild claims yet and I'm not sure why.

I move toward the iron staircase down to the main floor. A colorful section slows my feet, and the title on the nearest shelf catches my eye. "Hold a moment."

The group of mortals huddle together in the center of the square, eyeing the dangling ropes with trepidation.

"Fates. This many, already?" I count thirty-four mortals with glowing emblems on their hands, standing before me. In wagons behind them, bodies are piled. Too many to count. Wendeline has been busy.

"Four in this lot are tributaries. They must have tainted themselves within the last day because the keepers all fed recently without issue. The rest are regular servants," Boaz confirms, his hand resting on his pommel.

Regular servants who were determined to never serve as tributaries again. "And did they ingest it knowingly?" Or was it forced on them, like Sabrina?

"Does it matter? They wear the mark. They cannot be allowed to live, Your Highness. You've said so yourself."

"I know what I said." I move toward the group. The stench of piss grows stronger as I approach, the dark spots on the sandy ground marking those who've lost control of their bladders.

Most of them bow, despite their predicament. They're a mix of ages, from elderly to barely past Presenting Day. One of them—a wiry old woman with spotty skin and no cuff in her ear, a Rookery inhabitant, surely—sneers. Defiant, even in her last hour of breath.

"Why did you take the poison?" I ask to no one in particular.

Silence answers.

"Really? *No one* has a good reason for wanting to commit murder? I find that hard to believe." Because, despite not wanting to spare their blood any longer, what they've done is tantamount to that.

"These here didn't have nothing to do with it, Your Highness." A gray-haired man waves a hand at three women in their early thirties, gripping each other's arms. One of them is pregnant. "I knew their keepers would be knockin' on their doors soon enough again, so I put some in their drink. Please, spare 'em. I beg it of ya. I'll take whatever punishment you wanna give, but show them mercy."

Echoes of "Mercy, please!" rise from the mortals, churning my stomach. I have to turn away. Battles with enemies holding swords, I can handle. Helpless, unarmed mortals begging for their lives, on the other hand …

"Silence!" Boaz barks, the ring of steel from his blade sliding out of its scabbard quieting the crowd immediately.

Heavy footfalls sound then as guards lead eight more mortals in at sword point. Three are children. One is too young to comprehend what's happening. Certainly, too young to ingest the poison on her own. Her blue eyes are wide as she takes in the people, her thumb stuck in her mouth.

She reminds me of Gracen's daughter.

A mixture of nausea and anger hits.

What if Romeria is telling the truth? What if the poison flowing through these mortals' veins means nothing in just days?

And what if Gracen somehow finds out that I knew?

She would see me as a monster, and she would be right to.

I gave the order to execute children the night of the royal repast, as a show of zero tolerance, and those faces have lingered in my mind ever since. I can't make that same decision again, not if there is a chance.

And yet I find myself in an impossible position. Letting these mortals walk free will only encourage others who may have been hesitant. What's more, the keepers will slaughter them. It's no longer safe for them in the streets.

And what if the curse is *not* lifted on Hudem? What if that is a stalling tactic?

Damn you, Romeria.

Damn you and your letter.

"Long live, Princess Romeria!" the spotty old lady from the Rookery shouts. "May she reign over all—"

Her words are cut off by a dagger through her throat, earning gasps and shrieks.

I sigh. Boaz's aim has always been true, whether it be blade or arrow. In this case, it wasn't needed, and now the mortals are only more agitated.

"If the mortal admits to malicious intent when Wendeline is marking them, hang them outside their doors and be done with them." There can be no mercy for them in my kingdom. "The rest, bring here, but do not execute them yet. Post guards at all arena entrances. Feed them and do not harm them."

Boaz scowls "Your Highness, they are tainted."

"Yes, I understand that," I say with forced patience. "What about the children you have gathered in the ballroom? How many are there?"

"I have not counted, but many. We have targeted the areas of the city known for larger households first, to avoid a rush of dosing."

"As always, you are strategic." Sometimes too much. "And their keepers?"

"Most complied. A few rebelled, and I made swift examples of them. Resistance should be minimal going forward."

"I don't need the whole of Cirilea against me, Boaz."

"What of the children? Who have you placed in there to care for them?" Kazimir speaks up.

Boaz shrugs. "Let the older watch the younger."

"Babes watching babes," Kazimir mutters. "Brilliant."

"I am not a nursemaid," Boaz barks. "I am tasked with bringing them here, not minding them. What of these? How long are we to keep them corralled here?"

"Until the dawn after Hudem." When Romeria's fantastical claims will either be real or not. I peer up at the tower and catch a flutter of black hair moving in the window before it's gone. "And then we will have ourselves the grand execution that you are so desperate for."

40
ROMERIA

"Good morning, Eden," I call out, strolling past the menacing gargoyles.

She falters in her step, alarm plastered across her face. "Good—morning?" She notes my clothes, the ones she laid out for her queen.

I smile as I push through the doors and walk along the path. The morning sunshine feels natural against my cheeks, as if there is nothing between my skin and its rays. After months of being stuck wearing someone else's face, I can finally enjoy being back in my old one for a little while.

And it's not only my face. The voice I recognize as Romy's is in my ear, the reflection in the dressing mirror showed a familiar body.

Ahead, in the training ground, wooden swords crack. "Congratulations. You've just been gutted," Jarek declares, stooping to collect the practice weapon and handing it back to Brawley. "Again! And this time, remember that you are not a tree. Move your damned feet!"

Brawley jumps at his bark, fumbling with his sword only to drop it.

"Don't take it personally. He's always extra cranky in the morning," I call out.

Jarek has daggers within each grasp before he's even spun around, his menacing glare leveled on me. "Who are you?"

I mock gasp. "You don't remember me? I'm insulted. And we had so much fun that night."

His eyes flash with shock before narrowing. He juts his chin toward Horik and together they take measured steps, approaching me from either side. "How did you get in here?"

"I walked in."

"Into Ulysede." He purses his lips with doubt.

"Yeah. There was no one out front. You should have better security. Who's the commander in charge of this place, anyway? They're doing a shitty job."

Jarek's fists turn white around his dagger hilts.

I've provoked him enough. "Relax, it's *me.*" I reach up and slip the mask off my face.

Jarek's rigid body sinks with his sigh. "*Romeria.*" He sheathes his blades.

Horik's deep bellow of laughter trails him as he wanders back to their pupils.

"I had to test this thing out." The sun glints off the metal. "It works!"

"Do you realize how close you were to a blade through your chest?" he snaps, holding his hand out. "Let me see that."

"Be careful. It's old."

He studies it. "Vin'nyla's wings. Where did you get this?"

"From Lucretia. I went to see her last night—"

"You went down there *without me*?" His face morphs with anger.

I hold up my hands in surrender. "Hey, I came to your door, but you were *busy*." I give him a knowing look.

"Then you interrupt me. You *do not* go down into that serpent's tomb alone."

"Aye, aye, Captain." I mock salute, allowing irritation to bleed into my tone. I knew Jarek would be annoyed when he found out. I didn't expect him to scold me like I'm a child. "Lucretia's not going to hurt me. Besides, I can defend myself."

"Against that thing? I doubt any of us can." He hands me the mask back, his temper ebbing.

"She was asking about you. I think she has a crush." I should probably warn him that she's also a pervert who can travel unseen through wards and bedroom doors, but I resist the urge. It's best he doesn't know that, unless I want to spend my nights with Jarek standing over my bed.

"Whose face was that, that you were wearing just now?" he asks, a deep furrow across his forehead.

The doors swing open before I can answer, and Zorya and Gesine rush out, Eden close behind. She must have run to the library in a panic. Zorya's hands are filled with swords and the caster's eyes glow green, likely with a shield.

"It's okay, it's me. I was wearing this." I wave my hand, the mask's silver flashing.

The one-eyed warrior relaxes her fighting stance, and Gesine releases her hold of her power as they take the path toward us.

"A token from Vin'nyla. May I?" Gesine collects it from my grasp to study it. "Magnificent."

"Lucretia has five more hidden in the crypt. I don't know what they do, but if they're anything like *this* one ..."

"Did *you* know she went to the crypt alone last night?" Jarek's tone carries accusation as he glares at Gesine.

"I stopped at the library to tell her, but she was *busy* too." Seems *everyone* was busy last night but me.

Gesine's cheeks flush as she hands the mask back to me. "I imagine there is still much the oracle hides from us."

"You have *no* idea."

Jarek's head cocks, his glare lethal. "What is that supposed to mean?"

I sigh heavily. If he was mad before, he'll be reaching for my neck soon. "Those nymph engravings? They're doors to other stones. One of them opens to the nymphaeum in Cirilea."

Jarek's features go slack. "You didn't—"

"I went through it."

I press my hand over the stone that leads to Cirilea, and childish laughter curls in my ears. "Lucretia said most of them don't work anymore."

"Since the great rift, I would imagine." Gesine studies another stone closely. "These markings are familiar."

Jarek scans each one. "They all look the exact same to me."

"Not if you have spent years staring at one of these, trying to make sense of it." She taps the wall. "This one leads to Nyos, I am positive."

I test the carvings. "Nothing."

"It is too bad it no longer works. We could have had a doorway directly into Mordain."

I snort. "Yeah, because I'm sure they'd roll out a warm welcome for me if I showed up there."

"Master Scribe Agatha would. She would have loved to meet you. She would have kept you safe."

"Where is this eel you keep talking about, anyway?" Zorya scowls at the emptiness around us, deftly spinning a karambit between her fingers.

"Serpent," Gesine corrects her. "And not even that. She is a sylx, and I'm sure she is close by, waiting to reveal herself when she feels the time is right."

"No rush." Jarek's shrewd gaze searches the shadows as if he can make out her hiding spot within them.

Lucretia's location doesn't matter. "I'm going to Cirilea again tonight," I announce.

That jerks his attention back to me.

I can already hear what he's going to say. "I need to find out what Atticus is doing about Queen Neilina and the poison."

"You already know what his solution is for the latter. You've seen the executions."

"That was before we wrote to him." Zander and I didn't hold back much in our letter, but we have no idea if Atticus listened. He may not trust me, but will he send an army north in the chance that we're right? Will he stop slaughtering mortals, knowing that what flows through their veins won't matter after Hudem? Will he do *anything* at all? "Zander is heading to the rift to try to stop Neilina. He needs to know what kind of help he can expect against her, if any. The only way to find that out is in Cirilea. And I can't sit in Ulysede while the world around us burns. Not when I can help."

Jarek sighs, but he doesn't argue. "Can others pass through this with you?"

"Yes, but—"

"Then I am going too."

"They'll recognize you." I wave my mask. "I'm wearing this so no one recognizes me. If the guards see us together, the mask won't help."

He sets his jaw with determination. "I can blend in."

"*Really*?" I eyeball all six-foot-something of him—leather and blades and long braids. "Because I'm pretty sure you can't be anything *other* than a legionary, Jarek."

"You are *not* going through there alone, Romeria," he growls. "Talk some sense into her, witch."

"In this, I must agree with Jarek." Gesine smiles apologetically. "There is too much at stake if you are caught, and you still have much to learn where your affinities are concerned. Jarek's sword by your side, where your powers may not help you, will be invaluable—"

"Fates!" Jarek shouts.

I spin around, panicked.

He's holding Lucretia in the air by one arm, his hand clamped around her neck.

"Put her down," I warn evenly.

But she's not struggling against his grip. "You do not like me like this?" She manages through a strangled voice. "How about now?"

My jaw drops as Lucretia morphs into a perfect replica of Eden, right down to the beauty mark on her cheek and her doe eyes.

Jarek's face twists with horror, and he releases his hold instantly. By the time Lucretia's feet touch the stone floor, she's already back to her previous form.

"So you can do *that* too. Good to know." I spare a shocked look toward Gesine. Apparently, I need a lesson in sylx abilities.

"Do not sneak up on me like that. *Ever*." Jarek snarls.

Amusement flashes in Lucretia's yellow eyes. "Your advisors provide you with sage counsel, Your Highness," she purrs, seemingly unbothered by Jarek's reaction as she strolls around Gesine, her billowing sheer dress—crimson, this time—dragging along the stone floor behind her. "Use those most loyal to you. Allow them to protect you. That is what they are here for. To sacrifice themselves for their queen."

"No one's sacrificing themselves for me." But it would be nice not to face Cirilea alone.

"Pan would offer much assistance in gathering information. He was helpful in Norcaster, was he not?" Gesine suggests. "And no one knows his face."

"His mark glows, though." After the tournament, I'm sure everyone in Cirilea knows what that stands for.

"I can cut off his hand," Zorya offers, her suspicious gaze on Lucretia, who's doing her usual slinking around.

"Or I can temporarily conceal it for him," Gesine counters, with an admonishing look at her new not-so-secret lover. "If you can get outside the walls of the castle, you have allies in Cirilea.

People who can help you gather information, if they don't already have the answers."

"I can get us outside the walls from the royal garden. And inside the castle. Annika showed me a path the night she helped me escape."

"And you assume she did not inform her brother that you know of that? That it won't be either sealed or heavily guarded?" Jarek counters.

I honestly don't know if she would. Annika has surprised everyone more than once. "But there's no reason they should think I'm in Cirilea. Worst case, we turn back."

"No, worst case is you are shot with a merth arrow and die."

"So, you're in a glass-half-full kind of mood. *Great.*"

Jarek ignores me, shifting to Gesine. "Who is this ally you claim we have?"

"A Seacadorian mortal who lives in the Rookery and leads much of the mortal cause. His name is Seamus Potter—"

"Seamus Potter!" Jarek barks with laughter. "You expect us to rely on *Seamus Potter*?"

"I take it you know him?" I ask.

"Of course, I know him. He's a petty thief. How he hasn't been hung yet is beyond me."

"Hey!" I waggle my finger at Jarek's face. "Not *all* thieves are untrustworthy."

"That one? I trust less than *her*." He juts his chin toward Lucretia, capping it off with a severe glare. "He was likely peddling the poison and tainting unsuspecting souls. He could already be dead."

"Well, whatever else he may be, he has already been an immeasurable help to us," Gesine says. "He is the reason we found each other in the first place, Romeria."

"I asked Bexley for help."

"And she relies on Seamus for many things. If you can get to the Goat's Knoll, ask the bartender for him. He's a small man with carrot-colored hair and a weathered face. I am sure he will be more than happy to help if you give him my name."

Going there means seeing Bexley again. Even with my mask on, that seems risky.

Still, a buzz of adrenaline stirs inside me. There are so many people I have wondered about, and ever since last night, my mind has been spinning over the possibilities. How is Dagny and her family? And Corrin? Did Atticus mark them as enemies? Does Annika think I'm a traitor? Does she hate me? Even Wendeline has been in my thoughts every day. What has Atticus done to her? What did she tell him?

"We cannot simply stroll in. We need a plan," Jarek says reluctantly, and I know I've won him over.

"It is best you visit the tavern after dark," Gesine adds.

"Fine. We go tonight." That gives us hours to prepare.

Jarek sighs. "Zorya, go and find the imbecile."

41
GRACEN

"I suppose it's as good a use as any?" I watch with reluctance as three servants pack crates with the wrapped cakes and confectionaries that I've spent weeks preparing. I'd worked so hard on those, knowing they would be served at the royal wedding feast. The cellar shelves were full of them, but they are dwindling.

"Last wedding, the cakes went to the soldiers too," Fikar says.

"Yes, it is becoming a habit around here. Maybe a sign that the Ascelin princes should not attempt to marry," Corrin says beside me.

"Either way, the soldiers deserve sweets too." Fikar grins at me as he passes, his skinny arms straining against his load. The other two follow closely after, each sneaking a cake.

Corrin scolds them but lets them go with their pockets bulging.

The castle cellar is vast and filled to the brim—with preserves and root vegetables, browning onions dangling from nails on the wall, casks of wine and mead, barrels of grain, and more cured meat than all the stands in the Cirilean market put together.

Every time I find my way down here, I marvel at the amount of food available and the lack of punishment for servants should they indulge. Not that I've seen anyone ever take advantage. Most came from outside the castle household and realize what a plum position they have here. *I* certainly do. In Freywich, we all knew the keepers' cellars were overflowing, and yet we were lucky to get a second helping of stale bread and cold stew made from blemished fruit. But I'm not the only one with that past; there are plenty of stories just like mine. I can only hope my children find roles within the royal household and remain here.

"Not those! Take the ones on the left. They'll be spoiling sooner!" Corrin hollers at two servants who hold bushel baskets of potatoes.

"When does the army leave?" We've been tasked with collecting as much food as we can spare, to send along with them.

"Within the hour, which is why we're loading up the wagons as fast as we can."

I hesitate. "Will the king be going?"

"I imagine so. He has led those men for decades, and they will look to him to lead now. Though, you would have to ask him yourself to get a sure answer."

If he's leaving within the hour, I suppose I won't have a chance. Will he be fighting too? I would assume so.

What if something happens to him?

The knots in my stomach tighten.

Corrin's gaze drifts to my neck. I stole a glance in a mirror this morning to confirm that the marks, though barely noticeable, are there. "Are you relieved to hear that?"

Do I want him gone, is what she's asking.

It would make things less complicated, with Sabrina in my room and all my conflicting thoughts. When I woke up this morning, after tossing and turning for hours, my worries were even heavier. "He has been kind to me," I say out loud, as much to answer Corrin's question as to remind myself of the other side of Atticus. Not that it eases my conscience much. I am being lavished by his mercy, but what about all the other mortals? It doesn't seem right.

Corrin makes a sound I can't interpret.

Now that Fikar and the others have left, I have a chance to ask. "Have you heard anything about marked mortals being executed in the square?"

The look she gives me answers that question. "What did you expect to happen, Gracen? He cannot leave them to roam the city streets."

"I suppose not. What about the children I've heard have been taken from their families? Is that also true?"

Corrin's face hardens. Another confirmation.

"Where is he keeping them?"

"In a ballroom in the castle's west wing, under guard, from what I've heard, though I haven't seen them myself. Many more come in by the hour, with no one minding them." She tsks. "The children are alone and terrified."

My hands press against my mouth. "I don't understand how he could do this." It's not the Atticus I know. Am I a fool?

She steps closer to me. "Because no matter how charming he may be to get what he wants from you, he will rule this realm as he sees fit, for the good of *his* kind. He is *not* his brother, and we are mortals. Chattel to them, and nothing more. You have his blessing, where most do not. It is best you keep your head down, do your job, and do not share your opinions on his kingship. That is how I have survived. That is how you and your children will survive."

I nod.

"Now come, let us see what turnips we can spare."

We are halfway to the root vegetables when a flurry of *Your Highness* sounds, and servants rush to bow.

Even with all my inner turmoil, my heart leaps in my chest as Atticus strolls in, Kazimir trailing him. Here I was, only moments ago thinking I would not see him again. Worrying, if I must admit.

His blue eyes quickly find me, and dimples appear with his easy smile.

Memories of last night—of his strong hands on me, his tongue along my skin—are still ripe, and capable of feeding fantasies I've never had for *any* male. But the reality of what he does when he's not with me douses any flames that might erupt.

Corrin makes another one of those grumbles I can't read, but I doubt it's approval for this visit or the king's intentions. "Your Highness, I did not think you would ever be able to find your way here."

"Would you believe I used to sneak down here all the time as a child to steal sweets from that room?" He points to the one holding all the cakes.

"I do recall your mother the queen mentioning something about your impish ways. Though, that was many years ago before my time, given I am only a mortal and you are *elven*. What can we help *His Highness* with?"

I can't help but think Corrin's words are meant to be a reminder to me—of our stark differences.

Of our impossibilities.

Atticus will reign long after I've grown old and died. And he will have lost interest in my aging body before then.

His lips curl, as if he can read the intention behind her words and finds them amusing. "I must speak to the baker for a moment. In private."

She claps her hands. "Everyone, fill your arms with a load of supplies and come with me."

The five servants scuttle to comply, and in less than twenty seconds, everyone is gone, including Kazimir.

"I can clear a room like no one else." Atticus rounds the table where I stand. "How are you, Gracen?"

My nerves spike. Is he angry with me for not attending him last night? Is that why he has sought me out down here? "I am well, Your Highness."

His eyebrow arches. "Are we back to that?"

"Atticus," I amend. Suddenly, I'm as anxious as I was that day we ran into each other in the library. Speaking of which … Tucked under his arm is a leather-bound book, and an excuse to steer the conversation. "Have you visited the library today?"

"Yes. In fact, I've been there for hours, since well before dawn, scouring."

After he gave up on waiting for me? How long did he actually wait, though? He's the king. I doubt long at all. "And did you find what you wanted?"

"No. But I did find this." He slides the book out and sets it on the table.

"What is it?"

"Open it and see." Atticus shifts to stand behind me, his arms bracketing either side of my hips as he rests his hands on the table. "Go on."

I'm acutely aware of how close he is. With tentative fingers, I flip open the first page to see floral penmanship. "*Samara's Quest*," I read the title out loud.

"I stumbled upon a section in the library with fictional stories written by mortals."

"*Written* by mortals?" I momentarily forget my nerves as I smooth my fingers over the cover. It's simple in design.

"Yes. And it made me think of you and that book you learned to read on. It might not be as exciting as Hania's adventure, but I thought you would like it."

"You remembered." I figured he wasn't even listening.

His soft chuckle curls in my ear, sending a shiver down my spine. "Why would I not?"

I peer over my shoulder and up into his eyes. "Because you have more to focus on than my prattling."

His smile is lazy, teasing. "I *much* prefer listening to your prattling than all the lords and ladies in Islor, actually."

"Thank you, Atticus, for this gift." It'll be only the second book I've ever read. "I will take extra care and return it to the library as soon as I'm finished," I promise.

"No need. And if you enjoy it, maybe you can teach your children to read with it. I'm sure they would like that." His gaze drifts to my mouth. "Why didn't you come to me last night?" There's a vulnerability in his voice that I have never heard, and coupled with that look, it's enough to make me confess to everything.

My throat bobs with my hard swallow. "Sabrina was upset. She's having a difficult time adjusting to her new role, and I thought it would be best to remain and comfort her."

"That's very kind and selfless of you." There's a pause. "Is that the only reason?"

No. Though at this very moment, as I stare up into his eyes, and my pulse drums in my ears, I can't find any reason at all for not returning last night. My mind is drawing a blank.

I pull my focus away, to turn the pages. They are old but pristine. I doubt the book has ever been read by anyone but its author. It's such a sweet and thoughtful gesture.

But how can Atticus be so thoughtful and sweet to me, and so cruel to others?

"I heard ..." My voice fades as I lose my courage.

"You heard what?" There's an edge to his tone.

I swallow. "That you are leaving to fight in the east within the hour?" It's the truth and yet not what I intended, and something tells me he knows that.

"They are leaving shortly. I will ride at dawn. I would much rather remain here to ensure Cirilea's strength, but I must lead my men as we deal with traitors in the east. I cannot allow this level of treason."

"Will it be dangerous?"

"As dangerous as any battle is. Why? Are you worried for my safety?" There's a hint of humor in his voice again.

I twist my body until I'm facing the Islorian king. "Of course I am. I do not wish to see harm come to you." That, I can at least say honestly.

He pauses. "You've heard about the children too." He must read the agitation in my every limb.

I nod.

"And what have you heard about the mortals?"

"That you are executing all who the priestess marks as infected. That your king's guard is taking children from their beds in the night, without explanation, and leaving them alone in a room."

"And you are bothered by it."

Corrin's warning is a shrill scream in my ear, and yet I can't abide it. "Very much so." Atticus did tell me to speak freely.

"As you should be." His jaw tenses. "It bothers me too."

"Why can't you leave them be? The ones who aren't tributaries, I mean. What flows through their veins should no longer be of consequence, as long as they contribute to their household as intended."

"I wish it were that simple. But the mortals who show as infected can no longer remain with their keepers. They will not be welcome there anymore."

"And the children your king's guard has taken?"

"Will either be fed the poison unknowingly or become tributaries far too young, with or without my blessing. The safest place for them right now is in the castle."

I'm beginning to see his rationale, even if it's hard to digest. "For how long?"

"Until I know for sure they are safe," he answers cryptically. "But I've ordered Boaz to stop executing the ones who didn't knowingly consume it, and to keep them in the arena under protection." He watches me, as if weighing my reaction.

"That's … good." For now.

"The reason I came here, Gracen, is that the mortal children in the ballroom need care, and I would like you to be in charge of it."

"Me?" I squeak.

"I cannot think of a better person for this particular role." His eyes drift over my face. "I trust you to ensure they are cared for properly while they are held here. I trust you, period."

I feel lightheaded. "Of course, Your Highness. Yes, I will do it."

He smiles. "I will advise Boaz that he is to accommodate all of your requests, whatever they may be. Blankets, food, additional support … whatever you deem necessary, he is to comply without question. You give the order, and it is done."

My mind spins. Me, giving orders to others? I cannot fathom it. But for these children, I can do it. "Can I go see them now?" They must have been in there for hours.

His hand folds over mine. "Shortly. If you'll allow me another moment of your precious time." He grazes my cheek with the backs of his knuckles before smoothing his palm over my neck.

I swallow. "Did you need me?" I reach for the collar of my dress, ready to unfasten and push it away, to give him access, glancing cautiously toward the stairs at the other end of the cellar.

"Kazimir will not let anyone enter. And, yes, I *need* you, Gracen. But not like that." The intent in his gaze is potent, intoxicating.

My body flushes with anticipation. "Thank you, Atticus, for the book, and for trusting me with so much." I stretch up and press a chaste kiss against his lips. When I break free, he chases, his other hand finding its way to my hip as his mouth collides against mine, as if he was restraining himself but can't anymore.

Our tongues tangle much like they did last night, his powerful body enveloping me, his hand venturing from my hip to my backside, down to my thigh.

"Can I?" I reach out with a tentative hand, curling a short wisp of his hair between my fingertips.

"You don't have to ask for permission, Gracen," he whispers against my mouth. "In fact, please do not. And you may touch me anywhere you wish to."

Unable to resist, my fingers crawl up his stately jacket, over the fine embroidery, the detailed gold buttons, before I shift my focus wholly to the strength of the male beneath, and the urge to feel him.

"I don't normally *take* as I did last night."

I peer into his eyes to find them blazing. "What do you mean?"

"I mean, you didn't give me a chance to thank you properly."

His lips find my neck. I close my eyes and revel in his tongue against my skin again, as his mouth moves downward, tracing my collarbone. His fist balls up material from my skirt.

"But you will give me that chance tonight when you come up to my chamber."

I tip my head back. "I will do whatever you wish."

"*I wish.* But in case there is any doubt, that *is* also an order." He pulls me close until I feel the press of his hard length against my stomach.

"Yes, Your Highness." My voice has turned heady, desperate.

His teeth scrape along my jawline, but then he pulls away with a deep groan. "I know you are anxious to see the children, so I will not hold you any longer. Tonight, at midnight." With one last kiss against my lips, he strolls out, humming.

And I'm left standing there, dumbfounded by what just happened.

Corrin sweeps in moments later. "What did he want?" Her gaze automatically shifts to my neck.

But my thoughts are already racing forward. "The children will be hungry," I hear myself murmur. "Let's get Fikar back in here with some more crates."

42
ZANDER

"This is the halfway mark," Radomir announces, pointing at the narrowed path and a portico high above us. The same odd alphabet that marks the sanctum in Ulysede and countless books in its library shows here, linking Soldor to ancient times far beyond our comprehension.

Perhaps Gesine can find some knowledge on it.

Torches burn every ten riders for the safety of the horses, but even I appreciate having the extra light to marvel on this mine that the saplings have used for centuries, many of its walls and stalwarts not only intact but in pristine condition, the arches and details still distinguishable as if many millennia have not passed, and the earth running alongside the city did not crack open from the angry might of a god.

I peer behind us at the snaking lines of soldiers, all with a guarded eye on the enemy that rides at their side. We've been moving for hours through this vacant tomb, no hint of life beyond ours to be seen. I sense fatigue. "The horses could use a break."

"There is a spot just ahead. It should accommodate everyone once we are through. I will warn you, though, it opens into the rift and there is a water source there, so we may find ourselves with company."

"Who knew, even demons from the Nulling suffer from thirst." Abarrane draws a second sword with a grimace. Rings of metal echo through the cavern as others follow suit.

"Company such as …" What should we be preparing for?

"Mostly shadow dwellers and things with too many legs to count. There may be the odd hag or nethertaur. Once, though, we encountered a wyvern. She was a mighty beast, but she left us alone. They do not have a taste for our kind." He flashes those jagged teeth.

Elisaf surveys around us. "Why do I feel like bait?"

Kienen steps forward. "Your Highness, allow my strongest with the affinity through first. We can slow anything down should it be waiting until enough reinforcements fall into place."

"We do not need your affinities where our blades will do," Abarrane scoffs.

I sigh with forced patience. "And I would rather we not waste our blades and energy when their affinities may do." I nod at him. "I accept your offer with my appreciation."

"Aziel, Dorian," Kienen calls out, beckoning the soldier he left in charge earlier and another. The two shift out of line, snapping fingers that draw ten more Ybarisans with them. They pass by us to join Radomir at the lead.

Abarrane studies Kienen through narrowed eyes. "Do not do anything that might bring this place down on our heads."

The corners of his mouth curl. "Give me *some* credit that I can wield my weapon with skill, Commander. I think I've already proven that."

"You've proven nothing to me. But after you." She bows dramatically, and then watches his back as the Ybarisans move through the passage on their horses in double file. "He is too eager to please you."

"Maybe he thinks that's the way to your soft, warm heart."

She snorts and goads her horse forward, her swords drawn as if expecting an imminent attack.

We follow, the legionaries surrounding Telor and me, their heads on swivels.

On the other side, the mine opens into a massive, open space. The ceiling soars high above, visible thanks to dull daylight reaching in from the gap in the wall. The sound of rushing water pulls our attention to one end where a waterfall pours down rock and flows into a stream. Aside from the cauldron of common bats that hang from the crevices high above, there are no signs of Nulling beasts. Kienen and the other Ybarisans are already stooping to splash their faces.

"Radomir has spoken truth so far," Telor admits.

"Yes, in this, he has proven his worth."

"I am sure Neilina found him worthy too," Abarrane reminds me before dismounting and leading her horse to water.

"Find a spot to refresh your horse and yourselves if needed, and then move out of the way for others!" My voice booms through the cave as I follow my own orders, smoothing a palm over my stallion as he bows.

Radomir finds me there. "Have you ever been this close to the rift?"

"Aside from the actual crossing above? No, I cannot say I have." Certainly not this deep.

"Come." He beckons me with a nod, picking a path through where the water is shallow.

I follow, the stream ice-cold against my leather boots, Abarrane's eyes boring on my back. I cast a hand, telling her to remain where she is, as we move toward the gaping chasm ahead.

"This has been one of my favorite places to visit for years."

"The rift?" I am not one to fear heights, but standing at its brink has always reminded me how insignificant we all are. Even approaching it makes my legs wobbly.

"The glance of daylight." He looks up. "We are so deep here that it is filtered. It does not burn us. Until days ago, this was the most I'd seen in centuries."

I edge in closer, to get a better view above to where—so very high up—a faded blue sky peeks. It must be midafternoon by now.

The stone gives way beneath my foot.

Before my heart has time to leap into my throat, an arm seizes mine and yanks me back to safety.

"My thanks," I offer through an exhale.

"I have seen more than one fall into the void to catch a glimpse." He slides off his helm, revealing his grotesque face. "Who knows if they've ever found the bottom."

All around, in every direction, is jagged stone where Aminadav's fury carved through. "I'd ask if you regretted your choice to turn on your own kind all those years ago, but I feel as though your bargain with Queen Neilina has already given me your answer." He was willing to do anything to lift his curse.

"I did what I needed to survive. Yes, some of those things are unforgivable. Some will always be seen as a betrayal." His black eyes land on me. "I know what you think of my kind, and I do not blame you. But many could argue you and Romeria have also done something unforgivable in order to survive."

"I will not have our decisions for the realm be questioned by a sapling." I snap. "We did what we needed to for *everyone* in Islor. Do not mistake that for selfish gain. And do not forget, for you to survive, you need *us*."

"Regardless, soon your realm will be crawling with beasts, the likes of which we have not seen in two thousand years. Many will not listen to your reasons. Many will still see you as the enemy of Islor."

He is not wrong in this. "That is a burden I am willing to carry, if it means the slaughter of both mortals and immortals for blood ends." It might also mean the end of any hope to reclaim my throne. But that is a problem for another day.

Radomir observes the soldiers crowding around the stream, the delineation between sapling and Ybarisan and Islorian fading as they all search for a space. "Allow me to show you something that may be of interest to you first. This way."

I feel the legionaries' watchful gazes on me as I follow Radomir away from the gaping hole, toward the opposite side. Several have nocked arrows in their grips.

Radomir chuckles. "They do not need to fear me. Dragging kings into corners to trap and feed is beneath me. I will even wait here if it will appease them. I merely wanted to show you this, seeing as you and your queen are so entwined with these nymphs and casters." He gestures toward the alcove.

"Fates. What is this doing in Soldor?" I approach the four pillars and the engraved stone ahead, the telltale nymph scripture unmistakable. It looks identical to the nymphaeum in Cirilea. "I thought ours was the only one."

"This one does not see Hudem's light shine upon it."

"No, I guess not. So then, what is it for?"

"I was hoping you would know."

"I do not." Would Gesine?

"I'm sure it will reveal its purpose soon enough. But we would be wise to move on, as the path ahead narrows and I think our luck with visitors may run out soon." Radomir saunters away, granting me a moment alone to ponder how much we still don't know about these nymphs and their capabilities.

I leave with Soldor's nymphaeum at my back, worry lingering for what could be ahead.

43
ROMERIA

Cirilea's nymphaeum is empty tonight.

Releasing my hold of my affinities and my grip of Jarek's and Pan's arms, I step away from the stone wall, allowing myself to breathe in the cool air and acclimate myself to the expansive royal garden. An odd sense of déjà vu hangs thick in my memory, of the night I first entered this world, so long ago.

Beside me, Jarek grinds his molars.

"Do you need a minute to adjust?" I ask pointedly. The morels I swallowed an hour ago will mask my Ybarisan scent, and Jarek has crossed that threshold in Ulysede a dozen times to build up his tolerance, but who knows what passing through this stone does to an Islorian immortal's cravings.

"No. Let's get this over with."

I nod toward the blade in his hand. "You should probably put that away. No one walks around the royal garden with their sword drawn."

"*I* do," he retorts, but slides it back into its scabbard before charging out onto the path, his eyes scouring our surroundings. In his double-breasted suit and with his long hair flowing freely, Jarek blends in more than I thought possible. Of course, beneath that cloak and finery is a lethal form strapped with a dozen daggers of various shapes and sizes.

"You know, you make a pretty nobleman, *Lord Barwin*."

His gaze drags down the moss green dress beneath my cloak before settling on my new face—my new *old* face. But he says nothing in response.

Pan hangs back four steps behind us as instructed, dressed in simple wool breeches and jacket. Appropriate attire for a tributary trying to blend in. As Gesine promised, the glowing symbol on his hand has all but vanished beneath whatever masking trick she used. Her abilities seem endless. "Whose face are you using, anyway?"

Jarek shoots a warning glare over his shoulder. He gave Pan strict instructions not to speak, but he should have known that wouldn't last long.

"Sorry, *Lady Barwin*." Pan drops his voice to a whisper. "Whose face is that?"

I smile. "A girl I used to know."

"A mortal girl? 'Cause she's *real* pretty. If she's a mortal girl, you think I could meet her some—"

"Stop talking," Jarek barks, his head on a swivel as he looks for any threat.

"Relax." I hook my arm through his. That only seems to make him more uptight. "We are a noble couple out for an evening walk with our tributary. We haven't done anything wrong. And I promise, none of them have ever seen me before."

"That is the issue. No one would forget that face. They'll remember not having seen it before anywhere in the assembly."

"Why? Because it's so striking? Is that why you've been staring at me nonstop? Aww. Do you have a little crush on my old face?"

His dark chuckle sends a shiver down my spine, but I don't miss the hint of pink in his cheeks. "Is that truly your face?"

"Yeah. Why?"

"No reason. This way is fastest." Jarek nods to our right.

I groan at the cedar maze. "Are you sure you know your way through there?"

"As sure as I know the weight of my sword. Both of you, stop talking." He leads us down the narrow path, the hedge towering over us on either side, the scent of cedar mixed with cold air a soothing combination. The way he takes each turn without hesitation proves his word.

"How do you know your way around here so well?"

"There is much to do in this garden at night." He smirks.

"If I recall, there's only *one* thing to do in this garden at night." All those evenings I stood on the balcony, watching nobility disappear with their tributaries. "It seems different now though, doesn't it? So ... quiet." There were always couples and groups wandering around. Lanterns would burn along the path, lit at twilight each day by the casters sweeping through.

Now they sit cold, and there are no couples, no laughter, no sound.

"Yes, it does," Jarek agrees softly.

We round the corner and come face-to-face with a guard.

I plaster on a smile, even as Pan plows into my back. "Good evening, guard."

His expression doesn't soften. "Who are you, and what are you doing in the royal garden?" he demands.

Jarek offers a stiff nod. "Lord and Lady Barwin from Eldford."

"Never heard of it."

"Not our problem you don't know your way around Islor."

I press my elbow into Jarek's side in warning, but then cover the move by slipping a playful hand into his jacket, over his taut stomach. "It's near the border with Kier." And fictional, but Jarek swore these guards don't know half the lordships on the map.

"In the *east*." His eyes thin, and I sense we've said the wrong thing.

With lightning-quick speed, Jarek has drawn the merth dagger tucked under his sleeve and sliced it across the guard's throat.

The guard drops, clutching his wound as blood pours. In seconds, he stills.

"Did you have to kill him?" I hiss.

"Yes." Jarek wipes his blade on the guard's pants before slipping it back into its sheath. "There was no reason for him to react like that or question us in this matter unless something is very wrong within these walls." He heaves the body by the armpits, tucking the corpse as far under the cedar overhang as it will fit. "That will work for now, but not forever."

"And when they find him? The gardens will be crawling with guards."

"Then let us get moving."

I sigh. One problem at a time, Zander always says. "Just get us to the tunnel in the hedge." We continue along the path, tension gripping us. For once, Pan doesn't need to be reminded to be silent.

Jarek guides us all the way to the edge of the hedge before he stalls, signaling us with a hand gesture to stay back as he surveys around the corner. He flashes an arched-brow *I told you so* look at me. "The grounds ahead are *heavily* guarded, especially around that tunnel. Much more than usual."

I curse. Annika must have told Atticus. Did Gracen realize it was me she saw last night? And if so, did she tell him? Is that why they're watching it so intently?

"I count four ahead, but there are likely more on the other side that I can't see." He draws a sword. "If this does not work, we will have a problem."

"It'll work." It has to. "Pan, remember the plan." We went over it for hours this afternoon.

"Aye." He has adopted the legionaries' lingo.

"Just like riding to Norcaster that night. Not a single word from you. Not a sound." If I can duck past warriors while riding a horse, I can certainly do it now. "Stay close to me."

I close my eyes as my adrenaline races, my affinities burning under my skin. I should have practiced this more. Then again, I've been using my cloaking ability in desperate situations for years without realizing it. It shouldn't be an issue.

This is as desperate a situation as any.

"Get to the tunnel ... get to the tunnel," I chant in a whisper, reaching out to cling to Jarek's arm and Pan's shoulder, hoping that connection is enough to provide us the cover we need. I don't have a manual for this special skill of mine.

"Now," Jarek whispers, both hands gripping weapons.

As one, we head out along the path. Ahead, four guards pace in their stations. One is only ten feet away.

I ignore him and keep my thoughts and focus on only one goal—getting to that secret tunnel without notice—and as we pass them, taking the path that leads toward the castle.

I sense more guards in my peripherals—far more than I've ever seen guarding the castle—and my fingers dig into Jarek's forearm as I try to calm myself.

He doesn't so much as flinch.

Jarek waits until the sentry closest to us turns before he shifts the branches to the cedar hedge. We slide into the space between them and the wall until we're safely in the tunnel.

My body sinks with relief.

The door Annika and I took that first night that leads to the castle's undercroft is behind us. Jarek tests the handle before pushing it open and passing through. In moments, he returns and nods at Pan, a signal that it's clear for him to go.

I squeeze Pan's arm, a silent gesture to be careful. Between Jarek's and my knowledge of the castle's interior, we planned various routes to the stable where Silmar sleeps. I know the stable boy can be bought with gold, and Pan's easy nature will get him talking.

Still, I feel uneasy, sending him alone inside. But he is a survivor, just like I am, and he's been in too many sticky situations to count. He always finds a way out.

With a grin, Pan pats his shirt pocket where I stuffed several coins with Ulysede's mark and then disappears into the castle.

I wait until he's gone before refocusing on our own path. Jarek holds his finger to his mouth, but I don't need a reminder. We move along in the hedge, all the way to the steps down. When it's safe, I weave a ball of light and let it float ahead to illuminate the narrow tunnel.

Jarek curses as he stoops to fit. His shoulders graze either side. "No wonder we didn't know about this one. No worthwhile soldier can fit through it."

"Right. The big brave warrior is afraid of tight spaces. I forgot." I've never seen Jarek as agitated as moving through the wall into Bellcross. "It's not long." And we might have bigger worries ahead. "If Annika talked, the sanctum might be guarded too."

"Those guards back there were not for us. They are for whoever is in that room above. A prisoner, I imagine."

It dawns on me. "In my old room. Who do you think it is?" Maybe Wendeline? I pray she is alive.

"It is not our concern." We reach the end of the tunnel and the stone wall. Copying Annika, I yank on the lever with both hands. The ceiling above shifts with that familiar scraping stone sound. I move to climb through, but Jarek seizes my hips and pulls me back. "No" is all he says before hauling himself through.

The sanctum is empty and dark.

Not a single flame burns. The lingering scent of incense is gone, and urns of flowers hold shriveled blooms. They look weeks past their prime, forgotten. An eeriness slips over my spine, something ominous hanging in the air. There were casters living and worshiping within the sanctum when I was here. Women who had nothing to do with Wendeline's lies and treachery.

There's no sign of them now.

"Leave your dress behind this pew. We'll come back for it later," Jarek instructs, shedding his fine jacket to reveal the leather vest and the arsenal strapped to his form.

The guy is a walking lethal weapon, and he is here, by my side, putting himself between me and danger at all times. It still feels foreign. "Thanks for coming with me, Jarek."

"As if I had much choice with your stubborn ass."

I shimmy out of the long skirt to reveal my own breeches and tunic. While the need to look noble worked in the castle, blending in as a commoner will allow us better movement outside of it.

I look up to find him watching me, but he quickly shifts, adjusting his cloak. "Ready?"

"Yeah."

His hand is on the door when it stalls.

"What is it? Do you hear something outside?"

He hesitates. "This face of yours … the one you used to wear. I *have* seen it before."

I frown. "Where?"

"In my dreams. *Nightly,* since we entered Ulysede." He peers over his shoulder at me, concern in his expression. "What does that mean?"

"I have no idea. What kind of dream?"

He shoots me a knowing look.

"Oh." *Oh.* "If it's since Ulysede, then it has to be the nymphs messing with your head somehow. Maybe Lucretia." But how does she know my old face? Today is the first day I've worn the mask.

He curses under his breath. "But why? And does it not concern you that they can get into our heads?"

"Gesine said the nymphs like chaos." What they think they'll achieve by filling my commander's head with visions of Romy Watts, I can't guess. Maybe this is something innocent. But I don't need Jarek worried about dreams. I waggle my eyebrows. "So, you're having dirty thoughts about me, huh?"

His deep, dark chuckle vibrates in my chest as his sooty eyes rake over my face, rolling over my mouth. "Maybe don't mention this to the king. I'd prefer not to die the moment he hears about it."

"I wouldn't want that. How could I tease you mercilessly then?" I poke him in the ribs, earning his smirk as he pushes open the door.

Together we stroll out into Cirilea's city streets.

44
ATTICUS

"How *do* you manage to stomp your foot with each step and not look like a beast walking?" I muse. "You must teach me."

Annika's angry footfalls grow even louder, echoing through the hall. "Neilina agreed to this brainless proposal of yours?"

"Not yet. I doubt she has even received my letter." I hesitate. "But I did receive one from Zander."

She gasps, grabbing hold of my forearm, forgetting her anger for the moment. "Is he well? *Where* is he?"

"Can you pretend for a moment that he isn't your favorite brother?"

Her lips twist with disdain. "He's not trying to marry me off to a Ybarisan."

"He *would* if it made sense politically," I counter. "He and Romeria are in the Venhorn Mountains with her Ybarisan soldiers. Romeria received a letter from Neilina, confirming their coming attack at the rift on Hudem."

"*Romeria* is your source?" Her mouth gapes. "And you believed her?"

"I have no choice. It's too big a risk not to."

"And what of the eastern lords? Did she tell you about that plot, as well?"

"No."

She hums. "Bexley, then. She's always had a soft spot for you."

I ignore her. Bexley and what the east is doing isn't important, and besides, they'll be dealt with accordingly soon enough. "Even if Neilina does agree to my proposal, we cannot trust her to honor that deal."

Annika throws her hands up in frustration. "Then why are you wasting my time with this Ybarisan prince?"

"Why not? You have something better to do?"

"Yes. Find myself a new tributary." She's trying her best to hide the fact that discovering her usual tributary—a young mortal named Percy with a brilliant smile and an empty head—had been tainted didn't scare her. It scared me. Annika is all the family I have left within these walls, even if she despises me.

"Aren't you glad I had Wendeline mark him?" Percy was fine yesterday morning but woke up with his mark glowing. At least we know the priestess's brand works as it should. Who poisoned him, though, no one can figure out. Saoirse has an ironclad alibi, and she wouldn't admit to a conspirator within our household upon questioning, but she also hasn't admitted to hiding the vial in the library and had the gall to demand we reveal her accuser.

"I hear Dagny's son might be willing."

Annika's brow furrows. "She has a son?"

"Dear sister, sometimes you are so oblivious, it frightens me."

"Regardless, why are you dragging me here? Execute him and be done with it!"

"I didn't execute Wendeline, and she proved useful. Maybe Tyree still has value as well. And who knows? You two could fall madly in love with each other as Zander and Romeria have."

She rolls her eyes. "Yes, you need a battalion of guards to keep him from escaping, but I'm sure he will take one look at me and decide he's ready to abandon his scheming, murderous ways."

I ignore her sarcasm as we close in on his rooms, though her words are a stark reminder that I have ten soldiers on one prisoner when they're needed elsewhere. "Any issues?"

"None, Your Highness. The prisoner just finished his evening meal," a guard answers.

I nod toward the door, a wordless command they know to follow.

The three guards unlock it and enter, their swords drawn and ready.

A cool breeze flows in through the open balcony. Maybe ordering Wendeline to seal it as she did with Romeria would be a better plan.

"Behave," I warn Annika.

In moments, Tyree strolls through, the points of the swords pressed against his neck. He has bathed—thankfully—and changed his clothes into a simple black tunic and breeches. Where his arm was mangled by merth blades to hinder his affinity, silver scars remain.

"Seems pointless for you to have your caster heal me, only for these guards to injure me again, doesn't it? Or do you plan on having her heal me regularly?"

I wave a dismissive hand and the guards step back, removing their blades but keeping them at the ready.

Tyree's blue eyes shift to Annika. "My bride-to-be. Are you as thrilled by this match as I am?"

"I would rather suck on a vat of Romeria's blood than consummate that union," she snarls.

"I promise, your tune will change." He scrapes his gaze over her frame, a secretive smile on his lips.

I'm no fool. My twin sister is desired by most males who cross her path, not only for her royal position, but even more, her beauty.

But if there is one thing she doesn't react to well, it's cocky males. "We've intercepted a letter from your mother," she says with haughty indignation. "We know her plans to cross at Hudem, and we are already preparing to meet her there and crush her. So there is no use for you but kindling for a pyre, which is what you will be if my brother *ever* suggests I stand in a room with you again."

A strangled sound escapes me.

Tyree's smile grows wider. "I like a good challenge."

"There is *no* match between us, and there *never* will be," she hisses.

"Fates, why must you be so damned difficult," I mutter as she spins and stomps out the door.

Tyree's gaze trails after her, amusement shining in them. "I like her more already."

"Leave us," I command the guards.

They march out without another word.

"She doesn't have much respect for you, does she?" Tyree folds his arms, adopting a casual stance. "What kind of king can't control his own sister?"

"Speaking of sisters, how did it feel to have Romeria seek you out in the dungeon and pump you for information for her new love?"

A muscle in Tyree's jaw ticks, the only sign that my words pierce him. But I was there at the end of that exchange; I saw how he smashed her face against the bars in a fit of rage.

In the next moment, it's gone, replaced by an arrogant smirk. "I hear you are having issues with your eastern lords. How very terrible."

Those idiot guards must be gossiping again. "Nothing that isn't on its way to resolution soon."

"Resolution?" He snorts. "Islor is already on its knees, and you scramble with futile marriage proposals that will not solve your problems. My father was as foolish, and that landed him in a grave. You need better advisors, Atticus."

"And what would you propose, as my wise advisor?" I ask with exaggerated flourish.

Tyree strolls over to take a seat on the couch, slinging his arms across the back on either side. As if he hasn't a care in the world, as if I might not drive a sword through him at any moment. "Release me, and I will find my sister, so I may deal with her for her betrayal to Ybaris. That is one less traitor in your midst."

I laugh. "You mean, so you can round up your Ybarisan soldiers and help attack from within? That is possibly the worst advice I've ever received."

He shrugs. "Worth a shot. Though I do know my sister better than anyone else."

"Your sister the princess, perhaps. But not *this* Romeria. She is an entirely different person, and she is far more resourceful than you give her credit for."

His eyes narrow. "What do you mean by that?"

"You think because I moved you here, we are suddenly trading secrets like bedfellows? I can just as easily send you back to the tower. Or the dungeon."

"I hear it's full."

"Then a pyre in the execution square it is."

"You are not foolish enough. Just as you are not foolish enough to believe that caging those lords will stop others from rising in their place. The stewards probably already have."

"They haven't heard about it yet. I've made sure of that."

He studies his fingernails. "When will you admit it?"

"Admit what?"

"That you betrayed your brother to steal a broken crown. How does that feel?"

His words pierce me deeper than I expected.

"A formidable battle commander, you might have been, Atticus, but you have no hope of defeating my mother, not with the full force of Mordain behind her. She is too cunning for you."

"Perhaps. But you will never get the satisfaction of being alive to see it." I stroll out before I make good on my promise right there, pulling the door shut tight behind me. How did he—a prisoner—get the upper hand?

"You are to stand guard at this door, not chatter about the state of Islor for our enemy's ears," I hiss.

The guards bow and begin offering apologies, but I'm already gone, charging down the hall. Before I see Gracen, I should expel some of this rage.

45
ROMERIA

"Keep moving," Jarek warns, nudging me along past the man's naked corpse.

Sadness and anger burns inside me as I huddle in my cloak. "That's *three* bodies on this street alone." Why can't they at least give them the dignity of clothes? But I know the answer already. Clothes have value for the living, not the dead. And besides, they've been hung for a crime. They don't deserve any dignity.

"And we're likely to see more. Are you surprised?" From within his cowl, Jarek glowers at a man walking across the street, but then dismisses him as nonthreatening. "Atticus wants to send a clear message to the mortals."

"That he's cruel and coldhearted?" Zander would never have done this as king. "I told him the poison wouldn't matter after Hudem. That's *days* away now. Why won't he listen?"

"Because *you* are the one speaking, and it takes courage and honor to put bitterness aside. But these people are beyond your help. Focus on those you *can* help." He grabs my arm and leads me across the street, down an alleyway to connect to the corner where the apothecary sits, as dark and lonely as it seemed that night so long ago, when Gesine waited within.

We stall there while Jarek surveys the scene. "I expected

Cirilea's army to be crawling through the streets, but there is nothing."

Nothing but an eerie foreboding. It's hazardous for me to be back in Cirilea. And yet I miss the city—the people, the liveliness, the edge of danger that seemed to linger everywhere I went.

We keep moving at a clipped pace toward Port Street, my legs struggling to keep up with Jarek's. Beneath the near-full moon, I can just make out the *Silver Mage*'s tall mast on the water. People loiter on the street in clusters, but the mood is far more subdued than the night Zander, Atticus, and I came here in search of hints to finding Ianca. There are no banjos, no buskers, and only a few drunks stumbling about.

"My God." My feet freeze in place. Naked bodies hang from lampposts like wreaths at Christmastime. I want to look away, but I can't. "There are so many of them."

Ahead, two solemn women attempt to get a man down, one struggling to hoist him up by his legs while the other pokes at the rope loop with a broom. A ratty wool blanket is tucked under her arm.

Jarek shakes his head "It'll never work."

"No. It won't. So help them."

"That will draw attention to—"

"*Help* them. Please." I peer up into his eyes, pleading.

With a heavy sigh, he draws his sword. "Step aside."

The women huddle into each other and move away, afraid.

Half climbing, half jumping up the brick wall of the building, Jarek cuts the rope with one powerful swing.

The body collapses to the cobblestone with a thud, and the women rush in to cover him with the blanket. "Thank you, sir," the younger one offers, tears in her eyes as she collects the corpse's hand.

That's when I see the dull mark on hers. "Where did you get that?" I point to it. "That emblem."

"The priestess. She is going around Cirilea, marking all the mortals. She marked my Wilkins too." She holds up the man's hand to prove her claim. "Only, his glowed before. That's why they hung him. Because he took the poison and then he was foolish enough to admit it. I didn't even know he'd done it!" Tears roll down her cheeks, reddened from the cold.

An odd mix of vindication and horror swirls through me. Wendeline is still alive, and despite his childish response to my letter, Atticus listened to me.

He *listened* to me, but he's still executing mortals. Using *my* help to do it.

"We must keep moving," Jarek warns.

"I'm sorry for your loss," I offer the women and continue on, my teeth clenched. Only, the next body over catches my eye, the flames from the lantern casting a glow on her face. I recognize her, even in death. "*No.* Cecily." Why would they hang someone from the Rookery? Those people don't have keepers anymore.

A dull emblem marks her hand. It must have glowed once too.

"You knew her," Jarek asks.

"She helped us escape from Cirilea in her skiff. Is that why she's dead?"

"No, this corpse is fresh. Likely died today. And by a dagger through the neck." He points to a wound beneath where the rope cuts into her skin.

That's some small consolation, though. Why go to the effort to strip and string her up, then? And where is her husband? Arthur, that was his name. I scan the faces of the nearby male bodies, but I don't see him anywhere.

"Come." Jarek's arm curls around my waist as he urges me to continue. "Atticus will have spies in these streets. Lose your tears. They do nothing but draw notice and cause trouble."

"I'm going to kill him," I growl, brushing away the wetness on my cheek.

"We are here for information, not assassinations, as much as that would please me." In a rare show of affection, he squeezes me to his side once before releasing me.

"*This* is what Ybaris has caused. This is the result of that fucking Ybarisan queen's schemes and lies," I hiss. "It's the mortals who suffer most, yet again."

"Not for much longer, if what Lucretia says is true."

"Yeah, then we'll have Malachi and a pile of monsters to deal with."

"One problem at a time, Romeria. That is how we deal with it." He points ahead. "The tavern is there. Go on your own and find a table. I'll be in shortly and will take a seat nearby. Stay out of trouble, and remember—"

"*I know.* This is a bad idea and don't trust anyone."

He smirks. "I wasn't going to say that."

"Oh, really?" I peer up at him, hidden within his cloak. He's said it a dozen times.

"No." He steps in closer and drops his voice. "I was going to remind you that you are the queen of Ulysede now, and you do not bow for anyone."

His words catch me off guard. "A hidden kingdom that no one knows about, Jarek."

"Aye. Perhaps it is time for that to change." He studies my face for a moment, before releasing a long sigh. "Also, this is a bad idea and don't trust anyone. Especially not the tavern owner."

I give him a playful punch in the ribs. "Don't worry, I've already crossed paths with Bexley more than once."

"Then you know to be careful what you say in front of her. She has everyone's ear, including the king's." With that, Jarek breaks away from me and heads across the street to peruse the women standing on the balcony, looking to bait their next customer.

The Goat's Knoll smells of mead and melted wax, and hasn't changed any. To my relief, Bexley isn't at the door, and the girl who is seems more interested in her cross-stitch work than greeting customers.

I move past her and straight to the burly man behind the bar.

He smiles at me. "Haven't seen your pretty face around here before."

"That's because I'm not from around here. I just arrived today, for the royal wedding."

"Just today, huh?" Something flickers in his eyes that makes me think I've stepped in a lie.

Always offer as little as possible, Romy. I force a grin as I chastise myself for forgetting my skills.

"What can I getcha?"

I set a gold coin on the counter, face down to hide Ulysede's emblem. "A mug of mead and a chat with Seamus."

"The mead I can do. The other thing, though ..." He looks me up and down and pours my glass from the barrel tap.

I fish a second gold coin out of my pocket and place it on the counter next to the other. "Tell him I'm here on behalf of Cordelia." The alias Gesine used when she arrived in Cirilea.

He sets the mug on the counter and when he pulls away, the coins are gone. "Enjoy your drink."

"I'll enjoy it more with company." I head for an empty booth near the hallway Zander and I used to escape last time. Sliding in, I survey the room. It's only half full, the mood somber compared to the last time I was here. People hunch and whisper, casting sly glances around. A few have dull emblems on their wrists, marking them as both mortal and untainted. They'll fetch a premium rate for their blood if their keepers don't lock them in cages. With all the bodies hanging outside, I imagine that might start soon enough.

Only two more days, I remind myself.

Two more days and these people's blood will no longer be a commodity.

But Atticus can kill a lot of mortals in that time.

Kaders is here, in a booth across the room, sharing a drink with a woman in a long, sable-colored dress. I'll bet he'll be sailing back to Seacadore soon.

A tall, cloaked figure catches the corner of my eye, and a wave of comfort washes over me. Jarek takes a stool at the bar. Our gazes touch only in passing, but I know he could reach my side in a split second if I was in trouble.

I'm halfway through my mead and wondering if I should order another when a mortal slips into the bench across from me, a mug in his fist. He fits the physical description Gesine gave me of Seamus—small, wiry, with bright orange hair and deep lines across his forehead.

"The south wind blows tonight," he asks, his lyrical Seacadorian accent reminding me of Elisaf.

"And the north wind answers," I respond without missing a beat, armed with the necessary code words passed along from Gesine.

He takes a long sip of his drink. "Been waitin' to hear from you. How can I be of service to Cordelia?"

I dig into my pocket, relieved he won't make me jump through more hoops to prove myself. Gesine did warn me Seamus is wary of strangers, especially elven ones. But he's also a thief, and thieves are wary of everyone. "You can provide us with information." I show off a stack of gold coins within my fingertips.

His eyes sparkle. Thief language is universal. "On?"

"What's happening around Cirilea, on King Atticus and what he's been up to, that sort of thing."

"Nothin' good." Seamus collects a peanut from a bowl on the table and cracks its shell between his thumbs. "For starters, the city gate's been sealed since yesterday, with no one in or out, not even messengers, so I wouldn't be runnin' around, announcin' you've arrived today. That'll earn ya attention ya probably don't want."

I curse, hazarding a glance toward the bartender.

"Don't worry. Lombard's trustworthy. *Somewhat*, anyway."

"What else? What about all these dead mortals hanging everywhere?"

"Aye, the king's guard takes down one corpse and replaces it with two." Seamus stuffs the peanut in his mouth. "Supposed to be scarin' people into not takin' the poison, but it's not workin'.

People are feelin' hopeless and gettin' angry. And now that the caster's comin' around, testin' mortals—"

"Wendeline?"

"Aye. The one who marked the tainted ones at the royal repast. The king rounded up all the others and executed them the next day. She's all that's left."

No wonder the sanctum was so empty and cold.

"Honestly thought she was dead along with the rest of them. But then all of a sudden yesterday, they started bringin' her around, from house to house, markin' mortals. The ones that glow, they either throw up on a rope or haul 'em to the arena. Don't know why the difference. Maybe they're runnin' out of lampposts. She's at it all day and night. I assume it'll be till every last mortal is marked."

And every tainted one executed swiftly.

Damn Atticus. "How many mortals have been taken?"

"Enough to line the streets with bodies. But what's worse is he's takin' the children. All of 'em. Any his guard comes across."

"He's hanging children?" I can't hide my horror.

"Not sure what he's doin' with them, but they leave and they don't come back. He's probably keepin' them locked up so they can't be tainted." Seamus chugs his mead. "People are scared. A lot of servants who aren't tributaries took the doses, not wantin' to get caught with the vials. They thought they'd be safe enough, and now the priestess is marking everyone. They made plans to escape before Hudem and hide in the hills."

Memories of the marauders who captured Pan and me stir. "The hills aren't safe."

"Safer than what's goin' on in here."

"They need to go north." Jarek's right. What's the point of being a queen if I can't share my haven with those Islorians who need it most? "There's a city in the Venhorn Mountains that will take all of them. Every mortal. They will be free of this blood curse there. The queen who rules it will give them homes."

Seamus grins. "That sounds like a fairy tale."

"It does, doesn't it?" That's what it felt like the first time we walked through. "But it's real. I've been there. Cordelia is there now."

"Ain't that somethin', then. But it don't matter unless the king opens the gate, and I don't see that happenin'." He looks around. "There's been talk of raisin' arms, of fightin'."

"Against the king's guard?"

"Aye. The Cirilean army left this morning, and the eastern army that was camped outside left yesterday, so the odds are better."

My heart races. The taillok delivered our letter yesterday. Would he have responded so quickly? "To the rift?"

"Maybe. I could probably find out."

"How many soldiers were there?"

Seamus notes the stack of gold sitting idly on the table.

I slide it across, and it vanishes in a quick swipe of his hand.

"A few thousand each, at least. The city feels empty without them."

Zander needs to know to expect them. "Going up against Boaz is a bad idea. It'll just get the mortals killed sooner."

"I'd rather die fightin' then hangin' naked in the street."

I check his hand. There's no mark on it. If there was, I'd bet money that it would glow.

"And it's not just the mortals. The keepers are angry for losin' servants, angry for their young property bein' taken away, and they're blamin' His Highness for not acting sooner." He drops his voice. "There're plans to storm the castle."

"When?"

"Don't know. Any day now. City feels like it's about to erupt."

This is not good. How many more innocent people will die? And what about all the mortals inside the castle? Will Corrin, and Dagny, and Gracen get caught up in it? If I could somehow get them past the guards and to the nymphaeum ... But that doesn't solve the problem of all these mortals in the city.

"What about the port?"

He shakes his head. "No ship is sailin' out of Cirilea without a sealed letter from the king himself and he won't be handin' those out. Believe me, the sea captains aren't happy about it either. I know most of them and they're itchin' to get out. Not that they'd be able to take too many with 'em."

"Some is better than none."

A bark of deep, booming laughter draws my attention to the brawny seaman across the way. "What about a ship that can fit hundreds in the hull." Maybe more. The *Silver Mage* is massive.

Seamus follows my line of sight and laughs. "You'd need a wagon of gold and your pretty face to convince that one."

"If I can get that?"

His chuckles die down as he realizes I'm serious. "*If* you can get that … There're a few of us who get things done around here. I trust them with my life."

A band of thieves. I'm sure I'll need more gold to buy their loyalty, but I'll take any help I can get. I need to get these mortals far away from Atticus *now*. I reach into my pocket to fish out the sizable ruby that I brought from Ulysede and set it on the table in front of him. "I will pay in gold and jewels for every one of those ships to take as many mortals as they can to Northmost. Half before, half when they arrive."

He licks his lips. "When?"

"Tomorrow. Be ready. As soon as you hear from me or my people, it's time." We need to come up with a plan. This is going to be tricky.

"Tell Lombard to fetch me. He's always here. Each captain'll need a letter to hand off to the guards. The Silver Mage though, you'll need to convince that one on your own."

"I can handle him." I know how to speak his language. "Will the guards let a flood of mortals onto the ships?"

"Nah, but we'll stir up a distraction." He beams, showing off crooked teeth. "Lot of people are gonna want on those boats, what with all the chaos. Hudem celebrations are canceled, the royal wedding has been called off."

"Called off by whom?" Was it Zander's words in the letter that smartened him up? Thank God Saoirse won't find her way to the throne.

"Officially, His Highness has thrown his betrothed into the tower for taintin' his tributary—"

"What?" I hiss. *Gracen.* "When?"

"The taintin' or the arrestin'?"

"Both."

"I don't know the former, but the Lady Saoirse has been in the tower two nights now."

A wave of relief hits me. I saw Gracen just last night, so it wasn't her who was tainted then. But that might explain why Atticus was feeding off her. The royal tributaries would be targets for someone looking to poison the king. A baker with three kids … not as obvious.

"Anyhow, I'd imagine Lady Saoirse's not too keen on weddin' the king anymore."

"And what about Lord Adley?" He's been angling for the throne forever.

"Aye, he's got big problems too. He's in a dungeon cell with the other eastern lords. At least, I think he is. Also heard that His Highness executed the lot. Haven't been able to firm up an answer. No one's allowed in or out of the castle these days."

Atticus had the balls to lock up Adley? That's something Zander wished he'd done, in hindsight. "Why were they put in the dungeon?"

"Because they were naughty," comes an amused voice, startling me. Bexley has arrived, in an emerald-green dress with a fitted corset, the swell of her breasts spilling out the top.

Seamus dips his head—in apology or submission, I can't tell—and then slides out and disappears as quickly as he appeared. The ruby is gone, but I expected as much. It'll help with whatever convincing he needs to do.

Bexley takes his place. "It is the biggest topic of conversation around my tavern these days."

I smooth my expression. "What is?"

She props her elbows on the table's surface and folds her hands together, those unusual violet eyes dissecting me. Tendrils of soft strawberry-blond hair cascade down her shoulders. "What the king has done, what he plans to do. So many questions, so many theories."

"And do you have any?"

"I have *many*. But I am far more interested in this unfamiliar face who has arrived in my establishment, wielding the name of a caster who was last seen with the Ybarisan princess. And on the same night that a famed legionary sits at my bar." She nods to where Jarek hovers.

Fuck. She is too perceptive. She reminds me of Sofie in that way.

"A *legionary*." I take a long chug of my mead, feigning calm. Meanwhile my heart pounds. "I've heard they can be vicious."

"I suppose we all have a vicious side." She smiles, showing off her white teeth. "You seem so familiar. Have we met before?"

"You just said my face was *un*familiar."

"And still ..." Humor flashes in her eyes. "Where are you from?"

"Kettling."

She crooks her head as she studies me. "I may have believed that, if you were not sitting with Seamus, who would never trust a Kettling immortal."

"It doesn't really matter what you believe." What would Bexley do if she knew who I really was behind this mask? I betrayed our deal. Would she want to punish me for that? "Seamus and I have a mutual friend who he does trust."

She seems to mull that over. But every expression, every word, every move feels calculated. "You know who I am." It's not a question.

"You said it's your tavern, so I assume you're the owner?"

Her secretive smile doesn't reach her eyes. "Why are you in Cirilea?"

"I came here for the royal wedding."

"Seems you have wasted your time traveling, then."

"So I've heard."

"What is your name?"

"What's yours?"

She pauses. "People call me Bexley."

Interesting choice of words. It's not a lie, but is it not her real name? It's the first time I've ever questioned that. "People call me Tarryn. Tee for short." The grifter's name that keeps on giving.

"There have been many strangers around here as of late. So let me ask you again, what are you *really* doing in Cirilea, *Tee for short*?"

"Are you always this untrusting?"

"I have not survived as long as I have by being anything but. I wonder, have you come here to cause harm to the king?"

"Would you care if I did?" I know Bexley and Atticus are close. They've probably fucked each other a hundred different ways before he was king. Now that he is king, she must value having his ear. But I'll bet a woman like her values the information she trades even more.

"You wouldn't be the only one. There are others loitering about, waiting for their chance." Her gaze wanders over her bar's interior. "But the king and I have an understanding, and having him seated on the throne is far more convenient for me than the alternatives. So, yes, I suppose I do care. Purely for self-interest."

"And what would he say if he knew you were in regular communication with Mordain's casters after what happened to his parents? Would he still be so *understanding*?"

Bexley's eyes flare —with alarm or surprise, or likely both. "What can I say but I appreciate *all* sources of information."

"As do I, especially when that source knows their information is too valuable to bury for their own benefit." I slide a gold coin across the table, making a point of placing it face up, so the two-crescent-moon Ulysede emblem shows. Based on our last negotiation, Bexley doesn't seem to care about gold coins. Secrets are her precious commodity.

She pauses, examining it for a long beat. "This is the symbol they are marking on the mortals."

"Yes."

"Where is this from?"

"A friend in the north."

Her lips twist. "I've heard a certain Ybarisan princess is in the north."

"She is."

"I have also heard tales of old beasts from the Nulling prowling in the open. Far more than usual. As if they're drawn to something. Or *someone*."

Bexley must have a source in Telor's army. Or the saplings. I'll have to ask Radomir when I see him next. But is she also hinting that she knows of a key caster? "Nothing that hasn't been handled. Why did the king lock up the eastern lords?" I divert the subject.

She studies me, as if trying to decide how I fit into a puzzle. More likely, she's weighing how much she can extract from me and how much it's worth to her. "They are plotting to divide Islor in two, claiming as far west as the Plains of Aminadav and naming Kettling as its capital city. The force gathering there is considerable, aided by soldiers from Kier."

The Plains of Aminadav. That's the most fertile land in all of Islor. "*That*'s where Atticus sent the army?" Not to the rift?

Her lips twitch, and I realize my mistake: you don't ever call a king by his first name unless you know him personally, and even then, not in front of others. "He sent the eastern forces camped outside the city north to the rift yesterday, but the Cirilean army has left today for the east. I imagine he will join them soon, if he hasn't left already."

I curse. "But Islor's armies will be divided, fighting two different enemies." With a third—far worse—one waiting.

"To ignore either would be a detriment."

"And we'll lose both battles because of it."

"Yes. Likely. Unless he finds powerful allies, and I would hazard his recent actions are eliminating that possibility." Her focus wanders over the tavern's interior. "The air in Cirilea has become ripe with betrayal and rebellion. After so many years, I sense my time here is drawing to a close."

That's how a person like Bexley survives—by getting out while she can. "What about Princess Romeria?"

Bexley's eyes snap to me. "What about her?"

"What do people around Cirilea think of her? Of what she and King Zander are accused of. Do they believe it?"

"It depends which side you are on. Most elven want them burned on a pyre for the chaos they've caused. And mortals ... well, they pray for help from the Ybarisans as they watch their brethren die and their children taken."

My chest tightens. "And which side are you on?"

"The side that benefits me."

I quietly wait for her to give a better answer. At least she's honest.

She flips the coin between her fingers, caressing her thumb over the emblem as if it might rub off. "I believe the exiled king and the princess together held many secrets. But plans to destroy Islor was never one of them. I hardly think their intentions will matter, though, if the fates are involved."

She's being far more candid than I expected. It makes me want to return the favor. "They *are* involved. They have been for a long time."

She lets out a long, slow sigh. "It sounds like Princess Romeria should secure allies wherever she can find them, then."

Either Bexley is fishing, or she's already decided I'm closely linked to Romeria. "She has found some unlikely ones, yes." I hesitate. Bexley once told me that she couldn't be trusted, but that she would never pretend otherwise. "Can she count on you as well?"

A grim smile of satisfaction tells me Bexley got the answer she wanted. "I could be her greatest one. But I could also be her worst enemy." Something blazes in her eyes. "I never give valuable information without gaining something equally valuable in return. That is true for anyone who enters my establishment, whether it be pauper or prince, or a princess masquerading as a commoner."

Is she talking about the last time we met here? Or has she figured me out, here and now?

"It is also true for those who seek information from great distances, like the scribes of Mordain, who have been *very* eager to learn all they can about Cirilea and the late High Priestess Margrethe. They know far more about both the past and the future than anyone gives them credit for. All they need is to utter the word *prophecy,* and I listen *very carefully,* and I learn of things about the fates and the nymphs that would strike fear into the hearts of many should they come to pass."

I steady my breathing. Bexley said *nymphs*. She must have learned about the prophecy from the scribes. She knows, and she's testing me. "Like what?"

"I think I have been generous already. It is your turn now." She holds up the coin between two fingers, the emblem out. "What does this mean?"

My gut tells me now is not the time to lie. "It's the mark of Ulysede, a kingdom built by the nymphs and hidden for tens of thousands of years."

"But it is no longer hidden."

"No. Princess Romeria opened it and now rules there."

She sinks into the bench. "Another ruler to vie for power."

"She's not fighting for power. That's not what she wants."

"And what does *Queen* Romeria want, then?" She closes her fist over the coin. "What does she hope to bring to these lands, besides more chaos?"

"The end of the blood curse through the nymphs. And eventually, peace."

Her nod is subtle. "She shares the same bleeding heart for the mortals as the exiled king. No wonder he is so smitten."

"The exiled king who deserves to be back on his throne."

"Time will tell if there even is a Cirilean throne before long," she says noncommittally. "I wonder what the current king would say about this kingdom within his, if he knew?"

"Who says he doesn't already know? Who says he didn't receive a letter from Ulysede yesterday morning?"

"Is that so?" She sneers. Atticus must have had the chance to but didn't tell her about the letter, and she's not pleased with that. "I suggest you exit out the side entrance before you risk notice." Her gaze flips behind me.

Nonchalantly, I glance over my shoulder.

Shit. Atticus is here. He's dressed in casual clothes, so he must have snuck past Boaz's notice. He won't recognize me, but he'll identify Jarek in a split second.

The warrior is already on his feet, preparing to leave.

"Thanks for the heads-up."

"See? Wouldn't it be wise for Her Highness to have me as an ally?"

"She was under the impression that you wouldn't be up for that." Whatever else she is, Bexley has always been helpful to me. "Also, she wanted me to pass on a message. An apology, actually. She couldn't keep her end of a bargain, but she would never have caused you harm."

Bexley studies my face as if memorizing it. "Go now. I do not wish to answer questions about you. And watch the bearded one by the door. He goes where the king does and always with his sword."

"Noted." I slip out of the booth, but instead of taking the hallway, I veer left, toward Kaders's table.

The captain of the Silver Mage looks up, sees my face, and raw interest sparks in his pale blue eyes as they drag over my chest. He hasn't changed a bit, his face still golden and weathered, his hair a wild mane of sun-kissed curls. "You here for a little deal? I don't have one of 'em fancy marks, but my wind woman checks my drinks for any *additives*, if ya know what I mean." His voice is gruff and laden with an accent. Skatranan, I think.

I know what kind of *deal* he's into. I set the point of a solid gold dagger I procured from my vault on the table next to his mug, for his purview.

His greedy eyes widen.

"Meet me in the alley out back in two minutes, and we can discuss." With that, I turn.

And bump into a broad chest.

Atticus's broad chest.

My heart pounds, but I feign indifference. "Pardon me." I move to step around him.

He steps with me, blocking my path. "I don't know you." He surveys my face with a mixture of curiosity and suspicion.

"And I don't know you." *But I could kill you where you stand.* My affinities crackle beneath my skin, waiting to be unleashed. But that would only complicate things. And besides, Zander doesn't want his brother dead. *In here, tonight, he's not the king,* I remind myself. I don't have to bob and bow and play nice. "Do you need something? Because I'm on my way out."

"Be safe out there. The city is dangerous."

"I gathered that. You know, with all the corpses everywhere."

A harsh look skims across his expression, but it's gone a second later, and a smarmy smile appears as he steps aside. "Have a good evening."

I duck down the hallway and out the back, allowing myself a breath once I'm leaning against the wall. A minute later, Jarek comes around the corner, having taken another exit.

"Bexley made you right away." And she might have made me, too, though I have no idea how.

"We need to go now."

"Not yet. I need to arrange something." Already I hear approaching footfalls. "I'll explain it as soon as I can," I say as Kaders steps out.

He takes one look at Jarek's imposing figure and starts to back up, shaking his head. "Uh-uh. That gold will get you what *you* want, but I didn't agree to *him*."

I press the dagger against Kaders's neck, stopping him in his tracks. "Would a chest of gold and jewels be enough?"

His gaze shifts warily between the two of us. "What are you lookin' to buy?"

Not what you think, you pig. "A ship out of Cirilea."

He barks with laughter. "They won't even let me step foot on it to get my compass. There ain't no ships leaving Cirilea anytime soon, not without a letter from the king himself, and I don't see him bein' keen on granting one to the *Silver Mage*."

It's what Seamus said too. "What if I can get that letter for you?"

"You two lookin' for a ride to Seacadore?"

"To Northmost, and I want your entire hull."

"To Northmost!" He chuckles. "If the sirens don't get us, the rocks surely will. That's a tricky port to navigate."

"You can't do it? Sorry, I thought you were a skilled captain."

"'Course I can do it!" He scoffs, insulted. "But not with *you two* on the ship."

"We won't be on it. You'll have mortals." A plan is forming, one I hope we can execute with the help of Seamus.

"How many?"

"As many as you can fit."

His gaze flickers between the two of us. "You plannin' on usin' a wagon to move that chest of gold, because that's how much you'll need."

"You'll have more wealth than you know what to do with. And an act of goodwill on your conscience."

He heaves a sigh. "Cirilea sure isn't what it was, and I'm hearin' whispers of a comin' war that I want no part of. When you wantin' to leave port?"

"As soon as possible. By tomorrow night at the latest."

Cirilea's army out of the city helps my cause. Hopefully, Atticus joins them.

Kaders puckers his lips. "I'm stayin' at the Trinket Inn. You get me that letter and the gold, and I'll get your mortals to Northmost."

"You'll get both. Have your crew ready, but don't tell any of them what for."

"Aye, I know what loose lips they have after a few pints." He turns to go back inside.

"I wouldn't, if I were you," Jarek warns. "There's only trouble to be had in there. Go back to your inn and get rested."

"Here. As down payment for our deal." I hand him the dagger.

He tests its weight in his palm. "Haven't seen quality like this before."

"And there's plenty more where that came from." Jarek steps in close, to loom over the captain. "But if you cross us in any way, I'll bury that in your stomach."

"Yeah, yeah, you Islorians and your threats. Can't wait to get away from this fates-damned city and you lot." Kaders ambles down the alley.

We move in the opposite direction.

"What was it you said? That we are just here to gather information?" Jarek sighs.

"Things change. The city's gates are locked, no one in or out. Wendeline is alive. Atticus has her marking all the mortals like I told him to and then executing any who glow. He's taking all the mortal children from their families."

Jarek curses. "He'll be keeping them in the castle."

"Seamus says people are pissed. There's talk of storming the castle, from both mortals and the keepers. I don't know ..." I shake my head. "I have a bad feeling in my gut about all this. We need to get as many of these mortals out of this city as possible."

"I can eliminate the guards, if you think you can blow through the gate."

"I don't know if I can. And that many? You're good, but you're not that good, and I won't risk losing you. Plus, we can't leave Cirilea completely unprotected." I download all that I learned about the coming war in the east. "The city needs their gate intact and the king's guard alive. The *Silver Mage* is our best plan."

"It won't fit everyone."

"No, but between it and the other ships, we should be able to move out a lot."

"You want to steal ships."

"No. Seamus know the captains. We're going to bribe them."

"And all this gold we'll need in order to do that, how do you plan on transporting it all the way from Ulysede's vault, down to the crypt, through the stone, and *all the way* down to the port?"

"That'll be tricky."

"More like impossible."

I bite my lip. A thought strikes me. "Do you happen to know where Cirilea's vault is?"

He chuckles. "So now we're thieves, working with thieves."

Like old times. I smile as I slide into a comfortable coat.

We exit out the alley onto Port Street.

Where the soldier with the beard waits for us, his sword drawn.

Jarek's blade is out before I can process what's going on.

"I was sure you were dead by now." The bearded male's attention is on Jarek, his stance set for a fight.

Jarek's returning grin is vicious. "I'd hoped you were."

"Seems both of us are disappointed, then." His hazel-green eyes flip to me. "You keep bad company."

"I've heard that once or twice before." Who is this guy? He doesn't look familiar, but Jarek obviously knows him. All I know is he's attached to Atticus. Did he come out here to wait for us on his own, or was he instructed to? I guess we got off too easy.

"This is Kazimir, His Highness's personal lackey," Jarek answers my unspoken thoughts. "I've heard he washes Atticus's ass crack for him on the daily."

"Only when he asks nicely." The male—Kazimir—holds his easy smile. A façade, surely. "Who are you and what are you doing with a legionary in our city?"

I mock gasp. "Is that what he is? Why didn't you tell me what you were?" I playfully smack Jarek's forearm.

His jaw clenches. He's never appreciated my charades. "I think you should be more worried about the mercenaries stationed in the windows across the street with their arrows pointed this way than a pretty female and her guard who wish to leave. I doubt they're here for us."

Kazimir curses and shifts as if torn between checking Jarek's claim and not letting us out of his sight.

"For real?" I whisper. I can't see a thing in those windows, but I trust that Jarek can.

"I saw them there before I went in. Told you this was a bad idea."

I yank on threads of Vin'nyla's affinity, forming a solid shield in front of us.

Kazimir's eyes widen, and I know mine are glowing silver, but I'm not getting shot by another arrow. Besides, with my mask on, he'll never know who I am.

A cloaked form barrels out of the Goat's Knoll in a rush then.

It's Atticus.

46
ATTICUS

So many unfamiliar faces in the Goat's Knoll tonight.

Or perhaps I never paid enough attention before. Any one of them could be plotting against my seat on the throne as we speak.

I steal a glance over my shoulder to Kazimir.

He jerks his chin out the door. There's something out there that has interested him.

Fine, I say with a subtle nod. I can handle myself within these walls if needed.

Bexley's thoughts are lost in a gold coin when I slide into the booth across from her, but she snaps out of her daze. "Back so soon?"

"What can I say? I missed you."

"I wouldn't think you've had time to miss anyone, as busy as you've been."

I offer her a sly smile. "Aren't you the one who told me to give them something to fear?"

"You've certainly done that. There isn't a lord or a mortal who isn't terrified. The only ones who seem content are the ones who wish to see you fall." She feigns casualness, but I sense rippling tension in her. "The streets feel oddly vacant now that your Cirilean army is gone. When do you plan to catch up with them?"

"At dawn. It's time these eastern soldiers heard the truth from their king, not lords who fill their heads with lies and lofty dreams." Fates knows what Adley and the others promised them. Land? Wealth? A cure for the poison?

"And what will you do about Neilina?"

"I have to hope the forces there can keep her occupied until I lead the men from the east." I hate relying on my brother, but if anyone can succeed, he will. "We will form a second front to assault those who make it through."

"And what are your plans for Ulysede?"

I should have known that name would reach her ears soon enough. She's Bexley, after all. "How did you hear about that?"

"*Not* from you." She taps the table with her coin. "Though you had the perfect opportunity to share those details."

"So you could peddle them to the highest bidder?"

"Why are you here tonight?" She snaps. "What is it you wish to gain from me?"

She's angry. That's fine. I don't have time to play games. "Who vies to take Lord Adley's place, now that he and Lady Saoirse are locked up?" It's not his son. They found his head the morning after Zander left, amongst the fallen bodies. I heard I have Abarrane to thank for that.

"I'm sure the list is long."

"And which names are at the top?"

"Good question."

"Stop toying with me." My patience is running short. "Do not forget to whom you speak."

"I speak to a commoner who has found his way into my tavern, looking for information. Perhaps he'll find someone *peddling* it." She raises an eyebrow. "But when you see the king again, please tell him to reconsider who he paints an enemy to Islor, because I suspect he will desperately need one in particular before long." She sets her gold coin on the table. "And I would stop executing mortals if I were you."

"I have." At least the ones who don't openly defy the rule of law.

"It was mildly pleasant knowing you, Atticus." With that, Bexley is gone, slipping out of the booth and gliding through the darkness toward the door.

Leaving me alone with my dour thoughts.

It was mildly pleasant knowing me? Past tense?

What does Bexley know that she refused to tell me? I survey the Goat's Knoll, looking for an immediate threat, but I see none. Still, my hand lands on the hilt of my dagger for comfort. I have half a mind to haul Bexley into a dungeon to see if she'll be so surly when her wrists are shackled.

The gold coin she left behind gleams under the firelight. I collect it and flip it over within my grasp as she did. My stomach clenches as I take in the two crescents, intertwined. This coin must be from Ulysede, which means there is someone from there within my city.

I scramble out of the booth and charge out the front door intent on finding Bexley and interrogating her.

Instead, I find Kazimir armed and facing off against the raven-haired beauty I bumped into earlier, and a tall, cloaked form at her side.

Her eyes glow silver.

"You're a caster." Surprise fills my voice. And she's with Jarek —a legionary. I'm reaching for my sword when a searing pain slams into my chest.

47
ROMERIA

Atticus drops to the ground as people around us scream and scatter. They have no idea they're looking at their fallen king.

"That landed true and will likely be merth." Jarek's attention is still on Kazimir, who stares with a mix of shock and horror.

Atticus isn't moving.

"Fuck!" I rush to his side. The arrow protrudes from his torso, right where his heart would be. I check for a pulse. It's barely there.

Atticus deserves to die for all the mortals he's executed, but I know Zander wouldn't want this. "I'm doing this for your brother, not you." I reach for Aoife's healing thread. But Lucretia's words come back to me. I don't have time to knit this idiot's flesh back together with one affinity. I have to do this quickly or not at all.

"If you want him to live, I suggest you focus your energy on the enemy about to run out that door," Jarek warns Kazimir, a moment before a dark-haired man dashes out.

Kazimir charges him.

"Hurry up!" Jarek barks at me.

"Then get this thing out of him!"

He rushes to my side and yanks on the arrow, pulling it free. Even covered in crimson, the metal gleams, silver and deadly.

Without the arrow to plug it, blood pours out of Atticus's chest in a steady rivulet. I clamp my hands over the rush and summon all my affinities, allowing them to coil together in one thick silver thread. The sound of clanging steel fades from thought behind me as I sink my power into his fatal wound.

In seconds, the still body beneath me shudders to life. Atticus gasps for breath.

"The king's guard is on its way!" Jarek shouts.

Hyacinth-blue eyes that remind me of Annika's blink before focusing on me. "You."

He has no idea who I am. "I think you'll live, though you don't deserve it. Get Wendeline to fix up anything I missed." Horse hooves pound against cobblestone, warning me that we've run out of time. But on impulse—or maybe because a spiteful side wants Atticus to know who saved his life—I lean in to growl in his ear, "By the way, I don't even know how to play draughts."

Jarek yanks me away, and we run for the alley.

48
GRACEN

My dress is covered in spit-up, snot, and urine, and my back aches by the time I tuck in the last of the restless children, a four-year-old girl named Nora whose parents were taken to the execution square. She wouldn't stop sobbing until I promised her she will see them again.

I pray that wasn't a lie.

Corrin meets me by the doors, her hands on her hips as she surveys the ballroom of sleeping bodies. "I visited a barn much like this once." She picks a piece of straw from her lips with a grimace. "I will be smelling and tasting hay all night."

"It's better than them sleeping on the hard marble floor." When the guards first opened the doors, I was greeted with children huddled in clusters—the older ones cradling hungry babies in soiled diapers. They weren't making a sound, terrified.

The sight made my eyes well instantly.

My first order of business was to send the guards off to haul in hay bales. They did so without complaint. Then I enlisted the castle staff for food, supplies, and comfort. It's taken the entire day, but everyone has settled, and perhaps they're a little less frightened.

"This was a difficult task, Gracen. You did well." Corrin wears grim satisfaction.

It's not often she praises anyone, and my heart swells with pride. "It was a team effort." Dagny and the seamstresses scoured the castle for blankets. Fikar lugged in jugs of water, taking breaks in between to play jester, wearing away the children's fears with card tricks and silly faces. Sabrina led groups to the latrine and distracted the little girls by braiding their hair and singing songs. Corrin went on a hunt for suitable milk for the babies. I nursed two who aren't my own.

"They gobbled up those wedding sweet cakes of yours quite happily."

"Better to go to children than the soldiers, I thought."

"I agree. They've got plenty of barley and wheat flour to make their flatbread." She worries her lip. "Still, we have three hundred and seventy-four mouths to feed here and, I'm sure, more coming tomorrow. We will run out of wedding cakes."

"Then I will bake bread." I squeeze Corrin's shoulder. "I am staying here tonight in case anyone needs me." Or until Atticus summons me to his chambers. A nervous flutter stirs in my stomach at the thought, but I push it aside. I have too much to focus on here with these children to allow heady thoughts to intrude.

"And you will stay with her," Corrin declares as Sabrina joins us.

She must be as exhausted as I am. "Yes, of course. Suri and Lilou are already down." She looks around. "Have you seen Mika?"

"Not in a while." I groan, my head falling back in frustration.

Fikar is passing by. "He said somethin' about the horses earlier."

"I'll bet he's visiting Silmar." Mika dreams of sleeping in the stables like the older boy does.

"I guess I'll wander out that way and look," Sabrina says, but I'm already moving toward the door.

"No, it's okay. I'll hunt him down. The guards can be surly, but they know me by now. I could use the fresh air, anyway."

Corrin shakes her head. "That boy … one day he's going to get himself into mischief he can't get out of."

My trek through the castle toward the stable crosses paths with Dagny, her arms loaded with linen scraps.

Her round face splits into a wide, genuine smile the moment she sees me. She's always a ray of sunshine, even when life feels so bleak. "Found some more cloth we can use for diapering the wee ones."

"That's perfect. Thank you, Dagny. You've been an enormous help."

"Of course. Don't mind at all." She glances around before whispering, "A far better task than making a wedding dress for the demon."

I chuckle. "Maybe we should use that fabric for the children." What must be going through Lady Saoirse's thoughts at this very moment, locked in that gray tower, awaiting her punishment?

"Not a bad idea." She nods, and then her face morphs with giddy excitement. "Guess what! My Dagnar was summoned by Princess Annika herself. She's lookin' for a new tributary, and she heard he was keen to stay within the castle employ. Imagine that!" She squeezes my forearm. "If my boy's gonna serve, who better than the royal princess?"

"That's great news." I think. Is this coincidence or Atticus's doing?

Dagny frowns. "What are you doing around this end of the castle, anyway?"

"Looking for Mika *again*. I think he's out with Silmar."

"That boy! He's a handful!" She chuckles, strolling away. "Oh! And I think I found a nice new dress for ya! Come by tomorrow and I'll size you up for it."

I don't ask where the dress might have come from. With all the dead mortals, I'm sure I already know. My stomach rolls with the thought.

No one else walks the castle halls tonight. By the time I round the corner that leads to the stables, an eeriness clings to the air.

"Servants aren't allowed in these parts!" the guard stationed at the door barks, but then he blinks and his stiff body relaxes. "Oh, *you*. Let me guess, you're on the hunt again."

I wouldn't be surprised if every guard in this place had been tasked with tracking down Mika at one point or another. I offer an apologetic smile. "I think he went to the stables. If you wouldn't mind escorting me out there so I can check—"

"Go on, then." He waves me past, not wanting to be bothered.

"Thank you." With a curtsy, I slip through the heavy door and into the night, wishing I'd grabbed my cloak.

Ahead, the soft whinny of horses carries. The first time Mika ventured out here, he followed Silmar after mealtime. He never would have found it otherwise. It's not the main castle stable that the soldiers use, but a small one outside the curtain wall, with a door and a narrow tunnel through the stone that leads to it. If I had to guess, it's here in case someone in the castle needs to escape quickly and without notice.

I pass through the tunnel, absently thinking that perhaps a guard should be stationed here.

"… a magic potion hidden behind a book. But then Mama said I couldn't tell anyone—"

"Mika!" My alarm flares as his words sink in.

His curly brown mop whips around. "It's okay! Silmar says the king chopped off Lord Danthrin's head, so he can't make us go back to Freywich!" he exclaims with too much glee.

But it's not Silmar who Mika is speaking to. It's an older teenage boy with brown curls and big blue eyes. Much like my son's, oddly enough. I've never seen him in the castle before, and alarm bells ring instantly.

"Mika, come here *now*."

He drags his feet, as if they're tied to hefty stones. "But it's okay. This is Pan."

"We don't know Pan." And any stranger lurking around at night when the castle gates are closed, especially in these times, is likely up to no good. Silmar is one stall over, brushing a horse's coat, seemingly unconcerned.

"But he knows Eden."

That startles me. "Eden?"

"Yes, milady." Pan bows and when he stands again, he's grinning so widely, his dimples divot his cheeks. He has a sweet face, but I've been fooled by his sort before. "Mika and I got to talkin' about Freywich, and I said I have a friend from there. Actually, I know a boy from Freywich too. A stable hand named Brawley. Big, strappin' guy who's learning how to use a mace. I wanna learn, too, but Jarek says I'm liable to crack my own head open. He's probably right."

I falter, my mind trying to pick through his rambling for the important details. "You know Eden and Brawley?"

"Yes, milady. They're doin' well. Happy as can be. You're Mika's ma, right?"

"Gracen. Yes."

"Gracen!" The rambling boy's jaw drops. "Well, I'll be. I was hopin' to find you. Eden talks about ya all the time. Says you make the best pastries, and you were always takin' care of her. She knew I was comin' here tonight and wanted me to give you these." He fishes out a pair of knit baby booties from his pocket and hands them to me. "She was working on a sweater, but it got left behind in Freywich. They left in a hurry."

I study the stitching. Eden was practicing her knitting when we left. She's improved greatly. But … "I'm sorry, *who are you*?"

"I'm Pan." He takes a few steps and drops his voice to a whisper. "Romy rescued me from my keeper in Bellcross, just like she rescued Eden and Brawley from Freywich. And you guys, too, from what I've heard."

That first day, in the assembly, Lord Danthrin was lamenting how Princess Romeria had stolen his servants. This Pan fellow may very well be speaking the truth. "Romy?"

He holds his hands in the air in surrender. "I mean, *Princess Romeria*. Actually, *Queen Romeria* now. She's got a castle and everything!"

"Can we go?" Mika tugs on my skirt. "Please, Mama! I wanna see Eden and Brawley!"

"No, Mika. We can't." For so many reasons. Even having this conversation could be considered treason. I glance over my shoulder, afraid the guard is seconds from catching us. Or worse, Atticus will round the corner. What would he say? Pan shouldn't be here. "How did you get inside the city?"

"That's a long story. Me, Romy, and Jarek—"

"Her Highness is here?" I hiss. "Princess Romeria is *here*?"

"No." Pan looks like he swallowed his tongue.

"You're lying."

"No, I ain't. She's not right *here*." He points at the cobblestone beneath his feet. "But she wanted me to check on everyone in the castle. She gave me a list. Let's see, there was"—he peers up into the night sky as if this list is waiting for him there—"a lady maid named Corrin, a seamstress named …"

"Dagny?"

"Aye, that one." He waggles his index finger. "And her husband and son. Then there's a caster. Romy wasn't sure if she's still alive. And you guys, of course …"

"They're all fine." My heart pounds in my chest. All the castle staff who personally knew Princess Romeria. "We are all fine. The king has treated us well, though this poison has made life difficult."

"Yeah, Silmar was tellin' me about all the executions they've been doin' around here." He grimaces. "There's lots of them going on across Islor too. But don't worry, Romy wants to take you out of here and bring you to her kingdom."

"To Ybaris?"

"No. Ulysede. It's in the mountains, near the rift." He pulls a gold coin from his pocket and hands it to me. "You'll be safe there."

I stare at it in my palm, stupefied. I've never held gold before. It's a moment before I notice the engraving on the face—the double-crescent-moon emblem, the same one that marks our hands.

Faint shouts sound somewhere in the city, reminding me how dangerous it is to be caught talking to Pan. "You need to go. If they find you here, the king will execute you."

"Right." His face scrunches as he peers up at the imposing castle. "You wouldn't happen to know where they're keeping the caster, would ya? I haven't made it down to the dungeon yet, but—"

"Do not go down there. It's full of lords and ladies and guards. You will get caught, and you will be executed. But she is not down there anymore. I heard she's in the east wing of the castle when she's not in the city marking mortals. I do not know which room, and you will not be able to reach her. The castle is heavily guarded against anyone unfamiliar. You will get caught and—"

"Executed. I'm sensing a theme." He grins, despite the dour subject.

The wooden gate into the stable creaks open, and two cloaked forms rush through.

Silmar's eyes widen, but Pan waves him off. "It's okay, they're with me." To them, he says, "I thought we were meeting in the tunnel."

"Plans changed. We've got to leave *now*," the female elven declares, her voice stony.

I fumble for Mika, pulling him tight to my leg.

She freezes when she sees me standing there.

"Yeah. Look who I found!" Pan beams. "Small world, huh?"

"Gracen?" The elven woman pushes off her hood. Her hands are covered in blood.

I step back, ushering Mika behind me, and open my mouth to scream, hoping the guard inside will hear.

"*No, no, no* … it's okay. It's me." She holds up her hands in surrender. "It's Romeria."

"*You* are *not* Princess Romeria."

"I am, I swear. Here." She reaches for her chin, picking at it.

And suddenly Romeria *is* standing before me, holding a silver mask that she just peeled off.

I gasp.

"How did you *do* that!" Mika shrieks, earning both our shushes.

Finally, I remember myself and bow, urging Mika to do the same.

"We don't have time for that." She rushes forward, reaching for my hands before stalling, as if only then realizing hers are bloodied. She wipes them over her cloak. It does little good. "I am *so* happy to see you. I was worried Atticus would harm you or send you back to Freywich."

"No! He hasn't." I punctuate that claim with a headshake. "He's been good to us. Kind. And Lord Danthrin is dead. Atticus executed him." *For me.* He chopped off a lord's head for me, I don't say.

"He did, did he?" She looks down at my stomach. "*And* you had your baby."

"Yes. A little girl." I hesitate, dropping my voice. I know I shouldn't admit to this with ears around, but I can't help myself. If this is the only time I see her again, I need her to know. "She goes by Suri, but her real given name is Romeria. After you."

The princess's face softens as she absorbs that. "I'm honored—"

"The king's guard will be crawling over this place soon. We must go now," the tall, lethal-looking warrior declares in a raspy growl, watching the street beyond the wooden gate. Shouts sound nearby.

"Right." Romeria shakes her head. "Come with us to Ulysede."

"What? *Now?*"

"Yes." She waves me toward her.

"But I can't leave Lilou and Suri."

"We'll go and get them."

"Romeria," the warrior warns in a stern voice. "The longer we wait, the more people we have to kill to get out."

"I'm not leaving them here!" she snaps back.

I don't want them killing anyone. "It's okay. Besides, I can't leave. There is an entire ballroom of mortal children who need me."

"Where?" Her eyes widen. "Which one is he keeping them in?"

So she knows about that. "The west wing."

She nods slowly, as if fitting that information into a plan. "That ballroom has doors that lead directly to the royal garden, does it not?"

"Yes. They're heavily guarded, though."

"We'll be executed," Pan chirps.

Shouts sound again, closer this time.

The warrior draws two swords as if preparing for battle.

Romeria curses under her breath. "Okay. You will keep those children safe for me."

"Of course."

"And I need you to pass along an important message. Can you do that?"

"Mika, go on over there and help Silmar with the horse." I goad him forward with a hand against his back, waiting until he's out of earshot. "I owe you my life and that of my children. If you'll trust me with the message, I will get it where it needs to go."

She sighs with relief. "Tell Wendeline that we had it wrong and the door is already open, but the prophecy is real."

I repeat her words, an unease sliding over my spine. "I will deliver that." How, I have no idea, but I will figure out a way.

"I will see you again very soon. I promise." She slips on her mask and Romeria is gone, replaced by a stranger.

Pan offers a wave at Mika and Silmar, and then the three of them rush around the corner and are gone from sight.

I tuck the gold coin in my pocket and beckon my son.

He trots over, a dazed look on his face. "Did she tell you how she did that?"

"Using special magic that you can *never* talk about with anyone. I mean it, Mika. I don't care whose head has been chopped off." I collect his hand and tug him inside, equal parts furious with him and thrilled that his disobedience led us to the princess.

But what is she doing here?

And why were her hands covered in blood?

The guard ignores us as we pass him, sparing nothing more than a smug smile for Mika, but the boy's not paying attention, too enthralled by what he just witnessed.

I recite the message to Wendeline over and over in my head as we walk, praying I don't confuse or distort it. I wish I had paper and ink to mark it down, but those are next to impossible for a servant to find these days.

A rush of pounding metal boots sounds from the nearby main hall.

"Fetch the caster!" Someone shouts. It's Kazimir. "Drag her out of bed if you have to and get her to the king's chamber at once." Four soldiers rush past as we reach the entrance to the hall.

My mouth hangs with horror at the sight of Atticus's limp body held among them, his tunic soaked in blood, his face pale.

"You!" Kazimir points at me, his eyes wide with panic. He has a sword slash across his cheek. "He'll need a vein as soon as the caster is done."

"Right. Of course." I collect Mika's cheeks in my hands. "You go straight to the ballroom *right now*. Do you understand?"

His head bobs up and down, his bottom lip wobbling with fear.

"Go! Now!"

Mika tears away, and I follow Kazimir up the stairs.

Praying Atticus survives and that Romeria's bloody hands had nothing to do with this.

49
ROMERIA

Pan trips over the slain guard's boots and stumbles into the cedar hedge.

"Imbecile," Jarek mutters.

"I can't see anything in the dark!"

"Shhh!" I warn sharply, and Pan clamps his lips together.

I look over my shoulder for the hundredth time to make sure no one followed us. We snuck past the flock of guards, again using my cloaking skills. It seemed too easy. "At least they didn't find him."

"Let us keep it that way, or this place will be crawling with guards tomorrow." Jarek drags the corpse out and throws him over his shoulder like a sack of grain before continuing. "If we *must* return."

"Yes, we *must*." A surge of adrenaline charges through me as I think of the task we have ahead of us, and how much harder it could be now that Atticus—and the king's guard by default—know a caster is in their city.

I wish I hadn't had to reveal myself like that tonight.

I pat my pants pocket where the letters for the port guards are tucked away. We snuck into the war room on the way here, figuring the royal guard would be too busy looking for us outside the castle wall to think we might be inside already.

Jarek notices the subtle move, but he notices *everything* I do. "What did you write, anyway?"

"Hi, my name is Atticus, and I stole my brother's throne."

He snorts.

"I kept it simple and to the point. The ship is allowed to leave port immediately, by the king's order, and with mortal passengers." Hastily written and generic, but maybe enough to pass the guards' tests.

"If they don't pay attention to the bloody smears on the paper."

The reminder has me wiping my hands across my cape again in vain. "And if they do?"

"Then we put the lives of all those mortals ahead of them."

He's saying we'll kill them. I sigh. "Right." And Jarek *is* right, though I hate it. Never did I think I'd be adding murder to my résumé of crimes.

We exit the cedar maze and trek across the open grass, Jarek carrying the corpse. Moonlight shines from above, granting enough light that I can see the shadowy outline of the nymphaeum ahead. In two days, the second Hudem moon will shine so bright here, it'll seem like daylight.

And everything will change.

It's all I can do not to take off running toward the stone, so I can get back to Ulysede sooner, and write a letter for the taillok to take to Zander. My heart aches to see him again. The hours between now and dawn, when Gesine confirms he is safe, will drag mercilessly.

"I would have left him there to die." Jarek's gaze lands on my face. "What you did tonight for Atticus, I would not have had the fortitude to do."

"I didn't do it for him." I hope I don't regret the choice.

"Still. It takes a certain strength."

"Are you admitting that I'm stronger than you?"

His responding chuckle is dark.

Movement high in the sky catches my attention. "What is that?" I point upward. "Do you see that?" A large, winged black shape soars above us, circling. Unease slips down my spine.

Jarek curses and speeds up. "Run."

"Thank the fates!" Gesine exclaims as we spill through the stone and into Lucretia's crypt. "His Highness would have skinned me alive had you not returned."

Lucretia appears out of thin air a moment later. "The fates have nothing to do with this."

How she moves about Ulysede, I would love to know.

She winks at me as if she can read my mind. For all I know, she can. "Did you find the answers you sought, Your Highness?"

"I think so. A lot of them, anyway. Also, I'm pretty sure we saw Caindra." Jarek and I exchange a long look. He must be feeling what I am—relief that the dragon stayed where she was, circling above the city rather than diving into it. I can't imagine the devastation that beast could rain down on Cirilea.

"Yes, she will be able to find you anywhere."

"Wonderful."

"Isn't it?" Lucretia smiles, missing my sarcastic tone, or ignoring it.

Pan scampers away, finding a spot behind Zorya where he can gawk at Lucretia's sheer black gown and the feminine flesh beneath while trying to avoid her attention. The sylx seems to scare him.

Lucretia has no interest in Pan, though, her rapt attention on Jarek. "Who have you brought with you?"

"A willing male," Jarek says dryly, dropping the corpse on the stone floor. "Enjoy him."

She seems to study the dead guard, tapping his thigh with her toe. "Not much fight left in him, but I imagine he won't complain."

Zorya grimaces.

"Whose blood is that, Romeria?" Gesine's brow is furrowed at my stained hands.

"Atticus's." I describe what happened.

"They staked out the tavern, knowing he would come without the king's guard," Jarek says. "Paid mercenaries, likely."

"Atticus went there all the time to see Bexley." Much more often than Zander snuck out. If I were hunting someone, it's what I would have done.

"You see now, do you not?" Lucretia sidles up beside Pan, who visibly stiffens, before moving on. "What the Queen for All can do with her power and my masters' blessing?"

"All I know is he was breathing when we left." I hope I did enough to keep him that way.

"And Seamus?" Gesine's expression is hopeful. "Did you find him?"

"Yes, and he had a lot to say. I need to send a letter to Zander." And then we need a plan for how to get as many mortals out of that city before they are either hung or slaughtered in the brewing rebellion.

Gesine eases off the floor, collecting her stack of books. "Lucretia, it was a pleasure waiting with you." I can't tell by her even tone if she's being genuine.

"And I will see you later." Lucretia's yellow serpentine eyes sparkle with amusement as Jarek hauls the dead body off the floor. "*All* of you."

Pan is the first to run up the stairs, two at a time.

"What does she mean by that?" Jarek asks warily as we follow, stealing a glance behind him at the sylx, who watches like a hawk surveying a rodent.

"Let's just say I don't think we're ever truly alone around here."

50
ATTICUS

I feel hands on my body.

Multiple sets—strong ones, gripping my arms and legs without mercy; gentle ones, unfastening and peeling off my tunic; cool ones, grazing my tender skin.

"It was merth?" I recognize Wendeline's soft timbre.

The low hum of a male voice—Kazimir's—responds, but I can't make out what he's saying.

"Yes." I think I said that out loud. That burn, there's only one thing it can be.

I remember …

The gold coin.

Chasing after Bexley.

That woman with her radiant silver eyes.

Draughts.

She said something about draughts.

51

GRACEN

"You allowed His Highness to go out in the streets with a bounty on his head!" Captain Boaz roars.

"*Allow*? You think he asked for my *permission*?" Kazimir shouts back. The two commanding officers stand nose to nose, faces contorted with fury. If they were to draw swords, I can't say which would win the battle, but I truly hope we don't find out.

I slink back against the wall in Atticus's chamber, hoping to blend into the elaborate molding and gilt.

Captain Boaz edges closer to Kazimir, his stance menacing. "And where were you when this happened?"

"Ten feet away." But Kazimir adds quietly, "I should have known they'd be waiting there for him."

Captain Boaz shakes his head. His anger pours from his limbs, radiating outward. "Can you heal him?" he demands, his focus shifting to Wendeline.

"I will do my best." Her hands tremble as they hover over the wound on his chest. "How he survived this arrow, I do not understand. Whoever this caster was, she saved his life."

"That a caster and a legionary were there when the king was injured is too great a coincidence to be applauded. And he does not look *saved* to me," Boaz growls. "Remember, he is the only reason *you* are still alive." A not-so-hidden threat.

Wendeline dips her head, not meeting Boaz's eyes. Anyone can see she's afraid of him and with good reason, likely. "This will take me time."

"He has until dawn, when he must ride out to meet his army in the east. Until then, I have a legionary and a caster to hunt." Boaz charges toward the door. He noticed me at the last minute.

"Tributary," is all Kazimir says.

Boaz grabs my hand roughly, checks the dull mark, and then releases me and storms off, spitting out orders. "Send extra protection to Princess Annika. She is next for the throne. They may go after her too." The other guards filter out behind him, leaving the three of us lingering around the king.

Wendeline settles down on the bed next to him, her hands hovering over the gash in his chest—sealed but the injury visible. His skin is coated in blood. He looks so pale.

An ache grips my heart. "What happened?"

"The eastern lords hired mercenaries to kill the king. They were waiting for him to show up at the Goat's Knoll. They shot him the moment he stepped out." Kazimir sighs. "I was busy confronting a legionary I'd spotted and a female who was traveling with him. I should have been paying closer attention."

"You said she was a caster?"

"Apparently. I was sure she was elven, but then her eyes began to glow." Kazimir shakes his head. "When Atticus fell, she dove in to heal him, at least for a brief moment before the guard arrived and they ran."

Princess Romeria isn't a caster, though. She's elven. But her hands were covered in blood. "What did they look like? This legionary and the female?"

"Jarek is Jarek. A big, angry bastard. Lethal and impossible to mistake. The woman had dark hair. I have never seen that face before, though. I would have remembered." His eyes narrow. "Why? Have you seen something?"

I shake my head, perhaps too vigorously. "But I will be on the lookout." I shift my attention to Atticus, allowing my worry for him to bleed into anything else Kazimir might read in my pulse. "And the mercenaries? Will they try again?"

"That will be difficult. I killed them both." Kazimir peers at his friend and his jaw tenses. "He will pull through."

I can't tell if he believes that or if he is telling himself what he needs to hear. "Yes. He will." He must. And *I* must speak to Wendeline. Romeria's message burns in my memory, waiting to be relayed.

"He will need you as soon as he wakes."

My vein, Kazimir means. "I will have to step out to feed Suri, but—"

"Corrin will bring her up."

I nod. I suppose her cries won't disturb Atticus either way.

He frowns, leaning forward. "What is that all over your dress? Is that … vomit?"

I look down at the white milk stains. "Basically, yes."

His gaze shifts to the dark stain on my skirt. "And that?"

"Urine, from a diaper leak."

He steps back to appraise me with a critical eye, reaching for my hair. When he pulls away, there's straw between his fingers. "What in fates' name have you been doing all day long?"

"Comforting three hundred and seventy-four terrified mortal children."

"Commendable. Truly. But please do me a favor and use the queen's chamber to bathe. And change out of that."

My mouth drops. The *queen*'s chamber? "I can't do that!"

"Oh, but you *must. Please.* For him." He grimaces. "And me."

"A mortal baker in a queen's chamber. Mark this day for yourself. I know I will." Corrin sweeps into the bathing room, a white gown and robe draped over her arm.

I huddle in the grand tub, centered in a luxurious marble room that is truly fit for a queen and *not* me, my weary body begging for rest even as my mind is wired with worry. "Is she asleep?" I fed Suri while the bath was drawing. Hopefully, that will hold her over until dawn.

"Sound as a nethertaur, underground."

"You are comparing my child to a Nulling beast?"

"Your sweet baby? *Never*. That boy of yours, however ..." She snorts. "Do you need help?"

"No, I think I've found the last of the straw and vomit. If you wouldn't mind passing me that towel."

Corrin collects it, but instead of handing it to me as I climb out, she begins drying me off.

It earns my laugh. "I can do that myself."

"I know you can, but it has been an eternity since I helped anyone in this chamber. Princess Romeria did not care for any assistance at all. Though, she was never your typical elven royalty, was she," she adds, more to herself.

Corrin may not speak about the exiled king and Princess Romeria, but I sense she is loyal to them. What might she know of Princess Romeria's secrets?

Clearly the princess has a few. Somehow, she got into a city under lock, and with a new face and coins that bear the mark of the tainted. As far as Kazimir's description of the caster and the legionary, the looming warrior at Romeria's side when she came to the stable must be one and the same, and her hands were covered in blood. The more I think about it, the more I believe Boaz was right about coincidences—though wrong about intentions.

It is all far too coincidental.

Which means Princess Romeria saved Atticus's life, even though many could argue he doesn't deserve her grace. How would Atticus feel, knowing this? Would it change his opinion of her?

"Is the priestess finished?"

"I have not been there to check. I cannot imagine she will have the energy to continue too long tonight, though. They have been running her ragged, marking all these mortals, day and night. I hope she has enough in her for the king. Here, this should fit you well." She holds up the gown.

"It's beautiful." I test the material with my fingertips. It's made of silk with a wide collar and a delicate lace overlay across the waist. "I have never seen anything so fine."

"It was Princess Romeria's."

I pull my hand away as if burned. "Oh, I couldn't—"

"She will not mind, believe me." She eases it over my head. "A more generous heart for mortals, I have not seen before."

I slip my arms through the holes. The material tumbles to the floor.

"Take a look." Corrin gestures to the dressing mirror.

Even with only candlelight to illuminate the reflection, I feel transformed. Elegant, the silk subtly clinging to my curves. "I should hope Kazimir approves."

"Do not play games with me. There is only one immortal you seek approval of, and you will surely get it in that. I will not bother with more warnings because you will not listen to me." She gives me a knowing look before collecting my soiled dress from the marble floor.

But my mind is still lingering on the princess—on why she was here. "They are saying there is a caster within Cirilea, and she was there when His Highness fell."

Corrin's hands stall. "They did not recognize her?"

"No. Kazimir said he's never seen her before. She was with a legionary, and she tried to heal Atticus before the king's guard arrived and they ran."

"I imagine they will find her soon enough." She examines my soiled dress. "Well, it isn't a wonder the captain sent you in here."

I get the sense Corrin is dismissing the topic intentionally, but I don't push. We both have our secrets and perhaps it's best to keep them that way.

"The laundress should be able to get the stains out." Digging into the pocket, she pulls out the baby booties. "What are these?"

"Oh! Just someone thought I might like them." I scramble over a suitable lie. "One of Dagny's girls."

"That was nice of them. They'll keep Suri's feet warm at night." She sticks her hand in the other pocket.

I suck in a gasp as she pulls out the gold coin and holds it up to the light. I'd forgotten about it.

Her eyes dart to me but she doesn't say a word as she strolls over to the bathing chamber door, to chuck the soiled dress out while doing a quick scan. Seemingly satisfied, she pulls the door shut again and marches back, holding the coin between us, the double crescent moon facing me. "Who gave this to you, and do not dare lie to me, Gracen. I cannot protect you and your children if you do."

I swallow my growing anxiety. "From Princess Romeria. *Queen* Romeria now, apparently. Of some kingdom."

Corrin's eyebrows climb halfway up her forehead. "She was *here*? Inside the castle?"

"By the stables, when I went to look for Mika. It was her, but she had a mask on to disguise herself. Silver when it was off and a new face when it was on. It was like nothing I've ever seen."

"A fates' token, surely." Corrin's hands wring with her thoughts. "And the exiled king? Did you see him?"

"No. Just her, the warrior, and a young mortal named Pan. Very friendly. He's the one who gave me the coin and the booties, from an old friend in Freywich."

"You said a kingdom. Where?"

"High in the mountains, near the rift. Pan called it Ulysede."

"They traveled all the way back down here?" She purses her lips with doubt.

"I do not know. We had so little time to speak. They were running from the king's guard. Her hands were covered in blood." I drop my voice even lower. "I think *she* was the one who saved Atticus, Corrin."

Corrin bites her bottom lip. "Yes."

I knew it. "Now it is your turn to speak truth. What do you know about this?"

"Far more than I wish I did." She sighs. "They are one and the same."

My mouth gapes. "You mean Her Highness is a caster?"

"Yes, a powerful one, though no one here knows that. No one, except Wendeline, and she has suffered greatly to keep that secret."

Wendeline. "Her Highness gave me a message for the priestess that I must pass on."

"About what?"

Tell her we had it wrong and the door is already open, but the prophecy is real.

I falter. "It is best I do not repeat it. I do not want you complicit in this."

Corrin's face tightens. "Be *very* careful, Gracen. If the king suspects you are conspiring with her—"

"I'm not! Truly! And her message didn't sound like that. It was about prophecy."

"It will not look like nothing to the king, and certainly not to Boaz." She shakes her head, tucking the gold coin in her pocket. "I will keep this for now. I do not want you caught with it."

"But it is obvious that Her Highness does not mean the king harm."

"Is it?"

"She saved him! Why else would she do that? Maybe if Atticus knew it was Romeria—"

A knock sounds on the door, making us both jump.

"He is stirring," Kazimir says from the other side of the door. "He will need you shortly."

"Just dressing!" I call out, my voice strained.

Corrin rushes to fetch the robe made of the same silky material. "You listen to me." Her words are barely audible as she slides it over my shoulders. "We are mortals. We survive because we *do not* get involved in the affairs of kings and queens and their battles for power. Besides, do not assume you know her motivations. Maybe she wants Atticus alive so he can see Zander take back his throne. Or perhaps Zander wishes to deliver the killing strike."

I hadn't thought of those scenarios. But would she scheme with such calculation? "She told me to keep the mortal children safe for her. It sounded like she would be coming back for them."

"See? Who knows what she has planned, but I imagine it has to do with reclaiming the throne. She always was a cunning one. Both versions of her." Corrin shakes her head. "But, Gracen, if not for your sake, then for your children's, *do not* choose sides and do not get involved. Give the king what he needs and *nothing* more."

I nod, swallowing the guilt and fear that swirls inside me, knowing that I now hold secrets he may consider treasonous.

But I would never do anything to harm him. He must know that.

Corrin pushes the door open and lifts her chin. "Since when do captains hover outside bathing chamber doors? Is that not beneath you?" she asks crisply with that hint of arrogance. I don't know where she digs it up from. Sometimes I wish I had it in me.

Kazimir is already moving for the terrace. "Come. This way is faster."

"I shall take the baby down with me. I doubt she will stir again tonight." Corrin moves for the settee, where Suri sleeps soundly in her basket, a fire crackling in the hearth nearby.

I pause long enough to wonder when I tell my daughter one day that she slept in the queen of Islor's chambers, will she believe me? "Thank you." I read one last stark warning in Corrin's steady gaze before I follow Kazimir out.

The cold air bites at my skin as we move along a narrow passage that connects the queen's and king's terraces.

Kazimir steals a look at my ensemble, and I do my best not to shrink under the attention. I've been leered at by males, but this appraisal feels different. Appreciative. "Do you approve now?"

"Of the absence of urine and vomit? Yes." He chuckles. "Though I think I miss the perpetual streak of flour on your cheek."

"We could detour to the kitchen and fix that for you."

"And fool myself into believing it is me you are dressing for?" He winks before opening the door. His mood is much lighter than before. He's buoyed by relief for not just his king but his friend. "After you."

I enter Atticus's bedchamber as a guard is lifting an unconscious Wendeline in his arms, her limbs dangling helplessly.

Panic flares inside me. "Is she okay?"

"Wendeline is a lot tougher than she looks," Atticus croaks as a servant I've seen but never spoken to smooths a washcloth over his bloodied chest. Another carries a second basin of fresh water. "She will be fine in the morning."

Romeria's message will have to wait until then.

My joy to see Atticus conscious again pushes aside all other thoughts. He's still sickly pale, his lips tinged blue. But when his eyes roll over me, taking in my silk gown and robe, my stomach flips.

"Leave us," he commands softly.

The servants move instantly, collecting the basin of dirty water and scurrying out. It's as if they were waiting for the command and can't get away fast enough. How any of them can fear him so is beyond me.

And yet you feared him once too, I remind myself. Or at least, I feared his immense power.

"Here, let me continue that." I round the bed to his side and settle onto the edge, collecting a clean cloth from the stack and dipping it into the basin left behind. The water is still warm. I smooth it over his torso, uncovering taut muscle and golden skin with each stroke. "You bled a lot."

"So I've heard." He studies my face. "I like this version of you."

I blush. "I borrowed something from the queen's closet. My

appearance was not appropriate, according to *some*." I give a pointed look toward Kazimir.

"No, I meant how you moved in without hesitation. As if you have a right to me."

My hand stalls over his chest. Was I too brazen? Too presumptuous?

"No. I mean it, Gracen. Don't second-guess yourself." He closes his eyes and sighs. "And for the love of all the fates above, *please* do not stop."

Swallowing my nerves, I drag the cloth down his stomach, marveling at the cut ridges he showed off for me only days ago.

"The men who attacked me?" he asks.

"Both dead," Kazimir confirms. "They were waiting in the Jadelight. Rhodes is not here to confirm, but I would bet they were the mercenaries meeting with Danthrin. They each had a hefty purse of coin on them."

"Funded by Stoll and his supporters, no doubt. They probably thought they could kill me and the eastern lords would walk free. I should have executed them already." His chest heaves beneath my careful ministrations. "I suppose it was rather stupid of me to go there, in hindsight."

"Boaz certainly thinks so."

Atticus groans. "Do not let him in here tonight. I cannot deal with his reprimands."

Kazimir chuckles. "Don't worry. I've already received my tongue-lashing. I think he is too busy hunting for this mysterious caster and legionary to dole out more scolding."

Atticus's smile fades as a troubled look takes over. What does he remember? What does he think of his mysterious healer?

I wring out the soiled cloth. It's stained pink. "You know, a bath would be easier to wash all this blood off."

"If only I could get up." Atticus lifts his arm and then lets it flop back to the mattress as if to prove his point. "I did not feel this weak after the last merth arrow I took. This one is different."

More lethal, by the looks of the new silver scar next to the old one.

"You will be up and ready by the morning." Kazimir arches a brow at me as if to say "You know what he needs" before swiftly moving for the door. "Your Highness."

A king ready for battle in mere hours may be wishful thinking. Atticus looks seconds from drifting into unconsciousness.

The fire crackles and the water sluices in the otherwise silent chamber as I quietly work. Atticus's thoughts seem elsewhere.

I nearly lost him tonight.

Islor almost lost its king.

If not for Romeria, the very princess he has placed a bounty and execution order on.

Corrin's warning screams in my conscience, even as I gather the nerve to ask, "I heard this caster healed you outside the tavern. It sounds like she saved your life."

It's a moment before he sighs. "Yes, I've heard the same. Are you nearly done?"

He doesn't want to talk about it.

"I think that was the last of the blood." I cast aside the filthy towel for the servants to collect later.

"Good. I would not want to soil this." His gaze rolls over my outfit.

Neither would I, given it's not mine. Atticus is still half-dressed, and I don't think I could get his breeches off on my own without a tug-of-war. They can't be clean.

Heat floods my body in a rush as I slip off the robe and hang it on a hook on the bottom post of the bed, knowing what I must do.

"When I ordered you to come to my rooms tonight, this is not what I had in mind." He watches me round the bed to the other side.

"No, I suppose not." My hands tremble as I slip one strap of the gown off, and then the other, letting the material tumble to the floor.

"Fates." He stares at my bare curves. "Forget the merth arrow.

I think having you next to me like this and not being able to enjoy it is what will kill me."

My cheeks flush as I slip into bed, shimmying over until I'm lying next to him. "Come. You need to heal."

With a groan, he rolls me, his skin searing hot as his lips find mine. The kiss is soft and lacks its usual intensity, but I enjoy it all the same.

"Thank you for being here. For being willing." His forehead presses against mine. "I have always made a point of hiding vulnerability from my tributaries, but with you, I have no desire to hide anything."

"There's no need to." I enjoy seeing this side of him as much as the kingly version, save for the near-lethal injury.

"I promise, later, when I am able, I will not simply take from you. I will give you everything."

I don't truly understand what that means, but if it's anything like the feel of his lips, I am sure I'll enjoy it. I tip my head back, exposing my neck to him. The fear of that acute pain is gone, replaced by heady anticipation. I trust him not to hurt me.

His mouth finds my tender skin. Moments later I feel a sharp prick, but the sting fades almost instantly. I let my body sink into the mattress as I give Atticus what he desperately needs.

It's still dark when I stir.

Suri.

I bolt up in bed and swing my legs over the edge. And then I remember that I already fed her and I'm with Atticus in his chamber.

Cool air brushes across my naked skin. The terrace doors are thrown open, and Atticus stands outside under the moonlight. He must have gotten up to remove his breeches and boots because he wears nothing as he peers out over his lands.

I admire a shadowy view of his beautiful and strong form for a moment before I collect my robe and join him outside. "Feeling better?"

He inhales sharply. "You startled me."

"I didn't mean to." I didn't think that was possible for his kind, but he must be deep in thought. I hug the robe as I step out, fighting the urge to shiver. The stone is cold on my feet. "I'm glad to see you up."

"Thanks to you."

"I think mostly thanks to Wendeline." *And Romeria.*

"Do not trivialize what you give." He reaches for me.

I slip under his arm, and he sandwiches me between his muscular body and the terrace stone wall.

"Warmer?"

"Yes. Thank you. Are *you* not cold?"

"No. But I'll gladly take some of your heat." He steps closer.

My breath hitches at the feel of his hard length against the small of my back, but he only cocoons me within his arms. "What are you doing out here?"

"Thinking." He pauses. "If you had the chance to live for centuries beyond your mortal years, would you wish to, Gracen?"

"I ..." His question catches me off guard. "I've never considered it."

"Never? Truly?"

"No. We are not allowed to."

"But what if you *were* allowed to?"

I peer up to meet his gaze. "Is this a test?" Why would he ask such a thing?

"There is no wrong answer here. I am curious. What would your answer be?"

"I suppose ..." I think of Mika's big blue eyes and Lilou's cherub cheeks. "I live for my children. I cannot imagine making a choice like that. One that would keep me here centuries after they are gone." I shake my head. "No, that doesn't sound like something I would want to do."

"I knew you'd say that."

"You did? How?" I look up again, this time to see a sad smile.

"Because I know you better than you think I do." He tightens his arms around me.

It feels like an embrace between lovers. At least, it's what I've imagined. I've never experienced it before. Is this what they mean when they say the tributary-and-keeper relationship can be special? Intimate?

If so … I hope it is years before Atticus tires of me. But he *will* tire of me. I will grow wrinkled and gray, my body soft, and he will want a younger tributary to meet his needs. And I will become just the baker once more.

If this is how Atticus was with Sabrina, I can see why she is so heartbroken. Perhaps it is better that he moves through them quickly, so they can't grow too attached.

"I sense your worry." His voice is gravelly, close to my ear. "What is it?"

The king doesn't want to hear about my insecurities. "Do you think you will have the strength to lead this battle in the east?" I ask instead.

"I have no choice, but yes, I will have all the strength I need. Why? Are you worried about me?"

"Yes." I steal a glance over my shoulder at his handsome profile as he looks to the sky, but there is no hint of dawn yet. Still, it can't be far away.

A sly grin curls his lips. "I do not think you truly appreciate my skills. Though I suppose I can't fault you. You've never seen them firsthand." His hips press harder against my back, and another wave of heat rushes over me.

I want Atticus to touch me. It's an acute feeling, an acknowledgment deep inside my core, as I ache for him in a way I never have before. On impulse, I rock backward against him.

His shudder skates across my cheek. "Did you know there are a dozen guards right down there? You can't see them now. But in two nights, this entire garden will be bathed in a bright Hudem moon. You'll be able to stand up here and pick each of them out."

I suck in a breath as his hand slips between the folds of my robe. We won't be standing here in two nights. Atticus will be in battle, and I'll be fending for a horde of mortal children downstairs, worrying incessantly until his return.

"Before you came out, I was thinking that it's twice I've taken from you without giving you anything back. That ends now," he whispers, his mouth finding the tender skin behind my ear.

I revel in the feel of his tongue as his fingers graze over my inner thigh, sliding upward until they reach my center. He strokes me skillfully several times before slipping a finger inside. A moan slips free, my body slick and welcoming.

I must thank the priestess for her healing gift.

My legs tremble as I adjust my stance, granting him better access, my fingers enjoying the muscles that flex in his forearm. Never before have any of the males forced upon me ever bothered with such an intimate touch. I doubt they would be capable, but my needs never mattered.

With Atticus, he works slowly, circling my sensitive flesh with strokes of his thumb.

"Turn around," he whispers, his mouth pressed against my ear.

I do as ordered, allowing my robe to hang open as I face him.

His mouth crashes into mine, as if he couldn't wait another second, even as his hand never loses its pace, stroking deep inside me, building tension that begs to erupt. I grope his body aimlessly, absorbing every inch of hard muscle beneath my fingertips as wild desire claws at my inhibitions.

Eventually, I gather enough nerve to slide my palm between us, over the cut V of his pelvis. I wrap my hand around his hard length, marveling over his size, the velvety soft skin hot against my palm.

He groans as I grip him tightly and stroke as I was taught, from root to tip. For once, I actually *want* to do this. I want to drop to my knees and take him in my mouth. I *want* to watch the king of Islor fall apart under my touch.

"I need you to stop doing that so I can finish doing *this*." His tongue sweeps into my mouth as his hand works me over mercilessly, its tempo increasing.

I stall but don't let go, instead imagining it inside me. A rush of heat floods my lower belly.

"There it is," Atticus whispers, and I don't know how he senses it but moments later, a surge of ecstasy washes over me. I bite my bottom lip to keep my cries from slipping out as he coaxes wave after wave until my legs tremble.

Atticus hoists me in the air, guiding my legs around his hips. His tip rubs at my slick entrance—a tease of anticipation that I ache for—as he walks us back inside his chamber and shuts the door. I barely noticed the cold outside anymore, but the difference inside is stark. My bare skin promptly flushes.

"I've never met a mortal like you." He sets me down on the bed, my legs splayed and waiting, my silk robe fanned out beneath me. "I've never met *anyone* like you. You are so kind and gentle, and patient, despite all that you have been through."

"There are many like me."

"No." He shakes his head. "You have a way about you. A quiet bravery I admire." He kneels on the bed before me, his palms beginning at my ankles, smoothing up my calves, my knees, to my thighs. Gripping the backs of them, he drags my body down to where he can fit himself in between. His hands collect mine and pin them above my head.

"I've been thinking about this for days." Our mouths meet in the middle in a slow, tantalizing kiss that smothers my cries as he rocks into me, his fingers tensing around mine. My body accepts him—willingly, eagerly—as he sinks deeper and deeper, until I've taken all of him inside me.

His lips break free of my mouth to shift to my neck where he traces a line with his tongue. "This is what it's supposed to feel like," he whispers, his hips moving with skill, his hard length filling me completely with each thrust and yet not causing me the pain that so many others have.

"Atticus." His name slips from my lips as I lose myself in the feel of him where we're joined, all thoughts fleeing my mind.

"Say it again."

"Atticus," I echo.

It seems to spur him to go faster, harder, his lips a furious tangle against mine as our bodies meet with each thrust, my legs curling around his hips of their own accord as I feel myself growing impossibly wet for him.

My back arches as another flood of ecstasy hits, ten times more powerful than what he drew out on the terrace, rippling through me in crashing waves, my cries genuine and raw.

With a muffled curse, he slows, his shoulders tensing, his hands tightening. I feel his hard length pulse and my body welcomes his seed.

He collapses, bracing some of his weight with his elbows so he doesn't crush me. His hot breath skates across my neck. Surely, he needs my vein. I'll give it to him.

I'll give *everything* to him.

"Impossible," I whisper into the quiet dark as I stare up at the bed's canopy.

Atticus's heavy pants fill my ear. "What is?"

"It never could have felt like this with anyone else. Only with you."

"I think you are right." He releases my hands to pull my face to his for a kiss.

52
ATTICUS

"Oh, to be a king." Kazimir's helm is tucked under his arm, his admiring gaze on Gracen. "Each one of them is more beautiful than the last."

She sleeps soundly in my bed, her untamed curls sprawled across the pillow, the sheets strategically positioned to cover her mesmerizing body.

"Get out of here before she wakes and finds you hovering over her like a depraved soul." I shove him through the doorway to my living area, following him out.

He chuckles. "But I *am* a depraved soul."

I pull the door shut to not disturb her. "I know that, but she does not need to."

"Do you not plan on saying goodbye before we head off to war?"

"Of course I do."

"Well, you are running out of time, my friend. We must go. The horses are ready."

"Soon." I peer out the windows at the dawn light.

"Have you not recovered?"

"I'm well enough." I press a hand against my breastplate. The ache is still there, protected beneath armor, but it's dull and healing, thanks in no small part to Gracen's ready vein.

Rarely do I wake with a tributary in my bed and never intentionally. But this morning, when Gracen allowed me it, as well as another round of her supple body beneath mine, I was sure I wanted this—her—forever.

That's not something she wants, though. A truth that stung more than I expected it to when she admitted it upon questioning last night.

"This caster who supposedly saved me last night, is there any hint of her?"

"None. She and Jarek have disappeared without a trace."

I curse. "Jarek was Abarrane's second and loyal to Islor without fault. He would not part ways with her, and she would not abandon Zander." I could never understand that bond, and my brother swears their relationship never crossed boundaries.

"Those two were nowhere to be seen. But whoever this caster was, you can assume she is tied closely to your brother. And if that is the case, then why she didn't let you die is beyond me, but she has my thanks."

I don't even know how to play draughts.

Did I imagine it? No, I'm sure I didn't.

There is only one person that could relate to.

But it couldn't be …

Wendeline might know, but it would likely take cruelty to get the answer out of her, something I don't have time or an appetite for after she healed me last night, *again*. I've seen her weary before, but never unconscious.

I fish out the gold coin from my pocket and drop it in his palm. "Whoever she is, she gave this to Bexley."

His eyes widen. "Where would this come from?"

"Ulysede." Maybe I should have told Kazimir about the letter and its contents sooner, but I've charged him with enough already. Adding secret cities and prophecy to his plate didn't seem fair.

A knock sounds on the outer door.

"I'll fill you in on our journey." Which we must begin, caster or not within my city walls, if I have any hope of taking back Islor from our enemies. "Enter!"

Corrin sweeps in with a fussing baby in her arms. "Someone is hungry," she announces, strolling past us, her chin held high. "I assume she is in there?" She pushes through my bedroom door without waiting.

"Please, feel free." I wave my hand with embellishment.

Kazimir shakes his head. "A royal tributary with a baby. Only you."

"May I come in?"

Gracen looks up from the baby in her arms, shock splayed across her face. She wears nothing but the bedsheet, pulled up above the mounds of her breasts. "Of course, you may. This is *your* chamber." She surveys my polished armor as I approach. I haven't worn it since the night of the tournament, but it's like sliding on familiar old boots. Far more comfortable than Islor's crown. "You are leaving now?"

"Yes. My soldiers are waiting for me."

"I did not mean to sleep so late, but she is almost done and then I will vacate your rooms—"

"No." She thinks I'm here to kick her out of my bed. "Stay if you wish. And I hope to see you back here upon my return, dressed the same." Maybe she and her little family can move in next door, if I feel it is safe enough by then.

A blush crawls over Gracen's face, making her smatter of freckles stand out more. "When do you think that will be?"

"I'm not sure yet. Once I deal with the east, I must head north to see what awaits us there."

"So it could be awhile." She looks crestfallen.

"I will be back as quickly as I can." Sliding my finger under her chin, I lift her face to memorize it, dragging my thumb over her plump bottom lip.

I've known others of my kind who profess devotion to their tributaries. Even my brother kept the same mortal for almost ten years and then suffered from an odd melancholy when he released them from service. But I've never felt that bond they described.

Until now.

But if what Romeria claims is true and the blood curse will be no more, am I to lose this feeling, so soon after I've found it? Will whatever this is between Gracen and me become meaningless? Will she still feel the same way toward me? Just like this helpless infant relies on Gracen for her milk, an Islorian immortal king all but pleaded for her vein last night. She has seen firsthand the power she has over me, my weakness.

"Would you still feel the same way about me if I were not king?"

She meets my gaze. "Yes."

Not a moment of hesitation. "What if I did not take your vein anymore?"

Her brow furrows with confusion. "Then whose would you take?"

I sense a spike in her pulse, and it thrills me. She's jealous of the idea. "No one's."

Her frown deepens. "But—"

"Never mind. It's idle chatter. Nothing more." I lean down to kiss her, coaxing her lips apart to taste her mouth one last time before I pull away.

"I'll miss you," she says, and I sense a burst of panic inside her, as if she didn't mean to be so honest.

"Good. I'll make up for lost time when I'm back."

Heat ignites in her gaze with that promise.

"Don't look at me like that or I'll end up staying." The baby below stares up at me, her eyes unfocused as she suckles. "Lucky."

Gracen chuckles, but I'm not lying. I could easily find an excuse to abandon my responsibilities for another day or two. I nearly died last night. I would have if not for this mystery caster. I'm not eager to risk my life again so soon. Rhodes could hold the line until I arrive.

But time is not on Islor's side, what with Neilina threatening us as well.

With one last lengthy kiss, I peel away.

"Oh, Atticus?" she calls out when I'm at the door.

I'll never tire of hearing my name on her sweet voice. I want to hear it on her moans again. "Yes?"

"Some of the mortal children have ailments, and I was hoping Boaz could spare the priestess for an hour to tend to the worst of them. This morning, if possible. I'd like them to be comfortable."

"I will order him to do so."

A slow sigh slips from her lips. "Thank you. I appreciate that."

"Not as much as I appreciate your help with them." She took on a ballroom of children without complaint and with compassion I would never find in my kind. From what I hear, the crying has mostly stopped. "You know, you would make a good queen." It's a flippant comment, without any thought. But the moment the words are out of my mouth, I mean them. All the courtly requirements and political hoops, she could learn. Consideration for the plight of mortals as we navigate this potential new world, she could teach me.

She laughs, but the humor falls off when she sees me not joining in. "I am a mortal baker, Atticus."

"And I have never been one to follow the rules." Nor have I ever had these sorts of fantasies. Now, though, my pulse surges with anticipation.

I leave Gracen in my room and, for the first time in my life, I wish for a speedy battle just so I can return to her quickly.

A border of soldiers surrounds me as we approach the gate, their swords drawn and arrows nocked. The portcullis is already raised, with guards waiting to release the chain as soon as we're through.

"Do you feel it?"

"Feel what?" Kazimir's sharp eyes rove the windows and doorways. I know he blames himself for what happened last night. It will be a long time before we can pass a building without his extra caution.

"The energy in this city. It's off." I've patrolled these streets countless times on horseback as the commander of the king's army. Even at the height of paranoia and fear, just after Ybaris murdered my parents and Romeria was in the tower, when buildings smoldered and bodies collected, and a thousand whispers told a thousand different stories, it did not seem this tense.

"It's because of what happened to you last night. You are on edge."

"Maybe." But the air feels thick and heavy, the crowd barely restrained, their gazes full of poorly disguised malice.

It's as if something is about to explode.

It feels wrong to leave Cirilea in this state, and yet I have no choice. Much bigger threats to Islor await me out there.

Boaz stands at the gate with a small company of guards forming a ring, their swords drawn and aimed outward at anyone who might think to charge now.

"Fight well, Your Highness." He offers a curt bow. "The king's guard will hold your city until your return."

"I trust you will." I urge my horse forward, but then remember. "Send the priestess to administer healing to the mortal children in the ballroom this morning."

"*Healing*." His perpetual scowl claims his face. "What healing do they need? We have mortals left to mark—"

"We can spare an hour." Frankly, we can spare more. "Whatever she asks for, you give it to her. Understood?"

His jaw clenches. "As you wish, Your Highness." But it is clear he does not agree.

I knew there might be a day when I would have to reconsider Boaz's role in Cirilea. Perhaps when I return, I will make some changes. Until then, at least Boaz will follow my command.

"Let us make haste." My small processional of twenty soldiers moves ahead, past Cirilea's gate. The heavy chain sounds as the portcullis drops behind us, and our horses kick into a steady canter.

53
ZANDER

"Daylight up ahead!" someone shouts and a chorus of cheers echoes.

"Behold! The *other* east entrance to Soldor!" Radomir announces with too much energy after a day-and-a-half trek through a dark mountain. "You are almost free!"

And onto the next leg of what seems a futile task.

"Move!" Abarrane bellows, and a jumble of Islorians, Ybarisans, and saplings shift to one side as we head to the front.

At some point, soldiers weren't as focused on the rider next to them as they were on what deadly creature might wait for us around the next corner. Lines blurred and fears of one another relaxed.

Aside from a few small beasts that stayed away from our lengthy entourage, we didn't come across a single threat.

I imagine it would be a different story if Romeria were here.

"My kind will not be of much help to you in this next task, so we will remain within these stone walls." Radomir's cautious gaze is on the morning sun streaming in ahead. I've seen firsthand what it can do the moment it touches a sapling's skin. "I will meet you tonight at the first watchtower, when the moon is high."

"And I will attempt to ensure they do not kill you when you arrive."

"That would be much appreciated." His thin lips split wide. Now that I have seen his old face, he seems less of a soulless demon, but I can't allow myself to forget all the horrors these saplings have committed in the name of survival.

I hesitate. "Thank you for being our guide. I doubt we would have made it here without you."

"You certainly would not have. And if Her Highness's plans fail and the curse is not lifted, I think I shall regret ever leading you." He shifts away. "My people! Fall back and let them through!"

I squint against the morning light as we step out onto the stone.

"This must have been used for wagons coming in from the Ybarisan side, back before the rift formed," Kienen notes as we navigate our horses around boulders on a rough path hewn from use long ago and just wide enough for two mounts.

"There were no sides back then." And if Neilina has her way, there will come a day when there is no Islor.

We round a corner and get our first good look across the rift and into Ybaris, where the arid and damaged land on their side mirrors ours. Pre-rift accounts of this area told of rich valleys and fertile soil, but Aminadav's fury left an unsightly scar beyond the endless divide.

"Fates," Telor whispers, horror splayed over his face. "I have never seen an army like that."

Neither have I. Tiny dots merge over the land as far as we can see—of tents and wagons and Ybarisans willing to die for their slain royal family, thanks to the lies of their treacherous queen.

"Many of them are simple mortals, untrained and terrified. They will not be able to fight," Abarrane says.

"Many of them are elven soldiers and casters, trained and terrified, and they *will* be able to fight," Kienen counters, his posture rigid as he peers down upon Lyndel's forces below. They are trained soldiers as well, but they will be overwhelmed by the sheer volume of the other side. And all that stops them from crossing are two stone walls on either end of the bridge, each one erected when the two nations split. Neither will withstand the whole of Neilina's elementals.

Suddenly, I wish I had insisted that Romeria come.

"We do not want to fight them," I remind everyone. "As long as we can hold them off until Hudem's full moon, their attention will shift elsewhere." At least until reinforcements arrive.

A deafening screech sounds, and Telor's soldiers have their swords drawn in their next breath, their horses shifting uneasily. Everyone is waiting for that beast Romeria named a dragon to resurface.

But it's the taillok that soars above us, its iridescent feathers shimmering. Just as Gesine promised.

"Hold!" I shout as it swoops down to land on a nearby boulder.

Telor orders the soldiers to continue down the path as I dismount, my attention on the letter strapped to the taillok's leg, my relief bringing a smile to my lips.

It screeches again as I approach, its hooked beak looking primed to attack. "Any special instructions?"

"Do not anger it?" Kienen offers.

It watches intently as I unfasten the leather belt that holds the letter but makes no move.

"The witch is watching us?" Abarrane asks with mild interest. She would never admit that something tied to the casters and the Nulling might be useful.

"She is." Gesine will be able to relay my well-being to Romeria, who I'm sure shares my worry.

I crack open the seal and read the familiar scrawl.

And curse.

And curse again.

Nymph doors?

A war in the east?

A brewing rebellion in Cirilea?

Elisaf sidles up to me. "Anything interesting?"

"A thing or two." Or ten. Not *interesting*. Devastating. I hand it to him to read as my mind spins, the seer's stark prediction blazing prominently. *Islor must fall before it can rise.* If this is not its fall, then I can't imagine what else would be.

His eyes bulge. "She went to Cirilea?"

I don't know whether to be furious or proud of her. "She is fearless." Of course that snake was hiding something vital until I left. It's as if she *wants* to put Romeria in danger.

"When it involves helping others, yes."

Even ones who may not deserve it. My brother has ordered her death, and yet it sounds like she saved him.

Elisaf frowns. "She means to rob your coffers?"

I smile grimly. "That, I am *not* surprised about."

Abarrane has had enough of playing bystander. "Who is robbing you? What is happening?" she demands, and beside her, Telor and Kienen look as impatient to know.

I sigh. Where do I even begin? "I should have executed Adley the day I became king."

The rift lookouts spotted our lengthy processional not long after we emerged from Soldor. Telor ordered his men to wave their banner high. It seems to have worked, as only a small delegation rides out to meet us, rather than enough to match us in force.

Ulysede's banner, we keep lowered for now.

No one has tried to put an arrow into the taillok yet. It soars above us, waiting for my return letter while giving Gesine a bird's-eye view to relay back to Romeria.

"How long has it been since you were here last?" Telor asks.

"Too long," I admit. I entered this camp as the crown prince, and now I come as an exile. Never before have I felt this discomfort approaching my Islorian subjects, but I harden my resolve.

There can be only one outcome, whether they support me as king or not.

The sprawling elven barracks are to the right, the tributaries housed next to them in a fortified encampment fit for the criminals who are sent to serve as fodder. Mortal army quarters comparable to the elven are on the left, though the two sides merge in the middle for training exercises and daily life. I've always thought the divide pointless but, given the growing turmoil and the willingness to murder the elven for freedom, perhaps not.

Behind are the officer quarters—larger pavilions surrounded by guards. There is no pomp or luxury here, no silken tents. As is the way of life at the rift.

"Not much has changed."

"That we can see. Who knows what schemes live beneath our noses." Sadness marks Telor's face.

He must be thinking of Braylon. I've avoided mention of it until now, giving him space to mourn quietly. "That was not a mortal versus elven issue, Ailis. That was a son who was tired of waiting for his turn at power. He saw an opportunity and he took it." I add more quietly, "I know what that betrayal feels like."

"He always was ambitious. Perhaps he was right in his desires, if not his methods." He shakes his head. "I have toiled for days now how to tell Erwynn. Braylon and I did not see eye to eye on many things, but he was our only son. I fear she will not believe it."

"Lyndel is not even a half-day's ride from here. Do you wish to see her and share the news?"

"That is better left for another time. And besides, we have too much to focus on. If Braylon found soldiers willing to help murder their lord, what will *we* find in there?" He nods toward the mortal camp.

"The thought has crossed my mind too." These soldiers chose to join the rift army the day they came of age, knowing they would spend their lives protecting Islor. It is the trade-off for never standing on a stage on Presenting Day. But how many joined not for honor but solely so they never serve as tributaries? How many have lost loved ones to cruel keepers?

And now our neighboring army has offered a weapon and a promise, and perhaps hope to those who have wished for a different way of life for so long.

"I do not understand how these mortals can be so eager to tear apart Islor like this."

"One can love their realm but still see the weaknesses and beg for change. And they are not the only ones with a hand in Islor's demise. I would argue their cause is far more noble than what the eastern lords have been scheming, for power." Romeria's letter with news about Adley and the others was surprising, but not unexpected.

"You have always looked kindly on the mortal plight." He sighs. "It *does* feel like Islor has been brought to its knees to atone for its many sins, though."

My mind drifts to the past. "There was once a bard who visited the castle, years ago. His name was Phynys. A strong voice, entertaining lyrics. By the time he finished his performance, my mother's stomach would hurt from laughing so much." I smile, remembering the sound of it. It wasn't melodic or demure. The queen laughed as a drunken sailor might—loud and boisterous and with her whole body. "But he was also skilled at card tricks. One day, he dragged out a table and began building a house made from a deck of cards. It was tall and wobbly, and it teetered this way and that, and Phynys kept going and going. We knew that eventually it would fall, that a house of cards can only stand for so long. And it did. One piece tipped and the entire thing collapsed, scattering to the floor.

"More and more, I see Islor as that shaky house of cards that has reached the point of collapse we knew would come."

"You sound as though you are accepting defeat."

"Far from it. I simply see more clearly now. The Islor of yesterday is no more, and the Islor of tomorrow will only exist with help from Romeria and the nymphs, regardless of what new challenges come with it." Some, I have not been willing to admit to yet.

The group of twenty on horseback is closing in. A female rides at the center of the entourage, Lyndel's crest across her breastplate, the rift commander's stripe of feathers in her helm. Her golden arms are slender but ripple with muscle. "That is not Bragvam." A beast of a man who rivaled Horik's size and the commanding officer of the rift army as far as we knew.

"No, it is not. That is Gaellar." Telor purses his lips. "Which does not bode well for Bragvam."

The legionaries move into position, forming a perimeter around me as the soldiers reach us, their attention darting between us and the winged iridescent beast above.

"Lord Telor." Gaellar drops from her horse and bows. "We were not expecting you, and certainly not from that direction." Hazel eyes that match the color of her lengthy hair flash to me, noting the emblem on my breastplate. No one here has likely seen the mark of Ulysede yet, but an unfamiliar crest on a soldier's armor is always cause for concern. If she recognizes who I am, she says nothing.

"What happened to Bragvam?" Telor asks.

A solemn look fills her face. "We lost him to a wyvern three days ago. The second one we've seen in a week. This one was big. Sixty soldiers died before it flew away."

Beside me, Elisaf curses, and I can read his thoughts. "What color was it?"

"Orange."

Not the beast outside Ulysede's gates, then. Though, no one would mistake that as a simple wyvern.

Still, sixty soldiers dead. What will happen when there are dozens of similar beasts attacking? "Have there been any cases of poisoning here?" I ask.

"None yet."

Good, though that doesn't mean there aren't vials lurking. Soldiers are better at following orders than frightened mortals.

"You must order them to refrain from taking a vein until after Hudem." At which point, they will no longer need it.

She studies me again, then the legionaries, and then the long line of soldiers behind us.

"What news to report?" Telor asks.

"The Ybarisan army has been steadily growing each day. Bragvam sent more than one messenger to Cirilea, but we have not received word from His Highness."

"*His Highness* has been busy securing his stolen throne and condemning allies," I throw back. Though it sounds like he is facing a viable threat now.

Gaellar's eyebrow spikes. If she hadn't figured out who I was before, I'd say she has strong suspicions now.

I sigh. We don't have time for mocking and surely it won't win me support. "Queen Neilina plans to cross the rift on Hudem with a sizable army and all her elementals. Atticus has sent an army north. I imagine we will see their banner by midday tomorrow, if they ride hard. Bellcross has been summoned. When they arrive, I cannot say." I was hoping to see Rengard's purple banner flying, though I knew it would be an impossibility this early. If he makes it at all, it will be on Hudem's heels.

Gaellar shifts her attention to Telor. "If I may ask, my lord, who fights alongside us?" She won't be able to smell Kienen's Ybarisan blood from there, but she will soon enough.

Telor arches his brow with a "Do you want to tell her or should I?" look.

It's best to have this conversation now rather than in the center of camp, surrounded by peeled ears. "The true king of Islor with his legionaries, as well as soldiers granted by Queen Romeria of Ulysede, to help stop this attack." The sooner Romeria's new title spreads, the better.

The nervous glances swapped between the company of rift soldiers say enough.

Gaellar's eyes dash to Telor. "Ybarisans, my lord?"

"We are all allies in what is to come, which I fear very much," he answers somberly.

Her eyebrows pinch, but she nods. "At the rift, we do not burden ourselves with the battles of royal families, and we appreciate every blade that will join ours." After a beat, she adds, "Your Highness." She mounts herself with deft skill.

"I'm glad you feel that way." I hope she still does once the sun goes down and the saplings come out. "Now, if you'll show me somewhere I can pen an important message."

54
AGATHA

I groan as the wagon jolts over a bump, the pain shooting through my back. The journey from Argon to the rift is a smooth one, with relatively flat ground, but we are moving so fast that even little divots in the road feel like driving through craters.

Or perhaps it's that I'm too old for this because none of the sixteen other casters packed in here like hens in a coop on a cold winter's night seem to notice.

That is likely because they are too occupied with their terror over what lies ahead.

I shift the curtain aside to peek out the window. "Goodness." It has been decades since I traveled through Argon's lowlands, but I remember lush oat fields and fat grazing cows and crops of forest. Now the trees are black and withered, the soil barren, and the only thing feeding are crows on livestock corpses.

"The blight was especially bad this season." Josephine, a healer stationed in the midcountry villages, explains. "They had high hopes in spring, but then it seemed to ravage the crops overnight. Entire fields gone. The livestock became sick, many died. This winter will be difficult."

So many will starve. "It did not have to be this way."

"If only the Islorians were not so cruel," she says as if agreeing with me.

I resist the urge to correct her, but in the next breath change my mind. *This* is the problem. These lies Neilina has fostered in Ybaris have taken firm hold of the people living within because it is all they hear, and now they parrot them without thought. "It was not the Islorians who betrayed us. It was the queen and her incessant need for power, and her hatred for their kind."

It was already quiet in the wagon. Now, I can practically hear each one of them swallow.

"They killed His Highness," another caster—a young one I don't recall—speaks up.

"King Barris was murdered, yes. Fates rest his soul. I can promise you, though, that it was not by an Islorian blade, but by one much closer to him. You need only look to the next throne over."

Several jaws drop at my bold accusation. A few shake their heads in denial.

I sigh, unable to hide my irritation. "And where is the body of this supposed Islorian assassin?" Solange poked at this very issue in the guild meeting. "A murderer of a king would hang for all to see, I would think. Wouldn't you?" These casters should know better and yet they are like sheep!

"But they killed the princess and the prince—"

"The prince *may* be dead, and if so, he will have deserved it for his part in his mother's schemes. The princess is alive and well, and you will see her soon enough alongside the Islorians. What does that say to you, hmm?" Lorel will have me drawn and quartered when she hears of my words, but hopefully, I will be either across the rift or dead before that day. "We are heading into a war of Queen Neilina's conception and nurturing, and we are all fodder for her ambitions. Nothing more. Do not let yourself be misled by her battle cry."

Anxious glances flitter about the wagon. I can see they are equal parts frightened and curious.

"You are a *scribe*," Godwin, a pinched-face male caster whom I never liked announces. "How is it that you know such things no one else seems to?"

A smug smile stretches across my wrinkled face. Godwin's ego always was too big for his breeches. "It is *because* I am a scribe that I know *many* things no one else seems to."

"She speaks the truth about the princess," a soft voice calls out. A tiny caster with chocolate-brown eyes and hair as dark and rich as a crow's feather. "I have seen messages that speak to the princess bound to the exiled king. More than one."

A messenger caster riding with the healers for whatever reason. No matter, she helps my cause. "See?"

They don't see. Not yet. But they will soon enough. Fates help us.

55
GRACEN

The doors to the ballroom crack open and Boaz shoves Wendeline in. She stumbles, almost falls, before catching her footing. "Hurry up," he barks, earning her jolt and several wide-eyed looks from the children. A few younger and more fragile ones begin to cry, and Sabrina rushes to their side to calm them before they stir a chorus.

I truly hate Captain Boaz. If I had to spend time with him, I think I could hate him as much as I hated Lord Danthrin. I do not understand why Atticus would not replace him with someone more like Kazimir.

Wendeline's face is drawn, her eyes bloodshot as she surveys the mortal children huddled in their makeshift beds. They didn't give her enough time to rest. She looks minutes from collapsing. Finally, she spots me waving at her and she moves my way, her body hunched.

A mixture of guilt and relief swells inside me for my scheming this morning. I waited until Atticus was at the door before asking to send her, praying he wouldn't sense my inner turmoil, telling myself over and over again that some of the children *do* have scrapes and cuts. They could use her healing touch.

But that's not why I asked for her.

"You requested my help?" Wendeline says.

"Yes. If it wouldn't be too much strain on you."

"For the children? Never."

I feel Boaz's glare on my back as I lead the priestess toward a little boy with a festering scrape on his knee, earned long before he was brought here. "This is Edmun. We've put a poultice on the wound, but it doesn't seem to help." A foul odor lingers.

Edmun takes one look at Wendeline and begins to wail, tucking his hands behind his back in fear. He thinks she's here to brand him again.

"It's okay. She is going to make your knee better." I've seen the priestess work several times now—first on Mika, then on Atticus. Even on myself. Each time seems as miraculous as the first.

Wendeline smiles at him. "I promise, this time it won't hurt."

He sobs as she kneels in front of him, her eyes closed, her weathered hands hovering over the sore. The left one is still bandaged. I fear asking what happened to it.

I scan the small horde around us for the next needy child as she works her magic. Boaz hovers by the door, impatient.

Finally, she pulls away. "There. How is that? Better?"

He peers down at his knee where nothing but a pink scar remains. His head bobs, fat tears still rolling down his cheeks.

"Go and find Sabrina. I think she's brought in some more sweets." The last of them, likely. I'll have to find time in the kitchen to bake more.

He scurries off without another word.

Wendeline struggles to get to her feet, stumbling a step. "I just … need a moment."

I give her my arm and help her balance. This is my chance. "I have a message for you," I whisper the moment our backs are turned.

Her body stiffens. "He watches and he is suspicious," she warns on a breath, keeping her gaze ahead. She's terrified of Boaz, that much is clear. What did he do to her in that dungeon cell to make her frightened to even listen while we walk?

Can she listen while she pretends to heal?

"Here, this one." I guide her to a baby girl who has learned how to sit up, but cannot crawl yet. It has been a battle keeping straw out of her mouth. "She has that terrible rash on her arm," I say pointedly.

Wendeline collects her chubby limb, smoothing her fingertip over the baby's pristine white skin. "Yes, I see what you mean." She closes her eyes.

And I take a surreptitious glance around the ballroom as if scanning for other children with ailments before I crouch with my back to Boaz, pretending to distract the baby. "Romeria told me to tell you that you had it wrong. The door is already open, but the prophecy is real." I'd recited it over and over in my head, afraid I'd miss a key piece.

Wendeline's shoulders rise with a deep inhale, but she keeps her stoic position.

"I assume that makes sense to you."

She doesn't answer right away, continuing the farce for another ten beats before she opens her eyes and smiles at the baby, who coos back. "It's beginning to," is all she says.

I would be lying if I didn't say I was desperate to know what it means. But before I can ask, Boaz is suddenly there. "They will be fine with bumps and bruises. Weeding out murderers is more important. You are done here."

"The baker asked me to check on her baby who has been ill this morning," Wendeline says, her head bowed.

Wendeline's lie catches me off guard, but I recover quickly. "Yes. Vomiting everywhere." I point at the stain on my dress. It's not Suri's, but it's effective. Boaz grimaces and strolls back toward the door, barking, "Hurry up."

My stomach churns with nerves. *I* might vomit. I have never schemed like this before. I lead Wendeline over to Suri's basket, where she lays, swaddled in her blanket. She seems to like the buzz of the children's voices.

I collect her in my arms.

With her back to Boaz, Wendeline smooths her hand over Suri's forehead. "Keep your attention on her and listen. What I am about to tell you may be a great shock," she whispers in a rush. "Your child was born with an affinity to Aoife. She is the first of her kind in Islor in two thousand years."

I suck in a gasp under Boaz's steady gaze.

"If Her Highness's message is true, then great turmoil is coming, and I fear we are all in danger this close to Islor's throne. You must get her away immediately. *All of you* must get away immediately. There is no time."

"How?" I ask before I can stop myself.

Boaz is moving this way again.

"I do not know, but a terrible war is coming, and a new king will emerge." She switches to a louder voice—for Boaz's benefit, as if she could sense him coming. "Whatever it was, I think it has worked itself out already. I do not see any ailment that I can remove with my healing."

"Thank you anyway, Priestess." My voice sounds strained, but I hope it's believable.

"Done here?" Boaz grabs her arm and leads her toward the door.

I cradle Suri, struggling to keep my shock from showing. That look on the priestess's face that day when she marked us ... she saw this supposed affinity then. She knew Suri is a caster.

But how is it even possible? We are in Islor, not Ybaris.

My arms tighten around my baby.

56
ROMERIA

Jarek and I pace around my war room, waiting impatiently for Gesine to relay what she sees through the taillok's vision. "He is in the commander's tent at the rift now, writing a letter." Gesine's eyes are glazed over as she stares through me.

I imagine it's a similar scene on the other end, with that big Nulling bird staring at Zander. We've listened to a play-by-play since the first horse emerged from Soldor, the taillok observing from above as our little army navigated the terrain down to meet a group from the rift, then was escorted into camp. So far, it seems like Kienen and his men aren't being treated poorly.

"How long will that letter take to get here?" We need answers only Zander can give. He knows his castle better than anyone else. If there are other ways to move through it than what I know, he'll be able to tell us.

If he's willing to share.

"Mere hours. Not long. The taillok circled the entrance to Soldor for an hour before they stepped out." Long enough to show Gesine a dismal view of Ybaris's army, easily five times the size of ours.

"Mere hours is more than we have." I pace. Seamus and his

men are waiting to hear from us. Kaders is waiting for his gold. We need to solidify a plan and go.

"Can we send the taillok across the rift to peck out Neilina's eyes next?" Jarek says, earning my snort.

"Not without risking its capture," Gesine murmurs absently. "He is finishing now but, wait … what is he …" A smile curves her lips. "He is holding up the letter to the taillok. We will not have to wait for it after all."

So smart, Zander. "What does it say?"

Her eyes flitter back and forth as she reads. "He does not want you going back to Cirilea, but he knows you will go, anyway. He says to take the legionaries with you."

Jarek scowls. "As if I wouldn't know that."

"What else?" I push.

"There is a tunnel from a water fountain in the royal garden that will lead to the undercroft and put you close to the vault. Look for the three children and a fish. A lever on the back will open the passage."

So many secret ways to move around that city. And I knew he'd have an idea.

"There is one guard they change twice a day, on the sevens. You will need a key."

I curse.

Gesine blinks as she shifts back to us. "I can teach you how to make one, Romeria, with your affinity to Aminadav."

"*Really*?" Amazement washes over me. "Perfect."

"What reason did you give him for needing the vault?" Jarek asks.

"I told him I was buying off some guards to usher the castle staff through the royal garden to the nymphaeum. What?" I exclaim when Jarek's expression turns flat. "He doesn't need to be worrying about what I'm doing. He has enough going on at the rift."

A knock sounds on the door and a moment later, Horik ducks

his head to pass through, a small scroll in his hand. "It arrived by messenger bird."

Jarek frowns. "From where? Who else knows we're here?"

Horik shakes his head and hands it to me. "It's sealed. Marked with an *M*."

I've seen this seal before, on the letter Gesine sent to Margrethe, telling her to summon Malachi should anything happen to Princess Romeria. "Mordain's scribes."

"It found *me*. I spelled my letter to them with a tracer and hoped it would return. That writing on the outside is mine," Gesine admits as I pass her the letter. She cracks the seal and unfurls it with urgent hands.

"What does it say?"

"Nothing we do not already know. Neilina is crossing at Hudem with an army. Many in Ybaris believe you are dead, executed by the king of Islor, and they wish to avenge your death as well as that of King Barris." Her hands flop as if with disappointment. I'm not sure what else she was expecting.

"Anything else from Zander's end?" Horik interrupted us while we were gleaning what we could through the taillok's vision.

"He asked that you do what you must in Cirilea and then get back to Ulysede and remain there where you will be safe."

"While he's being attacked by Nulling monsters?" I wish there was a way to get to the rift in time.

"He is sending the taillok back now, but you've learned all you need, I think."

"Then let me round up Loth and Zorya so we can come up with a plan," Jarek says.

"And Pan. Don't forget him."

"I try to every day." The two legionaries leave, and Gesine and I are alone.

"So … nothing in there about how you need to kill me?" I nod to the scroll. They didn't know I was a key caster until Gesine sent that letter through Bellcross's fake priestesses. Will their devotion to prophecy weaken?

"See for yourself." She hands it to me.

I read both sides—Gesine's original message and this Caster Agatha's, who Gesine seems to trust beyond anyone else. There's nothing in here unless it's hidden between the lines. She left nothing out.

"Do you think they've figured out what Ulysede means?" One simple word scrawled at the bottom in a rush. That was the morning Ianca first said it, but we had no idea what she meant at the time.

"Master Scribe Agatha is wise. I would not put it past her, especially if news of the taillok's visions reached her ears."

Would they have had the same worries as Gesine had, about a key caster opening this secret nymph city and what it could mean for prophecy?

Gesine pauses, seems to choose her words. "Whether you like it or not, you are a caster and they are your people. You can choose to have some allies within Mordain or none, and I do not recommend the latter." A sad expression takes over her face. "There will come a time, and soon, when you need their help."

When Gesine is gone, she means. When I have no one to guide me through this new life, no one to interpret Lucretia's double-sided words, to translate all the books with knowledge locked in a foreign tongue. But Mordain is not my concern right now, other than what they are about to do at the rift, and if they harm Zander, then *I* will become very much a concern for them, and not in a good way. "Maybe you're right, but for now, I have you."

She dips her head. "You have me until I can no longer serve, Your Highness."

I leave the letter on the map table where it belongs for now—not a priority. Those trapped mortals are the only thing I care about today. "Ready to go back to Cirilea?"

She smiles. "Not in the slightest."

57
ZANDER

With cautious hands, I affix the letter to the taillok's leg, checking the strap twice to ensure it won't slip. I have no idea if Gesine was paying attention when I held the parchment up to the beast. I hope she was. I imagine that information is needed sooner rather than later.

I step away and the taillok tips its head back to release that earsplitting caw.

Abarrane throws the tent door open in a panic, her sword drawn.

It darts past her and in seconds, it's airborne, the beast's powerful wings propelling it high into the sky.

"I've asked for a return message by dawn. Please warn the lookouts so they do not try to shoot it down. It has proven invaluable to us."

"Romeria, even more so," Elisaf says. "Thanks to her, we understand Islor's current situation. We know what your brother's plans are as far as an army."

I sigh heavily. "Yes, and now that we know, there's no reason for her to endanger herself more." I wish she would remain in Ulysede.

"This urgency to get to your vault … Does it not seem off to you?"

"You mean that she would need my gold and jewels to bribe guards when she could fill her pockets with her own?" I chuckle. "This is Romeria. I am certain she is leaving important details out, and it's likely something I would not agree with. That, or she is getting her wish to give all my money away to the people of the Rookery." Her heart always bled especially for them.

"Jarek will take ten swords before he allows one to touch her. On that I stake my life," Abarrane says. "Trust that her commander will keep her safe."

"I pray you are right."

"Did you tell her about that nymphaeum stone in Soldor?" Elisaf asks.

"If I did, and those stones are doorways through, what do you think she would do?"

He smirks. "Use it to get here faster, possibly before Hudem's full moon."

"Exactly. We may not have encountered any beasts in Soldor, but a key caster in there will surely draw things from the depths that we do not wish to even know about, let alone fight."

"Still, we could use a caster's abilities on our side, especially one as powerful as Romeria."

"I know. But I fear what we are about to face may be beyond even her."

58

ROMERIA

"Doors." Gesine studies the nymph writing in Cirilea's nymphaeum stone with awe, moments after we pass through from Ulysede. "So many years, so misunderstood. By everyone."

"I have never met anyone so enthralled by these things," Zorya says. She, on the other hand, fidgets with her dagger, seemingly rattled by the sudden relocation.

Gesine smiles. "You have not met Master Scribe Agatha."

"And I do not plan to. One of you is more than enough." There's a slight teasing lilt in her tone, though.

"Let's go. We have a plan," Jarek orders, adding, "one that will likely go awry."

"It's a good plan! It will not go *awry*."

He leads the seven of us through the royal garden, taking a different route than yesterday. The legionaries fan out, Pan sticking with Horik and Loth, Gesine with Zorya. We didn't bother with the noble guises this time. Hiding one legionary is difficult. Four is impossible, especially when the king's guard is likely looking for us. Cloaks and blades will have to do.

My pulse races. Jarek's right. Too many things could go wrong.

I'm wearing my mask again, much to his chagrin. "Any good dreams last night?" I tease.

He sighs heavily. "It is not you. It is that face."

"Semantics." I duck as a tree branch flings back. "So, you did?"

"I already regret ever telling you."

"What happened in it?"

His responding chuckle is deep. "What's wrong? Missing the king too much that you need lewd visuals to get by?"

"Lewd? How lewd are we talking?"

"Lucretia has quite the imagination. You do not want me spelling it out."

"You're so sure it's her?" It probably is, but I get too much enjoyment from this. "Maybe it's just your secret crush on me."

He stops abruptly and I plow into his back before he spins to tower over me. "You are nervous about this absurd plan of yours. When you are nervous, you try to distract yourself with terrible humor."

"I wouldn't say *terrible*."

His gaze slides over my face. "When you wear that mask, I must keep reminding myself who you are. Be careful, or I might forget for a moment." He turns away as my mouth gapes.

Jarek and I are always tossing harmless banter, but that felt different. Charged. I don't know what kinds of things Lucretia is planting in his head, but I should probably order her to stop.

I follow him quietly the rest of the way until we rejoin the others.

"Three children and a fish." Jarek points at an elaborate water fountain with sprays of water jutting in various directions.

Just as Zander described.

Zorya pauses to scan the area for guards and then sprints in behind it and pushes on a block. A door swings open.

Pan's face makes a wide *O* shape. We're cut from the same cloth, he and I, in our appreciation for secret passageways.

Jarek snaps his fingers and our merry little band of thieves takes the stairs down to the tunnel into the undercroft of the castle.

The guard on duty watches as Loth and I approach the heavy iron doors. We keep our pace casual, unhurried. There's no one else around, but I would expect this area to be off-limits to everyone save for the royal family. Hence, my borrowed face. I hope Annika won't mind.

"Your Highness." The guard bows before his suspicious gaze flitters to the soldier beside me. Of all the legionaries, Loth stands out the least. Still, he stands out, and with each step closer, the guard's eyes narrow more. His hand moves for his sword hilt. "Princess Annika, do you require—"

Loth is so quick, I hardly notice him move before the guard crumples to the floor, rendered unconscious by a thump against the back of his skull.

"Thank you for *not* killing him."

The serene legionary dips his head.

"We have until seven tonight before the next guard arrives." A few hours to get in and out of the city. What trouble this might cause for Annika later, I don't know, but I didn't want to risk using Atticus's face, knowing he might already be gone to the east, a fact that the castle guard will be well aware of.

That is if he survived. I assume he has.

While Loth binds and gags the male, I channel Aminadav's affinity into the keyhole as Gesine taught me. The threads pour in like hot lava, molding into each intricate groove inside. I coax the threads to harden and break off the affinity, leaving a head much like any key sticking out. I give it a turn, and a click sounds.

"How many locks I did *not* have to pick over the years," I mutter, mesmerized by this newly acquired skill. I push open the heavy door with a smile of grim satisfaction.

"*That* is more than enough, and if it isn't, commandeer his ship and bury your blade in his gut," Jarek snarls, sizing up the chests of jewels and gold in Horik's and Loth's grips.

Both legionaries grunt under the weight of their parcels.

The bound guard in the corner is stirring, so we leave the vault behind, pulling the door shut and locking it.

I slip the key into my pocket, my nervousness giving way to adrenaline. "You guys should get moving. You know the plan." I hold up the letters sealed by "the king" before slipping them into Gesine's grip. "Get to the sanctum. I'm sure I saw a wagon there last night. Pan will get the horses from Silmar."

"Two lefts and a right," he echoes, repeating the direction we gave him to reach the stables from there.

Gesine already knows how to get hold of Seamus and then they'll head to the Trinket Inn to pay off Kaders. "We'll meet you at the port as soon as we're done here."

"Have fun fitting through that tunnel." Jarek pats Horik's shoulder as they take off, Zorya in the lead with her sword drawn. She'll get them there safely.

Jarek looks up the stairs to the main castle hall, his handsome face etched with worry.

"We'll be fine. Remember?" I wink and tap my cheek with my fingertip.

"Perhaps you should choose a less conspicuous person than Princess Annika?"

"You're right." And I know just the one.

59
GRACEN

"How is that stew coming along?" Corrin hollers at the kitchen door.

Sena leans over one of the pots and inhales. Three more simmer beside it. "Nothin' but water and tomatoes right now. Another hour, at least, I'd say."

"These poor people. If it were up to Boaz, they'd starve to death." Corrin fills her arms with loaves of bread until she's hugging as many as her short arms can carry. "I'll send Fikar in for it once it's ready." She struggles with the door handle before finally yanking it open. She storms off as quickly as she came.

I return to my task in time to watch the glob of applesauce slip off my spoon and splatter onto the stone floor.

With a sigh, I grab a cloth and kneel to wipe it clean before it ends up on the bottom of my shoe. That's the third spoonful I've lost. Either the fruit is too runny or I'm too scatterbrained, my gaze continuously veering toward the basket on the floor and the sleeping baby within it.

A sleeping *caster* baby, apparently.

How is that possible? And what does that mean that she has an affinity to Aoife? What will she be able to do?

Maybe Wendeline is mistaken. She has been under such duress

lately, dragged around Cirilea day and night, not to mention whatever horrors she faced in the dungeon at Boaz's hands. It is *far* more likely that she is wrong than that my daughter is the first caster born to Islor in two thousand years.

But what if Wendeline is right?

With the mess cleaned up, I pull myself to my feet.

Corrin marches toward me. "There you are. Just the person I was looking for."

"But you were just here."

"I was. You're right." She surveys the apple turnovers I'm making for the children. "Those look delicious."

What? "They're made with applesauce." Corrin despises apples, a fact she rarely neglects to mention. "Why are you acting so strange?"

She steals a glance toward Sena, who is paying no attention to anything but her stew. Still, she drops her voice. "We met last night in the stable. *Remember*?" Her eyes widen. "I figured this disguise would be safer to move around in."

Realization dawns and I gasp before I can help myself. "Your Highness?"

She gives me a wide-eyed warning glare.

"Sorry." I chastise myself. "You're back already."

"I told you I would be." She spots Suri on the floor and a smile stretches across her face. "That's my namesake?"

Despite my shock, I nod. "It is." And also, secretly, a caster. They have much in common.

Sena sets her gloves on the counter and, humming, strolls out the door.

Corrin—no, *Romeria.* Fates! What in Azo'dem is this mask!—watches over her shoulder until the cook is gone. "I don't have much time, but we're getting you and all the mortal children out of Cirilea now. I'm taking you to my kingdom, where you'll be safe from what's coming."

"A war." That's what Wendeline said.

Fear flickers in her gaze. "Yes."

We?

The legionary from last night is standing in a corner, ready to pounce on anyone coming through the doorway. He wasn't there a moment ago, though I've heard they move like ghosts. "How?"

"We're going to start a fire in the ballroom."

"What?" I gasp. "That will terrify the children!"

"A small one," she reassures me. "Just so we have an excuse to get them outside. If I can get them to the nymphaeum, then I can get them to safety."

I was just there with Atticus. It's a stone wall and an altar. I can't imagine what type of sorcery her plans involve. I don't need to know. "But a fire? There are over four hundred children in there now, and more arrive each hour as the guards continue to search the city. *And* it's full of hay."

"Four hundred." She curses, but then sets her jaw. "I can put it out with water."

"Because you are a caster," I say with hesitation.

A strange look passes over her face. "Yes, I am. Look, it's the only plan I can think of to get them outside without having Jarek kill every guard. I don't want that. *He* is fine with that." She nods toward where the legionary hovers.

I'm sure he could kill every one of them, but I don't want these children witnessing a slaughter, and the risk to them would be great. "The guards are only doing their jobs." And some of them have been relatively kind to me considering my impish child. Boaz is the only one whose loss I would not mourn. I bite my lip. "We just need to get them outside, right?"

"And to the nymphaeum, yes."

"Okay, I think I might have a better plan, one that doesn't involve burning down the castle or murdering people."

Corrin's—Romeria's—eyes light up. "I'm all ears."

I forgot how odd she was sometimes, with the things she said and the way she spoke, so casually, and unlike the stiff-backed nobility.

The kitchen door swings open. "I don't think those people can wait an hour for the ..." The real Corrin stops dead in her tracks, her jaw dropping as she takes in her doppelgänger standing next to me.

My stomach leaps into my throat as the legionary steps forward, his dagger out. "No!"

But Romeria grins and slips off her mask. "Let me guess. Stew. *My favorite*."

Fikar is collecting the soup bowls when Corrin clears her throat, giving me a pointed look. She isn't thrilled about this plan, but it didn't take much convincing to get her to agree.

It's time.

My insides turn somersaults as I make my way to the guard by the door. "I would like to take the children out for some air."

"There's plenty of air in here."

"*Fresh* air. They could use a walk to stretch their legs." I pray he cannot read my lie through my pulse.

He shakes his head. "You're not allowed to leave."

Princess Romeria gave me a short window to try it my way. I have no idea where she and that warrior went, but if I cannot convince this fool to let us out, I fear he will not live long. Knowing that bolsters my confidence. "His Highness put me in charge of these children and promised you would grant my requests. Did your captain not tell you this?"

"Grant you requests, yeah. Not let them leave."

"For a walk around the walled garden, with guards everywhere? Are you sure?"

He frowns.

But I haven't swayed him yet. "The last person who displeased His Highness where I was involved lost his head, and he was a lord. I would not want that to happen to you upon his return, when he asks if the guards complied and I am compelled to speak the truth." Fates, I think I might pass out. Where did the nerve to deliver that idle warning come from? "The garden is right there, and there is no escape. Where can the children possibly go?"

His lips twist. "This from the mortal who cannot keep track of one little boy?"

"To be fair, neither can all the guards in the castle, it seems." I dare a coy smile.

His eyes drop to my mouth and he smirks.

He thinks I'm flirting with him. I clear my throat. "Mortal children need fresh air. If they are cooped up for too long, they can become ill."

Doubt flickers across his face.

I rush to add, "And tiring them out now will help them sleep better later. Otherwise, they will become restless, and restless children can cry for hours. Imagine this many of them crying all night long."

That seems to push him over the edge. "You cannot manage all of them out there."

"I can!" I nod with confidence. "There are ten servants and enough older children to task each with minding two younger ones. Honestly, they are too scared to leave our sides, anyway. But if you would prefer to walk with us ..." I hold my breath, hoping he'll dismiss the offer.

He sighs reluctantly. Nodding toward two other guards nearby, he announces, "We're escorting them through the garden."

I stifle my regret—I hope I didn't just assign them all a death sentence—and clap my hands. "Children! Listen up!" Ears perk and curious gazes veer my way. "We are going to do something *extra* special now. Something that most mortals will *never* get a chance to do in their whole lives." I hope my attempt to inspire excitement works. "We are going to take a walk through the royal garden."

60
ROMERIA

We watch from behind a thick hedge as the glass doors to the ballroom open and children spill out, the older ones holding the youngers' hands, Gracen corralling them in her gentle manner, her baby cocooned within a sling over her chest to free her hands. Mika trails behind her, babbling to an attractive young blond mortal woman who holds Lilou's hand. Whoever she is, Gracen has entrusted her with guarding her kids.

"There are *so many* of them." I don't think I realized what four hundred children would look like. It's almost half the army Lord Telor brought to Ulysede's gates! "Is this insane?"

"Yes, but oddly usual for you, as I learned in Norcaster," Jarek mocks from behind me. "I count three guards escorting them. I will have to kill them."

"In front of the kids?" I cast a look over my shoulder. *"Come on."*

"Aren't you the one who wanted to set a room full of hay on fire with them in it?"

I throw an elbow back, earning a soft grunt. "I'll admit, that was a risky plan. But I didn't think I'd have an inside person." Gracen's idea is much better. That Atticus put her in charge and ordered the guards to comply earns him a point or two, though I can still never forgive him.

I gasp as another familiar face appears. "Dagny!" The seamstress marches along, prattling away. She has no clue this is anything other than a garden walk.

They turn onto the main path. In the far distance, I can just make out the clutter of guards near the east wing, watching. I hope none of them decides to step in, to question or to join.

Jarek curses. "That's the long way."

"It's the most obvious one. As long as they don't go into the maze, we'll be fine. Come on." Grabbing hold of his forearm, I let the familiar adrenaline wash over me. We cut through the garden, quiet and unseen as we follow them.

"It's time to turn around!" the guard closest to Gracen barks.

Shit. We're only halfway to the nymphaeum.

Gracen bites her lip, and I can almost see the wheels turning in her mind, looking for excuses to continue. "But they're enjoying themselves so much."

"The cedar labyrinth is ahead. We aren't taking them that far."

"A labyrinth?" Mika exclaims.

The blond servant shushes him and then grabs onto his hand as if afraid he might bolt for it.

"It has to be now." Jarek draws two throwing daggers from his belt, shifting his weight as he prepares to step out from behind the hedge. "I have the two on the left, you take out the one on the right."

"What?"

"Aim for his neck, as we practiced."

"I didn't practice hitting guards in the neck!" I hiss.

"Do your best."

I glare at him. "There are children here. I'm *not* throwing a dagger." Drawing on a thread of Aoife, I conjure a water arrow in front of us that will pierce the guard just as well.

"That works too. In three … two …"

A bell tolls. Not the slow and somber one that marks the hour. A rushed and furious clang, as if someone is swinging the rope as hard as they can. "What does that mean?"

Jarek curses. "The city is under attack."

"By whom?" *Oh no.* "Is that us?" Did Gesine and the legionaries get caught down by the port? If Gesine unleashes what she's capable of … I lose my grip on Aoife's thread and the arrow hits the grass with a splash. "What do we do?"

"We have our own task to complete. They will manage." Jarek steps out and, with strength and skill that seems impossible, he launches the daggers through the air, followed by a third. All three guards hit the ground.

Children scream.

"It's okay!" I run as hard as I can toward them, my hands up, praying we can get control of everyone before they scatter. On impulse, I peel my mask off to reveal the face some of them might recognize.

"Your Highness!" Dagny exclaims, rushing toward me, throwing her arms around my stomach in a hug so tight. "I thought I might never see ya again!"

Watching the friendly seamstress embrace me seems to calm many of the children, while others stare, dumbfounded by how I changed faces.

Jarek sweeps in, collecting his daggers and stirring new fears. Children begin to cry.

"We're not here to hurt you. We're going to get you back together with your parents," I say over the noise. *Eventually.*

A tall, skinny mortal man lingers nearby.

"Do you know where the nymphaeum is?" I ask.

"Yes, milady. I mean, Your Highness. Sort of, anyway."

"Okay. Start leading them in that direction, as quickly as you can. That way." I point to the route that doesn't take them anywhere near the maze.

He bobs and bows and then begins ushering the children away. They follow like ducks after their mother, quiet and focused.

Gracen's attention is on the dead guards. I can practically feel the guilt pouring from her.

"There's not much we could do about them, but my plan would have cost more, so thank you for your help."

The blond holding Lilou's hand gasps. "You *helped* the Ybarisan traitor?" She glares at Gracen with contempt.

Gracen shakes her head. "She is not what you think, Sabrina. I promise. She saved the king's life last night."

The woman—Sabrina—looks suspiciously from me to Gracen. "You are betraying His Highness." She lets go of Lilou's hand and backs away. "I am not going anywhere with her. I am—" She steps into Jarek's chest, her eyes wide with fear as she peers over her shoulder at him.

His jaw is taut. "You are coming with us or you will not leave this garden at all. Do not test me. We do not have time for that."

"Jarek," I warn steadily. Killing the guards was one thing, but killing this unarmed woman in front of the children will not end well.

Corrin marches up to her, her hands on her hips. "I was Queen Esma's devoted lady maid. Are you foolish enough to believe that *I* would follow a traitor?"

Sabrina's forehead furrows with uncertainty. The bell still tolls, a loud and frantic call to arms. Will it draw the guards away or out to us? We don't have time to find out. "Sabrina, help us get all the children out of here safely and then if you want to stay behind in Cirilea, you're welcome to. But I really don't think you'll want to."

Her gaze flitters over the children as they follow the man. Finally, she nods.

One problem averted. "Let's go."

"Thank God," I whisper to myself as the nymphaeum comes into view. The children are surprisingly quiet as we scurry across the field, little ones in the older kids' arms. My affinities sit beneath my skin, coiled and waiting.

"Your Highness!" Dagny grabs my wrist. "My Dagnar is in the castle somewhere. Albe too. I need to go find them!"

"You can't go back there. If the guards see you without the kids, they'll question you."

"I suppose you're right. Of course, you are." She worries her hands. "Do you think you could find them?"

"I've never met them. I don't know what they look like."

"Dagnar's like me, only much bigger!" She emphasizes that with her hands above her head.

"Okay, I'll try." I feel Jarek's glare on my back, but I ignore it. It's the least I can do for the seamstress after she risked herself playing messenger for me.

She squeezes my forearm. "Bless you, Your Highness. I've missed you so."

The bell continues to toll, a relentless gong. I'm desperate to get everyone through to Ulysede so I can come back to help Gesine and the others. I dread to know what they face.

The mortal man in the lead—Fikar, according to Gracen—reaches the stone first.

I run to catch up to him. "Everyone who's here, link hands!"

Nervous energy vibrates as the children reach for one another. I wait until the group seems large enough and then I grab hold of the nearest child and let the silver thread reach toward the stone.

Gasps and squeals sound as the children take in their new surroundings.

"Fates." Fikar stares, equally dumbstruck.

Lucretia appears a moment later, wearing a thick white smock, its collar snug just below her chin. "Satisfied, Your Highness?" She mock bows.

If I wasn't so anxious, I would laugh. I had scolded her earlier on perhaps choosing suitable attire for children. She went the extra mile. "Fikar, I need this space for more kids. Take them all up the stairs now. Eden will be waiting there for you."

I wait for his nod and then I send my affinity back through the stone.

A horde of children are already huddled, waiting. "Okay, next group!"

61
ANNIKA

Dagny's son looks like Dagny.

A male version, twice the height and burly.

But *still*, he looks too much like my late mother's seamstress for my liking. He's nowhere near as refined as Percy was. *Is*? What did Atticus do with my tainted tributary? He never told me, and then he just up and left for the east. The morning after getting shot by a merth arrow, no less!

I heard he spared Sabrina so perhaps he'll show the same compassion to Percy. Who knows, though? My twin brother is self-serving, and Percy doesn't have breasts.

Dagnar is a brute. I summoned him for a walk through the royal garden, and he arrived straight from the stable he'd been working in all day. It's as if all decorum around here has vanished as of late.

I sigh. The mark on his hand does not glow, at least. Perhaps all he needs is a change in wardrobe and a bath. And if that doesn't work, well … I suppose beggars can't be fussy and Islor's princess is now officially begging for a tributary.

If my parents could see this mess.

The guards ahead of us—there are too many of them lingering

inside the castle walls these days—are intently focused on the far west tower, where people filter into the garden.

"What is happening out there?" I ask out loud to anyone who might answer.

"It looks like the mortal children are going for a walk, Your Highness." By the guard's scowl, he doesn't approve. "Should we intervene and send them back?" He sounds eager for the order.

"I am sure they could use the fresh air. I know the feeling." Zander once sequestered me in my rooms for *weeks* because I helped Romeria escape the gray tower and her execution. I sniff. It seems he owes me an apology.

The children disappear down the path. There are *so* many of them. Honestly, what does Atticus think he's going to do? Keep a ballroom full so we never run out of tributaries? As if the city's keepers will tolerate that. The lords and ladies trapped here aren't pleased. I feel their harsh judgment on me as I walk through the castle, as if any of this blame rests on *my* shoulders.

This is *His Highness*'s problem. Not mine. "So, Dagnar, tell me about your day." I could not possibly care less, but I have enough tact to make polite conversation until I can sit him down and take his vein, and decide if I can tolerate this new match.

"It wasn't anythin' excitin', Your Highness. I got up, had bread with butter, went out to check on the horses ..."

I turn my head as he drones on so he can't see me pout.

We're approaching the first archway when the warning bell clangs. It makes my heart skip several beats. The last time I heard that sound was the day my parents died and Ybaris attacked us from within our walls.

Now what's going on?

A guard runs out of the castle, shouts something, and then charges back in. The others flock.

Dagnar scratches his forehead. "Don't that bell mean trouble?"

"Yes, it does." But with whom is the question. "Come on." We retrace our steps in a hurry to reach the two guards who remained.

"What is happening?" I call out to one of them.

"They're storming the castle, Your Highness," the one on the left says.

"*Who* is?"

"Mortals, keepers ..." He grips his sword.

Mortals and keepers. Of course. "It's finally happening." A wave of shock washes over me.

"What is, Your Highness?" Dagnar asks.

"Cirilea is revolting." The king's guard has been hanging people without trial, without mercy, and now they're marking common servants to be fed upon and taking their children away. Keepers have been dying horrifically for weeks, they're trapped in the city, and now their property confiscated. It was only a matter of time. "I can't believe Atticus left me here." Did he have any clue that this was coming?

"You must lock yourself in your chambers, Your Highness," the guard says.

"A lot of good that will do, if they want to reach me." And they will. I'm the only royal left in the household to accept punishment for all the disastrous decisions our family has made, beginning with Zander's betrothal to the Ybarisan princess.

"My ma was with the kids," Dagnar says, fear morphing his face. It's endearing, I'll admit.

"Go." I push him toward the direction they went. "These attackers are not here for you, but if they find you with me, I don't know what they'll do."

He falters.

"*Go!* Find your mother. That's an order!"

He takes off running without another look back. He wants to protect her far more than he cares to protect his princess, not that he could against a mob, anyway. That's fine, I can find my way to safety from here. I know this castle's secrets better than most.

A thud and clatter sound behind us.

I spin in time to see Tyree slash the throat of the charging guard. The other is sprawled out on the ground, unconscious.

And suddenly, I am alone to face off with the Ybarisan prince who has plotted my death once already, who just *jumped* from three stories up.

"I honestly thought the mortal might stay." He grimaces, favoring his right leg as he strips the guard of his weapons. "But I guess you don't inspire chivalry." He hobbles toward me, a dagger in hand.

I back away, fumbling for the small merth blade I keep tucked inside my cloak. "You can run. They won't chase you. My brother isn't here."

"And leave my bride-to-be?" He grins, but it's a pained look. "Do you think me foolish? I won't get out of Cirilea on my own." He darts forward, faster than I expected, grabbing hold of my arm and squeezing tight. "But I have a chance with a princess."

I swing with my free hand, stabbing my blade into the meaty part of his thigh, earning his howl of pain. Tearing it out, I make to plunge it in again.

In seconds my arms are tangled behind me and the knife I stabbed Tyree with is pressed against my throat. "That's not a very kind thing to do to your betrothed." He pants in my ear. "If you do not get me out of here, you are not worth keeping alive. Understood?"

I'm sure I hit an artery. Maybe I can humor him long enough that he'll bleed out. "The gates are sealed. No one in or out."

"I heard my sister escaped by skiff."

"The port is sealed too."

"I think we should try our luck, anyway, don't you?" My shoulders scream as he pulls my arms back tighter. "How do we get to the water from here?"

"I know a way." A long way that he'll struggle with, injured so. It might give me a chance to escape him. "I will get you there as long as you let me go."

"Bartering, are we? How about I promise not to kill you?"

"Do you actually know how to keep your word?" Doubtful.

"Let's find out." He gives me a shove. "Which way?"

62

ROMERIA

The sun is touching the horizon when Jarek and I push through Cirilea's sanctum doors, the children all safe in Ulysede, including Dagnar who we discovered charging through the royal garden like a wild boar, frantically searching for his mother.

Smoke and shouts and ringing steel greet us, spiking my adrenaline to new levels. It'll be dark soon and easier to move without notice, but for now, we draw our cloaks and hope for clear passage.

Jarek stalls, listens. "That's not coming from the port. It's coming from the castle. That is not us."

Both relief and new dread emerge. "Seamus said a rebellion was brewing." He hinted that any day now, the people would revolt. It makes sense that it would happen once the king and army had left the city.

"It appears it has finally come. The people feel they have nothing to lose."

"Will they get inside?"

"Eventually, yes. But that is *not* our problem. It works to our advantage. If the king's guard is defending the castle, they're not at the docks." Jarek scans the street before ushering me on with a hurried "Come."

The route to Port Street has become familiar to me. I run alongside Jarek, his blades drawn, my affinities simmering, through wafts of rancid air as we pass hanging corpses that need to be cut down and buried. Few people are on the streets, and they have no interest in tangling with two cloaked figures. Many are moving in the same direction as we are, their arms clutching children not yet taken by Boaz or whatever belongings they could grab on their hurried way. However Seamus spread the message, it worked.

The lower city buildings give way to a view of the bay, and a burst of joy hits me at the litter of skiffs already in the water, sailing out, loaded with people. "It worked. We actually pulled this off!" I manage between ragged pants.

"Do not celebrate yet," he warns. "The ships are still at port, including the *Silver Mage*." The biggest of all, by far.

We rush ahead toward the long line of mortals impatient to find passage. A guard lays facedown, a letter with my handwriting and the king's seal still in his grip. "I guess he didn't buy that?" The shallow waters below reveal hints of armor. More fallen guards, more letters.

My chest tightens.

"We tried the peaceful way first. You do not have to like it, but you must accept it." Jarek steps over the corpse. "They did what they had to do."

Not much is going according to plan today, but the mortal children are out and many ships' worth of innocent people will be sailing from here. That is no small victory.

We rush toward the *Silver Mage*, Jarek shouting, "Move!" Mortals huddle out of the way.

"No pushing! There's room for all of ya!" Pan calls out over the noise, trying to manage the crowd as Gesine and Zorya guide people along the boarding plank. Seamus and his people usher them downstairs.

"I wouldn't say that." Jarek regards the lengthy line and then the other ships. They're filling up, too, their decks swarmed with clusters of people as crews unfasten lines in a rush, preparing to sail.

At the *Silver Mage*'s helm are Horik and Kaders. "Why is Horik holding a sword to him?"

"Because he deserves it, but let's find out the reason." Jarek pats Zorya's shoulder once on his way past, hopping on the deck.

"Your Highness." Gesine dips her head in greeting as I follow Jarek, earning a few curious glances.

"Have you seen Wendeline?" I ask.

She shakes her head and my worry grows. Wendeline is the one marking all the mortals. She'll be a target for revenge.

I move past Gesine and grab Seamus's arm to get his attention.

He grins and clasps my hand. "The south wind blows tonight."

I return the smile despite everything. "And the north wind answers. You delivered on your promise."

"And you delivered on yours. The seamen were eager to leave, and when the bells started tolling, even more so. Only one was in too much of a rush to wait for gold and passengers. The *Tempest*." He nods toward a ship halfway out of the bay. "That surprised me. Aron'll do just about anything for a payday."

"Then Aron better hope he never meets me."

"He may be foolish enough to show up at Northmost, but knowin' him, he'll sail all the way to Westport."

At least it's only one ship out of more than a dozen. "Have you seen the priestess?"

"Not since the ruckus at the castle started and the captain dragged her back with him."

I curse. But maybe Boaz can keep her safe. I fetch an emerald I brought from Ulysede's vault and place it into Seamus's palm. "For your help leading them from Northmost to Ulysede. There's another to match when you deliver them."

His eyes widen. He quickly tucks it into his satchel with a nod and glances around. "I will do my best."

I offer another thanks and then rush up the stairs to the navigation deck where Kaders looks ready to piss his pants.

"He tried to sail off," Jarek explains.

"Aye, ya didn't say you'd be slaughtering half the king's guard!" Kaders scowls at the legionary.

My anger flares. "We paid you to take a hull full of mortals."

"An' the *Silver Mage* will never be welcome back after *this*." Kaders points to the castle, where an orange glow grows. "You didn't pay me enough."

I'm not about to be shaken down by this guy. "We made a deal, and you are going to honor it."

"This is still *my* ship!"

"And Her Highness thanks you so much for your service that one of her legionaries will accompany you, to ensure you have no challenges." Jarek drops a heavy hand on the captain's shoulder as he nods at Horik.

Horik dips his chin. "It would be my honor."

Kaders's face fills with confusion. "Her Highness?"

I slip my mask free for a moment, just long enough to watch the sailor's mouth drop. "*You*." He may not recognize Princess Romeria, but he recognizes when he's been duped.

Horik clasps hands with his commander. "Until next time."

"And there will be one," Jarek answers before we're moving again, rushing down the stairs. "The ship is almost full. They'll be sailing soon."

"Is it safe to have Horik so close to the sirens?"

"Kaders knows those waters and he will not risk his ship or himself. He'll sail along the shore and cut in before they reach the real danger." Jarek hops back onto the dock. "We've done what we can here. Seamus and his men will take care of the rest."

The others follow and, together with Pan, we rush down the dock toward the street.

"We need to find Wendeline! We can't leave her here." Gracen made me promise to bring her back. "And Dagny's husband is somewhere. And Annika—"

A deafening screech from above pulls everyone's attention upward, to the enormous dark silhouette that circles the castle.

My stomach drops. "That's Caindra." She's even bigger than we first thought.

"She's here for you," Gesine murmurs, a mix of awe and fear in her voice.

Jarek curses. "And she'll tear apart Cirilea. We must leave before she has the chance."

I open my mouth to protest, but he grabs my shoulders and meets my eyes, sincerity in his. "We will come back for the others when it is safe. You and me."

With reluctance, I mumble, "Okay."

We rush for the sanctum.

63
ANNIKA

Tyree holds me at dagger point as we watch the mortals flood the many ships and skiffs at the shoreline in the distance, our ship halfway out of Cirilea's bay.

"You're destroying my dress, mongrel," I snarl, fighting the urge to inhale the sweet orange blossom scent of his blood. It may be poisonous, but it smells divine. The worst sort of tease when I'm craving.

Tyree answers by tightening his grip around my waist. "Maybe you shouldn't have stabbed me with a merth blade."

"I suppose if you bleed out, it'll be worth the loss of fine silk."

His deep mocking laughter curls into my ear. "If only I had a belt. Oh, wait." He loosens his grip around my waist long enough to untie my sash and yank it through the loops. Wrapping it around his thigh with one hand, he orders, "Tie it."

He's already ruined my dress with stains, now he ruins its shape. "With pleasure." I grab each end and yank as hard as I can over the wound, earning his howl of pain. It gives me just enough leverage to elbow him in the stomach and break free. I get all of three steps before a heavy weight lands on top of me, pushing me down. My face smashes against the ship's wooden deck floor.

"Where do you think you're going?" His tone is mocking, his body pressed uncomfortably against mine. "We are at sea."

"Then there is no reason for you to be lying on me like this," I force through gritted teeth.

In seconds, I'm hauled back to my feet, and we resume our position of captor and captive, my own blade being used against me as I watch Cirilea shrink.

The *Tempest's* captain hops down from the navigation deck, studying my ruby ring in his grip. Tyree used it to barter our way onto the ship. I'd led him where he wanted to go and prayed that he would honor his promise and not kill me. He did something worse—forced me to leave with him.

"Winds are light. It'll take us at least three days to reach Northmost," the sea captain announces.

"*Northmost*. No, I want out of this insipid realm," Tyree growls. "You are taking us to Westport."

My mouth falls open. *Skatrana*?

"With the sirens? Are you mad?" The ship's captain shakes his head, holding up my ring. "Besides, this won't cover a trip like that."

He's arguing in my favor and yet my anger flares. "That ring will be the most valuable thing you ever hold in your pathetic life," I snap. It was my mother's. "The king will have your head for being a party to this, you know?"

The captain smirks. "Which king is that? The exiled one or the one whose city has fallen?"

I look back to my home, in flames. But it's the large shadow circling above the castle that catches my attention. I squint to try to make it out.

That isn't smoke.

64
ROMERIA

My lungs burn by the time we push through the cedar tunnel and emerge in the royal garden. The mortals and keepers have overwhelmed the king's guard and breached the castle walls with weapons. Through the windows are silhouettes of people *inside,* rushing along the halls, some chasing guards, others being chased.

"We are not joining this fight, Romeria," Jarek warns.

"But they're going to destroy everything."

"As will that beast above us if we do not get you out of here." He urges the five of us forward through the grounds.

It's unusually quiet here. The guards have abandoned their posts to fight elsewhere. The few left behind are dead. I peer upward in time to catch the corner of a wing before Caindra vanishes behind a plume of smoke and cloud. Jarek's right. With that in mind, I run alongside Gesine, who struggles to keep pace with the others.

Ahead is the infamous rose garden, a circular pattern of bushes and paths fanning out into hedge all around, the last of the fragrant blooms clinging to their branches. They still haven't rebuilt the water fountain Princess Romeria destroyed.

I've walked through this part of the royal garden more than

once since that first night in Islor, and yet now I am here again, my heart pounding in my throat. But at least I'm not alone this time.

"Go on!" Gesine goads, her words ragged between pants. "I will put up a shield from behind us if any guards should appear."

"We'll put one up together."

She smiles at me through her labored breaths. "Who knew … you would be … such a quick learner?"

"I could have told you that. But it helps that I've had a good teacher—"

A whistling sound cuts through the air, a second before Gesine gasps and falls.

I gape at the arrow protruding from her back, stunned for long seconds, before a "No!" tears from my throat, drawing the others back. But my attention is already behind us, on Boaz, who stands maybe fifty feet away, another arrow nocked and aimed at me. He never misses.

Footfalls close in behind me. Zorya and Jarek rush in on either side, swords drawn.

"Gesine!" Zorya calls out, anguish in her voice. It's the first time I've ever heard the warrior use her name.

Gesine doesn't respond.

Doesn't move.

"Where are they?" Boaz's voice booms and it instantly transports me back to the tower cell months ago.

"Where are *who*?" My fury bubbles beneath my skin with my affinities. I'm not the helpless prisoner I once was.

"The exiled king and his traitorous princess. I warned His Highness they would draw the armies out so they could steal the throne, but he did not listen to me."

He thinks we're behind this mess in Cirilea? It makes me want to laugh despite my dark mood. "Zander is at the rift trying to keep Neilina from taking Islor. Didn't Atticus tell you that?"

"Who do you think you are, to use their names so freely?" Boaz spits.

"Oh, I'm sorry, I thought you'd recognize me." I slide my mask up. "I'm the traitorous princess you've been looking for."

His eyes flare with a mix of hatred and shock.

But Gesine's still body fuels my rage. I'm not afraid of him. "Isn't this the rose garden you killed me in the first time? Because I'd like to repay the favor." With a primal scream, I hurl a blast of woven energy toward him. A flash of blinding silver light explodes much like it did the night of the grif, only I don't lose consciousness this time, indulging in the satisfying rush as I draw more and more from this deep well inside and channel my pain. Boaz has played judge, jury, and executioner for too long, eagerly delivering death while answering to kings and queens. He betrayed Zander. This world will be a better place without him.

"Romeria! Stop!" Jarek shouts in the distance.

I could continue this forever, and yet I need to save some sliver of affinities to get us back to Ulysede. I relinquish my hold and the brilliant light dims, leaving me to survey the damage I've caused. Boaz is gone as if he never existed, but so is the thick foliage, the hedges, the trees, the statues. Nothing remains but a charred path at least twenty feet wide leading straight to the castle. I've razed a large swath of the royal garden.

Zorya drops to her knees beside Gesine. "Save her!" she demands, snapping the back of the arrow off and flipping the caster over. The pointed head protrudes from her chest. Her eyes are vacant.

"I can't unless she has a pulse." My voice cracks over the words.

Zorya presses her fingertips against Gesine's neck. A pained cry of anguish erupts from the warrior's lips a moment later, confirming what I already know.

Just like that, Gesine is gone.

"They're coming." Loth nods toward the castle. The blast of my affinities must have drawn attention. Guards spill out of the castle and rush toward us, the path cleared for them. There are at least twenty, with more dripping out of the doors, one at a time.

"I don't think I have enough in me," I warn. "Not to fight them and get us home." What felt like an endless well inside is now hollow.

Zorya hops to her feet, drawing a second blade, her teeth bared. "I will give you a head start." She swings both swords, preparing.

"We are not staying to fight," Jarek barks. "You will die, and I am not losing another person today. Let's go!"

The warrior doesn't move.

"That's an order, legionary!"

With a roar of discontent, Zorya sheathes her swords and hauls Gesine up over her shoulder. She rushes past, her teeth gritted. A streak of tears mars her cheek.

"Romeria! Run, or I will carry you," Jarek warns.

My legs move of their own accord, and we take off in a sprint. Behind us, metal whistles and thuds to the ground, too close for comfort. I reach for Aoife's thread to form a shield but I can't seem to grasp it. Either it's spent or I'm too distraught by the lifeless body ahead.

Another deafening screech from above has me ducking and I sense Caindra sweeping down.

All this just to end up eaten by a dragon.

The ground suddenly trembles and I stumble, falling.

Jarek dives to haul me back to my feet in a heartbeat. He checks over his shoulder. "Fates."

I dare follow his gaze.

Caindra has landed in the charred strip, her massive body overtaking the royal garden, bending tree branches and hedges on either side. Shouts sound, but I can't see anything past her.

My fingertips dig into Jarek's forearms as my legs wobble under the ferocity of that stare. But she remains where she is, the finer details of her form hidden in the dusk.

"Why is she watching us like that?" I whisper.

"She's blocking their path," Jarek says. "She's helping us get away."

With a roar that makes me wince, as if she can hear and understand our words, Caindra swings her mammoth, spiked head toward the castle and opens her mouth. A stream of fire shoots from it.

"Go. Now!" Jarek has one arm around my waist, practically carrying me as we run the rest of the way to the nymphaeum. We've almost reached it when she emits another terrifying sound and launches herself back into the air.

I peer back at the empty space left. The guards who were there before are all gone. Jarek was right—she *was* helping us escape. If only she had gotten there before Boaz found us.

"Romeria, just a little more to get us home, okay?" Jarek coaxes my attention back to him, nodding toward the stone, his grip tight around me.

I manage to pull enough of my affinities to get us through the door.

Only when I touch Ulysede's stone floor again do I allow myself to dissolve in tears.

65
ZANDER

"The taillok will arrive at dawn with a message from Romeria, confirming all is well," Elisaf assures me as we stroll through the officers' quarters. Firelight and soft laughter surround us from all sides as soldiers attempt to shake the anxiety that gnaws at them, knowing this might be their last full night of life.

"I am sure you are right." And yet I worry.

We pass by Abarrane's tent, where Aziel and Drakon stand sentry outside, pretending not to listen to the heady sounds of coupling within, their hands gripping their pommels, ready to slay the other should there be any sign of treachery.

"How many gold coins do you owe me?" Elisaf whispers.

"It is you who owes me." A more predictable commander, I have never met. "She must have low hopes for our success tomorrow."

Elisaf's humor vanishes. "She's not the only one."

I sigh. "Come. We must be there to greet Radomir before someone mistakes him for the enemy and starts a war too soon." If they're not halfway through Soldor, having abandoned their loyalties.

Gaellar and her company of soldiers are already at the watchtower when we arrive, their swords aimed at the twenty saplings. Not one horse is able to stand still, sensing their riders' apprehension.

Radomir actually kept his word.

"What a warm greeting to the rift by our allies, Your Highness!" he declares with a flourish, flashing his jagged teeth.

"Weapons down," I order, moving between the two groups, ignoring the way the soldiers wait for Gaellar's nod before following. "They do not need an escort. They will remain with me until they return to Soldor."

"As you wish, Your Highness." Gaellar turns her horse. "With me!" They ride back toward camp as if wanting to get away from the saplings as quickly as possible.

I sigh. "You enjoy antagonizing people, don't you?"

"When they aim swords at me for no reason other than what I am? I thrive on it." Radomir is behaving far more like the arrogant sapling we first met outside Ulysede's gates, but I've seen the other side of him now, and I know there is an Islorian hidden deep inside, impatient to come out. His dark gaze scans the countless tents. "What news of the rift? Anything vital?"

"Several attacks by wyverns over the last few days."

"Given what's been crawling out lately, I'm not surprised. And the Ybarisans with you? Have they made them feel equally welcome?"

"Abarrane's welcoming one right now." Elisaf chuckles at his own joke.

I roll my eyes. "You cannot blame them for being apprehensive, Radomir. They don't trust your kind and you've given them no reason to yet. But they did not fire upon you, so I would say that's progress."

He studies the camp ahead. "Even so, I think we will return to

Soldor for the night. I would not want to be this close to freedom only to die before we have the chance to feel it."

"Suit yourself." Perhaps that is not the worst idea. Everyone is already on edge. "We will see you tomorrow as soon as the sun drops?"

"And it shall be the last time we must wait for that." He salutes and turns his horse, his companions following suit.

But an earsplitting roar in the night draws everyone's attention toward the gaping chasm, where a wyvern dives for a cluster of soldiers on horses. Screams sound as its claws rake across bodies, sending them sprawling. Other soldiers fire arrows at it that bounce off its orange scales like matchsticks.

My pulse races. "I'll bet that's the one that killed Bragvam." Back for seconds.

"Look at the damage just one can cause." *Imagine ten of them, a hundred,* Elisaf doesn't have to say.

I draw my sword from my scabbard. "This is the last thing we needed tonight."

"As one!" Radomir bellows, all hints of his previous humor gone. The group of saplings changes course, charging toward the rift, their horses' hooves a pounding thunder.

Elisaf and I follow a beat after, my affinity grasping for nearby flames.

The wyvern is circling for another attack. Gaellar races in with her men, shouting commands for the rift soldiers ahead to spread out. It's smart—grouping together will only ensure more die with each pass.

The wyvern must spot the gleaming Ulysede helms and shields approaching because it banks hard, swerving to meet the group head-on.

Radomir climbs until he is crouching in his saddle, a rapier in his free hand.

"What is he *doing*?" Elisaf shouts. "He is mad!"

"I do not know, but they have lived with these beasts for

centuries so perhaps we should trust that they know something we do not."

With a roar, the wyvern dives.

And I hold my breath, both with dread and fascination, watching as the beast opens its giant maw, intent on serving as many casualties as it can. But at the last moment, it seems to change its mind, pulling up, almost as if repelled. Radomir uses that opportunity to leap and stab the slender blade into its leathery wing.

The beast's roar rings of pain before it hits the ground, throwing Radomir off. The blade is still embedded deep within its left side, only the hilt protruding. It tries to take off again, but its injured wing drags.

Arrows rain down, pelting its body. It rears, facing off against its opponents from ground level. Even lame, it can still cause untold damage. We can't afford this.

I hurl a considerable fireball at its head, and then another. And another.

With a screech, the wyvern turns and runs for the chasm, diving over it without hesitation, vanishing from sight.

My body slumps with relief. Elisaf and I pivot toward where Radomir lies sprawled on the ground, but we aren't the only ones. Both his men and Gaellar rush in from different angles. We all reach him at the same time.

I dismount and run to his side, expecting a gravely injured sapling.

Instead, I find him laughing. "I told you they do not have a taste for our kind. They usually realize it at the last possible moment."

"Usually?" He raced in, *hoping* they would repel it before it delivered a devastating blow? I shake my head, though I find a new respect rising for the sapling leader. He did not have to put himself in harm's way, especially when he's so close to achieving his goals with or without us, but he did it without hesitation.

Maybe I have misjudged the sapling and this alliance after all.

Radomir pulls himself off the ground and peers at his bloodied hands. He must have cut them on the wyvern's scales. "There is a spot on the beast's wing that, if you penetrate it just so, you will immobilize it from flight."

"Where did you learn this?" Gaellar asks, her discomfort from earlier temporarily absent.

"You may defend the rift against these creatures, Commander, but we have learned how to survive *with* them for many years. It has not been easy."

She nods, and I see her mind churning.

What *I* see is an opportunity. "Perhaps you would be willing to spend time sharing knowledge with the soldiers here, so we are all better prepared." I imagine that is along the lines of where her thoughts are. I could order him to stay, but he might rebel. This way, he has a choice to help us and prove the saplings' worth.

Black eyes shift from me to Gaellar. "I have nothing better to do."

Gaellar dips her head. "It would be much appreciated by all."

The camp is unnerved after another attack by a wyvern, a dozen bodies—soldiers and horses—strewn like debris across the rugged dirt. And yet a cheer sounds in the night, followed moments later by more. Soon, an entire chorus erupts, the energy swelling.

I smile.

This is how we fight against the Nulling and Malachi.

United.

66
AGATHA

The sun is rising when our caravan reaches the caster pavilion, the trek through the thousands of Ybarisans slow and tedious.

I ease myself down the steps, my limbs aching in protest. Aside from a few short breaks when we watered the horses and relieved ourselves, the wagons have rolled night and day, their occupants sleeping where they sat. If Queen Neilina were wise, she would have had us leave days earlier, but she has no interest in prolonged travel, and her jeweled carriage has all the comforts.

I look up into the clear blue sky. "Not much time to spare is there." Even now, one can see the faint outline of Hudem's moon. It will intensify with each passing hour until it hangs so low and shines so bright, nothing can hide, the shadows non-existent.

"I have never seen so many people." Baedriya, the soft-spoken messenger who lent her support, says, her dark gaze raking over the sea of tents housing the poor souls who prepare to die for their treacherous queen. "I did not think there were this many in all of Ybaris."

"I fear there will be far fewer when the sun rises at dawn." Queen Neilina has promised them easy passage behind Mordain.

Many of them likely believe they will walk across the rift's pass and be handed land.

I lean down to test the patch of new grass sprouting beneath my feet. There are countless more poking through the dirt. Trampled beneath feet, but unmistakable. Nothing has grown here for two millennia and yet now there are hints of new life?

Would this have anything to do with the changes I fear are coming?

"Do you think if people knew that Her Highness summoned the fates, they would follow her?" Baedriya asks.

"People believe what they want to believe, even when the truth is laid bare, unfiltered and undeniable, before them." Lorel is not an evil caster, nor is she blind, but she chooses the path that ensures her position as Prime. She likely figures any hidden truths won't change the outcome. Maybe she's right. I could stand on the top of this wagon and shout them for all to hear, and all it would earn me is an arrow through my gullet.

The Shadows approach, riding two by two in a straight line, their identities concealed behind their fearsome-looking black armor. But I know Solange leads the escort with the queen and the elementals. She may not approve of our part in this war with Islor, but she also knows she has no choice but to follow orders. We are all pawns in Queen Neilina's game, and she will replace us as necessary.

The royal carriage slows, its frame winking with countless gems that mirror the castle towers. Neilina never leaves Argon without both the army led by Commander Tiberius and the Shadows. She rarely leaves Argon period, preferring the comforts of her pampered life rather than seeing how her people suffer.

"You should find Master Barra. I'm sure he has a task for you." I add as an afterthought. "May the fates be with you until dawn."

"And you as well." Baedriya bows and darts off.

The carriage door opens and Queen Neilina herself steps out, Aoife's token necklace a statement with its splendor. She has replaced her gold gown with one made of both gold and silver, perhaps a nod to Vin'nyla as she prepares to watch the battle unfold. I can guess without being told that she has no plans of joining, only claiming victory.

Behind her, Cressida steps out, her doe eyes wide and fearful.

My anger boils. That blasted royal demon. Can she be any more blatant with her scheming, keeping the innocent, collarless caster glued to her hip in case she must summon a fate?

The queen's gaze veers in my direction, and I duck behind our wagon, out of sight. Surely, she would question my presence if she saw me, and questioning done by her never ends well for anyone. I must do a better job of hiding until I can get across.

"Master Scribe!"

I jump at the husky voice and spin around to meet Solange's penetrating glare.

The Second towers over me. "I thought I saw you among the fray but couldn't make sense of it. What possible reason does an old scribe have for joining a war?"

I hesitate. Solange isn't known for her patience. If I tell the truth, this will go one of two ways, and if I lie, only one way.

With a huff, she grabs hold of my arm and drags me into a nearby tent, shooing away its occupants—messenger casters, all of them, their homing pigeons waiting patiently in wire crates. "Do not think because you are elderly and that the Prime is not here that I will not punish you myself." Sliding off her helm and mask, she sets them on a crate and wipes away the beads of sweat from her brow. "Did Allegra send you?"

My lips purse. I know Solange has little love for Ybaris, but beyond that, I don't know where she would stand on any of this.

"Do you think I have not noticed how much time you two spend together? All the corners the Second and the Master Scribe whisper in?" She shakes her head, her chestnut-brown braids slipping over her shoulder. "I suggest you start telling me what you know before the queen summons me and I am forced to reveal a conspiracy within Mordain's ranks without understanding it first."

Solange may hate the queen, but she follows rank and file, and she would go to Neilina out of spite to stifle the other Second's schemes. I have no choice. "The queen summoned Aoife twenty-five years ago, with the help of Caster Ianca, to create a weapon against Islor in the form of Princess Romeria."

Solange's nostrils flare as she struggles to control her temper. She already accused the queen of as much. "How about something that we don't all already know and are ignoring?"

"The scribes have never ignored it," I snap, my patience worn.

Solange folds her arms across her chest, a smug smile curling her lips as if she thinks she has walked me into a corner. "So, it is the scribes who conspire?"

"We do not *conspire*. We guide and we educate, and we prepare, as Ybaris's queen leads us to ruin and our own leaders bow to her perpetual deceit in favor of retaining their positions of power. We devote a life of servitude to knowledge while you all sneer and mock our purpose, and yet it is our work that uncovered the true danger behind the queen's treachery, that allows us to see that which you do not yet." I quote the line burned into my skull. "'When she rose again as a Daughter of Many and a Queen for All, only then could there be hope for peace among the peoples.'"

Solange's arrogance fades but in its place is not her typical biting anger. Instead, I see a hint of worry. "What do you mean by that?"

I sigh. Perhaps the one about to escort so many to their deaths should know what lies ahead. "I can explain everything, but it will require that you indulge prophecy."

67
ZANDER

I have seen more than a thousand of Hudem's moons in my life, and yet each time, my heart skips a beat as if spotting its sudden outline in the crisp morning sky is a surprise.

"Your Highness." Abarrane dips her head. "The saplings are safely in Soldor."

"Thank you for ensuring that." Not that I am overly worried about betrayal within the camp after last night's wyvern defeat. "Any sign of the taillok?" I have searched the sky, but there is still no hint of its iridescent feathers.

Abarrane shakes her head.

"Romeria may not have anything to report," Elisaf says.

"Nothing to report still deserves a report," Abarrane counters.

She's right. Worry gnaws at my conscience. I should have received a letter by now. Romeria would not wait.

Something has gone terribly wrong.

Elisaf pats my shoulder. "I will stand watch and let you know the moment it arrives. Get a few hours of rest while you can."

"I will not be able to rest. Besides, it seems I have company." I nod toward Gaellar, who marches toward my tent. *Her* tent, until I arrived.

"Your Highness." She bows, offering a sideways glance at Abarrane.

"Did you gain the insight you wanted from Radomir?" He sat with us for hours, answering questions and suggesting tips for the various beasts they've crossed paths with, until they had to return to the shadows. Even I learned a thing or two, and it was impossible to miss the sapling leader's light mood. If I didn't know better, I'd say he enjoyed the comradery, the respect.

"Very much, though I do not know how much use it will be for us. We have yet to see a nethertaur or a hag around these parts."

Abarrane clears her throat, a subtle way of expressing her displeasure with me for not revealing the truth.

She's right, but I ignore her for now. "Any sign of Queen Neilina?"

"That is why I am here. Our lookouts have seen her carriage arrive, along with her elementals and Mordain's Shadows."

My king's armor left behind in Cirilea still wears the battle-ax mark from the last encounter I had with one of those Shadows. They're daunting, as skilled with weapons as they are with their honed affinities. "I imagine she will want to exchange words before battle." I've never met Neilina in person, but I've heard she loves the sound of her own voice. I would be shocked if she doesn't seek the opportunity to meet me. "Keep a watchful eye and inform me as soon as their gate opens."

Gaellar's brow furrows. "Do you think that wise, to go yourself? If what you have told me about Queen Neilina is true, then she is not honorable. She will bring her elementals with her and use the opportunity to attack."

"Possibly. But I cannot hide. Besides, I welcome the meeting, so I can brief them on all the lies their precious ruler has fed them."

Peering over her shoulder at the arid fields filled with soldiers, Gaellar offers, "Many here feel that it is not much different in Islor."

I want to argue with her, but I can't because it's true. I've been at the root of some of those lies. But I'm not sacrificing others for my own gain.

Abarrane clears her throat … again.

Point made.

"How are strategic plans coming along?"

"Well, Your Highness, I feel we have the right plan laid out."

They cannot possibly have the right plan because they have no idea what's coming. "Gather your officers. We will meet in the command tent in thirty minutes." Maybe it's time for some candid truths.

That is what Romeria would do.

"If we leave a wide perimeter around our wall and then unleash several volleys of arrows, some of them will get through."

"But most of them will not."

"Bragvam said to aim for the Shadows, who will come in behind them."

Telor and I share an amused look as the officers around the table bicker.

"I thought she said her strategy was already laid out," Abarrane says mockingly, earning Kienen's chuckle.

Gaellar grimaces. I feel a pang of sympathy for her. She just inherited this position and while I'm sure she earned it, it takes time to prove herself against older, weathered soldiers who think they know everything.

"The last time Ybaris attacked—" one begins.

I bark with grim laughter, cutting him off. "You are strategizing maneuvers based on what they did the last time, one hundred years ago?"

The voices die down as stern faces stare at me. A few, I recognize, but most I've never met before. They don't know me any more than I know them, and by some of their expressions, my presence here is not appreciated. Some surely don't see me as king.

That's fine. They don't have to love me, but they damned well better listen to me. "Let me save you the trouble of too much quarreling. There is nothing about this battle that will resemble the last one, or any that Islor has fought in two thousand years. And that is because, at the height of the full Hudem moon, the Nulling will open."

Gaellar's face blanches. "There is a key caster?"

"There is, and it is Queen Romeria of Ulysede." I don't hesitate anymore. She is what she is, and I believe she is bound to be Islor's savior. "Because of Queen Romeria, we will finally have an end to this blood curse that has plagued us for too long. The Ybarisan poison will no longer be a threat to us."

Silence fills the tent as several sets of eyes flicker to the emblem on my chest. An answer to their unspoken question.

"But she's the one who brought the poison!" one of Gaellar's captains exclaims.

"Queen Neilina is to blame for the poison in Ybaris, regardless of how it arrived. And she should bear the full brunt of everyone's anger. You have heard many things over the last weeks and months. Some were outright lies, some were exaggerations. Know that what I say to you now is the truth and *only* that. King Barris was a good ruler. He and I wrote to each other several times over the years. He was a tough negotiator, but he was fair, and his love for Ybaris and its people was deep. We had every intention of honoring our alliance. My father, King Eachann, considered him a friend." An unexpected lump rises in my throat. "Islor had no part in his death, but I will gladly avenge it." I look to Kienen, hoping he sees the truth in my declaration.

"Queen Neilina never wanted an alliance and has been working against King Barris's wishes for years, going so far as to summon Aoife to create a poison meant to kill Islor's immortals."

"Yes, her daughter's blood!" the same captain complains.

"Yes, her daughter. But the Romeria who sits on Ulysede's

throne is not the one she birthed. One only needs to look to her caster abilities to know that. And this Romeria? She is the *only* being in our entire realm who can help save Islor *and* Ybaris."

"King Atticus has declared—"

"King Atticus is not here!" I bellow. "He did not come to help fight Neilina. He did not even answer the rift army's call for aid!"

A few beats of silence hang.

"And where is Queen Romeria?" another captain asks, looking around the tent. "If she is this powerful key caster who can save us, why is she not here to do so?"

I could have this officer dragged outside and flogged for the way he speaks to me, but it wouldn't help morale and, besides, he's right. As much as I don't want her in immediate danger, Romeria is the best weapon we have.

And she is not here.

I don't know where she is.

"The queen of Ulysede had another important task to attend to. She will join us when she is able." It's a white lie but also the truth. I know Romeria too well to believe she will remain in Ulysede while we are at war.

If there is a way to get here, she will find it.

68
ROMERIA

"The wielder of the elements was not long for this world, anyway." Lucretia weaves around where I sit on the floor, my back against one of the gargoyle statues. I've been here for hours while Ulysede's mortals help settle all those who arrived from Cirilea. Lucretia's frugal white smock is gone, replaced by gauzy black. She may as well stroll around naked. "I could sense the cracks in her affinities. They were waning quickly."

"Is that supposed to comfort me?" I would rather Gesine be here as a seer than not at all.

I can't even tell Zander the horrible news because she's no longer here to guide the taillok. He would have expected a letter from us this morning. He will be beyond worried about me—the last thing I want for him when his focus needs to remain on the rift.

"She died valiantly in battle. Is that not what these beings strive for?"

"We weren't in battle. We were running from it." I don't feel a millisecond of regret for Boaz's death. I hope it hurt, but I know he was gone in an instant. "And that's not what Gesine strived for." She loved history and knowledge.

She respected prophecy.

She was my friend.

A fresh tear rolls down my cheek.

Lucretia swoops in to catch it with her thumb. "My masters will be here soon. I have your outfit picked for you." With a sweep of her hand, she draws my attention to a gunmetal gray and gold dress with a fitted bodice. Ethereal-looking feather wings extend beyond its back, reaching halfway to the floor. They remind me of an angel.

I don't know whether to laugh or scream. In the end, I shake my head. "I'm in tears over my dead friend and you're trying to get me into a party dress? With wings? Do you seriously not care what is about to happen to all these people?"

"I do not fear as you do." She stands and glides over to the gown, her fingers running over the steely feathers. "I have faith that the Queen for All will triumph."

"At what cost?" According to prophecy, I'm supposed to bring peace, but the only thing I seem good at doing is bringing more death. "Besides, Queen Neilina has all the casters." I'm only one person.

"They bow to the throne of Ybaris. You are heir to that throne, are you not?"

"Apparently."

"If she were to die, it would be yours, and those casters would bow to you."

"Not you too." Radomir already made the not-so-subtle suggestion. "I already have one throne."

"You are Queen for All. The throne is yours to take."

"How?"

She cocks her head. "There is only one way. You know that."

To kill the queen. "I am here and Neilina is on the Ybarisan side." I point to the nymph doors. "Will one of those get me there?"

"Not close enough, no."

"Then what? How am I supposed to do this?"

A rush of footfalls sounds then. Jarek charges down the steps into the crypt, stumbling on the last one.

"What's going on?" Panic laces my voice. I don't think I've ever seen him out of breath before.

But it's Lucretia who speaks. "I imagine the answer to your question has arrived. You *must* wear that to greet her, so she knows you are ready." She gestures at the gown. "And do not forget your crown."

Eros doesn't break his stride once on our gallop through Ulysede.

"So, the wings ..." Jarek begins, but I shoot him a glare that cuts off any mocking.

I'm not in the mood. Lucretia was insistent that I must change, daring to invoke Gesine's name to convince me. Gesine would tell me to listen to the sylx and so I did. For her.

The wings are featherlight, their texture between my fingers silky soft. I barely feel them at all. The black dagger sheathed at the dress's belt, I notice far more. I'm fairly certain it's a token from Malachi, the material reminding me of the cuffs I wore in Cirilea for a time.

As soon as I reach the outer gate, Caindra tips her head back and roars.

I feel it in my teeth. "How does she seem bigger every time we see her?" Does she grow every time she eats someone? That thought makes me shudder.

"It is the first time we've seen her in full daylight." Jarek's eyes are wide—with appreciation or fear, I can't tell. Likely both.

"She's been doing that since she arrived," Loth says. "Roaring and stomping the ground."

All around her taloned feet are deep gouge marks in the earth, confirming his claim. It's like she's waiting impatiently for me.

"Open the gate."

Jarek gapes at me like I've just suggested he hold up his sword so I can run into it. "Are you mad?"

"I have wings on and I'm walking out to say hello to a fire-breathing dragon. No, I'm perfectly sane."

His lips press in a thin line. "I do not appreciate your sarcasm at the moment."

"Lucretia says Caindra's my answer."

"She's a serpent. You cannot trust her advice."

"I don't have a choice. She's the only one left who has any idea what's going on." My voice cracks. I swallow against the lump in my throat before I break down. "Caindra has had two chances to kill me so far, and she hasn't. She helped us yesterday. Remember?"

Jarek's shoulders sink but he doesn't counter me.

"Open the gate. Please."

Loth pulls the lever, and the portcullis ascends.

I inhale, searching for courage. My crown dangles from my fingertips. With reluctance, I settle it on my head. "Wish me luck." I step out.

Jarek moves with me. "Do not attempt to dissuade me." He shakes his head firmly. "Where you go, I go."

The dragon examines us through those menacing eyes. There's no way to read her. "She may kill you."

"I am not afraid to die for a worthy cause."

"Well, *I'm* afraid for you to die. I can't lose another friend."

He peers off into the distance, his lips parted as he weighs his next words. "You asked me why I am still here, why I did not leave once I figured out what you were." His Adam's apple bobs. "You are the worthiest of causes I have ever met, that I ever will meet, and I will follow you into the rift if you ask it of me. But do not *ever* ask me to leave your side."

His declaration sparks a sudden surge of emotion in me. Maybe it's because I just lost Gesine, but to have such loyalty after so many years of being alone is something I never imagined. "Just to the dragon will do for now." My voice is husky.

With a deep breath, together we walk toward her, my grip firmly on my affinities, my pulse in my throat. Her talons remind me of the taillok's, only twenty times larger. They look capable of shredding stone with a single swipe.

She makes a snuffing sound, then lifts her head to scent the air, but otherwise she doesn't move.

"Hello, Caindra."

Jarek snorts. "She doesn't understand you."

"How do you know?"

"Because she is a beast."

Caindra snarls, showing fangs the length of my leg.

"Uh … think you're wrong about that. Say you're sorry before she kills you."

He cuts a glare my way before offering a reluctant, "I apologize."

Her lip settles, her mood seemingly mollified.

I study her scales in the afternoon sun. They're not black after all, but a shimmering mix of indigo and rose gold, her horns a glossy violet tipped in gold. "You're beautiful." Scary as hell, but stunning, nonetheless.

She blinks and brings her head down to meet me at eye level. In her violet irises, I see a reflection of my dress.

On impulse, I reach out and touch her snout with a shaky hand. "Lucretia called you my answer."

"Answer for what?" Jarek asks.

Caindra's eyes are piercing as she watches us.

I was thinking about this on the ride here. "If I inherit the Ybarisan throne, I can order Ybaris and Mordain to stand down against Islor and help fight against the Nulling." It's the simplest, most straightforward way to keep Ybaris from attacking Islor. It might be the only way.

"That would require killing Neilina, which will be next to impossible, Romeria. She'll be protected by a wall of Shadows and elemental casters." He pauses. "Unless we can get *this thing* to attack her."

Caindra snarls again.

"Seriously, do you have a death wish?" I reach out to smooth my hand over her snout again. At some point, I released the hold on my affinities, and I only realize it now. "Sorry, he's an ass, but he protects me well."

Her nostrils flare and a puff of hot air hits me.

"You saw what she did in Cirilea with the fire," Jarek pushes. "She could wipe out even Neilina's strongest fighters."

"But we need them against the Nulling. No, *I* need to be the one to do this."

"Neilina's casters would kill you before you got close."

"Maybe not. As far as we know, Neilina still thinks I'm her daughter." And Gesine seemed to think that the elemental caster on the other end of the taillok might have held back details about what she saw that day Kienen brought it to Ulysede's gates, that I have allies within Mordain and Ybaris.

My gaze drifts over Caindra's wings, tucked at her sides. They remind me of a bat's—webbed and leathery. "If there was a way for Caindra to get us to the rift—"

My words aren't finished before a clawed foot curls around my body. With a deafening roar, her powerful wings beat the air as we climb into the sky. A scream of terror rips from my lungs.

69
ZANDER

The entrance to the rift's pass grinds open.

I marvel at the mechanics of the wall as we wait. According to old texts within Cirilea's library, King Rhionn returned from Ybaris not only with Key Caster Farren but also with several stone casters. He tasked them with building this great gate of sorts to match the one Ybaris built on their end, to keep the Islorians out after the blood curse arrived.

What they produced was almost identical. It's twenty feet thick and stretches thirty feet on either side of the bridge between realms, making it impossible for anyone to navigate around. It reaches a hundred feet high, making it equally impossible to scale over. Even an elven would break every bone in their body were they to jump. Nothing short of an army of casters could destroy this, or perhaps a pyre of wyverns.

The gate itself? Thick, impenetrable rock that works much like the tunnel in Bellcross's city wall, a puzzle of blocks that shift until an opening appears.

Two spiral staircases on either side give access to the parapet, where watchmen keep an eye on the other side's activities. They were the ones who sent word that the gate on the other side had opened, bringing us here.

Telor waits beside me. "Are you sure you wish to risk yourself this way? She cannot be trusted to respect the rules of war."

"No, she cannot. But I would not ask this of anyone else." And no one here has a chance at standing against Neilina. "My legionaries will join me." I nod toward Gaellar. "I am sure your commander will appreciate your guidance should something befall me."

"Nothing shall befall you, Your Highness," Abarrane says with grim determination, but even she wears a furrowed brow.

"Would you prefer me at your side or remaining here, Your Highness?" Kienen asks.

"It is best she has no idea we have joined alliances yet."

He dips his head. "Her affinity to Vin'nyla is strong. Do not get too close to her or she can steal the air from your lungs. Within fifteen feet is too close."

"I have heard the rumors." It's times like these when I wish I had been gifted a different affinity at birth. There are always air and earth materials to wield. But access to fire and water is never guaranteed. Still, we improvise. Behind me, several legionaries carry flaming torches, though the afternoon sun is still high in the sky. "Anything else I should know?"

"The Shadow leader's name is Solange. She is a Second in Mordain's guild, below only the Prime, and she has an impressive affinity to Malachi."

"Will she use it?"

"If Queen Neilina orders her to, yes. But she despises how little autonomy Mordain has, and how the guild constantly bends to the queen's will. She has long since wished to break free of Ybarisan rule, but it is impossible with this queen."

Wendeline once explained the complications around their union, how Neilina has held caster babies hostage in exchange for elementals and loyalty. "And you know this how?"

"The Shadows train with the elven warriors sometimes. Solange has been my opponent more than once." His gaze flitters to Abarrane, telling me all I need to know about the kind of sparring they've done. "Convincing her of the queen's treachery may carry some weight. Perhaps."

"I will keep that in mind. Thank you for the input, Kienen."

"Your Highness." He steps away.

And I can't help but marvel that not one but two unlikely allies have proven themselves invaluable during this journey.

Finally, the stone wall gives way to an opening and the path beyond—a bridge about forty feet wide that remained after Aminadav's smite. It's as if even in his fury, he left us an olive branch.

In the far distance, four rows of Mordain's Shadows ride in formation toward us, their black armor unmistakable even from here. Glints of gold gleam every so often, hints that Neilina is tucked in there with them.

I don't hide behind the Legion as we approach, remaining front and center, clinging to the nearby torch flames. Little good it will do if Neilina's elementals have a shield up.

High above on both sides, the vigilant spectators watch, searching for any hint of betrayal. Not that arrows or affinities could reach us in the center of the bridge, over the endless chasm.

The trek to the middle is long, with riders avoiding getting too close to the edge. Below is the Valley of Bones—an assumed resting place for all those who have tumbled into the rift during battle, though we cannot see the bottom from here.

"What is your plan?" Abarrane twirls a dagger between her fingers.

"To see what she knows of Romeria and to seed doubt in those around her." I will never be able to kill Neilina, but if I can convince her casters of her duplicity as we convinced Kienen, maybe we can win ourselves more unlikely allies on the other side.

"And do you really believe you can sway the Shadows?"

"I honestly have no idea, but this isn't a battle we can win alone." We may very well be heading to our deaths. But maybe I can stall them with the truth of what is coming.

The finer details of the lethal warriors are more recognizable now—the muted steel armor over black garb, the metal masks that cover all but their line of sight.

"They haven't changed much," Abarrane notes.

"Their uniforms have not changed, but the casters within them have." The ones we fought last died long ago from old age. Many of these will be young and inexperienced. None of them will have even seen war. Still, I wouldn't dismiss their skill. "Halt!" I call out ten feet from a center line carved into the stone.

The Ybarisans match the distance.

Both lines watch the other, waiting.

"Which king are you? The exiled one or the usurper?" a female at the front calls out, her husky voice hinting at humor. "We hear Islor can't decide."

I can only imagine what they've heard through their spies—a medley of lies mixed with some truth. "You must be Solange." I watch her eyes flare. She's wondering how I knew that, and what else I might know about her. "I did not realize the queen needed people to speak for her. Is she incapable or afraid?"

The taunt works. The line of Shadows shifts and Queen Neilina guides her white stallion forward, her metallic dress shimmering gold and silver in the sunlight.

My breath catches. Romeria—the old version—once told me she looked a lot like her mother. That was an understatement. Romeria is a nearly identical replica, only youthful. It's as if Aoife created a second version of her. In appearance, anyway.

Golden antlers are strung around her neck like jewelry. I've never seen a token so large before. What purpose it serves, I'm not sure I want to find out.

A caster came forward with Neilina, the telltale collar around her neck marking her an elemental. I can't see the emblems on her forearm to discern her affinities, but her blue eyes glow. I can only assume she's placed a protective shield in front of the queen.

"You *must* be Zander." Her cold, piercing blue gaze dissects me. "Have you come to negotiate the surrender of Islor?"

I laugh. "Only you would be foolish enough to think so."

Her returning smile is vicious, and I change my mind—Romeria looks nothing like this wraith. "Where is my beloved daughter? What have you done with her?"

I would love to provoke her with false horrors, but it wouldn't be wise. "She is safe."

Her perfectly drawn eyebrow arches. "In that gated city in your mountains?"

I keep my expression smooth. We already assumed she might have learned something through the taillok. The question is, how much? Did she hear that Romeria's eyes blazed silver? "Where no one can reach or harm her."

Her mouth seems to work around the words, but she doesn't release them. She has questions about Ulysede or Romeria—or both—that much is obvious.

I'm not here to answer them. "Your son, on the other hand, I doubt he fares as well."

Her lips curve as if she has a secret. "On the contrary, I just heard from the true king of Islor that Tyree is betrothed to your sister, Princess Annika."

I can't catch my shock fast enough, but I follow it with a genuine burst of laughter. *What the fuck are you doing, Atticus?* He must have offered the arrangement to keep Neilina on her side of the rift. Has he learned *nothing* of her deceitfulness? At least that confirms Tyree is still alive. Atticus kept him as a bargaining chip.

Neilina cocks her head. "Why does that amuse you so?"

"Considering how your family handles engagements, I would say the chances are slim of that one coming to fruition either." Annika is likely to stab him the first chance she gets. "By the way, thank you for your taillok. Caster Gesine is adept at wielding it. It has been *most* helpful to us."

Neilina's eyes ignite with anger. "Why am I not surprised those traitors ran to you?"

They didn't. They ran to your daughter. "Tell me, if Gesine and Ianca are traitors, what does that make *you*, given you broke

Mordain's sacred vow and forced Ianca to summon Aoife? Or what about how you murdered your husband?"

Neilina's mask doesn't break this time. She must have been expecting the accusations. "What did you think you would do? Meet me here to insult me and spew filthy lies, and my people would believe *you*, one of Malachi's demons?"

Not for long. "*Your* people. Interesting. They were King Barris's people first, were they not? You married into the throne. And they did love him so. I wonder what they would say if they knew the truth behind his murder. As for Mordain, I was under the impression that it was an independent realm with its own guild of intelligent and powerful casters, capable of governing itself."

"We have a mutually beneficial arrangement," Neilina says crisply.

"Is that what it is? It seems to me they are nothing more than instruments and slaves. But imagine how Mordain could fare with a different queen, one who would respect its independence." That last part, I say for Solange's benefit.

The Second's gaze narrows as she watches me.

What does she know?

Neilina's teeth grit. "It is clear you have not come to surrender, and you have wasted enough of my time. Norae, come."

The elemental dips her head.

The Ybarisan queen turns her horse and cuts through the lines, her back to us. "Shadows ... Rid me of these pests. It'll deliver a powerful blow to the rest of the fools about to die."

We draw our weapons and position our shields. My pulse races in my ear. "Did you hear that, Solange? Yet another order to follow from the Ybarisan queen who doesn't value your lives beyond how she can wield your power. There *is* a way out of this, a better option for Mordain."

I catch a spark of interest in Solange's gaze as the other Shadows wait for their leader's command.

Before she can give it, an ear-piercing roar cuts through the sky.

70
ROMERIA

Wind whips at my face while we soar through the clear blue sky, coasting over Islor's daunting mountain range as if they are nothing more than bumps on a map.

I'm cocooned protectively within Caindra's grasp, clinging to a talon that looks sharp as a blade but does not cut me. She's surprisingly gentle, holding on only tight enough that I can't slip free.

At some point, I realized she had collected Jarek, too, and I'm relieved, though he doesn't look as comfortable in the other claw. He hangs on to a talon, his legs dangling as if he might slip through her grip and plunge to his death at any moment. His face is drained of blood.

I imagine the difference in our treatment might have something to do with his calling her a beast several times. I can't wait to poke fun at him about it later when we are safely on the ground again.

Hudem's moon is out, sitting below the regular full moon. It's still dim but once the sun sets, it will bathe these dark lands in brilliant light.

And yet there is nothing to celebrate tonight.

I'm finally getting used to the feel of flying when Caindra

dives, and I scream, holding tighter to her as we approach the rift. I've only ever seen drawings of it and heard the stories. The real version is even more menacing—a yawning chasm in the world. It makes me wonder how the two sides didn't split apart and float away.

Dark masses swarm both sides.

Somewhere down there are people I care about.

People I love.

Shouts of alarm sound and soldiers scramble to get into position. It's pointless against Caindra. Arrows can't penetrate these scales. Hopefully, I can convince them to hold off and not attack.

She swoops down, coasting parallel to the ground but not landing.

My mouth gapes as she tosses Jarek like a castaway trinket. The fall isn't too far, and he rolls like a tumbleweed before coming to a stop. I can breathe again when I see him stagger to his feet.

Caindra banks left, narrowly missing the stone wall ahead. With one of her loud roars, she pivots again, plunging for the rift's pass where two distinct groups stare up at us, arrows nocked and blades drawn. The legionaries are unmistakable. Who the soldiers in all black are, I can't say, but I imagine they're the Shadows Kienen mentioned.

I spot Zander on our sweep past and my heart swells. I pray he sees me and knows that I've come.

Caindra lands on the other side of the Ybarisans. The stone bridge shudders under her weight, and several horses rear, sending their riders dangerously close to the edge.

She sets me down in front of her with a gentleness I would never expect, giving me her talons for support as I take a few steps on wobbly legs. "We'll have to work on the flying thing," I mutter. A puff of air from her nostrils answers me.

Ahead, two females sit on horses, their jaws dropped.

One is an elemental caster, her telltale gold collar marking her as such.

The other is a spitting image of Princess Romeria.

Of *me*.

No one ever warned me how much I looked like the evil Ybarisan queen. It's uncanny.

Behind them are the soldiers in head-to-toe black. They seem to struggle with where to focus—on the dragon or the Islorians. They're sandwiched between two powerful forces.

"Daughter!" Queen Neilina exclaims, as her eyes flitter between me—in my winged dress—and Caindra. "You have escaped."

Escaped? What did Zander tell her? I suppose I should play along. "With a little help." This is all happening so fast. If I could have planned this more, if I could have asked Gesine, I'd be better prepared. I'd know how to speak to my supposed mother. Did I call her Mother? Her Highness? Did I bow?

She slides off her horse and the elemental beside her follows, keeping the shield around them. Her delicate gold and silver dress shimmers in the sunlight. Aoife's token antlers around her neck are crude by comparison. They look more like a weapon than jewelry. "I did not think I would see you again." She walks casually—not like a mother rushing to embrace her long-lost child.

I match her pace, moving in, drawing on my affinities, weaving them into a tight silver cord. But thoughts of the royal garden loosen my grip. I cannot unleash that here. I'll kill everyone; I might even kill myself.

But does Neilina know what I am?

Who I am?

Does she have any clue that I'm here to kill her? My insides flip. The last time I tried to fool a family member of Princess Romeria's, it did not end well for me.

But if Neilina suspects anything, she hasn't hinted at it yet. She's too focused on Caindra, awe painted across her face. "Where did you find such a beast?"

I expect the dragon to respond with a snarl, but she remains quiet. "She found me." The truth likely serves me best here.

"How marvelous." She stops several feet away but doesn't

reach out, doesn't show any sign of affection. I'm thankful for it. "And she will listen to our orders?"

Our orders. She may as well say *my* orders. My irritation thrums. "If she feels like it."

Neilina sniffs. "I wish I'd known we had such a force before. I would not have needed to drag all these people here. Never mind that, though, they can wait until we obliterate the enemy's army and then cross. They will love me even more after that."

It takes everything in me not to grimace.

Neilina regards my dress, stalling on the wings. "This is an unusual outfit. What is its purpose?" She speaks calmly, as if unfazed by the clusters of Islorians behind her, swords drawn and braced for battle.

"I was told it would mean something to Caindra." I gesture behind me.

"By whom? Those two elemental traitors?" Her eyes narrow. "I want them brought back to Ybaris so I can hang them myself."

My fists clench at my sides as I struggle to control the sudden flare of rage, my affinities blistering under my skin, begging to be unleashed. "They are both gone, one to the change and one to an enemy arrow."

Behind Neilina, the caster holding the shield flinches. That news bothered her, which means she was an ally of Gesine's.

I'll bet there are more of them than I think.

"Just as well. You and I have much to discuss." Neilina gestures toward Ybaris's gate. "Come."

Would the old Romeria have bowed and followed? Surely.

No more than twenty feet away, through the crowd of horses and riders, I spot Zander, perched tall on his black stallion, his eyes locked on me.

I wink.

Neilina's jaw hardens. She must have caught that. "Why are Malachi's demons still alive?" she yells. "Finish them off!"

A ring of steel sounds.

"Stand down!" The bellow sails from my lips, and everyone freezes.

Neilina gapes at me. "How dare you counter my order?" She looks genuinely shocked, as if the very idea is preposterous.

"Because it's a bad order, given by a bad leader." And we don't have time to play this game. I let my voice carry. "Everyone here knows that it was not Islor who killed King Barris. It was you. And everyone also knows that you used your elementals to summon Aoife."

She stares at me as if I've slapped her. "Your accusations amount to high treason, Daughter."

I'm not your daughter! I want to scream, but that secret is best kept hidden if I want to claim this throne. "Not if they're true. Both crimes are punishable by death, even for a queen."

Worry mars Neilina's face. She is finally seeing this for what it is—a trap. Her chest heaves as she scrambles to find a way out of it. "The Islorians have turned Ybaris's princess against her own realm."

"No, I want peace for Ybaris, but it will never have that with you sitting on its throne." Zander is right.

"You are no longer my blood." She sneers at me like a cornered animal.

Suddenly, my chest feels like it's about to cave in, like someone is squeezing a fist around my lungs, keeping them from working. I release my grasp on my affinities as I gasp for the air that Neilina strips from me, vaguely aware of shouts in the distance and Caindra's roar.

But it's Lucretia's words that I hear.

The Daughter of Many does not choose one over the other. Let them merge until they are as one, and you will know power like none other.

With that kind of strength, I *must* be able to break this hold Neilina has on me.

I fight the panic and reach deep inside to grasp for the threads again. They rise to the call, coiling into a thick silver cord that I send toward Neilina gently, so as not to obliterate everyone behind her.

Her grip on my lungs vanishes, and I'm able to take a deep breath again.

Neilina gasps in horror. "Your eyes … they are silver."

She just tried to kill me—her daughter as far as she knows!—and she'll try again once this shock subsides.

Any reservations I might have felt about murder vanish. "Yes. It's quite the upgrade. You can thank Malachi for that." I slip the black dagger from its sheath. "But you should be more worried about my blade." I launch it at her like Jarek taught me and it lands true, sinking deep into her trachea.

She wheezes as she stumbles toward the elemental. Fitting, I should think.

"Kill … her…," she manages to croak.

But the elemental doesn't move, and neither do the Shadows behind her.

Neilina falls to her knees, clawing at the elemental's skirt.

The petite female looks from her queen to me, eyes wide with fright—afraid to save Neilina, afraid to let her die.

I won't leave the weight of that decision on anyone else. I gather a thread of Vin'nyla and launch it at my dear mother, sending her glittering form over the bridge's edge.

The Ybarisan queen falls without making a sound.

And I'm left to face off against Mordain, who has killed every key caster born in the past two thousand years. I swap one affinity for four and brace myself, waiting to see how this will play out.

The elemental is the first to drop to her knees. "My queen."

The masked soldiers behind follow, taking a knee, their hilts pressed against their chests. Echoes of the same words reach my ears.

Behind them, Zander and the legionaries stand, swords at their sides, their attention shifting between the casters in front of them and the giant dragon behind me.

I allow myself a deep breath of relief as Zander and I nod at each other. It's over. At least this part is. I fight the urge to rush for his arms.

As one, the Shadows rise and split into two groups, turning on their heels to form a path. One steps out of formation and approaches me. Zander makes to follow, but a swath of swords instantly appears, blocking his path.

"Allow him through," I order. "Allow them all through."

The swords drop instantly, and Zander rides along the makeshift aisle warily. The legionaries trail.

"Your Highness." The Shadow dips her head. "I am Solange, Second in Mordain's Guild of Casters and Master of the Shadows." Her voice is husky. "We are yours to order."

I study her, though it's difficult with only her eyes visible. Did Princess Romeria not know this caster and that is why she introduces herself? Or does Solange know that I am not really Princess Romeria? I have no idea who knows what within Mordain. Gesine would have known. She could have helped me navigate this.

Zander dismounts and passes Solange without a glance. Where I hesitated, he doesn't, his lips finding me in a deep kiss, the kind usually saved for private moments. It distracts me from all other thoughts. "I knew you'd find a way," he whispers when he finally breaks free. His eyes sparkle as they take in my face, my dress, my wings, before shifting his focus on Caindra, a hint of amusement woven into his awe. "You learned how to fly."

"More like cling for dear life."

He smooths his palm over his nape. "How did you manage this?"

"It's a long story." That I can't explain if I tried. Maybe Lucretia will be able to.

Hooves pound in the distance, drawing everyone's attention to Jarek as he races up the bridge from Islor's side. Even from this distance, I can make out the hard set of his jaw.

"He looks angry," Abarrane notes with a smirk.

"Yeah. Caindra's not a fan of his."

Zander chuckles, but his mirth slips away. "What I heard you say about Gesine, was it true?"

I nod, swallowing the lump that instantly forms in my throat. I'll explain it when we're alone and I'm not worried about crying in front of people.

Zander, sensing my anguish, wraps his arms around me, offering me a few moments of comfort as Jarek closes in.

My commander dismounts his horse to find my side.

I peel away from Zander's embrace. That will have to wait for later too. "I warned you not to call her a beast, didn't I?"

The legionary's steel-gray gaze narrows on the lingering dragon. He wears nasty, dirt-filled scrapes across his cheeks and neck from the tumble. His leathers protected him from worse. "What now?"

Good question. I didn't get past the part in the cobbled, spontaneous plan where I kill Neilina and assume her throne. But, honestly, now what? The sun has shifted in the sky, heading toward late afternoon. Hudem's moon is already brighter than when we arrived.

We are running out of time.

"Ybaris and Islor will not go to war against each other," I announce.

Several of the Shadows' shoulders slump. With relief or disappointment, I can't tell. "Unfortunately, there will still be a war, against the Nulling." I watch Solange as I deliver this news, wishing I could see her face to read it. But I see enough. "You knew this already."

She dips her head once. "I think there is someone you ought to meet, Your Highness."

Gasps sound as I ride through the Ybarisan camp on a borrowed horse, Jarek on one side, Zander on the other, the Shadows a blockade surrounding us. I don't know whether people's shock is that Princess Romeria is alive, that Queen Neilina is noticeably absent, or that Malachi's demons are on Ybarisan soil.

Or maybe it's the giant dragon perched on the top of the wall, her talons sending chunks of stone tumbling.

There are people wherever I look—many of them common folk, some children.

A regal-looking soldier with a gold breastplate rides forward, his lengthy golden blond hair swept back off his face. "Where is Queen Neilina?" he demands to know, sneering with hatred at Zander.

"Dead," Solange answers, with a note of pleasure in her tone. "Caedmon Tiberius, bow before your new queen."

This is the commander in league with Neilina? *This* is Princess Romeria's real father?

His jaw clenches. "Your Highness." His bow is delayed. The soldiers behind him follow immediately.

Do they know how deeply in bed he was with Neilina, both literally and figuratively?

What *I* know is that there is no way I can let him continue leading Ybaris's army. *My* army now. "Tell me, was it you or my mother who drove the blade into King Barris's chest?" I say it loudly, so all around us can hear. I watch his face as it morphs in stages—from shock to anger to grim determination.

He doesn't deny it, though.

I see the moment he makes his decision. He knows his days as commander are finished.

"Don't do it," I warn a second before he draws his sword.

Solange moves faster than any of the legionaries, driving a blade through his throat. He collapses with a gurgling sound.

Jarek inhales sharply. A tell that he's impressed.

Zander leans in to whisper, "You need to name a new commander for the Ybarisan army immediately. This cannot wait."

I nod, thankful to have him by my side. In this instance, the decision is easy. I know the perfect, trustworthy soldier. "Send two legionaries to get Kienen."

Abarrane nods at Iago and Drakon, giving the order.

"Good choice," he whispers.

"I know." I offer him a playful smile.

Solange wipes her bloodied blade on her uniform before tucking it away. "This way, Your Highness. She waits in a tent. I hope. She is a wily one." There's a hint of deference in Solange's voice, even as she mocks whoever I am to meet.

The Shadows lead me toward a cluster of tents. People outfitted in simple dresses and breeches rather than armor loiter around. They all watch with curiosity, anger, and fear as I pass, followed by a string of Islorians.

Solange stalls at a green tent. "There is not enough room for all of you."

"There is enough room for me." Jarek lifts the flap and barges through without asking or waiting for an order.

"He's still pissed about Caindra." I step inside, Zander and Solange on my heels.

In a wooden chair inside sits an elderly woman, her face creased with wrinkles that have seen many decades, her white hair pulled back in a wispy bun.

When she sees me, her cloudy blue eyes widen, flipping to Solange. "Your Highness!" She eases out of her chair with difficulty and bows. "I was not expecting you."

"Queen Neilina is dead. This is Ybaris's new queen." Solange removes her mask and headpiece, revealing a woman in her late thirties with tightly braided chestnut-brown hair. "This is Caster Agatha."

"Agatha." I know that name. "You're the Master Scribe."

Her face splits with a grin. "My dear Gesine has told you about me."

"Yes. Your letter arrived in Ulysede the other day."

"That took forever. I was wondering if it would make it." Her aged gaze darts behind Zander's and Jarek's looming bodies, searching. "Did Gesine not travel to the rift with you?"

The perpetual ache flares. "She died yesterday."

Agatha's shoulders sink. "The change?"

"No. An arrow from an enemy."

The caster's face crumples as she settles back into her chair, as if standing for that long is a strain. "She was a special one."

"She was," I agree. "She helped me learn so much about myself, and so quickly. She trusted you without hesitation. She told me *I* could trust you."

"I would never have expected an old scribe to voluntarily show up at the rift before a battle." Solange smirks. "When I spotted her, I knew she had to be up to something, so I pulled her aside for an explanation."

"I believe there were threats involved," Agatha retorts crisply.

The Shadow shrugs. "I needed the truth."

"You knew the truth already, but you and the Prime chose to ignore it."

"The Prime ignored it, leaving me little room to do anything at all," Solange snaps back.

"What did you tell Solange?" Zander asks Agatha, interrupting the bickering.

"Everything I know or suspect," Agatha admits, turning to me. "You have opened the nymphaeum door, have you not?"

I sigh. They have figured that out on their own. Gesine did say Agatha was smart. "Yes." They know this and yet no one has tried to kill me yet. "At the height of Hudem's moon tonight, Islor will be free of the blood curse."

"The nymphs have told you this?" Agatha asks.

"More like their spokesperson. A sylx."

Her eyes widen with delight. "I have never met one before."

"Be thankful for that," Jarek mutters.

"With the nymph's released, we are moving toward peace. The blood curse will be ended and the Ybarisan poison will be useless," Zander says. "But the Nulling will open."

"So we seal it like last time," Solange counters.

"No. It won't work. As long as the nymphs are here, it remains open." When Zander looks questioningly at me, I shrug and echo Lucretia's words. "It's all connected."

A heavy silence settles inside the tent.

Finally, Zander says, "Then our two sides must prepare to battle whatever comes out with everything we have."

I hear what he doesn't say. Malachi is a worry for tomorrow. I look to Agatha. "Why *did* you come to the rift ahead of a war?"

She chuckles. "I had high hopes of reaching this Ulysede and learning what I could to carry on the wisdom for Mordain. The scribes value knowledge. Of course, you know that. You've spent plenty of time with Gesine." She smiles sadly. "I realize how difficult the journey is, but the chance to witness prophecy unfold was worth the risk."

Difficult, but not impossible. "There are countless books in that library."

Agatha's face lights up.

So much information and no one to translate it for me anymore. What if there's a way to fight Malachi hidden within? But Agatha is one little old scribe. She would struggle as much as Gesine. "How many of you can read the ancient language?"

"Oh ..." Agatha scratches her chin in thought. "At least thirty of us."

Thirty casters to carry on Gesine's work. I owe it to her. "I have an urgent need for them. Would they be willing to come?" I expect to hear Zander's quiet warning about allowing more casters into Ulysede but he remains quiet. Maybe he's finally accepting what I did weeks ago—we can't do this alone.

"Would they be willing ..." Agatha cackles, an old lady's caw. "Write the letter and you will find them waiting at the rift within days."

"Then we will make sure you reach Ulysede." And Mordain's scribes will continue Gesine's work, as she wanted.

"If I don't keel over before then."

"Please don't."

With another cackle, Agatha eases out of her chair. "I know just the messenger."

"And I would be more than happy to send a message to the Prime, informing her of the change in rule." Solange's lips twist with satisfaction.

It doesn't take a genius to see that she doesn't get along with Mordain's current leader. Will I like this Prime? Or will I need to make swift changes there as I did with Ybaris's army commander? Do I even have the right? I've spent all my time avoiding Mordain and its casters. Now I must learn everything I can about them.

Another question for tomorrow.

First, we must survive the night.

"This is not how I anticipated the day going." Zander rides at my side as we cross the bridge back to Islor, the legionaries giving us a wide berth so we can talk. The sun has begun its descent, and two full moons hang bright in the sky.

My heart pounds with anticipation. "With me wearing wings and showing up on a dragon to kill my mother? Really?"

He reaches out to entwine my hand with his. The overwhelming relief he feels is palpable, even as we still have so much to worry about. "Kienen will lead Ybaris's army with honor."

"And what am I going to do? I have two thrones now, Zander."

"And I have none."

"Is this where you lecture me about sharing?"

His deep chuckle carries. "This is where I *could* say that I will help you. I know a thing or two about ruling." He pauses. "But honestly, *you* have taught me far more about leading people in the last weeks. I keep asking myself, 'what would Romeria do?' and the right answer always seems to come."

His words are sweet and unexpected, but I can't find too much joy in them. "I'm not sure *all* of my decisions have been the right ones." My brow furrows with worry. "When we left Cirilea, the keepers and mortals were storming the castle. I don't know what's become of it." I wanted to go back through the nymphaeum door the second I felt my affinities replenished to find Wendeline and Annika, but Jarek talked me out of it. All we needed was for one guard to see us vanish into the stone, and there would be a ring of soldiers waiting around it for us to come back through. *If* they're not all dead.

"We will march south and deal with it." Zander squeezes my hand. "But our focus is here tonight."

"One day at a time."

"Exactly."

Caindra's roar echoes as she leaves her perch on the Ybarisan wall, alarming the horses. My heart races as I grab my reins tight, fearing mine will either take off running or throw me over the bridge.

She swoops down to land in front of us, blocking our path and putting herself between us and Jarek.

Zander frowns curiously. "What is this about now?"

"I think she wants something." It's how she was sitting outside Ulysede's gate earlier, with her wings tucked against her sides. I dismount and make my way over to where she waits, nerves stirring at the sheer size of her. "Thank you for earlier. I couldn't have done it without you."

She brings her head down to meet me at eye level, like she did before, and I smooth my hand over her snout. "At least you understand me."

A puff of hot air breezes over my face.

And then I'm in her grasp and we're flying high into the sky once again.

71
ZANDER

"Romeria!" I bellow as the beast carries her south without warning.

Jarek charges up on his horse, his face hard with fury. "That's what she did last time. She grabbed us and *flew* away!"

"She will bring her back before Hudem's rise." Abarrane tries to assure me as we watch the dark form shrink in the distance. "She must."

I sigh. "I hope you are right. Until then, we must prepare."

72

ROMERIA

I can just make out Bellcross's purple banner as Caindra soars over the approaching army. Rengard answered Zander's call. It's impossible to gauge how far off they are from the rift—a half day, maybe? The Nulling will be open by the time they arrive.

Still, Zander's allies haven't abandoned him.

I smile, even as the soldiers below shout with terror, the dragon's massive body unable to hide in a cloudless sky. Caindra continues south and it's not long before I spot a second army, this one's banner green and gold. It must be the soldiers Atticus sent north. The company is comparable in size to Bellcross, and it'll likely arrive within hours after them.

Fresh fighters. That's all we can ask for.

In the far distance, a large swath of forest coats the land. That must be Eldred Wood, where we met the Legion after escaping Cirilea. Those days feel like an eternity ago.

Caindra banks right and turns back the way we came. A part of me wants to prod her to continue to Cirilea, so I can see the state it's in, but we don't have time for that now. She only brought me here to show me help was coming.

"Thank you!" I shout, though I doubt she can hear me. I settle into her grip and admire the view—of rolling hills and snow-capped mountains, of the two full moons. Despite the chaos that is coming, no one can claim that Islor isn't breathtaking.

Suddenly, Caindra dives to land in an open field, setting me down gently.

I find my footing in the grass. "Why are we here?" There's no one and nothing around. Not a single house.

Her head tips back and I brace myself for one of her terrifying roars, but it doesn't come. Instead, she curls her wings around her body, almost like a shield.

I watch with my mouth gaping wide as her massive form shrinks, turning and folding into itself much like Lucretia did when she morphed from her serpent form to the human female body she uses now.

In moments, Caindra is gone and a familiar face stands before me.

Oh my God. *"Bexley?"*

"I told you I could be your greatest ally, did I not?" She strolls toward me, her gown shimmering in hues of indigo and rose gold like her scales in sunlight, the neckline plunging as per usual. "I all but handed you a second throne today."

But … *"Bexley?"*

"Oh come, you cannot be *that* surprised, can you?" Her violet eyes flash with mischief.

"That you're a *dragon*? Yes, I am exactly *that* surprised."

"I will confess, I was startled to discover what you were too. I love this form, but I cannot sense caster abilities while I'm in it."

Lucretia's words stir in my mind. "You were hiding where everyone saw you but no one knew." As the owner of a seedy brothel, selling blood and flesh. And an Islorian immortal. "But you fed on mortals."

"It is the form I chose to take." She flashes a smile, just long enough to show her elongated incisors before they tuck back in. "I must say, I will miss it."

"You can't stay as her?"

She shakes her head, her expression growing serious. "With the return of the nymphs, I become what I am again. It is more difficult to change each time. Even now, my bones ache terribly and will until I return to my primary body. But I needed to take this opportunity to speak to you before I no longer can, about what is to come."

"You mean what's about to crawl out of the Nulling."

"Crawl, fly ..." She winces as she steps closer. "Long before Aminadav's fury split the earth, when the nymphs were here and the door to the in-between world was open, creatures would pass through and appear as if out of thin air, in random places. One here, one there. It was annoying, but it was manageable. They did not all come out of the rift in a flood, like cockroaches running from the light. That only happened with Farren's meddling. It seems as though the veil between the worlds is thinner in there, easier to emerge from."

It dawns on me. "You were alive when King Ailill was here."

"I have been alive for it all, watching these fools make the same mistakes over and over again." She sneers. "I will be at the rift tonight at the height of Hudem's full moon, and I will steer away the worst of them for the time being."

But not forever. "How?"

"By being *me*." There's an air of haughtiness in her tone. "You and the king and all your casters must take care of the rest."

I nod. "And what about Malachi?"

"What about him? Malachi is a fate. He will come, one way or another, but he will not crawl out like a common fiend. He will find a different path." She looks up at the Hudem moon. "We should return."

"Wait!" This is the last chance I'll ever have to talk to Bexley.

Her eyebrow arches.

"Did Atticus know what you are?"

"*That* is what you wish to know?" Her lips curl. "If your nemesis knew he was fornicating with an ancient creature?"

I guess that's not a worthwhile question when my time for answers is limited. "Will you still be my ally after tonight?"

"You are the Queen for All," she says simply, as if that answers my question, before stepping backward, into the open ground where she has room to morph back to her dragon form. The long grass is still flattened. "As far as Atticus is concerned, he had no idea."

"I can't wait to tell him he's into bestiality." I hold up my hands in surrender. "Not that I'm calling you a beast."

Her brow furrows and sadness collects on her beautiful face. "I fear you may never have the opportunity to do so."

73
ATTICUS

"My arse needs a break," Kazimir complains.

"Stop whining. We're almost there. The camp is over that ridge up ahead." We've been riding hard toward the plains. The journey has taken longer than I expected, mostly because the throb in my chest has been too much to bear at times. This is new for me—to have pain linger for so long. Feeding will help, but there are no options until we join my army where several marked mortals wait. *If* I can bring myself to take a vein from anyone other than Gracen. I sensed the jealousy that swelled in her with the idea that I would take from someone else. It was endearing. I don't want to disappoint her.

And after tonight, I might not have to.

Hudem's moon is a silver coin hanging low in the sky, casting its brilliant light over the rolling hills. It's a beautiful sight, and yet all I want to do is feel Gracen's naked body against mine. That I can't be there spikes my rage against these eastern traitors. But anger is good. Anger means I'll fight harder.

Ryker surveys the hills around us. "Shouldn't a scout have doubled back for us by now? They knew we'd be coming." The young soldier is usually the one I send between companies.

"Rhodes probably forgot." He's never led an army of men on his own before. Still, I goad my horse to pick up his pace.

We crest the ridge just as the sun tucks behind the horizon, its last rays bathing the ground ahead.

"What in fates ..." Kazimir gasps as we take in the disaster. The field is littered with bodies, some only feet away from us. Tents are slashed, cookfires smoldering. I see a few eastern and Kierish crests on armor, but there are far more of the Cirilean flame.

My Cirilean army, decimated.

Kettling's green-and-gold banner waves in the breeze high up ahead, staked into the grassy knoll. Next to it, the vibrant silver and red of Ostros flutters.

A sign of conquest.

A declaration of victory.

"They attacked a sleeping camp like cowards."

Here and there, soldiers wander, searching for dying combatants they can end suffering for and loot they can plunder. Some have noticed us and are sharing looks and shouts among one another.

"Your Highness, we must leave and gather reinforcements," Kazimir warns.

What reinforcements? They're all at the rift! But he's right, we can't stay here. "We ride back to Cirilea now." My voice sounds hollow as I give the command.

As one we turn our horses.

Three separate groups close in on us from various directions, fanning out. Where they were hiding, I cannot say. In the thicket and behind the hills, perhaps.

Hiding.

Or waiting for Islor's king to arrive.

Kazimir shares a somber look with me. "We cannot outride them." They are nearly all Kierish soldiers. Fierce mortals but mortals, nonetheless. There are at least two hundred of them to our twenty.

"No, we cannot." I draw my sword and everyone follows suit. I look up at Hudem's moon one last time. I suppose I will not get the chance to know whether Romeria told the truth or yet another lie.

But at least I will not have to endure the pain of losing Gracen.

74
ROMERIA

Thousands of soldiers stand in a grid formation, their knuckles white around hilts and handles and bows, their nervous gazes locked on the brilliant second moon above as it moves inch by inch, minute by minute, to the height of its power.

It's close now, and the energy that vibrates within this camp is electric.

No one knows what to expect. Will it be as bad as the bedtime stories of King Ailill's folly? Worse?

Bonfires blaze every twenty feet, fire readily available for arrows and for Zander, and to repel the Nulling creatures who naturally shy away. The saplings stand in their own clustered arrangement, the moon's reflection gleaming off their black eyes. Perhaps no one is as impatient to see the end of this blood curse as they are.

While I was soaring high with Caindra—Bexley!—Zander stood on top of a wagon and revealed what tonight's Hudem moon would bring, the good and the bad. But not the doom of Malachi. There is only so much truth people can handle at one time. In that, he and I agree.

"It is almost at its full strength," Zander says beside me.

My anxiety is a tangled mess. Now that we've told everyone about the end of the blood curse, I fear Lucretia has lied to me. But we will all know one way or the other very soon.

Jarek scowls at Caindra, perched on top of Islor's stone wall. "What exactly is it she said she was going to do?"

I tip my head back to regard her. She looks like the world's largest gargoyle. "Steer the worst of them away."

"But how?"

"By being herself. Beyond that, I don't know."

"The stairs are right there." Elisaf points toward the entrance at the bottom. "Why don't you go and ask her?"

"Because she can't answer. *And* she'll throw me off," Jarek grumbles.

My old night guard scratches his chin in mock thought. "I wonder why that is?"

I smile. "Glad to see you two can cut each other up even when the world is about to go to shit."

"If Caindra can deal with the wyverns, we can deal with the rest." Zander regards her with a curious frown. "I always knew there was something about Bexley."

"Nice try. You had *no* idea." I'm still struggling to believe it, and I watched her morph between forms.

Zander grips my nape with cool fingers. "Fine. But I'll admit, she was scary even as an Islorian brothel owner."

"She wouldn't even fit into the Goat's Knoll like *this*." I wonder what will happen to that place, now that she has had to say her goodbyes. Obviously, Zander will march back and reclaim Cirilea once we're done here. And then he and I can figure out how to clean up this mess Neilina made while preparing for Malachi. But we have Mordain and Ybaris and at least half of Islor behind us now. *Plus Caindra,* I remind myself. *And* the nymphs.

For the first time in a long time, I'm feeling hopeful. We can do this.

We must.

Caindra's roar fills the night sky.

"That's it." Zander peers up at the silver moon, so bright it's nearly blinding and so low, I think Caindra could fly me up to touch it. "It's at its peak strength."

I grip Zander's forearm. "Do you feel different? Do you feel the same change as within Ulysede?" My voice is urgent. I *have to* know this wasn't all for nothing.

I hold my breath for several long beats until a smile spreads across his face.

Loud whoops and cheers sound from the saplings who are saplings no more, their features that of the elven they once were, so many years ago. For many, who never stepped inside Ulysede, this is the first time seeing their comrades' true faces and an eternity since they've felt their own. Their hands fumble over their features. I'm sure I see a few tears streak down cheeks.

Radomir finds my gaze and offers me a deep bow and his sword pressed against his chest.

I dip my head in return.

Zander presses his lips against my forehead and whispers, "You gave them the sun back. That is something to be proud of."

My chest swells with exhilaration. All around us, elven discover the change, many sliding their tongues over their teeth. A soldier lies on the ground, unconscious, here and there. Did they faint from shock?

Even the mortals are embracing each other because, while nothing changes for them physically, a new freedom has emerged.

Caindra's second roar cuts off the celebration, followed by a third that sounds different—more menacing. Almost like a warning. There is no time for celebration.

"They're coming," I say, drawing on more of my affinities until I can feel them humming at my fingertips.

Moments later, a dark shadow shoots out from the rift, up into the sky. First one, then another, and then a dozen, then more, like a coven of bats, only *much* larger.

"Wyverns," Zander declares, and the bonfires around us surge.

So many wyverns.

But Caindra keeps roaring and they keep scattering, disappearing into the distance.

"Where are they going?"

"To become a problem elsewhere, I imagine. She is claiming her territory, and they are listening." Awe laces Zander's voice.

Except for one, it seems. A green wyvern swoops down toward the Ybarisan side, likely drawn to the caster affinities. A barrage of fire shoots upward from the ground, and the creature swerves to avoid it, circling wide to come back around and strike again.

But Caindra is faster, leaving her perch to swoop down over it. Her giant maw clamps over the wyvern's neck, severing it with a single bite. Two limp body parts fall into the rift. With a warning roar to others, she returns to the wall.

"If we didn't have her, we'd be screwed right now." There would be wyverns raining down hell on both sides and, despite Radomir's tips for incapacitating them, there would be a lot of lives lost.

I may be the Queen for All, but if I hadn't gone to Cirilea that night and sat down across from Bexley, divulged secrets, and offered her trust, would she have so willingly helped us tonight?

I guess I'll never know. I can ask her, but I won't get an answer anymore.

A horn blast sounds from one of the watchmen stationed at the wall. Something other than a wyvern must be coming.

My heart pounds in my throat as we watch a creature on four legs with blue-tinged scales and jutting tusks climb over the edge, shaking its body like a wet dog trying to shed water. It tips its head back and sniffs the air.

"It's a nethertaur!" I don't mean to sound excited, but I've faced one of these things before and I won, when I had no idea how to wield my affinities. "It's not as scary as a grif."

Several more climb out. Archers dip their oiled arrows into the flames, readying to fire.

Abarrane gestures with a mocking flourish as the beast closest to us charges, picking up speed. "After you, then, *Queen*."

My adrenaline soars as I hurl my affinities at it.

75
SOFIE

Malachi held out his hand, beckoning Sofie to him. "It is time."

Her pulse thrummed in her throat, in her ears, in her every limb as she approached the stone altar, knowing she would hold Elijah in her arms again soon, after centuries of longing.

"I am forever your servant," she whispered, reaching up to smooth her fingertips over his fearsome face.

"For an eternity." He gripped her delicate chin, holding it in place long enough to kiss her once before he banished her to the Nulling.

76
SOFIE

Dense fog swirls all around me, so thick, it leaves dew on my skin. No matter which way I look, I can't make out anything. I spin slowly, but nothing changes. No shapes, no forms, no shadows.

I remember this fog, in those moments after I discovered Elijah's still form on the floor of our bedroom, his soulful brown eyes replaced by a vacant gray haze, when I used my affinities to find him stuck in the Nulling, terrified.

My affinities are not with me now, and I feel their absence like an ice-cold blanket draped over my bare shoulders. Uncomfortable. Is that the Nulling's doing?

A sudden gust of wind brushes my skin, and then another, and another, almost like something is flying past me. Tentatively, I reach out, waiting. My fingers graze nothing but cool, damp air. In the far distance, a roar sounds, but here, I feel completely alone.

This is what my love has had to endure for over three centuries? How did he not go mad?

"Elijah?" I call out, then a second time, louder, "Elijah?"

Again and again, I call, taking small, cautious steps forward as if I might accidentally fall off an unseen cliff.

Suddenly, hands seize my biceps from behind, startling me.

I spin around.

My Elijah is right before me, exactly as I remember him.

"Sofie?" His face brims with incredulity, his hands fumbling over my face. "Is that really you?"

"Yes, Elijah. Yes!" I break down in tears and throw my arms around his shoulders, clinging to their strength.

He holds me tightly, sobbing. "How long has it been?"

"Too long, my love. Too long. You would not believe what I have gone through to reach you. What I have had to do." Centuries of groveling and bowing and giving myself to Malachi in every way possible. Can Elijah ever forgive me for that part?

His emotions settle, his body relaxing against mine as he strokes my hair. "Shhh ... There will be time for this later. We must leave the Nulling now."

I wipe away the tears with the back of my hand like a graceless child, though more trickle out. "Where? How do we get out of here?" Malachi never explained.

"Follow me." Collecting my hand, he leads me through the fog.

A stream of slow-moving water trickles ahead. I bend to splash my face with it. "Where are we?" We've walked for what feels like hours, that endless and unnerving roar growing louder until the fog gave way to this place. Here, the comforting buzz of my affinities has returned.

"In an ancient mining city named Soldor."

"In Islor?" We've passed through the Nulling's veil?

"Yes, and our path is this way, if I remember correctly." Elijah disappears around the corner. He was quiet as we walked, singly focused on finding our way. I welcomed the silence, reveling in the feel of his hand, stunned that he and I are finally together again.

"Yes. Come, my love. I have found it!"

I rush toward the sound of his voice.

Elijah stands within a sanctum, stroking engravings on a stone wall.

"How did you say you know about this place?" Malachi once described nymph scripture. I imagined it looking like this. But Elijah has been trapped in the Nulling for three centuries. He has never been to Islor before.

"I will explain later." Elijah winks. "Unless you'd like to live in a cave, we need your caster powers. All of them, and gently."

He is acting strange. Too calm and collected for a soul just rescued from the ether. Or maybe it's that I'm still in shock. I sigh, drawing on my affinities to bond them into silver cord. "Fine, but you will divulge *all* your secrets."

Humor flashes in his gaze as he takes my hand, kissing the back of it. "I will, my spitfire."

Nostalgia washes over me. Another familiar pet name.

I release my affinities into the stone and, in the next moment, the cave is gone and we are standing within another sanctum, this one outside. I look up into the sky and marvel at the magnificent second moon, bathing light over the towering trees and abundant gardens. Malachi told me tales about this special moon when he was preparing me to send Romeria here. It's far more magnificent than he described. "And where are we now?" The scent of spilled blood and smoke taints the air.

Elijah brings my hand to his lips again. "We are home, my queen."

77

GRACEN

I admire the Hudem moon's silver glow from my balcony as my three children sleep soundly inside. It bathes the city of Ulysede below—gleaming off the river, kissing the pastures beyond, highlighting the countless empty buildings that wait for inhabitants.

I've always thought this moon was beautiful, even if what it represented—more Islorian immortals to enslave us and claim our veins—was not.

But now, according to all the whispers I've heard since we arrived in this strange city, our veins will no longer be needed. Definitely not in this magical place, and supposedly not in Islor either. How, or why, no one is saying.

I look down at the emblem on my hand. It's the same as always. Sabrina's, though? It stopped glowing the moment we arrived. I have so many questions and no one to answer them.

Did Atticus know about Ulysede? About this place where there is no blood curse, no risk of poison? Did he know this as he was executing all those mortals?

I'm not sure what to think of this new life we've found ourselves in so suddenly. When Eden showed us to this grand room high up within the castle, I balked, insisting she'd been given the wrong directions, that there must be a servants' quarter for us. She smiled and then left us here and told us she'd check on us after she had all of Cirilea's children settled.

Since then, we've been permitted to walk freely about this picturesque castle, no guards to bark at us, no lords and ladies to send us scurrying. And yet no answers to the many questions Corrin and Dagny and I have. I have not even seen Her Highness since she transported us here and vanished into that stone. I heard whispers that she lost someone dear to her in Cirilea, a caster she could not save. I imagine she is mourning her loss in private.

I wish I could talk to her, though. I wish I could ask her about all the things Atticus has told me, so I can truly understand what is truth, and what is fear and anger.

Atticus …

My chest tightens with thoughts of him. What will he say when he returns to Cirilea and finds us gone? Will he be furious? Surely, he will feel betrayed by me. He will think I had been plotting with Romeria against him all along when that is as far from the truth as possible.

I hope I have the chance to explain, but I doubt it will matter.

I mourn the loss of his touch, staring listlessly at Hudem's moon when it seems to swell, its silver glow intensifying until I have to squint against it. I've never seen it do this before, but I've also never been in a secret city within a mountain.

A cracking sound cuts into the silent night. It's followed by countless more. The noise is coming from everywhere—above and below. With trepidation, I venture to the edge of the balcony to get a closer look.

The stone statues … they're all breaking apart, revealing curled forms within.

My jaw drops as they unfurl, their expansive wings stretching out around them.

With a chorus of unearthly shrieks that paralyzes me, the beings launch into the sky.

FATE & FLAME: BOOK FOUR

Book Four in the Fate & Flame series will release Summer 2024

Pronunciations

Romeria—row-mair-ee-a
Romy—row-me
Sofie—so-fee
Elijah—uh-lie-jah
Zander—zan-der
Wendeline—wen-de-line
Annika—an-i-ka
Corrin—kor-in
Elisaf—el-i-saf
Boaz—bow-az
Dagny—dag-knee
Bexley—bex-lee
Saoirse—sur-sha
Kaders—kay-ders
Malachi—ma-la-kai
Aoife—ee-fuh
Aminadav—Ami-na-dav
Vin'nyla—vin-ny-la
Ratheus—ra-tay-us
Islor—I-lor
Ybaris—yi-bar-is
Ybarisan—yi-bar-is-an
Cirilea—sir-il-ee-a
Seacadore—see-ka-dor
Skatrana—ska-tran-a
Kier—key-er
Mordain—mor-day-n
Azo'dem—az-oo-dem
Za'hala—za-ha-la
Caster—kas-ter
daaknar—day-knar
caco claws—kay-ko claws
Zorya—zor-eye-a
Jarek—yar-ek

Bodil—bow-dil
Horik—hor-ik
Sapling—sap-ling
Danthrin—dan-thrin
Ambrose Villier—Am-brose Vil-lier
Eden—ee-dun
Drakon—dray-kon
Brawley—bra-lee
Mika—mee-kuh
Iago—ee-aa-gow
Brynn—brin
Theon Rengard—thee-on ren-gard
Sheyda—shay-da
Ocher—ow-kr
Ianca— I-an-kuh
Ulysede—You-li-seed
Tyree—ty-ree
Oswald—oz-wald
Orme—aw-r-m
Fearghal—fer-gull
Golbikc—goal-bik
Isembert—I-sem-bert
Bregen—bre-gun
Eros—eh-rows
Fiach—fee-ock
Darach—dar-ack
Barra—bar-ah
Taillok—tie-lock
Sylx—silks
Phynys—fin-nis
Bragvam—brag-vam
Gaellar—gay-lar
Baedriya—bae-dree-ya
Cahill—kay-hill

ACKNOWLEDGMENTS

Readers often ask if I plot my stories, and my answer is always the same: I let the characters show me where they need to go. This book—and this world—is proof of that. Sometimes I feel like nothing more than the person at the keyboard, transcribing their words and coming along for the ride. This book has been a wild one, as all the pieces I imagined fitting in are beginning to do so.

I have a few people I'd like to thank as I finish up this beast of a novel and share it with you all (and I can't express my thanks enough to you, readers, for your willingness to continue along this journey with me. Some of you have been here since the very start):

Jenn Sommersby, you are an editing gift and a patient soul.

Chanpreet Singh, thank you for always making time for my manuscripts.

Hang Le, you continue to surprise me with your creativity and your talent. I can't wait to work on the next cover with you.

Nina Grinstead and the VPR team, I feel fortunate to have such enthusiastic, energetic, and supportive people to work with.

Stacey Donaghy of Donaghy Literary Group, this year marks a decade working with you as my agent. I can't wait to see what the next one brings.

My family, for being my anchor in this world, even when I'm living in another one.

ABOUT THE AUTHOR

K.A. Tucker writes captivating stories with an edge.

She is the internationally bestselling author of the Ten Tiny Breaths, Burying Water and The Simple Wild series, He Will Be My Ruin, Until It Fades, Keep Her Safe, Be the Girl, and Say You Still Love Me. Her books have been featured in national publications including USA Today, Globe & Mail, Suspense Magazine, Publisher's Weekly, Oprah Mag, and First for Women.

K.A. Tucker currently resides outside of Toronto.

Learn more about K.A. Tucker and her books at katuckerbooks.com